"*Point of Order* is that rarest of birds: an original legal thriller. Taking off from the profound idea that justice has something to do with who does the judging, this book will keep you on the edge of your seat even as it expands your mind. I couldn't put it down."
—Noah Feldman, Felix Frankfurter Professor, Harvard Law School, author of *To Be a Jew Today*

"The protagonist of this novel is a judge, and, improbably enough, so is the author. The result is a marvelous entertainment, a page-turning mystery full of romance and humor, which takes us inside the fraught and rather secretive world of a judge's chambers. . . . What impressed me most of all was the book's authority; it has the heft of authenticity."
—Tracy Kidder, Pulitzer Prize–winning author of *Mountains Beyond Mountains* on *The Hanging Judge*

"That rare gem: a crackling court procedural with authentic characters and beautiful prose."
—Anita Shreve, author of *The Pilot's Wife* on *The Hanging Judge*

"Novels have shown us what it's like to be a juror, an attorney, even the defendant, but this is the first I've read that puts us up on the bench—a knowing, nuanced portrait of a judge and the often imperfect system he watches over."
—Joseph Kanon, author of *The Good German* on *The Hanging Judge*

"A masterful work that took me inside the courtroom, behind the bench, and into the hearts and minds of a cast of unforgettable characters. . . . Thrilling, perfectly paced, beautifully written, witty, so very smart and so satisfying."
—Elinor Lipman, author of *Then She Found Me* on *The Hanging Judge*

"A compelling tale, with a cast of vividly drawn characters and a plot that twists and turns—it entertains, as a good novel should, but even better, it also informs, as only the best ones do."

—Jonathan Harr, author of *A Civil Action* on *The Hanging Judge*

"A debut that reads like the work of an accomplished master. A suspenseful page-turner written from the unique perspective not of a lawyer or defendant, but of the judge."

—Joe McGinniss, author of *Fatal Vision* and *The Selling of the President* on *The Hanging Judge*

"Written with precision and heartfelt passion for the law, this riveting courtroom thriller brings the legal system to life. Filled with memorable characters, infused with a deep understanding of the death penalty and the complex interchange between crime, the police and the justice system, *The Hanging Judge* is an electric story, well told."

—John Katzenbach, author of *Just Cause*

"Both an ode to the law in all its glory and a reflection on its sometimes tragic limitations, Michael Ponsor's *The Hanging Judge* will appeal to courtroom insiders as well as readers more generally drawn to a taut story well told."

—Madeleine Blais, Pulitzer Prize–winning author of *In These Girls, Hope Is a Muscle*

"Among its many virtues, [*The Hanging Judge*] will remind many readers that the judicial system is not infallible."

—Supreme Court Justice John Paul Stevens

POINT
OF
ORDER

POINT
OF
ORDER

A Novel

MICHAEL PONSOR

OPEN ROAD

INTEGRATED MEDIA
NEW YORK

978-1-5040-8282-2

Published in 2024 by Open Road Integrated Media, Inc.
180 Maiden Lane
New York, NY 10038
www.openroadmedia.com

In memory of
Chief Judge Joseph L. Tauro (1931–2018)
Mentor, colleague, and dear friend
and
Hannah Njoki Kahiga (1944–2012)
A joyful, luminous soul

And, as always and in everything, for Nancy
Still off the charts

POINT

OF

ORDER

§23 POINT OF ORDER

23.1 When a member thinks that the rules of the assembly are
being violated, he can make a *Point of Order* (or "raise a
question of order" as it is sometimes expressed), thereby
calling upon the chair for a ruling and an enforcement of
the regular rules.

Robert's Rules of Order (12th ed., 2020), 233.

PROLOGUE

Dominic O'Connell waited in the living room, forcing himself to stay calm. When the marshals came for him, he'd be ready. He'd gotten up at four, showered, and put on a suit and tie. Taken his pills. His lawyer, Sandy Tarbell, was over at the window, keeping an eye down the street. A leather valise on the coffee table held his toiletries and medications. They probably wouldn't let him take it, but it didn't hurt to have it just in case.

Julie came down, still in her robe, and stood in the entry. She asked Tarbell whether she should get dressed.

"No. You're perfect." Tarbell looked her over. "Just freshen up and give your hair a brush. I want you in the doorway when they hit."

Without saying anything, Julie slipped off. After a few seconds, there was the sound of water running. O'Connell gave his lawyer a look.

"People will sympathize with her, Dom, and that might help." Tarbell poked his chin at him. "And take off the tie, please."

"Why?"

"It's not how I want you to look."

"But—"

"Dom, if you'd listened to me a week ago, we wouldn't be in this mess. Don't give me a hard time, okay?"

O'Connell pulled off his tie and tossed it on the sofa. "I don't appreciate people telling me what to do."

"When a federal judge tells you to stay home, you stay the hell home."

"I had important business in Brooklyn. Face-to-face business."

Tarbell returned his gaze to the window. "I won't ask what the business was."

Around 5:15, it began to get light. For everyone else, it was going to be just another pretty June morning. At the sound of an engine, O'Connell went over to where Tarbell was standing and stooped to look through the blinds. Across the street, a van with a big antenna was getting parked. The square was so quiet he could hear the yank of the hand brake.

Two people, a man in jeans and a woman in a gray business suit, got out, and the man began setting up a tripod. The woman was holding something, probably a microphone. One of the neighborhood blue jays landed in a tree above them and began jeering.

Tarbell muttered, "Right on time. Hogan must have tipped them."

O'Connell blew out a breath, disgusted. It was a joke that Buddy Hogan, the U.S. Attorney, was gunning for him now. A decade or so back, when Hogan was a nobody, he'd made a safety donation to Hogan's first campaign for Suffolk County D.A., in case he won. Buddy was a punk even then, and he hadn't changed. Everything was politics.

He looked at Tarbell. "How'd you know they'd be coming today?"

"Friend owed me a favor."

"This early?"

"The feds always come at dawn."

After seven months of home confinement, his forbidden trip down to New York, even this close to his trial date, should have been no problem. He'd planned it out carefully, leaving after midnight and coming back very early, but someone must have gotten on the phone. One of these days, he'd find out who it was.

The bow window gave him a good view of his neighbors. The town houses around Louisburg Square were ripples of brick facade with tidy granite steps, pots of geraniums, and doors with shiny brass knockers. The grassy oval in the middle contained a few tall trees and a statue of some Greek on the south end.

Dominic O'Connell was not particularly happy with his Beacon Hill home. The old town house had cost him eleven million bucks, and it didn't even have a decent yard. But his wife loved it. The lady who wrote *Little Women*—he always forgot her name—supposedly died in one of the houses across the way. Julie liked that, and O'Connell had vowed that as long as he was alive and able, Julie would get what she liked. Today was going to be a big bump in that road for her. This, above all things, was breaking his heart.

"You think the judge will lock me up?"

"Most would. Yours, maybe not. We'll know in a couple hours."

O'Connell examined his attorney, this man he was depending on to save his butt, and wondered again if he had the right guy. He'd already fired two lawyers, and he didn't think much of this one either. All these years, he'd been the one in charge. Now, he had to stand here with his hands in his pockets, taking orders.

It bothered him that Tarbell was scrawny and that his weedy hair fell over his collar. Julie had mentioned that she and Tarbell had had a couple of dates back in high school. He couldn't imagine what she'd seen in him. Even fifteen years older, O'Connell could snap Tarbell in two without breaking a sweat.

"Classic perp walk," Tarbell was saying. "Typical Hogan bullshit."

He started to say something but stopped. What was the point?

"I told Hogan I'd surrender you whenever they wanted." Tarbell was still peering up the street, talking over his shoulder. "But Buddy wants to parade you on the evening news, in cuffs, looking like the fucking Boston Strangler."

Years ago, when O'Connell was a kid, the cops used to stop by his uncle Tommy's two, three times a month, all smiles, picking up their envelopes.

Tarbell broke away from the window and turned toward him, still going on. "Besides your idiotic trip to New York, Hogan's pissed that you canned Sam Newbury and hired me." He tilted his head in the direction of the van. "This is his bush-league idea of payback. We'll see about that."

The shadows of three black SUVs glided past the window. Soon now.

Julie came up behind O'Connell. No sound of her footsteps, just a hand on his shoulder. He turned to look into her eyes. Her dark brown hair had a few touches of gray now, and she was a little mussed and sleepy-looking. Perfect skin, trim as a cheerleader, and with a heart that could see right through to the bed he was born in.

Tarbell interrupted, pointing at the entry. "As soon as they hit the stoop, Julie, you need to pop that door open, okay? They'll have a no-knock warrant, and they'll be dying to smash it in." He shifted back to the window. "Plant yourself in front of them, in the camera line. I'll be right behind you."

Julie nodded, turned away from the lawyer, and spoke to him. "It's going to be okay, babe. We'll get through this." She squeezed his shoulder. "Breathe."

Nothing in her face was closed off or guarded. She was just with him. On the bookcase behind her was a picture of the two of them at a fundraiser for children's cancer, the Jimmy Fund, sitting at the head table with the mayor. O'Connell had just told another one of his famous stories, and they were all laughing their heads off. Good times.

"I know." He pulled in a deep breath and unclenched his hands. "It's just that . . ."

He couldn't finish. What he hadn't told her, what he hadn't been able to tell her, was that this morning had been on its way for a long time. More than fifty years, almost before she was born: an offense, his lawyers told him, with no statute of limitations, that time could never wash away.

You'd think he'd remember every detail of that night, the worst of his life. The fact was, though, a lot of it kept drifting. He remembered what had happened, of course, remembered that his uncle Tommy—Tommy Gallagher, the dear departed King of Southie—had let him drive the Fleetwood. He remembered that the cop Scanlon had given him a hard time for having an Italian first name.

So much of the rest of it, though—where they'd gone, how long it had taken—was mostly lost in the fog of years.

Car doors were slamming, and running feet were slapping on the steps.

Tarbell nodded at Julie. "Go!"

PART ONE

1

U.S. District Judge David S. Norcross was sitting at an outdoor café on the edge of the Boston Public Garden, having an early morning latte with his wife, Claire. At their side, in a stroller, was their infant son, Charlie, who was smiling up at the trees across Arlington Street and waving his hands as though he were conducting music. It was the beginning of a beautiful summer day, but Judge Norcross was not enjoying himself. His eyes swept the area, checking for escape routes.

Claire set her coffee down. "What's up, David? I'm doing my sparkly best here, but I'm getting nothing back." She reached over and patted his hand. "You okay?"

"Sorry, it's . . ." He dropped his voice. "I think we have a situation."

She pointed at his plate. "You haven't touched your sticky bun." Normally, he loved pastries. "Are you having a stroke or something?"

This little outing was supposed to be a treat before Claire dropped him off at the courthouse, and they separated for their workdays. Claire, who was on sabbatical from Amherst College, was going to introduce Charlie to a colleague she was coauthoring a book with.

Norcross had an early meeting scheduled with the Clerk of Court Warren Armstrong.

Now, they had a problem. Norcross picked up his cup, took a very deliberate sip, and set it down.

He spoke softly. "Listen. There's a man three tables away, behind you . . ." He quickly touched Claire's arm. "Please don't turn around. He looks like someone I sentenced a while back, and he's been giving us ugly looks. We need to get out of here." He glanced around for the waiter, who of course was nowhere to be seen.

The man at the far table rose, hesitated, and began walking slowly toward them. Except for a certain determination, his face was expressionless. His right hand was in his pocket.

"Here he comes." Norcross bent forward and spoke under his breath. "If things get, you know, just very calmly take Charlie, and . . ."

Claire nodded. "Right." Her eyes were a little wide, but she was steady. She'd do what was necessary.

He stood and took two steps, positioning himself to block Claire and the baby. The man was shorter than Norcross, but thicker. He was wearing a worn red feed cap.

"You're Norcross, right? The judge?"

He couldn't bring himself to deny this. "Uh-huh. That's right." He set his hand on the back of a chair, ready to shove it between them.

"You don't recognize me, do you?"

He put on a courteous expression. "I'm afraid I don't. Have we . . ."

The man took his hand out of his pocket and pointed at Norcross's chest. "You stuck me in jail for two years."

"Did I?" This was not very good, but it was all he could come up with.

In the center of the table was a pewter pepper mill. Casually, he picked it up and gripped it in his right hand. Norcross had played hockey in college and enjoyed his share of brawls. This guy, who looked slow, could probably be managed, unless he had a weapon. With the pepper mill, his first punch—if he could get it in quick— might knock the guy down.

The man looked Norcross over, sizing him up, then broke into a grin. "Take it easy, Judge. It was the best damn twenty-four months of my life." He slapped his stomach. "Look at me. I lost thirty-five pounds and quit smoking." He held out his hand. "Just wanted to thank you. Damien Collins?" He bent closer, raising his eyebrows. "Remember me? From Greenfield?"

Though the sentencing had to be three or four years back now, the judge's memory of the beefy Franklin County drug dealer returned as though it was yesterday. The Presentence Report, he recalled, had described Collins's attempt to bolt at the takedown. The DEA team had had to chase him halfway to Charlemont before his pickup went off the road. They had not been happy.

"Damien Collins, of course. By golly, you *have* lost weight." He put the pepper mill back on the table, and they shook hands.

Collins laughed. "Sorry if I spooked you." He nodded down at the table. "Glad you didn't bop me with that shaker."

Norcross waved his hand dismissively. "What was the charge again?"

"Cocaine. Possession with intent. The prosecutor wanted four years, the prick." He leaned sideways to look around Norcross at Claire. "Sorry, ma'am."

"That's right. So he did. So he did." The judge nodded. "And you live here now?"

"Yep. When I got out of Devens, they put me in Odyssey House out in Waltham for six months, and afterward I hung around. I have a girlfriend now and a little landscaping business. The whole bit."

"I'll be darned. You look great."

"Four years stone-cold sober this April."

Claire stood up. "So, David . . ."

"Sorry. This is my wife, Claire."

Claire smiled. "We should probably . . ." She pulled on the hair at the back of her head. Norcross could see she was rattled.

"Pleased to meet you." Collins nodded at the judge. "Your husband and I are old buddies." He looked down at the stroller and spoke to Claire. "This your boy?"

Claire was wrapping the sticky bun in a napkin. Her hands were trembling slightly. "Yes, this is Charlie." She put the bun in her purse. "He's seven months."

Collins turned to Norcross. "So, Judge, what are you doing here in Boston?"

Norcross was enjoying this—it was a relief, for one thing—but he could tell Claire wanted to wind things up. The waiter had finally noticed them, and she was taking care of the check.

"Just here for a few days. Borrowing a friend's place up on Commonwealth Avenue."

"Nice."

Boston was not Judge Norcross's usual duty station. His permanent assignment was in the federal court's Western Division, ninety miles out the Mass Pike in Springfield. He'd only come east for a few days to assist with a wave of immigration cases that was threatening to swamp the Boston court.

"So." Claire put her purse strap over her shoulder. "We'd better be running along, David, if you're going to make your meeting."

"Sorry, sorry. This has to be really weird for you." Collins put his hand briefly on Norcross's shoulder. "I'll let you go. Couldn't believe it was you, man." He turned and, as he walked away, spoke over his shoulder. "Be good."

Norcross called after him. "You too."

"I'm tryin'." They both laughed.

Claire and Norcross stood by the table until Collins turned a corner into the morning crowd and disappeared. Claire immediately dropped down on her chair again.

"Holy shit, David."

"Yeah. That was, uh, that was something."

"Does that happen very often?"

"First time for me. Hector Ramos mentioned it's happened to him twice. Occupational hazard, I guess. Still . . ." He wiped a hand over his face. "Wow."

"Well, I'll say again, 'Holy leaping shit.'" She stuck out her tongue and gave a muted Bronx cheer. "Give me a second here."

"Let me take the boy." As he unhitched Charlie and picked him up, his son grinned and gave out a happy chuckle. Norcross held him high in the air against the shimmering green trees. It felt incredibly good to be alive.

2

When Warren Armstrong leaned forward to make his pitch, Judge Norcross frowned and rocked back in his chair, as though he were trying to dodge a punch. The judge was a good guy, and Armstrong hated to jam him, but he had no choice.

As the clerk of the federal court in Massachusetts, Armstrong had two main jobs: keeping the district's five thousand cases moving and keeping his thirteen judges happy. It took some footwork to do both. Armstrong's résumé included a degree from Harvard and a solid background in court administration, but as a Black man, he'd had to endure a sprinkling of crap about affirmative action when he'd first come on. After nine years, that was mostly behind him. He was very good at his job, and everyone knew it. Still, it was always tricky to corral a judge.

"The chief asked me to feel you out on this. I realize we're asking a lot." He watched Norcross's eyes. "He'd have called you himself, but we have to move fast, and he's tied up with *Torres*."

Chief Judge Delmore Broadwater, nicknamed "Skip," exercised a loose supervisory authority over the court. His family was Olde Boston, and before becoming a federal judge, thirty years back, he'd been a staffer for Ted Kennedy in D.C. and later legal counsel for Governor Bill Weld in Boston. A chief judge couldn't force another judge do anything, but Broadwater was well connected, well respected, and, most important, well liked. His colleagues bent over backward when he asked for a favor, and Armstrong was counting on Norcross to fall in line. At the moment, Broadwater was bogged down in a twelve-defendant jury trial involving the Salvadoran street gang La Mara Salvatrucha, known as MS-13.

Norcross continued to look as though he'd tasted something sour, and Armstrong dropped his voice to press his point. "We've really got our backs against the wall here, Judge. Otherwise, I wouldn't, you know . . ."

Judge Norcross mostly sat out west in Springfield, and Armstrong hadn't spent a lot of time with him. He was the district's youngest judge, a tall, rangy man, with one of those rectangular Caucasian faces right between homely and good-looking. He'd grown up somewhere around the Great Lakes, and his midwestern manners hadn't left him—if you stepped on his toe, he'd apologize—but his politeness kept him a little tight-assed and tough to read.

Two things, in Armstrong's opinion, saved Norcross from being terminally bland. First, before law school, he'd spent two years in Africa in the Peace Corps. He supposedly spoke Swahili. Second, Norcross had been a widower when he came on the bench. Then, about a year ago, he'd surprised everyone by marrying a hotshot English professor from Amherst College. Recently, they'd had a baby boy.

Norcross's load of roughly a hundred criminal and three hundred civil cases kept him very busy out in the court's Western Division. He'd only volunteered to come east to Boston for a few days to assist with a surge of illegal reentry cases. What Armstrong was asking for now went way beyond that.

Norcross wasn't hiding his reluctance. "I thought Peggy Helms was handling *O'Connell*."

"As of this morning, she still is, Judge. That's the problem."

"I'm happy to take care of a few immigration sentencings, Warren. But a conspiracy-to-murder trial, empaneling in ten days? Give me break. Besides, *O'Connell* is a Boston case. I'm a Western Mass guy."

"I know it's asking a lot, but like I said . . ."

"The baby still wakes up twice a night, and Claire's book manuscript has to be at the publisher by August." Norcross squinted as though he had an itch and rubbed around his eye. "This would be really tough for us, Warren."

"What's your boy's name again?"

"Charles Lindemann Norcross, but we call him Charlie."

"Nice."

"It is nice. It's very nice." Norcross glanced up at the ceiling impatiently. "But now you're telling me that *O'Connell* needs to be redrawn, and I might have to spend two weeks here in Boston trying it?"

"Right. With Sandy Tarbell, we're thinking at least eight to ten trial days."

"And the thing is already a Boston media circus, right?"

"Can't deny that, Judge."

"So assigning somebody new to preside will make a splash."

"It will be noticed. I'm not going to kid you."

Dominic O'Connell was one of the city's prime notables, a poor kid from South Boston who'd started his own contracting business and made a fortune developing the city's shadowy waterfront. He was half owner of the Bruins now, and his picture appeared regularly in the *Boston Globe*'s "Style" section squiring his elegant wife to charity events. O'Connell's flair for good stories and funny, no-bull quotes had made him a favorite of reporters for many years—until the roof fell in. He'd been confined since last Thanksgiving to his Beacon Hill mansion, charged with conspiring to kill a Boston cop back in 1968. Then, a few days ago, he'd made headlines getting caught sneaking down to New York for reasons unknown but probably not good. Somebody dropped a dime on him, and the marshals grabbed him on a violation warrant. He was back in home confinement now, this time with an ankle tracker and a probation officer calling him every six hours. With all this publicity, selecting an impartial jury was going to be a bear.

Norcross shook his head. "Why change horses? Peggy Helms is as good as we've got. She's already handled most of the pretrial motions, and she's . . ."

"I know. I know, Judge." Armstrong hesitated. "But there's something I haven't told you." He made sure he had Norcross's eyes. "This needs to stay between us, okay?"

"Fine."

"Tony Helms has been battling pancreatic cancer, and the last couple days it's taken a bad turn. The docs say he's got two weeks, maybe three, tops." Norcross's face twisted into an expression of real pain. Armstrong had forgotten that he'd lost his first wife to some sort of cancer. "I'm sorry." He paused to let Norcross absorb the news. "They're, you know, they're not telling anyone for now. They want to keep the situation private and spend some time with their kids without a lot of public handwringing. The chief wants to protect them."

"Oh . . ." Norcross closed his eyes and shook his head. "I'm so sorry . . . That's just . . ."

"It wasn't a problem as long as *O'Connell* was a plea. But now that it's a trial, maybe going two, even three weeks with jury deliberations . . ."

"Right."

"We have to take the case off Peggy's shoulders. She'll need to be with Tony and their boys."

"Of course."

"Problem is, we can't tell anybody why, at least not right away, and Sandy Tarbell—"

"Tarbell will have a fit."

"Exactly. He'll be losing his favorite judge."

"Yep."

The Honorable Margaret C. Helms had been on the bench for decades, and she was famously ferocious in defending the rights of the accused. Defense lawyers worshipped her. Prosecutors preferred practically anyone else.

"It's worse," Armstrong continued. "O'Connell's last attorney, Sam Newbury, had a plea deal worked out with the government. Then, out of the blue, O'Connell fired Newbury for some reason, hired Tarbell, and kicked the deal over. When we transfer the case, it will look like we're hammering Tarbell for taking the case to trial."

"Terrific."

"Yeah." Armstrong sat back and sighed. "Where I am now, with Judge Helms unavailable, is I have only two judges besides you who can take *O'Connell*. Most of the others are already on trial or have recused themselves. They know O'Connell personally, sit on the boards of nonprofits with him, have investments in his projects, and so forth. Judge Helms won't give up the case unless we can find a replacement who can hold the trial date. She's kind of stubborn sometimes."

"Right." Norcross nodded. "We all love her, but she's a tiger."

"Exactly. She won't consider another postponement. There's no set rule, but the chief would really like to have at least three judges in the pool to make the draw credible. Ordinarily, I'd just draw it from the two we have, but given the nature of the case, and with Tarbell . . ."

"Who are the other two?"

"I'd rather not say, Judge, in case I'm ever asked about our conversation here. But I can tell you that our U.S. attorney will hate it if it's drawn to one of them, and Tarbell will go absolutely ballistic if it ends up with the other."

"I see. And then there's me."

"Right. You're my 'None of the Above.'" Armstrong tried a smile, which went no nowhere. "No offense. You're not from here, and you're, you know, your reputation is down the middle. Nobody's going to think . . ."

"None of the Above," Norcross said. "Very flattering."

"I'm not asking you to take the case, just let me put you in the draw."

Judge Norcross shifted in his chair, and something about this movement told Armstrong he had him. If judges shared a religion, one of its primary sacraments would be the "blind draw"—the neutral, random assignment of cases, with no manipulation or even any appearance of fooling around. Norcross would feel compelled to protect that. The situation wasn't fair, but neither was life.

"Fine. Toss me in the pool."

"You may not get it, Judge. There's only one chance in three. The computer might skip you, and—"

"Oh, I'm sure to get it." Norcross turned to look out the large window next to his desk. The view opened out onto an expanse of

Boston's Inner Harbor and a sky half filled with sodden clouds. It had been drizzling off and on, but at the moment the sun was sifting through, kicking splinters of silver light off the choppy water. Whitecaps were slapping against the pier. After musing a few seconds, Norcross shook his head. "I'm sure to get the darn thing. And I'm going to have a wife who will not be happy."

"We can put you up at the Seaport during the trial."

"I won't need a hotel. We're borrowing a condo on Commonwealth Avenue while Claire finishes up some research for her book. It belongs to a friend who's away right now."

"We can get you some help out in Springfield, if you . . ."

"It's summer, Warren. I can slide things around." Norcross tugged a file over onto his blotter, not pleased, but ready to move on. "So, you nailed me. Congratulations." Norcross's smile was quick and robotic, but it was a relief.

"Thanks. I owe you one. We may redraw it later this morning but hold off announcing the formal transfer publicly for a day or two. We'll need to do a press release." He hesitated. "Changing the subject, how is Angie Phipps taking care of you?"

Norcross looked up from his file, considering. "In court, she's fine. She's doing a good job keeping the session organized. I saw her in the clerk's office this morning, though. She was talking on the phone, and she seemed pretty upset about something. Just so you know."

Armstrong had assigned Angie Phipps as Norcross's temporary courtroom deputy while he was in Boston. She was technically a "floater," meaning a clerk with no permanent assignment to a particular judge—a sort of utility infielder who could babysit a visiting judge like Norcross as well as handle a variety of other tasks. When they had no visitors, Armstrong mostly used Phipps as an IT troubleshooter, something she was a whiz at. Like everyone, she had her problems.

"I have over a hundred folks to supervise, Judge, and at any one time at least five of them are melting down. My chief deputy is out on maternity leave. My jury administrator fell off a ladder and broke his leg in two places. Dumbass. We have a delegation from the Supreme Court of Belgium visiting, and Judge Ramos has drawn three patent cases in the last ten days. That's not supposed to happen when our case assignment software is working right. I asked Angie to look into it. If she can't figure the problem out, I may have to call on some D.C. techno jocks. I really hate doing that."

"Always something."

"Plus, my son called me last night." Armstrong knew he was going on too long, but he couldn't pass up the chance to massage Norcross a little more. "He just graduated from Georgetown, and now he wants to take a year off before business school to try being a rap artist. God help us."

"Well, good for—"

"He says it's satirical hip-hop, very issue focused." Armstrong shook his head. "The group is called 'Fig Jam.' His mom is ready to put her head in the oven."

Norcross smiled. "Following his dream, I guess."

"I hate figs." Armstrong stood up. He was late for the Belgians. "All those goddamned little seeds."

3

"Sorry I had to steal your client, Sam."

Sam Newbury and Sandy Tarbell were hurrying down Atlantic Avenue away from the courthouse. Newbury had very mixed feelings about Tarbell, and this phony apology didn't help. They'd just been before Judge Helms, where she'd formally allowed Newbury's motion to withdraw and approved Tarbell's appearance as the new defense attorney in *United States v. Dominic O'Connell*. Tarbell, as usual, had to be the big dog, walking fast and deliberately making it hard for Newbury to keep up. Tarbell's gray hair was tossing around in the breeze.

"Don't worry about it, Sandy." The two men paused for a red light. "Getting kicked off *O'Connell* is the best thing that's happened to me since my ex-wife went into rehab."

Newbury intended this remark to be funny, but Tarbell's expression didn't change.

"Glad to hear it."

"I'll send over the file. You'll have a lot to get through in a short time."

"I'll be ready." Tarbell sniffed. "In state court, sometimes you only get a weekend."

Newbury caught a glimpse of his reflection in the window of a parked van and was pleased to see that he was taller and better-looking than Tarbell. The Hermès tie his new girlfriend had given him looked good with the light blue summer suit.

Tarbell spoke, staring ahead. "I knew O'Connell's wife, Julie, a while back. I couldn't say no when she asked me to talk to him, but I never thought the bastard would hire me."

"You're damn lucky Judge Helms didn't detain him after the New York thing."

"Helms has a good head. She issued the warrant, had him dragged in at dawn, and blistered the shit out of him in open court. He got the point."

"Why in the world did he take off like that?"

Tarbell gave him a look. "I didn't inquire."

"Can't blame you." Newbury forced a laugh. Tarbell wouldn't tell him even if he did know. "By the way, I loved how you handled the grab. I couldn't have . . ."

"Pretty, grieving wife in the doorway. Works every time."

"Half of Boston now thinks Hogan's an asshole." Newbury smiled. "I love it."

The light changed, Tarbell bounded off, and Newbury hurried after him. Despite himself, he was a little in awe of Tarbell, who had ten years on him and much more experience in the courtroom. Newbury was a former federal prosecutor and now a partner in a Boston megafirm. He had developed a comfortable practice focusing on white-collar felonies committed by Boston's elite, who flocked to him looking for the sweetheart plea bargains he could negotiate with his old pals at the U.S. Attorney's Office. It was beginning to embarrass him that he hadn't tried a case—hadn't actually stood in front of a jury—in almost three years. On the other hand, his annual income was easing up toward seven figures.

Sandy Tarbell was a solo practitioner with a storefront office out in Jamaica Plain, a highly diverse neighborhood southwest of Boston's city center. Tarbell made sure everyone knew that he'd lived in JP for decades, from back when it was poor and crumbling. His work usually focused on the grimy-collar crimes poor people got arrested for: murder, rape, drug dealing, armed robbery, domestic abuse, and so forth. Tarbell's aversion to plea bargaining was legendary. The people he represented were mostly convicted, and in Newbury's opinion deserved it, but now and then he'd read of a miraculous "not guilty" Tarbell had pulled off. The word was that Tarbell, despite his high volume of work, was having trouble keeping up with JP's gentrifying rent increases.

"You finagled a hell of a deal for O'Connell." Tarbell rushed along, talking over his shoulder. His tone was grudging.

"Who told you that?"

"Julie. A plea with an agreed term of five years, right?"

"In the ballpark."

"For a conspiracy to kill a cop?" Tarbell shook his head. "Fucking amazing." He stepped off the curb and then jumped quickly back as a cab barreled by. Someday, this guy was going to get himself killed. "How'd you manage that?"

"Long story." He drew up next to Tarbell. "Didn't hurt that the U.S. Attorney's Office is petrified of Judge Helms."

Tarbell grunted. "I'd never get a deal like that."

Newbury glanced around and dropped his voice. "You're right. The deal was two inches this side of a miracle. Anyone ever finds out how I did it, I'll probably get disbarred. So why'd Dom punt me?" He looked down and rubbed the back of his neck. "I don't mind, but I'm curious." Newbury did, in fact, mind—a lot.

Tarbell waited a beat before responding. "Let's just say Julie was worried that even five years would have been bye-bye."

They crossed the street and continued walking, more slowly now.

"So you're going to try the case?"

"No choice." Tarbell glanced up. "Figure I've got one chance in ten."

"With Helms, maybe one in four." He paused. "She's your best hope."

"You don't need to tell me, Sam. This isn't my first rodeo."

They walked along in silence for another half block. Newbury took a breath and plunged in. "There's a little scuttlebutt I picked up about Helms you might want to know." Maybe he just needed to give Tarbell a jab.

"Yeah?"

"Bill Treadwell, our managing partner—"

"I know Treadwell." Tarbell's tone was disdainful.

"Bill's brother is head of oncology at Mass General. Apparently, Helms's husband, Tony, is in bad shape. I rushed the plea deal because I was afraid if things got worse—"

"Helms would jump?"

"Right."

Tarbell stopped and gaped at him. "You're kidding me." He actually stomped his foot, like an angry teenager. "Goddammit!"

"Yeah."

"If they fob me off onto some new judge now—"

"Could be just rumor."

"I'll do something. I don't know what yet, but I'll make the new guy wish he'd never been born." Tarbell looked up at the sky and repeated, under his breath. "Goddammit."

Tarbell picked up the pace again. A boiling energy was pouring off him. As the drizzle resumed, they reached a point where their paths diverged—Newbury's toward his neighborhood of glass, steel, and two-thousand-dollar suits, and Tarbell's to the "T" and on out to South Huntington Avenue. Newbury impulsively reached into his pocket and pulled out a card. "Not sure why I'm doing this, Sandy, but here's a little going-away present." He handed the card to Tarbell.

Tarbell looked at it. "I know this guy. He's a dirtbag."

"Big ugly law firms keep up connections with that sort. They can come in handy sometimes."

"I've heard some whispers . . ."

"If Helms jumps and you need a consult, call him. Use my name."

"What kind of consult?"

Newbury started to walk off. It felt good to let Tarbell be the one left standing in the drizzle for once. "You'll figure it out, Sandy. Just tuck the card away." He held his hand out, palm up. "For a rainy day."

4

Not long after his meeting with Armstrong, Judge Norcross took the bench for one of his immigration cases. He was borrowing the chambers and courtroom of a Boston colleague, Herb Conti, who was at a conference. As Norcross lowered himself into Conti's chair, he rolled his shoulders and shifted from side to side, trying to get settled.

"Ms. Phipps, call the case, please."

The big leather chair in Norcross's Springfield courtroom was as comfortable as an old slipper, and his bench was always neatly organized. Conti's bench was so cluttered it felt like a rummage sale. It overflowed with framed pictures of his children and grandchildren, a tarnished silver dish of paper clips and cough drops, scattered felt-tip markers and pens, and three plastic Star Wars figures in front of a card that said "We Love Grampie!!!" Norcross had barely enough clear surface to square up his yellow pad. Plus, the chair was tippy and too high.

Angie Phipps called out, "Court is now in session in the case of *United States v. James Okello*, 19-CR-30220-DSN."

As the attorneys took their seats, Judge Norcross scanned the nearly empty courtroom. This was going to be quick and ugly.

It would be quick because the defendant James Okello had already pled guilty to illegal reentry after deportation, and the sentencing guideline range was relatively low, only twelve to eighteen months. A midrange prison term would zip up the case.

It would be ugly because of the misery he would be inflicting on the defendant's family. A woman and three children, two girls and a boy, were sitting in the front row of the gallery, obviously Okello's wife and kids. The wife was petite, with short gray hair and a small, determined face. Making it all worse was that James Okello was from Kenya, where Norcross had spent two years in the Peace Corps. He'd loved Kenya. What he was doing felt like a kind of betrayal.

Sad as the situation was, it was just one more immigration heartbreaker, and not as bad as some. Washington's aggressive approach to undocumented immigrants had generated a tidal wave of illegal reentry prosecutions in Boston. Like most judges, Norcross found these cases depressing, but he felt obliged to pitch in. Boston judges had come west to help him out plenty of times.

After arranging a few documents in front of him, Norcross began. "As you know, we are here this morning, following the defendant's plea of guilty, to consider the appropriate sentence. I want to review with you what I've read in preparation. Please tell me if I've missed something."

Okello's attorney, a federal public defender named Tom Redpath, had placed a hand on his client's shoulder and was whispering to him, probably clarifying some last-minute detail. Okello was nodding, agreeing with whatever Redpath was saying. Good. This was going to be bad enough without dragging it out.

Judge Norcross moved at a trot through the preliminaries, summarizing the sentencing guidelines, the range of potential prison terms, Okello's record, and other details. He looked up to survey the courtroom from time to time. His brain, as usual, was in many places at once.

Two young Black men entered the courtroom and took seats behind the Okello family. One of them was especially striking. It had been drizzling off and on, and he took his time removing his raincoat, laying it across the back of the pew and tugging at his cuffs before getting settled. He was tall, and athletic-looking, with prominent cheekbones, and almond-shaped eyes. His charcoal suit and clerical collar identified him as some sort of minister or priest, and his very erect posture conveyed an unassuming but distinct charisma. The other man was shorter and potbellied, wearing a rumpled tweed blazer and prominent black-framed glasses. While the cleric's expression was calm, the shorter man looked edgy, glaring around the courtroom as if he were picking out someone to punch.

The defendant's wife turned and quickly shook hands with both men. There was a formality about the gesture that suggested they were not family or close friends. The tall man was probably acting in his pastoral capacity, to show support, which occasionally happened.

Norcross finished up his summary and turned to the assistant U.S. attorney. "I'll hear first from counsel for the government."

As the hearing unfolded, what struck Norcross most about the young cleric was his expression as he looked up at the bench. The man gazed at him steadily, as though he were trying to memorize his face.

The assistant U.S. attorney stepped up to the podium. "Good morning, Your Honor. For the record, I am Claudia Papadakis, and I am here representing the United States." She nodded over at the defendant. "I'll keep this short. When Mr. Okello was picked up last time, the government did not seek a prison sentence. He was only deported back to Kenya and ordered not to return. Clearly, this did not stop him from coming back again." She gestured at Mr. Okello. "There he sits. This time, we are seeking a modest, midrange prison term, fifteen months. We hope this will send Mr. Okello a stronger message. When he gets out, he will be deported a second time. Perhaps his memory of prison will keep him from returning again in violation of our laws." She paused to check her notes, then looked back up. "That's really all I have to say." Frowning, she sat down.

In brief chats at court receptions, Judge Norcross had learned that Papadakis's parents had immigrated from Greece to Gloucester, north of Boston, after WWII. She and the judge had enjoyed a polite connection over the fact that she had a little girl about Charlie's age. An intelligent, good-natured woman, Papadakis of course did not wish—no one wished—the Okello family any harm. Nevertheless, here they both were, doing something terrible to them.

When the defense attorney, Tom Redpath, stepped up to speak on behalf of Mr. Okello, Norcross felt a wave of nostalgia. Tom's father, Bill Redpath, had handled the defense in the toughest case Norcross had so far drawn, a death penalty trial that Bill had managed brilliantly. Not long after the trial's conclusion, Tom had moved from California to head up the federal defender's office in Boston. The younger Redpath was less weather-beaten than his father, and his shaved head and small twinkling ear stud marked the generation between them. At the same time, he'd inherited his late father's bearlike presence and his deep, weary voice.

"Whatever sentence you impose this morning, Judge, it will not be modest." Redpath gestured behind him toward the defendant's wife and children. "In fact, for the Okello family it will be a catastrophe." The two girls squirmed self-consciously; Okello's wife and son stared straight ahead with identical faces—half despair, half stone-faced rage.

"Let me tell you something about who these folks are." Redpath paused, creating an emotional platform for what he was about to say. The man in the clerical collar broke off staring at Norcross and leaned to one side, trying to get a better look at the defendant and his lawyer.

"The facts are pretty straightforward. James Okello was born in Uganda. After his father was murdered, his mother, Lavinia, fled the violence there with James, who was a young child. The two of them lived just over the border in Kenya for several years. Lavinia eventually made her way to Massachusetts through Canada, where she had an uncle who was a teacher. This was more than thirty years ago. She had a student visa, and, after it expired, she just stayed on. James went to high school here through eleventh grade, then dropped out to start working. His mother was very ill, and the family needed the money."

Tom Redpath had his father's knack for driving home an argument without wasting time, but also without appearing to hurry. Prior to his most recent arrest, Redpath said, Okello had been working two jobs—days with a successful cleaning service he'd started, nights as a dishwasher at an Applebee's. A broken taillight had gotten him stopped and handed over to the immigration authorities.

"James's wife, Beatrice, has a valid green card." Redpath turned to acknowledge the defendant's wife. Her face remained unchanged. "She works sixty hours a week as a home health aide. One of those women who makes life bearable for our parents and grandparents." At this, Beatrice dropped her head and pinched her temples between her thumb and fingers, as though she were trying to hold the sides of her skull together.

"James and Beatrice, like all parents, are very proud of their children." Redpath pointed to identify them individually. "Hilary, Hope, and Charles." Hilary, the youngest, was sitting on her hands, rocking from side to side and looking around the courtroom with frightened but curious eyes. Hope, a string bean of a girl with Coke bottle glasses, was squirming and fiddling with something in her lap. Her mother snatched whatever it was away from her and gave Hope a sharp look. The girl looked down, blowing out her cheeks and frowning. The oldest child, Charles, was teen-idol handsome.

"They are particularly proud of Charles, who just completed his junior year at Minuteman High School, out in Lexington. He's a straight-A student and an all-state soccer player." Hearing this praise of her older brother, Hilary leaned forward and smiled over at him. But the boy was looking away, and Norcross could see the shadowed muscles along his jaw twitching.

Redpath continued. "All three children were born in the United States, which of course makes them American citizens. They have never visited Africa or even traveled outside this country. Upon completion of his time in confinement, Judge, James Okello will be deported again. If he is caught returning to this country another time, his term of incarceration will eat up most of the rest of his life."

Redpath raised his voice. It was only a slight increase in volume, but it heightened the drama of his words. "Putting aside his decision to reenter this country, which he did out of love for his wife and children, James Okello has always been a law-abiding, hardworking man. But whatever you do this morning, his life here is now over."

Redpath turned to the side and stared for a count of three at the stenciled pattern over the empty jury box, gathering himself before he continued more quietly. "This family is identical to generations of brave immigrants who've come to this country. In a better world, we'd be welcoming them with open arms. I ask you to depart below the bottom end of the guideline range and impose a sentence upon Mr. Okello equal to the time he's already served. The result will be his release from immigration custody and immediate deportation. I don't need to tell you about the conditions in these DHS detention centers, Your Honor. They are awful places, and the less time he spends there, the better. If I could do more for the Okello family, I would. This all makes me sick, frankly, but it's where we are these days."

The wrap-up after this did not take long. Through his lawyer, the defendant waived allocution, his right to speak before receiving his sentence. Mr. Okello was naturally shy, Redpath said, and his English tended to break down when he was emotional. The defendant was leaning with his elbows on the counsel table and had his hands shading his eyes, as though he didn't want to see what was happening. In the end, Judge Norcross imposed a twelve-month sentence, the low end of the guideline range, giving Okello full credit for acceptance of responsibility and for the four months he'd already been detained. Redpath's eloquence had saved his client some months in prison but ensured that his separation from his family would take place promptly.

Soon after this, Angie Phipps called the recess. When Norcross stood to leave, he witnessed the familiar scenario: the defendant standing, stooped forward, with his hands behind his back as the deputy marshal applied the handcuffs, and Beatrice Okello twisted to the side, pressing her face into her son's shoulder.

Walking down the back hallway to his borrowed chambers, Norcross reflected glumly that, for better or worse, the memory of this proceeding would fade quickly, as new and harder cases crowded in before him. His job, as a colleague informed him after his appointment, was sometimes just to "rule and roll."

When he returned to his office, Norcross noticed one of Charlie's pacifiers sitting on the corner of his blotter. He had put it there when it fell out of his jacket pocket as he changed into his robe. He held it up and looked at it, smiling. It had not eluded the judge that Okello's son, like his, was named Charles. Claire had needed a ridiculously long time to convince him to become a father, and now he could not imagine what had held him back. He considered for a moment how it would feel to be parted from his boy. Unbearable.

5

Warren Armstrong made his way across the dramatic atrium of the Boston federal courthouse, dodging knots of lawyers, office staff, and reporters. He was, as always, in a hurry, but he couldn't help pausing to take in the view of the Inner Harbor. The dominant feature of the atrium was a tipped, curving glass wall—what the architect called a "conoid" structure—several stories high and longer than a football field. The vista beyond the glass reached over the choppy water all the way to the Tobin Bridge. Sheltered inside, and washed by the blooming light, the courtrooms rose above him in tiers, floor upon floor, each with its elegantly arched brick entrance. The place packed a wallop, and it kept him humble.

Out of the corner of his eye, he noticed Angie Phipps standing by the entrance to the cafeteria talking to a big-firm litigator named Vincent Seabury, a man he knew and didn't like. As he watched, Seabury leaned, grinned, and placed his hand on Phipps's shoulder, letting it linger longer than necessary. Armstrong changed course.

"Hey, Angie, just the person I was looking for."

Phipps, who was holding a file, looked relieved to see him.

Seabury's expression was more neutral. "Hey, Warren. What's up?"

"My cholesterol, Vinnie. How you doing?" Without waiting for an answer, Armstrong turned to Phipps. "'Fraid I need a quick word with you, Angie."

Phipps gave an apologetic look to Seabury. "Duty calls."

Seabury started to walk away. "Phone you later." It was not a question.

Armstrong called after him. "Oh, Vinnie." Seabury looked over his shoulder. "I heard your wife's a surgeon, right?"

Seabury's eyes drifted over to Phipps and returned to Armstrong, not happy.

"E.R. doc."

"Bet she's handy with a scalpel."

Seabury strode off, pretending not to hear.

As they walked toward the clerk's office, Armstrong spoke in a low voice. "If you're going to flirt with married guys, at least avoid the knuckle draggers."

"I was trying to be nice." Phipps frowned. "He didn't mention being married."

"I'm sure he didn't. Let me know if he comes up to you again."

"No need to go all daddy on me, Warren. I can deal with Armani."

"Armani?"

"It's my secret nickname for him."

"Because of his suits?"

"No, his cologne. Whew!" She waved a hand in front of her face. "Anyway, I'm seeing somebody. At least I hope I am. Somebody super single."

Everyone in the tight-knit court family was fond of Angie Phipps. She was very smart and always ready to pitch in.

Armstrong nodded. "Good. Just wanted to check and see if everything's okay."

"Everything's fine. Why wouldn't it be?"

"Judge Norcross told me he saw you on the phone this morning, and you looked upset."

"Don't remember anything." Phipps shook her head. "Maybe it was my crazy uncle Jack. He's tries to be nice, but he's kind of a nuisance sometimes. Talks and talks."

"Nothing up with Ronnie?"

Phipps looked troubled. "He was home last weekend. It was so-so."

As a teenager Phipps had had a baby, Ronald, who suffered from some serious disability. A couple of years back, she had moved him into a therapeutic community out in the western part of the state, but the boy still visited her from time to time, and his meltdowns tended to knock Phipps's life sideways.

"How about we try another Red Sox game?"

"Ronnie loved it." Phipps laughed. "But once was enough for me."

That April, Armstrong had gotten hold of four Opening Day tickets at Fenway, and he had asked Phipps if she and Ronnie, who was eleven, might like to go with him and his wife. He hadn't realized what he was taking on. Ronnie carried himself strangely and sometimes made loud, odd noises that attracted uncomfortable looks. Sitting in the bleachers, Armstrong had had to use his best "you got a problem?" glare to make sure their neighbors stayed polite. Then, in the bottom of the fifth, a grand slam home run landed in the bullpen right in front of them. The ecstatic roar of the home crowd set Ronnie off big-time. They left shortly afterward.

He gave Phipps a sharp look, moving to the topic foremost on his mind. "Have you had time to check out the CAP problem I mentioned?" The CAP was the court's computerized Case Assignment Program, which distributed newly filed cases randomly among Boston's federal judges.

"Warren, for God's sake, come on. You only told me about it yesterday, and this is three times you've mentioned it now."

"Sorry. It's a bee in my bonnet."

"Judge Norcross has a bunch of pleas and sentencings this week. Can I get back to you by Friday?" Phipps looked harassed.

"Make it Monday. I'm taking a personal day Friday to drop into my college reunion." Armstrong frowned. "Like I told you, something's wonky with the programming, and if we can't come up with an in-house fix, I'm going to have to call in an IT swat team from Washington. They're always a pain."

An attorney passed by and gave Phipps a long look. One of Phipps's problems, in Armstrong's opinion, was that she made herself too tasty for her own good. The bright teal and gold summer dress she was wearing looked very nice with her reddish-blond hair, but it was snugger than he would have advised, and its hem was a tick on the short side.

As they passed the public entrance to the clerk's office, Phipps turned away, shielding her face. "Oh crap."

The infamous Arnie Foster was loitering at the counter, drumming on the granite surface with his fingers. The set of Arnie's mouth made it clear that he was braced for combat. Fortunately, he didn't notice Armstrong and Phipps as they slipped by behind him.

Federal courts were lint traps for loonies. A steady trickle of them showed up waving illegible complaints and demanding relief from imagined injustices. Some of these, like Arnie Foster, were known as "radioactives," folks who'd decided that the CIA, or possibly the Federal Aviation Administration, had planted wires in their brains, or very small microphones in their dentures, to monitor and control their thoughts. They came to court seeking injunctions to put a stop to this. Most of the ninety-four federal district courts in the United States had radioactives. They ate up a lot of time.

"I thought Judge Helms threw out Foster's case." Armstrong used his card to buzz them through a locked entry into the maze of offices behind the public area.

As the door closed behind them, Phipps exhaled a sigh. "She did dismiss the last complaint, but he's filed a new one. Someone else is sticking bugs in his brain now."

"Who's doing it this time?"

"Michelle Obama."

"Uh-huh. She probably is."

"I just saw Judge Helms, and she's tossed this new one too." Phipps paused. "I love her. She's so smart. She knows what she wants to do, and she just does it."

"She's dealing with a lot these days."

Phipps waved the file she'd been carrying. "Anyway, now I'm going to have to give Arnie the bad news, and he's going to hit the roof again. It's like—"

"Let me handle it, Angie." He took the folder from her. "Nobody ever yells at me."

"Are you kidding?"

"Okay, hardly ever." Armstrong gave Phipps a fatherly pat on the shoulder. "But let me manage this one, okay? You just take care . . ."

6

Judge Norcross was poring over some paperwork to prepare for his next immigration sentencing when he heard a soft knock. His law clerk, Mossy Campbell, was standing in the doorway.

"Sorry to bother you, Judge. I was grabbing a sandwich, and one of the African guys from *Okello*, the one with the collar, came up to me in the cafeteria. He says he'd like to see you if you have a minute."

Norcross was very fond of Mossy. She was a superb researcher and writer, always in a good mood, and almost as tall as he was. Before law school, she'd been a star point guard on the University of Connecticut women's basketball team. He suspected that she could have made a lot more money playing professionally than working for him.

Despite his affection for her, Mossy's interruption at this particular moment irritated him. He had a pile of documents to work through, including the *Okello* Judgment and Commitment order, and he was concerned that the priest, or whatever he was, might want to discuss something about the case. He couldn't do that. Catching his look, Mossy hesitated and added: "He says his name is Reverend David Kamau."

Kamau must have taken special care introducing himself, because Mossy pronounced the man's name correctly. It rhymed with the comic-book sound of a rifle shot—*ka-pow!*—and was a very common name in the Highlands area outside Nairobi, where the judge had spent two years teaching after college.

"Did he say what it was about?"

"No, except that he brings greetings from . . . just a sec, he wrote it down." She looked at a slip of paper in her hand. "He brings greetings from the village of . . ." It was clear the name had her buffaloed. "I can't say it." She handed him the note.

The slip of paper made Norcross smile despite himself. It bore two words, *Mwi Muto*. This was the name of a little village not far from the Kenya Institute of Administration, where he'd taught.

"It's pronounced Mwee Moo-toe. A very pretty place." He looked at the paper, letting his recollection drift. "*Muto* means 'river' in Kikuyu, the tribal language of that area. The village sits above a stream." A silence grew as Norcross continued to stare at the note.

Finally, Mossy broke in. "So. What do you—"

"Sorry. Bring him around."

As he waited, Norcross had a passing concern that David Kamau might turn out to be someone he was supposed to know but wouldn't recognize after so many years. Fortunately, as soon as Kamau entered his chambers it was obvious that he would have been, at most, an infant or toddler at the time Norcross left Africa. Kamau carried himself very upright and held his raincoat folded over one arm. His dark, well-pressed suit set off his bright clerical collar. Some of the same intense expression that Norcross had noticed in the courtroom lingered in his eyes.

Norcross stood and held out his hand, "Hello. I'm David Norcross."

Kamau took the judge's hand firmly. "It is an honor for me to meet you, Judge Norcross. I am David Kamau." Typical of well-educated Kenyans, he spoke with a British accent. "Reverend David Kamau, I suppose I should say." He smiled faintly. "It's new, and I am still coming around to it."

Norcross felt awkward having his guest sit across from him at his oversize desk. Instead, he steered Kamau into a more informal alcove, where a sofa and two upholstered chairs were placed around a coffee table. Kamau laid his coat over the arm of the sofa and took a seat.

As he lowered himself into the wingback, Norcross nodded in the direction of the courtroom. "I noticed someone with you in court. Will he be joining us?"

"No, and it's probably for the best. We had a minor row."

"I'm sorry."

"It's not a problem. We're very old friends—we were at school together—and we'll soon patch it up." His deep voice made him sound older than his years. It was easy to picture him in the pulpit. "The passage of time has been kind to you, Your Honor. An acquaintance from the village had an old photograph of you. In it, you are very young." Kamau nodded at the judge. "But I easily recognized you even after so many years."

"It was a special time for me, certainly, and a wonderful place."

"Our family lived in Nairobi, and I mostly grew up there, but I spent many happy days in Mwi Muto with my cousins when I was a young boy."

"I'm not surprised. It was beautiful. The maize and coffee fields." Norcross paused, remembering. "So green."

"People told me that after your day teaching at the Institute you would walk over to Mwi Muto and teach English in the evenings. That was very generous of you." Kamau smiled. "My older cousins still sometimes talk about Bwana David."

"I loved it." After a few weeks in Kenya, the young David Norcross had begun giving English lessons to the elders of Mwi Muto three evenings a week. The village was a mile from the Institute over a dirt path. When the lesson was over, one of his students would sometimes invite him back for a meal of grilled goat's meat and homemade beer. Sometimes he'd end up spending the night. The next morning, David would retrace the red-earth trail along the stream back to the Institute. A damp mist would be lying in the low patches, roosters would be crowing, and the aroma of cooking fires would be in the air.

"It seems long ago now. Long ago and almost out of a myth." Norcross rubbed his eye. "But tell me about yourself. What brings you to the United States?"

Kamau explained that he had a fellowship at Harvard Divinity School. His grandfather had been Kenya's first postcolonial minister of education, and his parents had strongly emphasized academics. Prior to coming to the United States, Kamau had attended an elite preparatory school outside Nairobi before moving on to Magdalen College, Oxford, where he'd taken a First in theology, a rare honor.

"Well done."

Kamau waved his hand. "I'm making too much of myself." He looked thoughtful. "Perhaps I want you to be impressed, Your Honor—a barefoot child running around an obscure village in central Kenya, a little nothing who has grown up to be a very small something."

"Not so small. Young maybe." Norcross leaned back in his chair. "I'm afraid I need to mention one thing before we go too far. If you are here to discuss the Okello case, I'm sorry to say—"

"Oh my goodness, no." Kamau held up his hands. His palms were pink. "I understand that would be quite improper."

"Thank you. I'm relieved."

"Being here for the Okello family was rather a coincidence. I know them only slightly. I wanted to pay you a visit for an entirely independent reason."

"Ah." Norcross felt himself tighten, preparing for whatever this reason might be.

"I was feeling a bit apprehensive, I suppose." Kamau gave a short laugh. "I needed the Okellos to set me in motion."

"Did we overlap at all when I was in Kenya? I imagine you would have been just a child."

"No, I was born after you left. Up to now, I've only known you through the village chatter. You talk about myth, sir, but to me . . ." Kamau looked up, meeting Norcross's eyes. "I must confess that for me this is rather like encountering a figure out of folklore."

"Well . . ." Norcross said. "Here I am. Billy Goat Gruff."

They both smiled. Norcross had been wrestling with an urge to inquire about a woman from Mwi Muto he'd been close to. Now, he persuaded himself to speak. "I doubt you've met her—she would be a little older than I am, and she may not live in the area anymore—but do you happen to know a woman named Hannah Nyeri? We both worked at the Institute, and . . ." He hesitated, searching for the words. "We became good friends."

"Yes. Hannah," Kamau said. "Ms. Nyeri. Of course. I knew her." He leaned forward tapping his fingers together, collecting himself. The intense expression that had struck Norcross so strongly in the courtroom had slipped away as they'd been talking. Now, it returned. "Do you remember a rather quaint colloquialism we Africans have—the special use, sometimes, of the term 'late'?"

"I remember." Norcross began to feel a little sick.

"Then I must share with you the sad news that Hannah Nyeri is late."

Some central panel in Judge Norcross's mind cut out, and the room gathered itself into a stillness. Reverend Kamau was telling Norcross that Hannah Nyeri was dead. She was the "late" Hannah Nyeri. Norcross became aware of the faint whistle of the breath going in and out of his nose. David and Hannah had stayed in touch after he'd left Africa, with occasional letters and, later on, infrequent emails. Then, as life tumbled along, their youthful connection predictably dissolved. He hadn't realized until that moment how ardently he'd been assuming that Hannah remained in this world and that the two of them still shared happy memories of each other, even after so many years.

"I'm so sorry to hear that. I . . ." Norcross paused. "I thought . . . I thought very highly of Hannah."

"Yes, I . . ." Reverend Kamau looked down at the floor. "We all did." The silence resumed in the room and stretched out. After a while, Kamau smiled and said quietly, "Sometimes, you know, she would come to observe my cricket matches."

"You played cricket?"

"At school, a bit. And at Oxford."

"And your friend there in the courtroom, did he play too?"

Kamau took two or three seconds to absorb the question, then threw back his head and burst out laughing. "Him? Forgive me—the very idea!" He paused to take a breath, shook his head, and laughed again. "My poor friend could not, as we say, score a single off a slow long-hop." He wiped his eyes. "He is most definitely not a sportsman."

Kamau's laughter made Norcross smile too. He remembered how, while he'd been in Kenya, the faces of some of the men could move abruptly from austere—intimidating, actually—to irresistibly warm and delighted when something funny or touching came up. Despite his striking dignity, Kamau was still young. He might be a man of the cloth, but he liked to laugh, and he had a wonderful smile.

"Well, I'm not sure what a long-hop is, but . . ."

"I believe that, in your baseball, it might be called an easy pitch over the middle of the plate." Kamau tapped the tips of his fingers together and shook his head, eyes still twinkling.

Another silence followed, and the judge's sadness at the news of his dear friend's death returned. Its power took Norcross by surprise.

"Did . . . did Hannah ever mention me?" He waved his hand, trying to brush the question away, embarrassed. "I'm sorry. I don't—"

"No, of course." Kamau leaned back in the sofa, immediately becoming serious again. "Hannah was a happy woman, I think, very happy in her life in the years after you left." He looked up at the ceiling, gathering his words. "But, yes, I remember she did mention you once or twice. I don't recall the context exactly, but it was something to the effect that the two of you were very young. She was laughing—I can see her quite clearly. And I think she said something about, if you'll forgive me, something about your being 'a very sweet boy.'"

"Ah. Well, it was . . . It was . . ." Norcross hesitated, and then, with no idea where he was going, stopped. The two men subsided into silence again. The quietness between them did not feel at all awkward, and it dawned on Norcross that, in a surprisingly short time, he had come to like Reverend Kamau very much.

After a while, Kamau cleared his throat. "Perhaps I should tell you what prompted me to come here." He smiled. "Apart from our mutual affection for my little village."

"Yes. Great."

"I should have rung you up first. I'm sorry if . . ."

"No, no. It's okay."

"We have a small committee of foreign students at the Divinity School that sponsors speakers from time to time to address various topics, especially ones involving difficult moral or ethical issues." A look of unhappiness passed over Kamau's face. "A colleague from Nigeria had to return home, and the responsibility to arrange our next speaker has unexpectedly fallen on me."

"I see."

"Her application to extend her visa was denied, and she had to leave very abruptly." The shadow behind Kamau's eyes deepened. "She was escorted to her plane." He took a breath before continuing. "So. I was hoping you might honor us by coming to speak at our next program."

"Ah."

"You may choose any topic you wish, of course, but I know our membership would be especially interested in your capital case, your views on the death penalty, or anything you felt comfortable saying about that."

"You know about my *Hudson* trial?"

"I confess we do. We googled you."

"I see, of course. Well, I'd have to avoid certain areas, but . . ." Norcross paused, then gave himself a shove. "Yes, certainly, of course. I'd be honored."

"Or you could discuss immigration law."

Norcross broke in quickly. "I'll stick to the death penalty. It's easier."

"Unfortunately, with our summer schedule the timing is a bit compressed. Perhaps as soon as sometime next week. I'll need to confer with—"

Mossy Campbell stuck her head into the room, beaming. "Judge, just wanted to let you know . . ." She noticed Reverend Kamau. "Oh, sorry."

"It's all right. What's up?"

Mossy's eyes drifted over to Kamau. What she had to say was for Norcross's ears only.

Kamau immediately stood up. "I've taken up enough of your time, Your Honor." He nodded at the judge. "It's been a great pleasure to meet you."

"The feeling is entirely mutual."

They shook hands, and once more Norcross noticed the appraising look in Kamau's eyes, briefer this time.

"I'll consult with our committee and be in touch soon." Kamau collected his raincoat and umbrella.

"I look forward to that."

"I can find my way out." Reverend Kamau nodded to Mossy and was gone.

Norcross looked over at the couch where Kamau had been sitting and realized, feeling ridiculous, that he was hoping he'd see Kamau's wallet or cell phone on the cushion so he could run after him.

The first time he had caught sight of Hannah Nyeri, she had been walking along a hedge of bougainvillea next to one of the Institute's new brick classroom buildings. Two or three years older than David, she had a master's degree from Makerere University in Kampala, and she was one of the most popular teachers on the faculty. When he'd seen her, she'd been caught up in some earnest conversation with one of her students. Her quick smile as she passed was so bright and unexpected that it had made his head swim.

At this point, he remembered his law clerk, who was still standing in the doorway.

"Sorry. What's up?"

"Just wanted to let you know that they redrew *O'Connell*, and we got it." Mossy raised a fist in the air. "I'm so psyched!"

High-profile cases always excited the law clerks, and sometimes Norcross, too, but the news of the *O'Connell* draw, though half expected, landed on him heavily. The challenge wasn't so much in presiding over the trial, which would be hard but interesting, as in having to tell Claire that he'd be tied up in Boston for another two or three weeks. The first stage of the proceeding, jury selection, would be especially tricky and possibly protracted. He'd need to get Angie Phipps working right away, contacting counsel, rearranging his docket, and clearing the deck for action.

7

Dominic and Julie O'Connell were sitting kitty-corner at the end of their dining room table, playing Semi-Cooperative Scrabble, one of the games Julie had invented to keep Dom from climbing the walls during his home confinement. Her version cut down on competition by allowing them to look at each other's letters, make swaps, and total up a joint score.

Julie pointed at his letter rack. "I'll trade you my 'S' for your 'G.'"

Dom knew that his wife had overhauled the rules because she was better at Scrabble than he was, and she didn't want him to feel stupid. He'd told her, truthfully, that losing at the game didn't make him feel dumb; it just meant he was bad at Scrabble. He was smarter at other things, like impressing fat-cat investors, intimidating loan officers, or bringing the hammer down on sleazy subcontractors. Still, if she thought her version was more fun, Dom was happy to play along.

"You'd give up your 'S'?"

"That way I can do 'wedge' here, and you can do 'zeroes' on the triple-word score."

He examined the board. "You never cease to amaze me, sweetheart." He looked up at her, admiringly. "Very first time I saw you, I loved your 'S.'"

"Don't think I didn't notice."

Dom's first wife had been killed in an automobile accident a week after their thirtieth anniversary. Eileen's sudden death had shattered him utterly, and even his three daughters couldn't dig him out of the black moods that dogged him during the years that followed. Julie's arrival somehow performed the miracle he'd stopped hoping for, and did not deserve, bringing him back to life. Now, their own tenth anniversary was just around the corner. Whatever he did for her could never be enough.

She reached over and patted his hand. "Hey, I got an email this morning. You have another granddaughter on the way."

Dom lit up. "Chloe?"

"Yep. They finally did it."

"Wonderful!" A wave of delight broke over him. "Wonderful."

Nothing, other than Julie, made Dom happier than his grandchildren, especially the little girls, but he'd told his daughters that he did not want them or the grandkids anywhere near the courtroom during his trial. Things were hard enough. He'd made it clear that constant phone calls would not be helpful either. He knew that they loved and supported him, and that was enough. He let Julie keep everyone up-to-date.

The age difference between Dom and his wife had never bothered him or, as far as he could tell, Julie either. Even with his heart problems and all the meds he was on, the two of them had—with his doctor's approval and Judge Helms's permission—run a charity 10K together that April, finishing in the top half. Against doctor's orders, he could still bench press 175 pounds.

They made their trade and arranged their tiles. He let his eyes rest on Julie as she jotted down the new point total.

"Listen, honey, you should go to the Saltonstalls' party. Everybody will be—"

"No way." Julie shook her head without looking up.

Dom knew that she was still upset about his illegal trip down to New York. It had not been the brightest thing he'd ever done, but she'd never asked him a single question about it, never complained.

The fact was, he'd had to get out. All his life he'd been an outdoor, on-the-go kind of guy. Sleep had never been a problem for him, but now he spent the night tossing in half dreams, with old pieces of memory from the Scanlon ride sliding into place like tiles in a mosaic floor. Every night, the details of what happened got clearer.

"Yo-Yo Ma's in town, and he'll be there. You know how much he'd love to—"

"Wouldn't be any fun without you, babe." There was a sharp knock outside, and Julie jumped up to see who it was. "No Dom, no laughs."

They'd agreed that he would never answer the door, in case it was a reporter or some contract photographer trying to lure him into the entryway for a snap. Julie's happy voice was reassuring.

"Hey, fellas! What's up?"

"Hello there, Jules. God help me, have you gotten younger?"

He recognized the voice of his friend and business associate Rafferty. Before he was halfway through the entry, Rafferty had babbled out two or three paragraphs on how terrific Julie was looking. The man could talk. But there was at least one other pair of heavy male feet approaching, and when the group entered the room, Dom was pleased to see that it was a younger man, Aidan. Unlike Rafferty, Aidan was clearly in a foul mood, and Dom was pleased to see that too. He wanted Aidan in work mode.

They all moved into the living room, with Rafferty and Aidan taking seats on the sofa.

"So how you doing, Dom?" Rafferty turned to look at Julie. "Tell me the truth, Jules, he's driving you batshit, right?"

"Julie, would you mind making some lemonade for my good friends here?"

Julie got up, smiling. "Shall I put something in it?"

Rafferty waved a hand. He had a classic red face and a curly head of bright, coppery hair. "Nah, it's too early." Aidan, sallow as a corpse, said nothing.

Dom looked up at Julie. "Just lemonade, thanks." As she disappeared, he added. "Take your time, okay?"

As soon as they were alone, Dom turned to Aidan.

"I have a job for you."

Aidan didn't say anything, just cocked his head to one side, listening.

"My old lawyer, Newbury . . ."

Rafferty broke in. "Oh, Newbury, that dipshit. He's such a—"

"Shut up, Raff, okay?" Dom softened his tone. "You're a good man, but I want Aidan to take the lead on this one."

Rafferty leaned back in the sofa and held up his hands, palms out. "Your call, Dom."

"Newbury has something of mine. He knows it, and he's making me chase him." Dom's mouth tightened. "If he's not careful, he's going to make me lose my temper."

Aidan didn't change expression. "You want him brought here?"

"Yeah."

"No problem."

"Don't take any baloney from him. He knows why I want to see him, and I'm done asking nicely." Dom turned to the side, frowning. "I can't go into details on the phone, even if the son of a bitch would call me back. Sandy Tarbell says I should assume there's some guy next door with a headset, recording every word I say. I want Newbury here in person to—"

"Dom, what is this?" Aidan interrupted. "I don't care if you want him here to tie a bow on his dick. He'll be here. When do you want him?"

"Tomorrow at . . . wait. Damn." Dom thought for a second. Clanking sounds were coming from the kitchen, a spoon going around in a ceramic pitcher. He hated to put this off—he'd made his decision, but he didn't have a choice. "Sunday at three."

"No problem."

"Julie's got something with her book group then. You two come with him."

8

Warren Armstrong had not attended any of his previous college reunions, but he was delighted that he'd turned up for his twenty-fifth. Ridiculous situations enchanted him, and the chaos in Harvard Yard as his classmates assembled for their group photo was a spectacle he would not have missed for anything. The overwrought photographer was going bananas.

"People! People!" The poor guy was standing on a rickety platform of plywood and scaffolding, six feet off the ground, with his wide-angle camera set up on a stand. He was scooping his arms in the air as though he were trying to pull in a cloud of butterflies.

"Please. PLEASE! If you are standing beyond the end of the row of benches here . . . Sir? SIR! If you are standing outside the benches, which is where you are now, you are not going to be in the picture." Someone bumped the wobbly platform, and the photographer grabbed the tripod to steady himself. "Hey! Whoa!"

A high-pitched voice sang out. "Sorry!"

The crowd gathering for the picture comprised about three hundred alums and spouses, loosely, very loosely, assembled on the broad steps of Widener Library. Knots of six or eight people kept drifting off and then floating back to rejoin the main body. Half the assembly was paying no attention to the photographer, too busy hugging and slapping the backs of old friends.

As Armstrong stood on the edge of the crowd looking for a place to squeeze in, he noticed his handsome classmate Sam Newbury, blond head held high, striding along with his hand on someone's shoulder. Newbury, typically, had gotten himself picked to be class secretary, which gave him an excuse to hustle. Their class included an unusual number of big shots who might be useful to him, including a famous actor who drew a crowd whenever he stopped to blow his nose, a high-tech billionaire (supposedly the eleventh-richest man in the country), and a former All-Pro wide receiver for the Kansas City Chiefs. It was a networker's dream.

Despite his thick layer of New England upper crust, Newbury wasn't a bad guy. They'd both been in Eliot House, and Newbury had regularly let Armstrong use his vintage MG for drives out to Wellesley to pay visits to the undergrad who would eventually become his wife. Things were improving in those days, but not many rich white boys would do that sort of thing for a Black kid from downtown.

Newbury's sharp eye had no trouble picking out Armstrong, and he hurried over to him. Armstrong prepared to be greased.

"Hey, Warren, they let you out?"

"Once every twenty-five years, Sammy. How's it going?"

Newbury gave the person he'd been talking to a couple of quick pats and shoved him off toward University Hall.

"It's totally crazy. We're already behind schedule. The Secret Service needed half an hour for their damned dog."

"Their dog?"

"Sniffing for bombs. Sarah Blackwell insists on being in the class picture, and now we're waiting for her. They want her here and gone before anyone even notices."

"Sarah Blackwell was in our class?" Former Senator Sarah F. Blackwell had been appointed secretary of Homeland Security a few months back. "I thought she was a year ahead of us."

But Newbury was already trotting off. "Lunch next week? I'll call you." He pointed to a vacant spot at the end of a row of benches. "I'd grab that seat, Warren. We may be a while."

Only the first row was going to get to sit. All the rest of the alumni had to arrange themselves in tiers on the granite steps leading up to the library entrance. Standing up there was tough on the back, and people were beginning to gripe.

Armstrong lowered himself gratefully onto the bench. The delay had worked out well for him. He'd hung around court until the last minute, hoping to slip in a meeting with Chief Judge Broadwater. He'd wanted to let the chief know about an incompetent docket clerk who was threatening to sue her judge for age discrimination, and he needed to get clearance to bring someone in from Washington to look into CAP, the Case Assignment Program. Whatever the problem was seemed to be over Angie Phipps's head. But Broadwater had squeezed in a preliminary injunction hearing during a break in his criminal trial. It was scheduled to go thirty minutes and still droning on after ninety. Armstrong's last-minute dash for Cambridge had him arriving a couple of minutes after the time originally scheduled for the photo.

As an awkward young Black man from Roxbury, Armstrong hadn't found his time at Harvard easy. Even so, he'd retained a certain fondness for the place. Widener Library's twelve mammoth columns still faced the four columns of Memorial Church at the far end of the Yard. They were like two sets of teeth, secular and divine, grinning—or maybe growling—at each other. The crisscrossing tree-lined walkways were as graceful as ever. Sadly, several of the giant trees from his undergraduate days had fallen prey to disease and been replaced by honey locusts, maples, and other trees he didn't recognize. The scene was very pretty, very collegiate, but after all the years not quite the same. It was true that you could never go back.

"Excuse me, lady in the blue hat? No, no, the other lady in the blue hat." The photographer was pointing. "No, not you. YOU! Yes. Would you please take your hat off? I can't see the man behind you."

The photographer shook his head and muttered, "These people went to college? I've had Cub Scout troops . . ."

A vaguely African- or Middle-Eastern-looking man in green coveralls was walking in Armstrong's direction, awkwardly holding an overstuffed shopping bag in one hand and pulling a wheeled plastic barrel behind him with the other. Armstrong had seen the man earlier, one of the campus custodians, spearing discarded programs and scraps of paper.

The crowd was finally beginning to cohere, grumbling and shuffling, with two or three of the college's undergraduate interns nipping around the fringes like border collies. The photographer broke into a grin. "Yes! Thank you, Shannon. Now, in a minute I'm going to ask everybody to look at me, and—"

"Wait!" A portly man trotted up, wife in tow. "Is this the class picture?"

The photographer lowered his face into his hands.

An empty space next to Armstrong at the very end of the bench was big enough for one more person, if he or she was not too large. The custodian approached and placed the shopping bag there. It had a Harvard COOP label with a wad of crimson tissue paper stuffed on top. The custodian spoke in broken English, pointing in the direction of Emerson Hall, off to Armstrong's right. "She ask me. Save her seat."

Armstrong nodded and craned his neck but couldn't locate whomever the custodian was pointing at. There was a lot of milling around. "Well, if she wants to be in the picture, she'd better shake a leg." The custodian walked away, pulling his noisy trash receptacle.

A few seconds later, a broad-shouldered man in a navy suit and tie strode quickly up to Armstrong and pointed at the bag. "I wonder if we could move that, sir, and slip Secretary Blackwell in here." He had one of those button gizmos in his ear with a wire trailing down, obviously part of some security detail.

Having half agreed to save the seat for someone else, Armstrong felt conflicted. "Well, fact is, it's not my . . ."

"We can just put it here for now, okay?" The agent set the bag on the ground between Armstrong's feet. He called over his shoulder. "Right here, ma'am."

Sarah Blackwell had been editor of the *Crimson* when they'd been undergraduates, and Armstrong vaguely recognized her. He held out his hand.

"Warren Armstrong."

"Hello, Warren. How nice to see you." She shook his hand but did not bother to give her name. "What a lovely day, huh?"

"Yes. Very nice."

"Sorry to make you move your bag. My guys can be . . ."

"Thing is, it's not my bag."

The agent was standing six feet away, looking around at the crowd with a sharp expression. He must have overheard Armstrong because he immediately spoke up. "Whose bag is it?"

At this point, a voice burst through from the far side of the steps, several rows behind him.

"Hey, Armstrong! ARMSTRONG!" When he twisted around, he saw another old Eliot House friend, Louis Baptiste, his irrepressible roommate from Trinidad. Armstrong was inclined to wave him off and catch up later, but he knew the man would never give up. In their undergraduate adventures, Louis was always the ringleader. No girl could resist his accent.

"Come, man, we got space for you. Group portrait!"

Two other voices joined the summons, other Black Eliot House alums he'd known well.

"Stir yourself, you unruly thug!"

"*Fanya haraka!*" This was a Swahili phrase they'd been in the habit of using, meaning "Hurry up."

Armstrong sighed and stood. He knew resistance was futile, but he hesitated out of concern for the poor photographer. His path was going to take him in front of the row of benches, right past the center of the picture, where a group of alumni was holding the Harvard Twenty-Fifth Reunion banner.

The photographer noticed he was standing, getting ready to make his move. He put his hands on his hips and glared at Armstrong. "You're kidding, right?"

Armstrong was looking up to where his friends were, considering the best route to get to them. Secretary Blackwell was smiling up at him uncertainly.

"Sir! Whose bag is it?" The agent had taken a step closer.

Armstrong shrugged. He was reluctant to go off and leave the bag where anyone could take it. He picked it up and held it at shoulder height.

"Does this belong to anyone?" He looked around.

Sam Newbury had positioned himself near the top of the steps facing down at the photographer's stand, where he'd have a good view of everybody but still be in the picture. Glancing behind him, he noticed an attractive woman emerging from the library and descending in his direction. He started to smile, trying to remember where he'd seen her. On the step just above him, she paused to check her purse, looked annoyed—as though she'd forgotten something—and began to turn around.

The jarring sound of the explosion startled Newbury so badly that he stumbled backward and knocked the woman down. It was not so much a boom as a giant bang that left his ears ringing—like two iron freight cars slamming together at full speed. A few seconds later, as he untangled himself and scrambled to his feet, he caught sight of the Widener columns. In two places, bloody globs of something had spattered against them. Deep red trails were running down the granite now, like dripping paint. Dazed and apologizing, Newbury bent to help the woman. She looked confused, and on her left side a crimson stain was spreading.

Almost immediately, the screaming began, people shrieking for help and a hoarse male voice rising above the rest: "Oh my God! Oh my God! Oh my God!"

9

Norcross was bent over his briefcase, getting organized for his walk back to the condo, when Angie Phipps appeared in the doorway. He hadn't been expecting her.

"Did you hear?" She propped her hand against the doorframe. Her mascara was smeared, leaving a sooty smudge under one eye.

"Hear what?"

"There was a bomb at Harvard, I guess." She seemed dazed and shook her head in disbelief. "Sarah Blackwell was killed. The, you know, the . . ." She shifted her eyes to Norcross for help.

"Right. Homeland Security. Good God, that's awful, Angie."

"There's hardly any details." She took a shaky breath. "It's on CNN."

"Do they have any idea who did it?"

"Warren Armstrong was at Harvard this afternoon."

"Oh man! I don't like that." Norcross slid a clump of memos into his briefcase. "Did you try his cell?"

"No answer."

"Well, Harvard's a big place. Still." He stopped fiddling with his papers and looked at Phipps. "Are you okay, Angie?"

"At least two other people were killed they said, not just Black-well, and a bunch of others are critical." Her mouth twitched down. "Warren has always been, you know, really good to me."

"Oh, Angie, I'm sorry." He stepped toward her. "I'm sure he's okay. The chances are very slim that anything happened to him."

"He was always really great about Ronnie."

"I'm sure he's fine. It must be crazy over there." He snapped his briefcase shut. "Just keep trying, okay? And when you get him, please ask him to call me."

"Okay." Phipps started to turn away, but stopped herself. "I almost forgot. The African guy in court the other day? In *Okello*? Not the tall one, the other guy—the shorter one with the glasses—dropped this off for you." She handed him an envelope.

"Thanks. I'm running late." He slipped the envelope into his jacket. "Keep trying Warren, will you please?"

Phipps nodded, turned, and hurried off. It was sweet of her to be so worried, except that now Norcross was worried too.

From his years at the law school, Judge Norcross could easily picture Harvard Yard, very serene. The thought of some terrible violence there was sickening. About Blackwell herself, he'd always had fairly neutral feelings. Some of what she said made him uncomfortable, but she had a reputation as a hard worker, and the blow to her family would be horrible. Did she have children?

Norcross called Claire, partly to make sure she knew what had happened and partly just to check on her—foolishly, since she was miles away from Harvard Yard—but his calls to the condo's landline and to her cell phone only got voice mail, and a text got no blips.

As he was hurrying down the back corridor toward the judges' elevator, he ran into Peggy Helms. She was a glamorous-looking woman in her midseventies, always fashionably dressed and with a perfectly coiffed swoop of snow-white hair. Today, she was wearing a navy suit, a thick gold necklace, and large glasses with bright red frames.

It was a wonderful thing, and a bit amazing, that his strong-minded judicial colleagues, appointed by five different presidents, for the most part sincerely liked one another. The vast majority of their cases touched on no hot-button issues, and everyone pulled together to get the work of the court done. Occasionally, some sharp differences arose—the discussion of cameras in the courtroom had been especially fierce—but the shared pressures of the job gave them a kind of sibling bond that smoothed over rough patches.

Next to Skip Broadwater, of all his colleagues Norcross was fondest of Peggy Helms. Even in the face of the news about the bombing, he felt his heart lift when he saw her stately figure coming down the hallway toward him. She had a stride like a dowager runway model.

As they came closer, she raised her eyebrows. "You've heard, I suppose?" She had a throaty voice.

"Yes. Do we know who did it?"

"Just another twisted soul, I imagine, who thinks he's saving the world." Helms shook her head. "Or taking his revenge on it. It's so sad."

"Angie Phipps says Warren was in the area." He pushed the elevator button.

"Really? Where?"

"Somewhere at Harvard. We're trying to get a hold of him."

"Marvelous. Something else to worry about."

"I'll be glad to get home."

"Please say hello to dear Claire. You have a real treasure there." After a pause, Helms added, "Sorry you got *O'Connell*, David. It nearly killed me to drop that case, but I hated even more that it landed on you. You're not even from around here."

"No problem. It's just another trial. My law clerk is ecstatic, of course."

"They always are, bless their greedy little hearts."

"Stupid of O'Connell to fly the coop like that." The elevator arrived, and Norcross followed Helms inside.

"Silly man! Two weeks before trial—what could have possessed him? I put the fear of God in him. I doubt you'll have any more trouble of that kind."

"Some of the papers were disappointed that you only put him on the ankle tracker."

"I know. The *Herald* wanted him dangling upside down over a brazier." She adjusted her glasses. "I'm keeping all my other cases, of course, but that one—now that it's a trial and not a plea—I simply couldn't . . ." She trailed off.

"Please, Peggy. Don't worry about it."

"Will you be able to hold them to the trial date?"

"Absolutely. You fixed the day, and that's when it goes."

"Good." Helms looked relieved. "Something funny's going on with that case. Somebody's playing games."

"The games tend to stop once the jury is in the box."

"Exactly."

After another pause, Norcross took a breath and said, "I'm, um, very sorry about Tony."

"Thank you." Helms pressed her lips together. "Perhaps we could talk about that some other time."

"Of course." He cleared his throat. "I know how it is."

She lifted her eyes to him. "I know you do."

At the ground floor, Norcross got off, and Helms gave him a brief, stoic smile before continuing to the basement parking area.

Two Boston patrol cars sat by the curb outside the courthouse, their blue lights flashing. A court security officer in a navy blazer stood just beyond the doors, hands behind his back, bouncing on his toes nervously.

"What's up, Johnnie?"

"Oh, hi, Judge." The CSO gestured toward the patrol cars. "They're setting up a security perimeter as a precaution, and we're calling in some additional staff to keep an eye on things."

"You guys are moving fast."

"This Harvard mess has given everybody the jitters. Can't help remembering the Marathon."

"Thanks. We all rely on you."

Norcross knew it was not rational, but he was increasingly anxious to get home to Claire and Charlie. He considered calling an Uber but decided it wouldn't save much time. The downtown streets were a maze of one-ways, and some of them might be blocked. At a brisk pace, he could be at the condo in less than half an hour.

On the sidewalks near the courthouse, more people than usual seemed to be on their cell phones, even the people in groups. There was a continuous wail of sirens, sometimes from cruisers barging through the red lights right in front of him, sometimes moaning in the distance. Radical groups, the judge recalled, would sometimes space out a series of explosions. It felt as though anything could happen.

Walking quickly along, he checked CNN on his cell. The photographs were horrific, but he could find no names of victims other than Blackwell. He increased his pace, eventually crossing Tremont Street at the Park Street T Station and making his way through the Common. He knew the terrain from when he'd worked in Boston as a young lawyer, and ordinarily he would have enjoyed being part of the bustling scene. Today it was all a blur.

He was marching up Commonwealth Avenue, on the wide tree-lined walkway in the middle, when he noticed a young woman sitting on a bench near the statue of Alexander Hamilton. She was reading a book and rocking a stroller with her free hand. As he drew nearer, the judge looked down at the infant and saw, to his surprise and delight, that it was his son, Charlie. The boy had hold of his bare foot and was studying it. When the young woman lowered her book, he recognized their neighbor's daughter and their sometime babysitter Brandy Kim.

"Brandy, hi! I didn't know . . ." He bent over the stroller. "Hey, buddy! How you doing?" Charlie glanced up at his father briefly before returning to his foot.

Brandy stood up, giving him a polite smile. "Hello, Judge Norcross. Nice to see you."

"Didn't know you were on duty."

"It was last minute. I was around, so I'm helping out."

"Uh-huh. Where's Claire off to?"

"She had some research thing." Brandy looked at her watch. "She should have been back by now. It must be taking her longer than she—"

"Did she say where she was going?"

"One of the libraries?" She gestured down the street. "Harvard, maybe?"

Everything got very sharply focused and distinct: the outlines of the shadows on the sidewalk, the smell of exhaust from a truck grinding by, the weight of his briefcase in his right hand. A couple of blocks away, someone gave an angry blast on his horn.

"Harvard." He needed to be very controlled. "Well, let's get Charlie inside, why don't we?"

He crossed the street, carefully looking both ways, pushing the stroller ahead of him, feeling the touch of each step on the pavement.

In the condo foyer, he turned.

"Listen, Brandy. You might not have heard, but there's been some kind of incident at Harvard, and I'm a little worried about Claire."

"Incident?"

"Some kind of terrorist incident, I'm afraid. Yes, I know." Brandy looked stricken. "Could you hang around and keep an eye on Charlie while I make a couple calls?"

She nodded down at the stroller. "Sure. I could put him down for his nap."

"Great. Great. Sorry if I seem distracted. I'm sure everything's fine. I'm just being, you know, a worrywart."

The condo was on the first floor, and after some fumbling, Norcross got the door open. As of this moment, everything was still okay. While Brandy steered the stroller into Charlie's room, Norcross made another call to Claire but got no answer. He followed up with a call to his security contact at the U.S. Marshals Service. They might have the names of some of the other victims. The phone rang a long time, and as he waited, he paced over to the windows looking out onto the street. The breeze was tossing the trees around as though nothing had happened.

A sudden thumping rose outside the door and then the clatter of a key in the lock. He killed the phone, tossed it on the sofa, and, three seconds later, there stood Claire.

The wave of relief brought a mist to the judge's eyes. By some very fast, very blurry sequence of movements they were immediately in each other's arms, holding on for dear life. He could not remember anything feeling so good.

"Christ! Are you all right? Were you at Harvard?"

Claire tipped her head back. A tear was running down her cheek, but her mouth was tipping into the start of a smile. It was like rain with the sun shining.

"David, you never swear. You . . ."

"I do, Claire." He pressed her against him. "I just save it for appropriate occasions."

Claire made a smothered noise—half groan, half laugh—as she mashed her cheek into his chest. "You are so bizarre, David, and I love you so much. Yes, I was there. I was—"

"Good God! Are you okay?"

"I don't know. I-I think so—" Claire interrupted herself. "Where's Charlie?"

"He's fine. He's in his room with Brandy. She's putting him down for his nap." He touched her cheek. "If something ever happened to you, I couldn't . . ."

"I know." She dropped her head onto his shoulder. "Neither of us could."

Nothing took place after that for some time, except the distant sound of traffic and the two of them inhaling and exhaling and pressing into each other. Finally, Claire spoke into the side of his neck. "It was awful, David. It was the worst thing I've ever . . ."

"So you were there then. At Widener?"

"The most horrible, horrible thing . . ." She took a deep, gulping breath and began to tremble. She pushed away from him, holding his arms, and spoke to the floor. "No." She shook her head. "I'm . . ." She stepped away and began flapping her hands as though she were trying to flick something off her fingertips. Her voice went up toward a squeak. "I'm not going to fall apart again."

"It's okay. It's okay."

"On the way over here, I think I scared the hell out of the guy who gave me a lift. I was sort of out of control. I couldn't stop—"

"You had a ride?"

"Yes, some very nice guy. Sam, um . . ." She turned her head to the side, thinking. "What was his name? It's a street in Boston. Wait." She held up a finger. "Sam Newbury. He was there too. He fell on me, actually."

"Sam Newbury, the lawyer?"

"I guess so. He said—"

"Blond, toothy guy?"

"I suppose." She gave a sort of laugh. "He did have incredibly white, even teeth. I remember that."

"That's him. He was at my old law firm."

Claire's speech picked up speed. "He said he recognized me from some bar association thing I'd been at with you. I was a total drooling mess. It took me most of the ride to regain my sanity."

"I'll have to find a way to thank him." Norcross looked around the room. "Can we sit down, please?"

"I can't right now." Claire put her hand on her chest and took another deep breath. "I really need a shower. I have to get out of these . . ."

There was a rustle behind them, and they turned to see Brandy, looking uncertain. She'd had the good sense to give them space, but it had been a while now.

"Sorry. Are you okay?" She held up her phone. "I ought to get home. I need to make some calls."

"Oh, Brandy," Claire said. "Thank you so much."

They agreed to settle up the next day, when she was scheduled to babysit again. Brandy had been a trooper, but the privacy after the door closed behind her was very welcome.

Norcross touched Claire's hair. "I tried to call you."

"I was in such a hurry that I left my stupid phone on a shelf in the library. I just needed a quick check on a facsimile of the Harley manuscript—this thing I'm working on—and I was rushing down the steps when I realized I'd left it, and . . ." She paused. "And that's when it happened. It was so loud it hurt. I could barely hear afterward. And then the . . ." She put both hands on Norcross's chest and looked up at him. "We can talk more after my shower, okay?"

As she turned, Norcross saw that the side of Claire's tunic was spattered red. "Claire, for God's sake, you're hurt. We need to get you to a—"

"That's the thing. It's not my blood!" Her voice went up. "It's not my blood, David. See?" She pulled up her tunic to show her unbroken skin. "It must be somebody else's."

"Oh God."

"I have to take a shower." She looked up at him, her voice shaking. "Seriously. I promise I'll be better afterward." She lifted the hem of her tunic and dropped it. "I really have to get out of these clothes." Flecks of blood were on her leggings too.

Norcross cupped her face in his hands. "It's okay. We're safe now. I love you."

"Thank you. I know you do." She looked into his eyes. "But I need to wash. I need hot, hot water."

Norcross nodded. "I'll find a bag for your clothes. Do you want some brandy or something? That's supposedly good in an emergency." His eyes wandered to the kitchen. "There probably isn't any."

"Tea, I think, after my shower. Any kind of herbal tea." She started to take her tunic off but got tangled.

"Here." Norcross helped Claire pull the tunic off over her head, noticing with something like an ache the tender, familiar contours of her shoulders. So vulnerable.

Claire threw the tunic on the floor and walked quickly off toward the bathroom, calling back. "Maybe some rum in the tea if you can find any."

As Norcross was rooting around under the sink looking for bags, he heard the shower kick on. Almost immediately after that, his cell phone rang. It was Chief Judge Broadwater.

"Skip?"

"Hi, Dave, this will have to be quick." Broadwater was the only one who ever called him Dave. Somehow, it was reassuring. "I'm contacting everyone to pass on some very sad news." He cleared his throat. "Can't bring myself to do it by email."

"Okay."

"There's no easy way to say this. Warren Armstrong is dead. He was among the people killed at the Harvard bombing."

"Oh, Skip."

"Apparently, he was sitting right next to Blackwell." Broadwater sighed deeply. "Rotten luck." After a pause, he continued. "I'm going to talk quickly here, because if I don't, I won't get through this. Warren and I go way back. I knew him in the governor's office when he was an intern, and it was clear even then that he was the real deal. I have a lot of calls to make. I'm . . ." He paused again to breathe. "I'm pretty cut up, to tell the truth."

Norcross sat down on a hassock in the living room. "I can't believe it. I just saw Warren Wednesday. He was twisting my arm to take *O'Connell*."

"Yes, I'd asked him to talk to you. I was supposed to see him today, but I got tied up." Broadwater broke off, and Norcross could hear him breathing hard again. "I can't go into details right now. If I start . . ." A silence followed. Broadwater must have turned away from the phone. Finally, he pushed on.

"The other thing I need to pass on is that they've got the bomber. It will be in the papers tomorrow and probably all over the internet any minute now. Turns out he's a Kenyan named Kahlil Khan, a Muslim."

"Uh-huh." Norcross immediately thought of Reverend Kamau. It was inconceivable that Kamau would be involved in this, but the coincidence startled him.

"The bomb may have been remotely detonated, which would mean that Khan was working with at least one other person." Norcross could hear a siren on the other end of the line, probably right below Broadwater's chambers. "They've traced him to a town on the Kenyan coast, Lamu or something."

David broke in. "Yes, it's on the Indian Ocean." He and Hannah had spent a week in Lamu in a beach cottage during the Institute's August vacation. The Asian housekeeper had noticed them holding hands and left a sprig of jasmine on their pillow.

"Mike Patterson from the FBI gave me a summary briefing. Seems Khan had a brother Hussain, who was deported this spring and found dead in Nairobi soon afterward. Kahlil may have been angry at DHS, and the court, too, which upheld the deportation order. It's possible that Hussain and Kahlil had a connection to the radical group Al-Shabaab. They've been active in the coastal areas of Kenya. Something like that. It's all still a muddle."

"Right. Sounds like it."

"I'm saying this, Dave, so you know that other bad guys may be out there, and they definitely know how to make things that go bang. We all need to be on our toes."

"Sure. Of course." Norcross got up off the hassock and walked over to the window. The trees were still tossing in the gusts of wind. "Can I contact anybody? I'd like to give you a hand here."

"Thanks, but I need to do this." Another pause followed while Broadwater may have been considering whether to say more. "Yes. Well. You're my first call. I need to go. Goodbye for now."

Norcross switched off his phone and stood staring out the windows. He needed to get Claire and Charlie out of Boston as soon as possible. He heard a heavy thud in the bathroom, like the sound of a large shampoo bottle hitting the floor.

10

The news of the death of Warren Armstrong, first on the internet and then in a blizzard of texts, transformed Angie Phipps into a zombie. As she steered through the Friday evening traffic, she stared blankly forward, telling herself: Just be empty. Do not feel. Do. Not. Think. If she started, she'd go straight into a light pole.

Except for alternate weekends, when her son visited, she lived by herself in an apartment on Memorial Drive in Cambridge. Her windows faced out onto the Charles River through a band of sycamores. When she got home and closed the door behind her, she flopped into a chair and gazed for half an hour out over the water, seeing nothing. After a while, her brain began to sputter, and unwelcome thoughts began making their way in.

She couldn't do anything right. She was too gabby and whiny. Her hair was all wrong. She overdid the flirting, like with Vinnie Seabury. She was a slut.

Her eyes drifted over to the bookcase where a large framed photo of Ronnie, with one of his big grins, sat on the top shelf. She retrieved it and sat back down, holding it in her lap. Ronnie's father had taken off halfway through her pregnancy. Who could blame him? She'd been impossible. She'd smoked weed all the time, which probably was the cause of Ronnie's problems. Warren had always kept an eye out for her. Tears started trickling down, and she lost track of time.

Eventually, she noticed the clock and remembered that her boyfriend, or the man she was determined to have as her boyfriend, would be arriving for dinner in less than an hour. She immediately leaped up, put the photo back on the shelf, found a Kleenex, and blew her nose very hard. One of the strengths she'd acquired during her years as a single mom was the ability, when she felt overwhelmed, to shift things into compartments. Now, she moved Warren's death into a small, quiet room and turned the key. Outside this room, nothing awful had happened. Her grief, guilt, or whatever it was could wait.

Scrubbing her face with a cold washcloth, Angie reassured herself that meal preparation would be simple. She'd decided that morning on an easy Mark Bittman recipe—citrus chicken—with basmati rice, green beans, and a salad. Nothing fancy. Carl would bring the wine. She was okay.

Carl Alberti worked for the Bureau of Alcohol, Tobacco, Firearms, and Explosives, known as the ATF, with an office in the U.S. Attorney's suite. He was seven years older than she was, two years postdivorce, and killer handsome. They'd met in an elevator at the courthouse and immediately clicked. Alberti had teased her about a book she'd been carrying, and she had mocked his neon-orange running shoes. Their one fling, in his car, had been quick and fumbling. She was determined that this particular night would be one he'd never forget. She'd bought silk underwear especially, emerald green.

The book she'd been carrying was titled *So What's Wrong with You?* by Sophia Antelope. It was a ridiculous, made-up name, but a lot of what Sophia wrote helped Angie in her big project—her voyage to a better life. Ronnie had arrived when she was only sixteen, and his severe needs had eaten up more than a decade of her life. Her big break had come two years ago when, with some help, she'd gotten Ronnie into a private residential program out in Berkshire County, in Lenox, where he was doing well. Then, she'd invested in a completely new wardrobe and leased herself a red BMW. She'd started taking self-defense lessons, learning some karate moves, which gave her the chance, once a week, to kick and shout. The move to the nicer apartment on Memorial Drive followed. It was way past time, she'd decided, to take some risks. Go a little wild.

Occasionally—like when she had to deal with the CAP—she could still feel the ground trembling under her, but she was making steady progress, and she loved the new her. Without Sophia's encouragement, she might never have found the courage to manage Helms, Norcross, and the other Honorables, and she might never have spoken to Carl Alberti or had the nerve to diss his comical shoes. She might never have done a lot of things.

She was juicing a lime when the phone rang. Her heart sank when she saw it was Alberti.

"Hi, Angie. You probably know why I'm calling."

"Yeah, but tell me anyway." She could hear he was talking from his car.

"You heard about the Harvard bombing?" Alberti had the tail of a Boston accent, and it came out in the way he pronounced "Harvard." It was incredibly sexy.

"Uh-huh."

"Well, we're all flat out now. Afraid we'll have to postpone our dinner." He paused when she didn't say anything. "I'm sorry." After another silence, he added, "Really sorry, believe me."

"You could come by for a drink later on if you wanted."

"Nah, it'll be really late." Alberti burst out in a different tone. "Oh shit!"

"Shit?"

"I'm on the Southeast Expressway. Something's tying the traffic up again."

"Ah."

"That's why I said 'shit.' I wasn't saying 'shit' about . . ."

"It's all right. You can say 'shit' whenever you want to." She waited a beat. "You're a big boy."

"Shit, shit, shit."

"Well, shit." She sat down on the bench in her breakfast nook. "Listen." She steadied herself and took a breath. "Come by any time tonight, whenever you're done. I'll be up."

"Nah. It could be, like, two, three a.m., or . . ."

"Any time, Carl."

"And I might be really wiped out."

"Uh-huh. And I might be in my lavender teddy." There was a thoughtful pause on Alberti's end. "But if it embarrasses you, I can take it off."

She could hear Alberti breathing. There was increased traffic noise in the background, the sound of cars accelerating.

"You're bringing me good luck, Angie. We're moving again."

"See?"

"Maybe I could squeeze in a visit, if you're sure you don't . . ."

"I'm sure. Let me give you my address."

"I have it."

"You do?"

"We know where everybody lives, Angie. Part of the job." The noise on Alberti's end continued to increase. "Listen, I have a call coming in here. I have to go."

"So, see you later maybe?"

"If I possibly can, I'll move mountains."

Apart from the accent, Carl had a romantic way of talking about things like moving mountains that made Angie's pulse quicken. As soon as she got off the phone, she turned on her Keurig. She was generally an early-to-bed girl, but tonight she was going to need her caffeine. After that, she began working through outfit changes. The big question was whether to stay in work clothes, switch into her date outfit, or put on her silk pajamas and dressing gown. The old Angie Phipps would definitely have gone with the pj's and the tousled-hair look. In the end, she decided on a yoga suit—cotton drawstring pants and a light top with the zipper pulled down enough to be interesting but not trashy.

It was, as Alberti had predicted, somewhere in the wee hours of the morning when Angie's intercom gave a short buzz. She had been dozing, and the sound was so brief that she wasn't sure at first whether she'd really heard it. Alberti must have been trying not to wake her if she'd gone to sleep. As she hurried to the door, she wondered how she would ever manage a relationship with someone this nice.

Alberti was wearing black jeans and a wrinkled blue polo shirt. In the doorway, he looked tired, and he did not lean forward to kiss her. Once inside, though, she got a long hug.

"You okay?" he asked. His rumpled, sympathetic face was unbearably sweet.

She lifted a shoulder. "Been better, to tell the truth."

"Listen—I should have said this before—I am really sorry about Warren Armstrong. I know how you felt about him. This must be just . . ."

"It's the worst, the worst, worst thing." She closed her eyes and shook her head. "I don't know if I can talk about it. What I could really use now is another one of those hugs."

"At your service."

This time, the experience was longer and squishier, and when they'd finished, they kissed. It was a nice enough kiss, but not necessarily a prelude to anything.

"Can I get you something?"

"Love a beer, if you've got one." Alberti walked into the living room. "Wow. Nice."

"Thanks." She went into the kitchen and got two cans out of the fridge. "You must have had one hard day."

"Yeah." He shook his head. "George Thomas, the guy who played for the Chiefs, is probably going to lose a leg. I just came from trying to ask him a couple questions. I've been interviewing some of the other injured too." He gave a tremendous sigh. "I have to say, yes, it's been one of the toughest days I've had since I began doing this work. Toughest days of my entire life, really."

She put a hand on his shoulder. "I'm so sorry. It must be . . ." She trailed off.

"Yeah, it is."

"If you just want to go to sleep . . ."

Alberti gave her his slow smile. "Let's see how this goes."

They sat for a while without saying anything. Two or three lonesome cars went by on Memorial Drive, out very late or up very early.

Nervously, she placed her hand on top of Alberti's. She was relieved when he responded by lacing their fingers.

"I don't know if I'm allowed to ask." She took a quick swallow of her beer. "But how are things going? Any progress?"

"There's a lot up in the air that I can't talk about, but a few things will be public by tomorrow." He blew out a breath. "It looks like a straight terrorist hit. The FBI has grabbed the guy who placed the bomb, somebody named Khan, a Kenyan."

"You're sure it's him and not just . . ."

"Harvard's security cameras suck, but you can see him well enough, about three minutes before the explosion, taking the hand-off from some female."

"Really? A woman?"

"Yeah, and a little too well-dressed for the occasion." He looked into the distance. "Then Khan wheels his barrel over and puts the bag down on the end of the bench next to Armstrong. It's blurry, but—"

"So it wasn't just, like, some local crazy?" Her hand shook as she placed her beer on the coffee table.

"Negative. The bomber may be part of a local cell. His brother was deported a few months ago and ended up dead in Kibera, the big slum around Nairobi. We're combing the Boston area for other possible coconspirators, especially Kenyans." He looked at her. "I'd better leave it at that. There's a lot we still don't know."

"It must be so hard. I can't imagine." She laid her head on Alberti's shoulder. He bent down and kissed her. This time, the kiss had more pepper.

"Listen, Angie. Couple things." His face was close. "First, most important. You've been on my mind a lot. Even with everything else going on."

"Me too." She lifted her head. "I mean, I've been—"

"I don't want you to think that this is, you know, some wham-bam-thank-you-ma'am kind of thing for me. It's maybe more than that, okay? For me anyway."

"Yes. Me too."

"And I'm thinking I'd like to take it a little slow, if that's all right with you."

She felt her heart sink. This could mean a lot of things.

"Sure. We can . . ."

"So what I want to say is this."

"Okay."

"This is kind of strange, I know . . ." He paused. "But would you like to go to the aquarium with me some time?"

"Oh Jesus!" She sat up and started to laugh. "Mary and Moses."

"What?"

"You about scared me to death. I couldn't imagine what you were going to say. Do I want to go to the aquarium? Carl, that is so sweet."

"Well, I've been around Boston my whole life, and I've never been, and I was thinking you might want to go and maybe we could have dinner somewhere afterward. Things are crazy right now, but I'm starting my days very early, and I might just be able wangle an afternoon off some time, and . . ."

She took Alberti's hand. "Yes, Carl, I will. I want to. I will go to the aquarium with you, and I will have dinner with you afterward. We will have a real date."

"Great. I think it would be—"

"I've taken Ronnie there, like, sixteen times. He loves the aquarium."

"Oh." Alberti sounded disappointed.

She gave Alberti a kiss on the cheek and patted his hand. "The experience will be completely different with you, believe me. Can't wait to show you the octopuses."

"We could try something else."

"No way. We're going to the aquarium." She hesitated. "But you said there were a couple things."

"Yeah, the other thing is that I have to be up in four hours. Will you forgive me if I take off?"

"You can sleep here if you want. I promise not to . . ."

"I have to get home. There's stuff I need."

"Okay." She paused. "But will you do me a favor?"

"What?"

"When we go to the aquarium, will you not wear your orange shoes? They attract flies."

"Those shoes are awesome, Angie, but I only wear them to jog to work. If you let me take you to dinner, I promise to look civilized. More or less."

"Thanks, I'm, um . . ." She saw him glance at her top, obviously tempted. "Listen, we could—"

"No. No." He got quickly to his feet. "I have to hit the road."

When she stood, he surprised her by putting his arms around her and giving her a five-alarm kiss that made her knees wobble.

Alberti looked over his shoulder as he walked toward the door. "I'll call, okay? Or text you?"

"Please."

As the door was closing, he stuck his head back in. "By the way, I love your outfit." He nodded at her breasts. "Especially that zipper."

After Alberti had gone, she changed into a shapeless flannel nightgown, slipped under the covers, and lay for a while staring at the ceiling. It was the weekend, and her Saturday karate class wasn't until eleven o'clock. Her brain eventually began to slow down. Sometime later, she allowed herself to peep into the little room and found that the ghost of Warren Armstrong was sleeping, at least for now.

11

About the time Angie Phipps was cranking up her Keurig and choosing her outfit, Sandy Tarbell's brother, Graham, was looking for a parking place in the murky neighborhood where Sandy kept his office. After buzzing through the front door and groping his way in the darkened foyer, Graham found Sandy bent over his desk in a puddle of amber lamplight, furiously copying something out of a volume of the *Federal Supplement*. Sandy nodded at the chair opposite without looking up.

Graham took the seat as directed. "How you doing?"

"Not too good." Sandy pushed a clump of gray hair back off his forehead, still scribbling, and still not looking up.

"Same-old, same-old, huh?"

It was not pleasant for Graham Tarbell to come to his brother for help. The two of them ought to have had a lot in common—they were both attorneys, and they shared most of the same DNA—but their lives had long ago diverged into entirely different worlds. For reasons Graham never understood, Sandy had taken up criminal defense here in Jamaica Plain, while Graham managed his own midsize downtown firm, Tarbell & Knight, which did exclusively corporate work.

All this made things awkward enough, but what really irritated Graham was Sandy's hair. Six years younger, Graham was as bald as a marble, except for some salt-and-pepper fuzz over his ears. Sandy, in contrast, sported this dramatic steel-gray mop, white over the temples—perfect for his man-of-the-people Andrew Jackson act. Whenever Graham got together with him, Sandy was constantly raking his fingers back over his ears, showing off.

"How about this Harvard mess, huh? Pretty bad."

Sandy didn't respond, and Graham waited, forcing himself to be patient while Sandy finished up his note-taking. Disaster loomed, and he needed help from the world on his brother's side of the tracks.

Sandy finally stopped writing and snapped the lawbook closed. "Yeah. Crazy times."

Graham decided to lob Sandy a question that would let him have the floor first. "How's that big case of yours going? What's the client's name again?"

"That's why you came here, huh? To inquire about my law practice?" Sandy frowned, and his voice dropped to a mutter. "Dominic O'Connell."

Growing up, Sandy generally treated his baby brother like a nuisance and a sissy—called him "Graham Cracker" or just "Crack" for short. Still, whenever Graham needed something badly enough, Sandy would usually come through and was sometimes even kind.

"That's right. I remember," Graham said. "The murder conspiracy thing." A police siren burst out, close by, and Graham jerked around to peer out the window before continuing. "So, how's it going?"

"The 'murder conspiracy thing,' huh?" Sandy made air quotes. "I guess that's what you'd call it." He turned to stick the lawbook onto the pile behind his desk. "Right now, I hate everybody. I lost my judge this afternoon, and I'm totally fucked. Somebody's going to pay."

"Sounds bad."

Sandy nodded over at the far corner. "You want some coffee? It's cold, but we could use the micro."

"I'll pass."

"Remember Julie Kelleher?" Sandy picked up a pencil and began drumming on the desk with it.

"Your first big crush? Didn't you two take me out on the swan boats?"

"She's O'Connell's wife now, his second wife. She called me up out of the blue." Sandy turned to stare into the inky window. The siren was disappearing into the distance. "God, it was good to hear her voice again. When I saw the caller ID, I almost peed. She's still beautiful. Hasn't aged a single day."

"Must be nice for O'Connell." Graham forced a chuckle. "Pleasant young addition to the other side of the bed."

Sandy spoke up sharply. "She was forty when they got married, and she had her own business as an event planner—biggest in Boston. If he'd wanted a bimbo, he could have had one."

"Well, as they say, hope springs eternal. Maybe if O'Connell's out of the picture, you could . . ." Sandy had just wrapped up his second divorce, so he was unattached, though rarely without company when he wanted it.

"Shut up, Crack, would you please?" Sandy said this in an offhand, inoffensive way. "Anyway, O'Connell had this big-firm lawyer, Sam Newbury . . ."

"I know Newbury. He's a good guy."

"Right. Just your type. Anyway, he'd worked out a deal to plead O'Connell to five years, which for conspiring to kill a cop is ridiculous. There were only two problems."

"Okay." Graham's wife would be sitting up, waiting for him and worrying. Sandy was a night owl, and he could talk forever.

"First, O'Connell has already had two heart attacks. He takes, like, sixteen pills a day, and he sees his doctor every couple months for monitoring. In federal prison, the medical unit will give him two aspirin a week, and he'll die. It helps with their space problem."

"Julie, I take it, was not happy."

"He wouldn't last a year, and she knew it." Sandy combed his fingers back over his temples. "I need this case like a hole in the head, but she sat right in that chair and cried her eyes out. Who can stand that?"

"Not Sandy Tarbell, that's for sure."

Sandy shrugged. "It's not the worst weakness you can have, especially when I have a second reason, a better reason, to grab the wheel here."

"He's loaded and can handle your fee?" O'Connell Construction was one of the biggest contractors in the booming Boston market, with juicy connections inside the mayor's office and the statehouse. Graham Tarbell would have given his right testicle to have OC for a client.

"That's very nice, I admit. But, more importantly, I think I can see a way to get him off. It's a slim chance, and it just got slimmer, but . . ."

"So what's his defense? Everyone says it's open and shut."

Sandy began tapping again on his desk with the eraser end of the pencil. "Come to think of it. Let's change the subject." He leaned across his desk. "So, tell me, Crack. What brings you to my grimy neighborhood at this late hour, huh?"

Graham laid out his tale of woe, and Sandy seemed to listen carefully, nodding from time to time. Compared to the melodrama of the O'Connell case, Graham's situation sounded thin. No one had died, at least not yet. No old lover's heart was being broken. Still, for Graham it was a catastrophe.

When Graham was done, Sandy was quiet for a while. Then he resumed tapping absently on his desk. "This is not my briar patch, but here are a few thoughts, for what they're worth. If your case ends up in court—"

"They'll be filing any day now."

"Then your ass will be riding on two or three things. First, your judge. You're going to want to know everything about him, or her. Is he a Shriner? Get yourself a Shriner lapel pin, or whatever they wear. Then, there's the jurors. You'll want a consultant. Pack the box with as many Cambridge liberals as you can find. Then there's—"

Graham broke in. "Give me a little credit, Sandy, okay? This is Trial Practice 101. The case can never go to trial. If it does, my client's dead, and I'm dead with him. The judge and jury won't matter." Graham hesitated, taking in his brother's expression. "Or am I wrong?"

"You are wrong." Sandy jabbed at the air with the pencil. "The problem is you corporate types don't get into an actual courtroom often enough. You just take a bunch of depositions, wait three years, and write a check."

"That's garbage, Sandy. We know which judges we like, and we know which ones we'd break a leg to avoid. But I still don't see—"

Sandy snatched the sheaf of papers off his desk and waved it impatiently. "Okay, just to take an example, here's the O'Connell indictment. On the surface, it's pretty complicated, but in a few days now my trial will boil down to two simple things. First, who gets on the jury. I'll be looking for nice overeducated folks from Wellesley, Newton, and Brookline. Norm Angelini, the court's jury administrator, fell off a ladder and is home with his leg in the air. I sent Norm some flowers. I may drop by his house with a pizza. I need to know where the jury summonses are going, the neighborhoods the jurors are coming from. To hang the jury, all I need is one."

"Okay, and the second thing?"

"The judge's instructions, particularly the one on reasonable doubt and the one on weighing the credibility of a government cooperator."

"Who's the rat?"

Sandy's landline rang. "I don't like that word. I've had too many of them for clients." He picked up the phone. "Yeah? Uh-huh. You're very welcome." He paused. "No problem. Happy Birthday." He laughed. "No, I'm *not* kidding. Bye-bye." He hung up.

Graham looked at Sandy. "Calls at this hour?"

"Returning a favor."

"Okay. So, who's the whatever, the cooperator, this time?"

"Burned-out ex hit man from Philly with terminal cancer, who's fingering O'Connell as the wheelman in the Chunk Scanlon murder. If the jury has a reasonable doubt about Mr. Philadelphia's credibility, then O'Connell walks, and maybe I get a big wet kiss from Julie. If it doesn't, then O'Connell dies in prison because he screwed up fifty years ago when he was a teenage moron." He scooted forward in his chair. "Now, everybody in my world knows that you can count on Judge Margaret Helms, God bless her, to hammer those two instructions home hard. She uses more or less the same words as the other judges, so if you read the transcript, they don't look much different. But little touches in Helms's phrasing, the way she comes down on certain words, the eye contact, her crusty schoolmarm voice, the way she leans toward the jurors at certain moments—all this means that what she says will get inside the jurors' heads and stick. Up until lunchtime today, I was feeling just a little optimistic. I know Helms. I could build my defense on what I knew she would say. Even better, I could build it on how I knew she would say it. Now, I've somehow got fucking Davie Norcross, from the fucking boonies, who I know fucking nothing about."

"So what happened?"

"It's obvious. Buddy Hogan and Sam Newbury had worked out a cute little plea bargain. The trial was off, and the summer vacations were on. Then here comes Sandy Tarbell, who kicks over the deal, and all of a sudden Helms is out and Norcross is in. They're giving me the shaft. Simple as that."

"Okay, Sandy, look. I sympathize, but—"

"I hate the motherfuckers. They're sticking it to me, which means they're sticking it to Dom, and that means they're sticking it to Julie. I'm not going to let that happen. I'm going to—"

Graham's patience collapsed, and he broke in. "Fine, Sandy. Fine. Go for it. But—not to be self-centered—what about me? What about my little ten-cent disaster?"

The two brothers looked at each other for several seconds.

"Okay, Graham, listen. I'm going to ignore my better judgment here. After you leave, I'm going to get on the phone, okay? Tomorrow or the next day, you'll get a call from someone you wouldn't ordinarily touch with the blade end of your nine iron. Here's his card."

Graham looked at the card. "Jack Taylor? He's a zero."

"Don't let this guy fool you. He has claws. He'll suggest some fancy lunch. Do the lunch, but keep your mouth shut. Then come back and tell me what he's selling." Sandy pointed at Graham, doing his typical older brother thing. "Don't—do *not*—bite on anything without talking to me first. I mean it. You're a babe in the woods here. That's all I'm going to say, except that we have to agree that this conversation, the one you and I are having at this very minute, never happened."

"Why?"

"You'll find out why at the lunch."

12

As the image of the alumni arranging themselves on the steps of Widener Library burst into chaos and flying debris for the eighth or tenth time, FBI Special Agent Mike Patterson closed the screen and looked around the table.

"So. It's been . . ." He checked his watch. "Twenty hours. Where are we?"

At Patterson's request, two men—Assistant U.S. Attorney Bob Schwartz and Carl Alberti from the ATF—had joined him in a small conference room at the Boston courthouse for a private spit-balling session.

Alberti pointed at the screen. "One more time. Just the handoff."

Patterson ran the video back to where it showed a well-dressed elderly woman approach Kahlil Khan in Harvard Yard and hand him a large COOP bag with paper handles. They watched again as the woman patted Khan on the shoulder, pointed to a spot outside the picture, and bustled off in the direction of Memorial Chapel.

Patterson shook his head. "If that's a female, I'm my grand-mother."

Bob Schwartz might technically be overseeing the investigation, but Mike Patterson was the oldest, most experienced, and most senior member of the trio. As an "ASAC" in the FBI's Boston field office, he was one of four assistant special agents in charge, with shared responsibility for hundreds of agents and staff covering the states of Massachusetts, Rhode Island, and New Hampshire. Within two hours of the bombing, the Boston SAC, with the blessing of the attorney general in Washington, had designated Patterson to coordinate the Joint Terrorism Task Force, or JTTF, that was handling the overall investigation of the Harvard bombing.

"The scarf's a giveaway." Alberti pointed at the screen. "It's probably there to hide a man-size Adam's apple."

"Our people in Washington are running over profiles of subjects known to dress up as women. Nothing helpful so far." Patterson peered discontentedly at the blank screen. "Of course, we can't be absolutely sure that's not a female."

"I can." Schwartz spoke up. "Our delivery guy, as they say, ain't no lady."

Bob Schwartz was the head of the Criminal Division of the U.S. Attorney's Office in Massachusetts. To Patterson's relief, Buddy Hogan had made Schwartz the government's primary trial attorney, the lead prosecutor in the bombing investigation. Schwartz was an interesting man. The first thing people noticed about him was that he was very short—when he was seated, the tips of his toes barely brushed the carpet—and that he had an unusually round head covered with short silver hair. Boston defense lawyers mockingly called him "The Pawn," since he looked just like the chess piece, but his fellow prosecutors had responded with their own nickname, "Checkmate."

Schwartz deserved the compliment. He was, hands down, the most effective prosecutor in New England and one of the best in the country. In court, he never used notes, and in his openings, he always employed the same reliable kickoff joke. Standing in front of the jury box, he'd bounce up on tiptoes, wave his arms, and ask the jurors: "Can you all see me okay?" This always got a laugh, and from then on everyone was on his side. He'd advance through the evidence one square at a time—nothing fancy, no soaring rhetoric, but, like a pawn, never retreating. In seventeen years as a prosecutor, Schwartz had lost exactly once. Patterson had shared counsel table with him on six trials now, all tough cases, all ending in guilty verdicts.

Patterson leaned forward, moving his eyes from Schwartz to Alberti. "Okay, what's the sequence here? We've got maybe ten minutes before someone finds us and starts thumping on the door. Who's doing what?"

It was a relief for Patterson to have a private sit-down like this, with two people he knew and trusted. The regional JTTF was one of over a hundred such entities, national and international, working under the director of national intelligence in Washington. In the terrorist context, these task forces were essential. Scattered efforts by different law enforcement agencies in the past had resulted in failures to share information, unhelpful rivalries, and wasted resources. At that moment, two floors below, a couple dozen state and federal investigators, along with clerical staff called in on a Saturday, were hard at work drafting reports, making phone calls, and bumping into one another. Coordinating all this would soon be absorbing as much of Patterson's time as the actual investigative footwork. Even now, he could feel his phone vibrating with an incoming message. He ignored it.

Schwartz pointed at the screen. "First thing we do is tell Harvard to stop buying its security cameras at Sam's Club." He picked up a rubber band and began fiddling with it.

"I'll pass that along." Patterson nodded at Alberti. "What have your people got for us about the bomb, Carl?"

"We flew all the pieces we could recover down to TEDAC, and they put them under their microscopes or whatever." TEDAC was the Terrorist Explosive Device Analytical Center in Huntsville, Alabama. Patterson had visited the facility twice during trainings. "They've confirmed that the device was probably a jerry-rigged standard military-issue M67 fragmentation grenade."

Schwartz was fashioning his rubber band into a cat's cradle. "Jerry-rigged?" He was a good lawyer, but Patterson hated it when he started fiddling.

"Whoever built it modified the timer, maybe with parts from an M68."

"Baby steps, please?" Schwartz was watching his hands. One of his knees was bouncing.

Patterson broke in. "The M67 has a straight M213 pyrotechnic fuse with a delay of four seconds. You fling it, duck, and wait. The M68 is designed to detonate on impact, but it has a backup timer that triggers after a few seconds if it doesn't explode when it hits."

Patterson had a long career with the FBI, but he was also, proudly, a colonel in the army reserves with two tours in Afghanistan.

Alberti picked up. "Our people think Khan and his friends must have figured out how to extend the delay, or incorporate a remote detonator, to give Khan time to do the set and get clear."

"Huh." Schwartz noticed Patterson's dark look, dropped his rubber band, and sat back, interlacing his fingers. "Sounds more complicated than necessary."

"Not just complicated—harebrained. If the bag gets dropped, or jostled, or they take too long to place it, wham!" Patterson slapped the table. "Plus, the tactical approach here seems odd to me. The M67 has a kill radius of maybe ten feet with an injury range of forty to fifty. If Khan and his friends just wanted to take out Blackwell, they had safer and more reliable ways to do it. If they wanted to kill a whole bunch of people, they could have used a more powerful explosive and gotten more blood for their bang. For example, they could have—"

Alberti broke in. "Three dead and eleven critical is not bad, Mike."

"The M67 has about six ounces of explosive, which was more than they needed if they only wanted Blackwell, but too little for your standard crowd bombing."

"Yeah, but—"

"This could be some nutcase working out of his basement just as easily as an organized group like Al-Shabaab." Patterson frowned. "Getting hold of a grenade is not that hard, unfortunately. A lot of them went missing in Iraq."

Alberti nodded. "You think this might be a couple lone wolves? Like the Tsarnaev brothers?"

"Could be. Or maybe someone trying to look like them who just gets a kick out of killing people. Or has a beef with Harvard."

"I don't know." Alberti frowned. "A couple of our guys met with the head of security at Harvard and, beyond the usual stream of cuckoo shit, nothing credible was on the radar. We have a military grenade, a bomber whose brother just got deported, and a high-level target. Seems obvious to me they were terrorists going for Blackwell."

"Hold up a second, Carl." Schwartz nodded at Patterson. "Remind me what you've got on Khan, will you Mike? I'm going to be in court in an hour for his initial appearance."

"On a Saturday? Who drew the case?"

"Broadwater."

Patterson nodded. "Well, that explains it."

"Yeah. He's appointed Tom Redpath to represent Khan. I spoke to Redpath an hour ago about having his client sit down with us. We're working on a proffer letter."

"Let me know how that goes." A proffer letter could be the crowbar that cracked a case open. It allowed a witness to sit down with the government in a safety zone, disclosing what he knew but with the assurance that nothing he said would be used against him in court.

"Absolutely." Schwartz pushed himself forward in his chair. "But tell me again about Khan, Mike. What's his vibe?"

"He's no mastermind. We were at his apartment in Cambridge-port forty-five minutes after the bomb detonated. Two state troopers pulled up as we were going through the door. We found Khan sitting under a light bulb at his kitchen table, eating an egg salad sandwich, totally clueless as far as I could see."

"Does he speak English?"

"Some. Scared to death. No idea what was in the bag, he said. Just doing some old lady a favor. He admitted knowing about the explosion—he'd just gotten around the corner of the library when it went off—but he didn't realize it was connected to the COOP bag. Couldn't even give us a decent description of our supposed bag lady."

"Follow-up?"

"Nope. Redpath's shut Khan down. We've got him parked in Plymouth. No way we want him on the street."

"Broadwater will never release him. Redpath won't even ask." Schwartz picked up his rubber band again. "Tell the truth, I'm more worried about Khan's safety. We don't want somebody sticking a spoon handle into him before he talks."

"He's in solitary. The guards tell me he sits and stares a lot."

"So what's bothering you, Mike? You look . . ."

"Well, we've still got a lot to follow up on. I've got thirty-four agents out there right now, talking to everybody we can find who was at the reunion. It's a top priority, but it may take a day or two. I'm not saying this wasn't terrorism, but it feels odd. Nobody's claimed responsibility—"

"Give them a day or two," Alberti said.

"And the bag arrived early. How did they even know Blackwell would be sitting there?"

"I'm betting the answer died with the Secret Service escort. Maybe he said something that Khan or his friends overheard."

Schwartz's eyes had been going back and forth as he followed the debate. "Okay, what about our third victim, Armstrong? Any reason to think somebody was after him? Or maybe after someone else at the scene."

"It's hard to say," Patterson said. "I'm going to be canvassing Broadwater and some of the other judges to see if there was anything unusual going on with Armstrong. Any threats or problems of any kind."

Alberti broke in, "How well did you know Warren Armstrong?"

Patterson looked at Alberti, suppressing a prickly response. "Not that well."

It annoyed him that people assumed that, because they were both Black, he and Warren had to be buddies. It was certainly true that, even after decades of posturing, too few African American men or women held senior positions in either the FBI or the administrative hierarchy of the federal judiciary. He and Armstrong had had that uphill climb in common. Their personalities had been so different, though, that they never became more than acquaintances. He'd considered Armstrong a little too much of a player, always trying to keep his judges contented and off his back. Armstrong had probably thought Patterson too brass-assed and judgmental. The fact was that neither of them would have been successful if they had exchanged positions. Their strengths were too different. Now, there was one less member of a cohort that was already way too small.

Schwartz pointed at the screen. "Okay, let's assume that Khan, intentionally or not, was just the mule here. What do we know about his connections?"

Alberti opened his file. "Mike and I have our people out buttonholing every East African in the greater Boston area, especially the Kenyans. There aren't that many, and we're running backgrounds on all of them."

"We have to do it, of course, but I don't know . . ." Patterson sat back and shook his head.

Alberti held up a piece of paper. "I've contacted the Kenyan embassy. There's a student at Harvard Divinity School who comes from a very wired-in Kenyan family. My embassy contact hinted he might have some slippery connections back home. He's my first stop."

"Uh-huh." Schwartz closed one eye, aimed, and shot his rubber band at the clock on the far wall. It hit the target, bounced, and fell into the coffeepot. "Damn."

"Leave it," Alberti said. "It'll improve the flavor."

Patterson spoke. "My bet is Khan is telling the truth. He never had any idea what was in that bag. If so, there goes our Muslim connection."

Alberti raised his eyebrows. "Kind of rough locking Khan up if he's totally innocent, Mike."

"Funny. His lawyer said the same thing."

Schwartz broke in. "Hey, at the moment I don't personally give a damn if Khan is innocent. He's safer in Plymouth, and he's staying put. For the time being, we need everyone to assume we think he was in on it."

"Fine, but I'm going to look into my nutcase theory." Patterson nodded at Schwartz. "You know what they say. The only thing more dangerous than organized crime . . ."

"Right." Schwartz nodded. "Is disorganized crime."

"To me, everything points to a terrorist connection." Alberti gathered his papers and began putting them back in the accordion file. "And it's very well organized."

"There's also always a chance this was a screwup. Maybe the bomb went off early. Maybe they killed the wrong person." Schwartz stood up. "I have to get ready for court. But you know what else worries me?"

"What's that?" Patterson asked. There was a sharp knock on the door. His phone was vibrating again.

"Maybe they ain't done yet."

13

It was Sunday morning, and David was bent over the high chair, happily airplaning a spoonful of banana mush into Charlie's mouth.

"Brrrrrrooww! In for a landing."

Bananas were Charlie's favorite, and as soon as he swallowed, he opened extra wide for another delivery. The boy's eyes, staring up at his father, were alight with happy expectation. David stirred up another spoonful and took off again.

"There you go, buddy." David was whispering. "Mommy's sleeping. So we men need to be superquiet." He scraped up a half teaspoon of overflow from Charlie's chin and was just inserting it when the condo's landline burst out.

"Oh no! Daddy has to get the stupid phone." He snatched it up quickly.

"Uncle Dave? Hello?" It was his niece Lindsay.

He tried a half whisper. "Hi, Lindsay. Listen, I need to talk—"

"Hello?"

He spoke louder. "I need to keep it down here . . ."

Charlie brushed the spoon and the baby food jar off the high chair tray. The clatter and the spray of banana onto the floor made David wince. Charlie peered down with an intrigued expression.

"Just wanted to check on how Claire's doing."

"She's better, thanks. Still sleeping." David glanced in the direction of the bedroom. No sound. "How's it going with Marlene?"

Lindsay, a sophomore at Amherst College, was the daughter of David's difficult older brother, Ray, who lived in Washington, D.C. She was coaching at a girls' softball camp for the summer and dog-sitting the judge's yellow Lab at their Amherst house while he and Claire were away.

"Marlene's bummed. She misses Claire, I think."

"Not me?"

"She's ambivalent about you, Uncle Dave. She thinks it's your fault she's stuck here with me."

"Always the bad guy." He wedged the phone under his ear and grabbed a paper towel. "Story of my life." As he bent down to mop up the banana and to retrieve the jar and spoon, he heard the door to the bedroom squeak. Claire was moving around.

"How's the wrist?" Lindsay sounded concerned, which was very sweet.

Claire had sprained her wrist when she fainted—or, as she insisted, slipped—in the shower. David had wanted to take her straight to a hospital until she pointed out that they'd be over-whelmed after the bombing. A teleconference with Claire's doctor in Amherst was reassuring, and afterward David had run out for a Velcro brace that went from Claire's knuckles to her forearm. Friday night, Claire had popped two Advil PM, gone to bed early, and slept for ten straight hours. Saturday had also been very quiet, with naps and a stream of phone calls from worried friends.

"It's improving." David licked off the spoon and scooped up another mouthful for Charlie. "But she keeps taking the brace off."

"God, the thing at Harvard must have been . . . I don't know. I keep trying to imagine it, and I can't. How is she doing? I mean, really."

Lindsay's mother had died and her father had been badly injured in a freak plane crash when Lindsay was in high school. She and her little sister, Jordan, had stayed with David for a few months after-ward. Following a rocky start, Lindsay and Claire had become close.

"Yes, it was beyond awful. She's still, you know . . ." He was going to say more about Claire's emotional state but held up as she drifted into the kitchen. She was in her flannel bathrobe and flip-flops. He gave Charlie a final scoop of banana. "There you go, my man."

Lindsay's voice brightened. "Prince Charles is up?"

"Yeah, we're finishing breakfast. He says hi." A car horn tooted on the other end of the line, in the background.

Claire kissed David on the cheek and walked over to the coffee maker. David had already brewed a pot, and when Claire saw it, she put her hand on her heart and bowed toward him in a gesture of gratitude. The feeling of her coming into the room, retrieving a mug from the cabinet, going to the fridge, getting the milk out—all the familiar, morning movements—filled David with a calm sweetness. They were happy together.

"My ride's here. How long do you think you guys will be in Boston?"

"Up until Thursday, I think, finishing up a few things." David set the banana jar on the counter. "That okay with you?"

"Anything's okay with me."

"I may need you to dog-sit again starting next week for a trial here. It may go two or three weeks actually." David began wiping Charlie's face with the end of the paper towel. "It just came up." Charlie scowled and twisted his face away.

"No problem." The horn sounded again, a little louder. "Gotta run. Love you."

David put the phone back. Claire climbed up onto one of the stools by the kitchen island, took a swallow of coffee, and looked at her husband wearily.

"A two- or three-week trial? What's that about?"

David made an effort to sound casual. "It's that contractor who supposedly conspired to kill a police officer back in the sixties."

"Dominic O'Connell?" She sipped her coffee again. "Mr. Bean Town? Isn't that one for the Boston judges?"

"Yes, but I volunteered."

"You volunteered? Oh, David, for heaven's sake." She set her cup down with a clack.

"I know, but they were up the creek. Sometimes you have to step up."

"I can't believe it." She shook her head. "You do these things, and you don't even talk to me first."

"Warren only asked if he could put me in the draw." He paused. "It was less than a fifty-fifty chance that I'd actually get it, but the computer spat my name out. I'm sorry."

The mention of Warren Armstrong brought the conversation to a stop. Claire closed her eyes, dipped her head, and took a deep breath. "Well, you may be back here on your own." She looked at him. "I'm about done with urban life for a while."

Charlie was observing the two of them carefully, picking up on the change in the mood. His face contracted, and he began to slide toward tears. His bananas were gone; his world was falling apart. Claire held out her arms. "Here, let me take him."

David lifted Charlie out of the high chair and handed him over. "It's just that . . ." He felt terrible.

"I know, I know. You wanted to help Warren out." She set Charlie in her lap and began bouncing him. "How's my boy? How's my boy?" Charlie's face relaxed a little. She kissed the side of his neck, and he let out a short squeal of pleasure.

"It wouldn't have felt right to refuse, Claire, not after he came to me."

Claire waved a hand. "Right. I know. Just give me a minute to absorb this, okay?"

The door buzzer interrupted. The sound was especially piercing and aggressive.

"Who on earth?" David crossed the room and pushed the intercom button.

"Hello?"

"Hi, David, it's Monica."

"Monica?"

"Don't hate me! I have pastries."

David gave Claire a questioning look. Monica was an old friend of hers from grad school, a professor at MIT now. She and Claire were finishing a book on medieval lyric poetry together.

Claire responded to David's wordless inquiry with a resigned shrug. He buzzed Monica in, and a few seconds later she came through the door like a blast of wind.

"I know, I know, I should have called first, but my phone's disappeared again, my marriage is on the rocks, and I'm not in my right mind. Oh crap, you're still in your bathrobe, Claire. I'm so sorry. You must hate me. What an intrusion!" Monica waved a hand. "Oh, go ahead and hate me. I can take it. The world is such a mess. Here, look what I brought." She waved a bakery box tied up with brown string. When she noticed Charlie, she broke into a grin. "Oh my God, Claire, he's getting so big!"

Charlie was staring up at Monica with his mouth open, fascinated. She was not a small woman, and she was wearing a billowing ankle-length crimson tunic. David could not imagine anyone but her ever putting such a garment on, let alone going out in it. Charlie was gazing at her as though she were a giant red balloon that had just magically landed in his kitchen.

Monica put the box on the island and untied the string. "Ta-da! Croissants, scones, and cinnamon muffins. I could have gotten bran, but they're so goddamn virtuous. They taste like sod."

David peered into the box. "Wow. Monica, this is really spectacular."

"Give us a hug here, David." Her vast embrace carried a wave of lilac talcum. "The world out there is just going crazy. MIT is suspending classes tomorrow." She stepped back and studied him. "I've come to hear about Claire, but I have a few questions for you first, Your Honor. We have an Iranian family one floor down, the nicest people, and they're not even going out of their apartment, not setting one foot out, until things cool down. I took them a casserole, and there was something chalked on their door I won't even quote. They've lived in our building longer than just about anybody, and they have to put up with this garbage. Can't you judges do something about this?"

"Well, Monica, to begin with . . ."

"Hold on." Claire interrupted. Her expression of wonderment was almost identical to Charlie's. "Your marriage is on the rocks? Has Bernie . . ."

"Lost his mind? Yes! Yes, he has. And you know why? Because his mind is so fucking tiny it could fall down a heat transom. All he can do is rave about immigrants, especially Kenyans, and how we should never have let them in, not even the guys who repainted our hallway, and how they should all be deported, and how fed up he is with the government, the politicians, and everybody he can think of. We had a big fight this morning. I had two choices: bury a meat cleaver in Bernie's forehead or get out of the apartment." She paused and looked at Claire intently. "How are you managing? God, you must be . . . Are you okay? Here, have a scone." She held out the box.

David broke in. "I have a great idea. It's a beautiful Sunday morning, and I think Charlie and I will go for a ramble."

"Aw, man, he's giving us space to talk!" Monica dropped her voice and pointed at David. "He's such a sweetheart! Can I marry him too?"

Claire looked unconvinced. "I'd think about it, Monica. He's just found time to inform me of another case he's taken on here. Some new adventure."

"What case?"

"Well," David began. "It's not really . . ."

Claire sighed. "The Dominic O'Connell thing."

Monica's eyes went wide. "Really? Oh my God, you have that case? David, so many people are going to hate you! I'm not kidding. Even my brain-dead husband loves Big Dom. Half of Boston thinks this is some typical Buddy Hogan political stunt. Did you see the thing on YouTube where he got arrested, at five in the morning or something, with his poor wife standing right there in her bathrobe? It was like the Gestapo. Of course, the other half wants to skip the trial and just drop O'Connell into a giant food processor. Before you know it, they'll be writing things on your door, too, kiddo."

"Huh. Well . . ." David had his back to Monica and was trying to yank the awkward stroller out of the broom closet. "I guess we'll have to see."

Not long after that, much to his relief, David extricated himself. He and Charlie crossed the street and wheeled their way down the grassy mall that divided Commonwealth Avenue. Sunlight was casting blotches of dancing shadow on the sidewalks, and the lush trees were rocking overhead, sifting the air.

Few other pedestrians were out. After the Harvard bombing, many people had made prompt exits for Maine or the Cape, and those remaining seemed to be keeping inside. It would be a relief to get Claire and Charlie—and, come to think of it, himself—out of the city and safely back home to Western Massachusetts for a while.

Charlie and David always loved their walks, and today, despite everything, was no different. As they rolled along, their relationship was not so much as parent and child, but simply as two human creatures who happened to be of different sizes and ages, wordlessly enjoying the same sequence of vivid moments together. Their heads lifted in unison to follow a burst of pigeons flapping up. They jumped simultaneously when a motorcycle suddenly took off with a jarring roar. As they circled the statue of a revolutionary war general, Charlie turned and gave his father a careful look, as though he were sizing him up. It occurred to David that someday not that far off, if they were both lucky, Charlie might be the one doing the pushing, and old Judge Norcross would be the one getting wheeled. That wouldn't be so bad. He had a child now, someone who carried the Norcross DNA and who might be channeling some trace of his father into his own children.

Farther along, they came to the piece of statuary David secretly treasured the most, the bust of Patrick Andrew Collins with his spectacular mustache, mayor of Boston from 1902 to 1905. The unpretentiousness of Collins's epitaph always moved him: "A talented, honest, generous, serviceable man." David felt that if he were remembered just for those four qualities, even for a little while, his time on the earth would have been justified. The word *serviceable*, in particular, reminded him of Warren Armstrong's "None of the Above." It was probably the highest compliment he could hope for as a judge.

He and Charlie continued across Clarendon Street and then Dartmouth and stopped to stare up together at the statue of the great abolitionist William Lloyd Garrison. Garrison was a hero nowadays, but in his lifetime his fierce opposition to slavery had provoked the Georgia legislature to put a price on his head and persuaded even many Bostonians to despise him. Nevertheless, he kept speaking out and writing. They couldn't shut him up.

Garrison's statue was, of course, in some sense a memorial to the law's failings. In Garrison's day, the federal courts had supported slavery, and northern judges, even those who personally opposed the law, enforced the Fugitive Slave Act and ordered escaped men and women to be returned to their so-called owners. Norcross could not help wondering how much of his own work—his enforcement of the country's heartless immigration laws, his regular imposition of brutal prison sentences—would be revealed after he was gone as indefensibly cruel and unjust. His work was essential but morally complicated, and he himself was unlikely to be remembered, when the decades rolled by, as any kind of hero. The most he could hope for was to be generous and serviceable, bending his historical moment toward the ideal of justice as far as he could.

Garrison's statue depicted the man seated at his ease, with his left leg comfortably extended. David recalled how well-groomed and simple his life had been before his fluky meeting with Claire and the arrival, after some foolish agonizing, of his splendid boy. His life now was a treasure beyond anything he'd ever dreamed, but like his profession it was complicated and fragile. Among other things, he'd have to figure out how to be a serviceable dad. In that effort also, he knew his performance was bound to fall short of anybody's ideal.

Charlie was beginning to wave his hands and squirm against his shoulder straps. Nap time was approaching. They needed to get back.

14

Nothing in Sam Newbury's comfortable life had remotely prepared him for the sour-faced man who stepped into his path on Congress Avenue, nodded toward a car idling at the curb, and said, "Mr. O'Connell wants to talk."

He couldn't help smiling. It was like a movie. "Absolutely. I'll give him a ring first thing tomorrow morning."

"Uh-huh. Get in." The man opened the rear door and pointed.

As Newbury stared into the car's black interior, his heart took a little hop and his palms began to sweat. This was happening way too fast. He knew very well what O'Connell wanted to talk about. He'd been dodging his former client's calls for more than a week.

Looking around, he saw a big man with curly red hair leaning against a street sign, his arms folded. When their eyes met, the man lifted his shoulders with a kind of *Ain't life a bitch?* expression. Newbury wondered if he should try to run, start screaming for help, or do something, but everything he could think of seemed incredibly undignified and weird. What did a person do, actually, in a situation like this?

Up to thirty seconds ago, he'd been hurrying toward his office, completely preoccupied by the aftermath of the Widener bombing. He'd been up half the night making phone calls, passing on information to family members, doing his class secretary thing. The conversations had often been hard, but people had been grateful. He'd had a phone message from David Norcross, thanking him for rescuing his wife, and he was planning to call His Honor back and see if he could lure him out for a drink sometime soon. These social connections—as his mentor Bill Treadwell liked to tell him—wouldn't necessarily make judges decide in your favor, but they might make them less inclined to rip you to shreds. Every little bit helped.

Now, he had this to deal with, for God's sake. People hurrying by weren't even looking at him.

"Fine." He smiled more broadly. "I'll call him right after dinner. Promise."

He couldn't phone 911. Given what he'd been up to, the last thing he wanted was the police poking around.

The sour-faced man shook his head. "Don't screw around here, Mr. Newbury. You're smarter than that."

He made a show of looking at his watch. "Look, I have an appointment. I don't want to be rude, but . . ."

"I bet I can be ruder than you." The man stepped closer. "Want to find out?"

"But . . ."

"Come on, blue eyes, I'm being nice here. Just get in the fucking car, okay?" He pointed again.

So Sam Newbury got in the car.

The red-haired man climbed into the driver's seat, and soon afterward the sour-faced man entered the passenger side. "What'd I tell you? Easy-peasy." He heard the locks snap. Childproof.

Newbury wiped his palms on his knees and began composing what he would say to buy time with O'Connell. He prided himself on being quick on his feet.

In fact, after they entered O'Connell's office in the back of the house on Louisburg Square, Newbury didn't get a chance to say much of anything. As soon as he opened his mouth, the red-haired man stepped up, gave him an apologetic look, and punched him hard in the upper diaphragm. Then he shoved Newbury backward onto a black leather love seat. The blow knocked the wind out of him so thoroughly that he squeaked when he tried to inhale.

O'Connell was sitting at his desk, a dark silhouette against the big windows behind him. "That's for not answering my calls." He pointed a finger at Newbury, speaking mildly. "Please don't ever do that to me again, Sam, all right?"

Newbury tried to answer—he'd crafted his excuses, and they were good ones—but he couldn't form the words. He'd never been punched like that before.

The red-haired man looked down at him kindly. "Short breaths, Sammy. Don't try to talk." The other man was leaning against the closed door. When he saw Newbury looking at him, he yawned. O'Connell leaned forward and put his elbows on his desk.

"A few months back, we gave you a large sum of money. Remember?" When he struggled to answer, O'Connell leaned a little closer. "Do you hear me?"

Newbury nodded and managed to grunt.

"Good. And you promised me something in return, remember?"

He took a ragged breath. "Yes, but . . ."

O'Connell picked a glass paperweight up off his desk. It was the size of a lemon and had a flat bottom. He held it up. "No 'buts,' okay? Please?" He put the paperweight down and continued. "You haven't delivered what I paid for, so, obviously, I want my money back."

"But, it's . . ."

He dodged barely in time to avoid the glass lemon, which whizzed past his ear and hit the wall behind his head with a loud bang.

O'Connell rocked forward, half standing, and put his hands on the desk. "I said, 'no buts,' Sam. Didn't you hear me?"

"But, how—"

"Every goddamn penny, Sam. You understand?"

"I know, but how am I supposed to—"

The red-haired man spoke. "Just transfer it back into the account you pulled it from." He bent and picked the paperweight off the floor. "We'll take care of the rest."

"I don't—"

"I'll be generous. You got a week." O'Connell sat down and waved a hand, dismissing him. "Next time, I won't call first."

"Come on, Sammy." The redhead put a hand on his shoulder. "Let me give you a lift."

15

Jack Taylor's invitation to lunch arrived, as Sandy had predicted, very soon after Graham's late-night visit to his brother in Jamaica Plain. Now, Graham found himself in a private dining room at a pricey Back Bay restaurant picking at a lobster salad, with Taylor sitting opposite him. The guy was a scuzzball, one of the last people he wanted to be seen with, but what he was saying was very tempting. He couldn't resist listening.

"So, like I said, just speaking hypothetically, how much do you think one of your big-boy clients would put up, in a jumbo case, to guarantee the federal judge of their dreams?" Taylor was a very large man, built like a block of concrete, and his oversize legs, squirming under the table, made the ice in their water glasses tinkle.

Graham tried to sound skeptical. "Legally speaking, corporations may be people, Jack, but I don't think they have dreams."

Taylor squeezed one eye closed and twisted a pinkie into his ear, as though he were trying to engage the ignition of his brain. "Well, they sure have nightmares, don't they?" He gave an awkward grin. "I can hear them moaning in their sleep sometimes, the poor babies."

Graham turned to look out the window. The room had an impressive view over the Charles River Basin.

When the silence lengthened, Taylor pressed again. "So, seriously, how much?"

"We'd lay out a bundle to dodge a couple of those yo-yos. I can tell you that." He raised his eyebrows at Taylor, half joking, half inviting him to keep talking.

This was enough. "Okay. Let's play a game." Taylor picked up his napkin and folded it in half. "We've got eleven federal judges sitting in Boston, right? Thirteen in the District of Massachusetts, but we'll leave out the ones in Worcester and Springfield. And let's just say you have the mother of all class actions about to run up your tailpipe. Write down the name of the judge you'd most like to have the case drawn to. Just kidding around." He pushed the napkin toward Graham. "If you were God."

"That's a cloth napkin, Jack." He nodded at the table. "We aren't at Burger King here."

The decades since Graham had started Tarbell & Knight had been brutal sometimes, with many fourteen-hour days, but in the end the firm had succeeded beyond his wildest hopes. To reward himself and to celebrate his twenty-fifth wedding anniversary, Graham had bought his wife a five-bedroom Victorian farmhouse on Martha's Vineyard that spring. The place was a reach financially, but it was the summer home of their dreams: four acres on the water. His son, Bobby, would be bringing his wife and the grandkids to visit that August for two weeks. Alice was in heaven.

Now, everything he'd worked for was helplessly rushing toward Niagara Falls. For weeks now, Graham had been hearing nothing but the roar of the cataract around the bend.

Taylor pulled a Sharpie out of his jacket pocket and pushed it toward Graham. "Go ahead. Write. They got plenty of napkins."

Graham did not even look down. Whatever he did, he was not going to scribble on something and create a piece of evidence. In fact, at that moment an urgent voice inside his head was shouting at him to get the hell out of there. But he couldn't bring himself to walk. He had to sit, wait, and see what Jack Taylor had to offer.

His looming catastrophe came down to simple arithmetic. Tarbell & Knight these days had twenty-seven lawyers and forty-one support staff. The firm covered its massive overhead easily because of one major client, a tech conglomerate called Cimarron Systems, started by a nerdy genius Graham had met in high school at Boston Latin. Every year, this one client generated millions in fees. Losing Cimarron would kick the legs out from under T&K.

Now, a firm out of Los Angeles, a well-oiled corporate assassin, had Cimarron in its crosshairs. His geeky pal from Boston Latin was a genius with computer code, but he tended to veer toward insane optimism when it came to his business. As the L.A. litigation group pointed out, Cimarron's press releases and SEC filings last year had wildly exaggerated the company's short-term prospects, luring in hundreds of millions from deluded investors. When quarterly earnings came in well below—hugely below—predictions, Cimarron's stock price plunged, and these investors got royally skinned.

The California law firm had assembled an angry mob of plaintiffs—pension funds, labor unions, billionaires, and even a couple of very pissed-off movie stars—and it was poised to file a class action lawsuit, charging both his friend and the company with civil securities fraud. If it lost the imminent legal battle, Cimarron's exposure, including punitive damages and attorneys' fees, might stretch to over a billion dollars. Graham Tarbell's golden goose had its head on the block, and if the axe fell, T&K would almost certainly go down too.

He did not bother to deface the napkin. He knew the judge he'd want.

"If I were God? Margaret Helms."

His voice did not quite sink to a whisper. That would be giving Taylor too much. But his volume was low enough, he hoped, to duck under the recorder Taylor could be wearing. Jack Taylor was exactly the borderline type who might have fallen into legal problems of his own. If he was in trouble, the FBI would be quite happy to give Taylor a slap on the wrist, providing he delivered them a medium-size fish like Graham Tarbell. What he was flirting with here, bribery and conspiracy to obstruct justice, was serious criminal conduct, felonies that could get a person sent away for many years. This could be a setup.

Taylor retrieved the Sharpie and put the napkin back in his lap. "Right. I figured."

Graham spoke louder. "But this is all just talk, right? I heard Helms was off the draw, anyway. Her husband's sick or something."

"Not true. It's only *O'Connell* that's getting transferred. Over to what's-his-name." Taylor pursed his lips trying to remember. "The horse-faced guy from Springfield."

"Norcross."

"Right. But she's still taking on new cases, same as ever. Any lawsuit that comes to her now won't go to trial until long after Tony Helms is under sod."

"How the hell do you know all this?" His tone was borderline offensive. He didn't care.

Taylor looked back, unblinking. "I just know."

Graham imagined the pleasure of sharing the news that Judge Helms had drawn the Cimarron lawsuit—sitting at the head of some polished conference table with the company's management group and his law partners. The delicious sense of mastery.

"Sooo." Taylor drew out the word. "Let's just call this a gentlemen's bet. You'd like Helms . . ."

"We're not talking about contacting any judge." Graham pointed at Taylor and spoke even louder. "Even hypothetically, I don't want you to think for a second that—"

"Fuck, no!" Taylor looked sincerely appalled. "Approach Helms? You think I have a death wish? I'd be in cuffs in ten minutes."

"Yes, well—"

"Besides, who needs to contact anybody? Did you read her decision in *Hasbro*?"

"Can't remember. I may have glanced at it."

Graham had in fact read this decision three times. Helms famously despised class actions, and her fiercely written sixty-page opinion in *Parker v. Hasbro* had torn up and dismissed a lawsuit almost identical to the one Cimarron would soon be facing.

If Cimarron got a dismissal from Judge Helms, the California plaintiffs would of course try to appeal. That didn't worry him. T&K's litigation team could drag out the appellate process for years, giving Graham time to negotiate a bird-in-the-hand settlement that his client could survive. These tactics might not amount to Justice with a capital "J" as it was taught in law school, but it was how lowercase justice worked in Graham Tarbell's corner of the world.

"So, like I say, we'll call this a gentleman's bet," Taylor continued. "Let's say I'm betting this case coming up against Cimarron—"

Graham broke in sharply. "No idea what you're talking about, Jack. What case coming up against Cimarron?"

For a space of two, three, four seconds, the two men were eye to eye, each reading the other perfectly. The interval was not long, but for Graham it was enough to nail down two things. First, Taylor was not playing. This was for real. Second, from this point on, there would be no references to reality, not even in private. Graham could trust Taylor for that. Everything would be coded, even when they were alone, to protect them both.

"Just picking one of your clients randomly, Graham. Could be anybody. But, like I say, just for fun, let's assume somebody, whoever it is, gets nailed with a monster securities fraud lawsuit. Bankruptcy looming right over the horizon. If this should happen, I'm ready to bet that the case will get drawn to the Honorable Margaret D. Helms. If I hit, one chance in eleven, you pay me three million bucks. If I lose, I give you four season tickets to Fenway Park, box seats, nine rows behind home plate." Taylor held out his hand. "Deal?"

"This is not a very good bet for you, Jack."

"Let's just say I'm feeling lucky." He withdrew his hand and gave Graham a steady look. "I've come up aces a few times now, Graham, and I play this game with only a very small, very elite clientele." He reached out again, grinning. "So, deal?"

Graham looked at Taylor's hand. Sandy's warning not to agree to anything without speaking to him first flickered through his mind. Screw him.

"One million."

"Two." Taylor kept his hand out, still with the smile.

"Six seats. I'll want to take the grandkids."

"Done."

Graham could not help being impressed, when they shook, that Taylor's oversize hand was as smooth and dry as a dollar bill.

16

The next day, Judge Norcross woke up to the sound of the birthday song. When he felt a warm bite on the tip of his earlobe, he opened his eyes and found Claire leaning over him. A tray carrying a cup of coffee and a muffin sat on the nightstand. The muffin held a burning candle.

"Happy birthday, Your Honor." Claire's song was a whisper, and her damp breath lingered on his cheek. "Happy birthday to you!" The aroma of coffee and the faintly sulfurous smell of the expired match hung in the air.

"Wow." As Norcross continued to wake up, a few details came into focus. Claire had changed into her special silk nightgown, she'd put on a little makeup, and she was wearing a wonderfully transparent smile. He stretched and enjoyed the easy surge of blood as the new day worked its way into his brain. The sun was making a dusky triangle on the far wall.

Claire sat down on the edge of the bed. "Charlie's asleep." She put her finger on the bridge of his nose and drew it down into the depression above his upper lip. "So I'm bringing you a birthday treat."

"But it's not my birthday."

"Really." She kissed him. "Oh gosh."

Norcross laughed and raised himself on one elbow. "Where. Where'd you get the muffin?" By this time, pretty much every cell in his body was doing the Wave.

"Charlie was up very early, and we took a sunrise walk over to a coffee shop down the street." She kissed him again. "They open at six."

He broke off a piece of the crusty muffin top and popped it into his mouth. "Terrific special treat." The sugar crunched sweetly. "Thank you for . . ."

Claire leaned closer. "The muffin isn't your special treat." Norcross glanced over at the clock—it was a workday—but Claire put her hand on his chest. "We have loads of time."

They tumbled into an extended, increasingly ardent spell of kissing and floundering with clothing. At one point, Claire gave out a little squeak of pain.

"Oh no, your wrist."

"It's much better. See?" She held up her hand and wiggled it around. "We don't have to rush back to Amherst. It's just a little . . ."

"Are you sure? We could always wait until . . ." By this time, Claire was half naked.

"David. Make your wish." She leaned toward him, whispering. "I'll blow out your candle."

A half hour later, the two of them lay in each other's arms, the two sanest people in the Greater Boston Area.

Claire pressed her cheek against his chest. "It's been a rough time." Her voice was a murmur.

"Very rough." It had been only four days since the Widener bombing.

"We need to remember that life has other things too."

Not long after that, Norcross showered and put on his suit and tie while Claire went to check on the baby. He made his signature mushroom and cheddar omelet as an inadequate expression of gratitude for their morning frolic, and the three of them settled comfortably around the breakfast table, Charlie in his high chair. The boy was in his usual morning good mood, smearing egg on his face and happily lobbing bits onto the floor. Halfway through the meal, Norcross noticed that Claire seemed to be hesitating whether to say something. After a short interval, she spoke.

"A strange thing happened when I went out for the muffins this morning."

He finished chewing. He had a bad habit of talking with his mouth full, especially when his mind was in four or five places at once. "Really." He swallowed and waited.

"I know this sort of thing bugs you, so I wasn't going to mention it."

"Uh-huh."

"When we were out, some guy took a picture of Charlie and me. With his cell phone."

"Really." He put his fork down.

"I don't know if he saw me noticing. It was just, like, a couple seconds, walking toward us, and then when he got close . . ." She raised her hand as though she was holding a cell phone. "Click. Click. No smile, no eye contact, and off he went."

"What did he look like?"

"Ordinary. Jeans and a T-shirt. Sunglasses. A cap from some sports team."

"Man?"

"I think so, but whoever it was may have had, I think, a ponytail."

"Facial hair? Beard or mustache?"

"Hmm. Not sure." Claire took a bite of toast. "Maybe a mustache?" She waved her fingers under her nose. "Kind of wispy? I don't know why I say this, but he seemed foreign-looking."

"Dark glasses, you said?"

"Yep." Claire looked up at the ceiling and closed her eyes. "Probably."

"Did you see where he went? Did he get in a car, for example?"

"I didn't bother to look. Sorry. He was like a tourist snapping a picture of a typical American." She smiled. "Maybe he just thought I was hot."

"You're right. This does bug me."

"Should we do anything?"

"I'll mention it to our security people. Please tell me if it happens again."

While he was loading his briefcase and preparing to leave for his walk to the courthouse, Claire jumped up from the table.

"There was something else." She picked up an envelope from the sideboard. "I found this in the pocket of your jacket when I was putting together the bag for the cleaners."

He took the envelope and opened it. "Do you want me to drop the cleaning off? It's on my . . ."

He stopped speaking as he read. It was the note Angie Phipps had given him on Friday after the bombing, before they had learned about Warren Armstrong's death. The words were neatly typed on heavy stationery and did not take up much space on the page.

Dear Honorable Judge Norcross,

My name is Godfrey Mungai. I accompanied our friend Reverend David Kamau to your court two days ago. My purpose in writing is to ask if you would kindly meet with me, please. I have reasons to believe that Reverend Kamau is in grave danger. I am hoping you will be willing to help him, given your situation. Thank you.

The note ended with Mungai's email address and phone number. Claire had been watching as he read. "Important?"

"Not sure." He slipped the envelope into his pocket. "I better hit the road."

Norcross was a fast walker, and as he made his way along the bustling sidewalks to the courthouse, various things were sloshing around in his head. He'd spoken with Reverend Kamau the previous afternoon, discussing his talk at the Divinity School next Monday, and he'd even mentioned having Kamau come out to Amherst for dinner, with no hint by Kamau of any problems. Norcross recalled that, at their first meeting, Kamau had mentioned something about a "row" with Mungai. Did Mungai have some kind of agenda? It seemed best to wait until he'd touched base again with Kamau before responding to the note.

As he hurried along, Norcross was fielding other distractions, including a motion to dismiss in a product liability case. The legal issue was dry and complex—a question of personal jurisdiction over a small manufacturer in Rhode Island—but the fact pattern made him squirm. Plaintiff, a fifty-six-year-old carpenter, alleged that a negligently designed nail gun had discharged spontaneously, firing a two-inch roofing nail into his groin.

At a busy corner only a few blocks from the courthouse, Norcross glanced up to confirm that he had the walk sign and was just stepping off the curb when a powerful hand grabbed him and jerked him backward, so roughly that he nearly lost his balance and fell on his behind. At the same moment, a bike messenger pelted by in front of him, close enough to touch.

The kid shouted back, "Eyes open, Roscoe!" and barreled on, pumping hard.

The rescuing hand gave his shoulder a pat, and Judge Norcross turned to see that it was the FBI agent Mike Patterson.

Patterson pointed at the retreating bike. "Want me to pop him?"

"Wow, that was close. Thanks."

Although their relationship had some constraints—judges and law enforcement agents worked in different, sometimes conflicting, worlds—Norcross and Patterson could almost be described as friends. They'd known each other while Patterson handled criminal investigations in Western Massachusetts. Over time a personal relationship had grown up.

"Actually, I was hoping to run into you, Judge."

"Sure. Better than running into that bike." Norcross was taking a minute to recover from the near miss and, equally, from the sneering comment thrown at him by the messenger. People didn't talk to him that way. "How's Margaret? Is she still knocking them out of the park?"

Patterson's daughter Margaret and Norcross's niece Lindsay had both played on the Amherst Regional High School girls' softball team, Margaret as the team's ace pitcher and Lindsay as the catcher. Senior year, the team had won the Western Massachusetts championship and gone on to finish second in the state.

"Very proud. She just picked up a Stanford book prize for excellence in her writing."

"Good for her. She's doing physics, right?"

"Right. When I tried to read her paper, I understood about half of it."

The breeze picked up as they crossed the Fort Point bridge, rippling the water and blowing a sandwich wrapper around in crazy circles. The seagulls wheeled and complained.

Norcross let them walk a little way before tackling a new topic. An Old Town Trolley, bursting with tourists, ground its way past them. "Listen, Claire mentioned something that kind of worries me."

"How's she doing? We heard she was at Harvard last Friday."

"Still recovering. It was really awful for her."

"Please let her know I'm thinking about her." Claire and Patterson were both baseball fans and had bonded during the girls' softball games.

"When she and Charlie went out this morning, some guy with a ponytail took pictures of them, she says."

"Hmm."

"I don't like that."

"Don't blame you." Patterson looked up at the sky, thinking. "Send me an email with the details, will you? Location, time of day, description and so forth. I'll do a report, so we'll have something in the system."

"You'll have it by lunchtime."

"Not much else we can do. I'm assuming she doesn't want anyone detailed to her?"

"No, that'd be overkill, and she'd hate it."

At the foot of the bridge, they turned left and soon the redbrick bulk of the courthouse came into view. Clouds were drifting across the glass facades of the neighboring buildings.

"I had you on my list to talk to, Judge. You met with Warren Armstrong a couple days before the bombing, right?"

Norcross remembered their talk now with sadness. "Yes, he was hitting me up for the O'Connell trial."

"Uh-huh. You'll be seeing me in court on that one, Judge, with Claudia Papadakis. I'm filling in as case agent."

"Thanks." Norcross appreciated Patterson mentioning this. They'd steer way clear of the topic now.

"Did Armstrong seem concerned about anything when you talked to him? Anything in particular going on?"

"Let's see." Norcross reeled his mind back to when Warren was sitting across from him. It seemed like an hour and a lifetime ago. "I remember he talked about his son."

"Uh-huh. Dougie, the wannabe rapper."

"It was driving him nuts." They were approaching the front door of the building. A white-haired court security officer was standing outside, hands behind his back, looking around. "Are you thinking the bomber might have been targeting Warren?"

"Not really. Just checking on everything."

"Will you make today's memorial?"

Chief Judge Broadwater had arranged an informal ceremony for Warren that morning in the Jury Assembly Room. It was for the court family only, getting the judges and staff together to grieve and support one another. The death had hit everyone very hard. Warren's wife and children would be attending.

"I'll be there." Patterson held the door as they passed into the building. "Anything else you can think of?"

"Warren had some staffing problems, some people out. And there was a computer glitch he had Angie Phipps trying to figure out." Norcross smiled. "Judge Ramos was drawing too many patent cases."

"Hmm. I'll check with Angie about that."

They parted ways, and Norcross took the elevator up to his chambers. When he arrived, he found a yellow message slip waiting on his desk. It was from Godfrey Mungai, leaving his number and asking again for Norcross to call as soon as possible. The note said it was an emergency.

17

Carl Alberti pulled into the parking lot outside the Plymouth County Correctional Facility. He'd gotten word from the shift lieutenant that Kahlil Khan was going to be seeing a visitor, a subject by the name of David Kamau, and he'd hurried south to intercept him. Kamau was the shadowy character identified by the Kenyan embassy. The man's visit to Khan just a few days after the bombing deepened Alberti's suspicion that the Harvard attack was choreographed by an East African terrorist cell.

As he waited in the parking lot, he shot a quick text to Angie Phipps, telling her he was thinking of her and asking how she was doing. It was going to be a while before he'd have an opening for their aquarium date.

Before Angie had time to respond, Alberti saw a tall Black man with a clerical collar exiting the jail's front entry. A gray Corolla immediately pulled up to the curb. Before Kamau could enter, Alberti drew up alongside, blocking the Corolla in. He lowered his window.

"Excuse me? David Kamau?"

The tall man looked at him. "Yes?"

"Could I have a minute?"

A shorter man with glasses, also Black, got out of the Corolla, slamming the door too hard. The man started to say something, but the parson, or whatever he was, put his hand on the man's shoulder.

"How may we help you?" He sounded British.

Alberti exited his vehicle and approached. "Carl Alberti. I'm a federal agent working with the Bureau of Alcohol, Tobacco, Firearms, and Explosives." He held out his identification.

The shorter man glanced down at his ID and scowled. "The bureau of what?"

"Alcohol, Tobacco, Firearms, and Explosives."

The taller man raised his eyebrows and smiled. "That's a very long title. You must have many responsibilities."

"I understand you are Reverend David Kamau. Is that right?"

"Yes."

"And you are?" Alberti looked at the shorter man.

"Am I obliged to tell you?"

Alberti gave a short laugh and shook his head. "No, but I'm going to find out, and, if you tell me, it might make things easier for both of us."

Kamau peered down at his friend, still with an amused smile. After thinking for a few seconds, the shorter man grudgingly gave his name. "Godfrey Mungai."

"Could I have a spelling on the last name?"

Mungai spelled his name. He was clearly not happy to be doing this, but it was hard to tell whether his response meant anything. It could just signify that he was uncomfortable with law enforcement in general, which was probably understandable. Foreigners frequently reacted this way.

Alberti put his identification back in his pocket. "Reverend Kamau, could I have two minutes of your time? Privately?"

Mungai glanced nervously up at his friend before turning back to Alberti. "Why?"

Alberti continued to address Kamau. "Could I?"

Kamau nodded down at Mungai. "We won't be long."

Alberti did not want his questions interrupted with any coaching or indignant commentary from Mungai. He also did not want to put Mungai in a position to testify about the contents of his conversation with Kamau, possibly offering a version that would conflict with his. He'd been trained to keep things simple, and he wanted to be the only witness to what Kamau said. In the event of some disagreement, it would be his word against Kamau's.

They spoke at the far side of Alberti's car, out of Mungai's earshot. Alberti began with easy things, confirming Kamau's address, phone number, and email, even though he already had these. Kamau answered truthfully.

"I understand you have some connection to Harvard Divinity School."

"That is correct. I have a two-year fellowship."

"May I ask how it is that you know Kahlil Khan?" When he noticed Kamau hesitating, Albert added, "Just a routine question. We're contacting anyone who might know him, trying to find out as much as possible about his background."

"I see." Kamau nodded. "Well, to be candid, I don't know him. Or, rather, I didn't know him until an hour ago when we met in there." Kamau nodded in the direction of the jail.

"May I ask what made you decide to visit him?"

"I was contacted by the Kenyan embassy and asked to check on him. Khan's English is not fluent, and they were concerned about his condition."

"How was he?"

"Not happy, of course. But today was not my first visit to a detention center. This one is reasonably clean, Mr. Khan is getting adequate food and water, and he has no medical problems so far as I can see. He does not appear to have been beaten yet or suffered any other abuse, but he is very frightened. His area of the facility is uncomfortably warm and close. The ventilation and air-conditioning do not appear—"

"May I ask what you and Mr. Khan talked about?"

Kamau stopped and looked at Alberti for several seconds before replying. "I'm afraid I can't reveal anything about the substance of our conversation, Mr. Alberti. It is true that I am ordained in the Church of Kenya and Mr. Khan is a Muslim, so I am not technically his formal religious confidant, but the situation still . . ."

"No problem. No problem. Don't worry about it."

At this point, Mungai called out. "David, we need to go." He pointed to his watch. "Chika needs her car back."

Alberti spoke reassuringly. "I really appreciate your help."

"Of course." Kamau gestured over at Mungai. "I am afraid I have to go. Our friend will be waiting."

As Kamau walked away, Alberti called out. "Sorry. One more thing. Do you remember the name of the person from the embassy who called you?"

Mungai had gotten into the car and was starting the engine.

"Grace Otieno. At least, that is the name she gave me." Noticing Alberti's expression, Kamau smiled again and raised his voice so it would be heard over the car. "O-T-I-E-N-O."

"Thanks."

Kamau bowed, perhaps sarcastically. "Please let me know if I can be of any further help, Mr. Alberti."

Alberti got into his car and swung around to the staff parking area, leaving Mungai room to get out. He watched through his rear-view mirror until the Corolla had disappeared, then got on the line to the Kenyan embassy in Washington, D.C. By good luck, he was connected directly to the staff member he'd originally spoken to. His contact quickly confirmed that there was no one by the name of Grace Otieno working at the Kenyan embassy.

18

Judge Norcross rarely acknowledged it, even to himself, but in all the frantic world he never felt so much at peace, anywhere, as he did in the courtroom. A blessed calmness always fell upon him in the silence right after his court clerk reached her crescendo—"God save the United States of America and this Honorable Court!"— and he lowered himself into his chair. Today was no different. For these few seconds, he felt like a perfectly shaped gear in a well-lubricated machine. This was where the universe wanted him. He fit.

He let his eyes travel over the gallery, nodded at counsel, and said in a deliberately firm, deliberately good-humored voice, "Good afternoon. Please be seated."

It was unusual for him to be starting his court day this late, but the Armstrong memorial and the thorny jurisdictional memo in the nail gun case had eaten up the morning and part of the afternoon. Now, here he was, ready to hear arguments on a raft of motions in *O'Connell* that needed rulings before the trial. The court stenographer's fingers were poised over her machine, all eyes were on him, and time itself waited for his signal to resume.

Then, the moment passed, everyone sat down, and the usual melodrama came tumbling vividly in. To his left, Attorney Tarbell returned to rifling through his papers. Next to him, the defendant O'Connell leaned back and crossed his arms with a disgusted expression. Two men, one with striking red hair, sat behind him in the front row, obviously associates or henchmen of some sort. To the judge's right, Assistant U.S. Attorney Papadakis struck a posture of relaxed attentiveness, her hands folded on the table, with Mike Patterson seated next to her. The pews in the gallery were dotted with clumps of spectators and journalists, including not only the regulars from the *Globe* and the *Herald* but reporters from the Associated Press, the *New York Times*, and, he'd heard, even a stringer from the *Philadelphia Inquirer*.

Judge Norcross slid his yellow pad into position and leaned forward. "Ms. Phipps, call the case please."

In a slightly ragged voice, Angie Phipps called out, "Now before the court is the case of *United States of America versus Dominic O'Connell*, criminal action 21-10231-DSN."

The memorial that morning had been heartbreaking for everyone, but Phipps had taken it especially hard. About a hundred judges and staff had attended, listening to praise and reminiscences about Warren Armstrong from Chief Judge Broadwater and Judge Ramos, the two members of the court who had known him the longest. This had been tough enough, but then Armstrong's son, Douglas, stepped to the podium to speak. He'd barely gotten a word out before Phipps's grief became audible, and she slipped out of the room. Now, as Judge Norcross looked down to review the outline he'd prepared, he saw Phipps at her desk below him, pouring herself a cup of water. Her hand was steady. She must have recovered somewhat.

"We're here today to address a number of pretrial motions. Most of these I'll be handling on the papers. Only two or three impress me as requiring any extended oral argument."

At these words, Sandy Tarbell's chin bobbed up, and his eyes widened in anger. Tarbell had filed twelve motions. He obviously had plenty to say about every single one of them.

The judge peered down at Tarbell with his own steady, quelling expression, until the defense attorney's face relented a little, but only a little. Attorney Tarbell was obviously ready for a tussle, maybe even looking forward to it.

Norcross's mind shifted—he'd deal with Tarbell later—and he turned to Assistant U.S. Attorney Papadakis. "The motion that jumped out at me first was the government's request to take a deposition of its key witness, Brian Shaughnessy. I was surprised to see this. We're on the eve of trial here. It's a heck of a time to schedule a deposition."

Depositions were common in civil litigation—meaning, usually, lawsuits between private parties over money. They typically took place in an attorney's conference room, with a stenographer to record the lawyers' questions and the witness's answers under oath, and to prepare a transcript. The deposition provided a preview of the witness's testimony, and the transcript could be read to the jury if the witness died or was otherwise unavailable at trial. Since no judge was present to keep things on track, the value of these civil depositions depended on the opposing attorneys behaving themselves, which they sometimes didn't. Descent into bluster and bullying was not uncommon, especially with incompetent lawyers.

The Federal Rules of Criminal Procedure made depositions in *criminal* cases very rare, and for good reason. Brian Shaughnessy was a crucial witness against O'Connell. A deposition of him would give Papadakis an advance opportunity to smooth out Shaughnessy's testimony before trial. It would also give Tarbell a chance to intimidate Shaughnessy with a barrage of sharp, possibly improper, cross-examination outside of Norcross's control. With no adult supervision, the whole thing could collapse into a table-banging mess.

As Papadakis got to her feet and made her way to the podium, she did not exactly take her time, but she did not hurry either. To Judge Norcross, she conveyed an impression of relaxed, even-tempered confidence, a welcome counterbalance to Tarbell's manic aggressiveness.

He pressed his question. "As you know, Ms. Papadakis, Rule Fifteen permits a criminal deposition only in some exceptional circumstance. What's yours?"

"Mr. Shaughnessy's dying, Your Honor. That's our exceptional circumstance."

"We're all dying," Tarbell muttered, ostensibly to his client but loud enough for the assistant U.S. attorney, the judge, and the reporters to hear.

Papadakis looked over at Tarbell for a beat of two seconds, sighed, and turned to Norcross. "True, but Mr. Shaughnessy has late-stage lung cancer, and I have a letter from his doctor confirming that his condition is precarious. May I approach?" She stepped forward and passed the letter to Phipps, who set it on the bench in front of Norcross.

Tarbell hopped up and began, in a grating voice, "Could I please . . ." He stopped short when Papadakis flipped a copy of the doctor's letter onto his desk.

"Sorry this is arriving so late, Judge. We had trouble getting the doctor to respond. It was only emailed to me this morning."

The door to the courtroom banged open, and to the judge's discomfort, Reverend Kamau's friend Godfrey Mungai entered. He took a seat in the row at the very rear of the courtroom, pushed his glasses up his nose, and looked around with his usual suspicious expression. Mungai must have decided that the judge was ignoring his messages and that he needed to come harass him in person.

Unfortunately, as Norcross was peering down, Mungai glanced up at the bench, and the two men unintentionally locked eyes. After a short, awkward interval, Mungai nodded curtly, as though he and the judge had just tacitly agreed upon something. Norcross had no idea what that might be.

Papadakis was continuing. "To be honest, Judge, in twelve years as an assistant U.S. attorney, I've never taken a deposition in a criminal case before. I know it's a potential headache." Papadakis was a good lawyer, and Norcross could tell that this concession was in response to something she had read in his face. He turned away from Mungai and quickly rearranged his features to make himself more inscrutable.

"This is a unique situation for two reasons." Papadakis held up a finger. "First, Brian Shaughnessy is our key witness. We of course have other evidence clearly establishing Mr. O'Connell's guilt." At this, Tarbell smirked and whispered something to O'Connell. "But Mr. Shaughnessy's testimony is at the center of our case. Second, Mr. Shaughnessy really is very ill. As the letter demonstrates, he could die at any time and die quickly. In these circumstances, the rule supports a deposition to preserve his testimony for the jury in case he can't come here in person." Papadakis tipped her head at Tarbell. "I realize that my friend at defense table probably thinks a deposition would be the worst thing since the wreck of the *Edmund Fitzgerald*, but—"

Tarbell piped up without standing. "No, no, no, I'm fine with it." In response to Norcross's frown, he scrambled to his feet. "Sorry, Judge. Just as long as I have an unrestricted opportunity to cross-examine. And, by the way, this so-called *other* evidence? That's pure bull. Brian Shaughnessy is what they've got, and all they've got, and he's a boiled-in-the-bone liar."

At these words, Norcross noticed the heads of the reporters bobbing down as they typed on their iPads. "Pure bull" and "boiled-in-the-bone liar" were tidy phrases to work into the lead of the next day's news story, as Tarbell undoubtedly knew. One of them might even make a good headline.

Norcross had been glancing over the doctor's letter as Tarbell spoke. "It says here that Mr. Shaughnessy's condition has been stable for the past eight weeks."

Papadakis nodded. "True, Judge, but the doctor also says—"

Norcross tapped the letter. "The doctor also says that in the absence of a sudden downturn Mr. Shaughnessy can manage the trip up from Philadelphia and take the stand here in person."

"But, Judge, look at the last sentence. Dr. Aziz concludes that he could go into crisis at any time and, if that happens, he might slip into a coma within hours, or even—"

Tarbell, still standing, broke in. "It hurts, Your Honor. It really hurts me to say this, but I agree with Ms. Papadakis. A deposition is needed to preserve Shaughnessy's testimony. I'm prepared to make myself available at any—"

"Nope." Norcross shook his head. "Sorry. Not going to happen."

The two lawyers both said "But . . ." simultaneously.

"Not until we have stronger evidence of Mr. Shaughnessy's decline."

Papadakis kept her face calm. "I understand. We'll request reconsideration, if necessary." Tarbell wasn't ready to give up. He held his hands up to the bench. "Your Honor, I'd object strongly. In fairness to Mr. O'Connell—"

"You have my ruling. Let's move on."

Tarbell stared at Norcross with his mouth open, then flopped back in his seat. "Let the record note my objection."

"Your objection, as you know Mr. Tarbell, will be preserved without the need for any formal notation. We'll move on."

Judge Norcross, as usual, had made his ruling without conveying any hint of ambivalence, but also without any absolute conviction that he was right. His decision was rooted in his instinct that the deposition would be a bad idea, particularly with a lawyer like Tarbell. It was obvious to him that the more prudent route was to deny Papadakis's motion and let her bring it back if Shaughnessy began slipping. On the other hand, if Shaughnessy suddenly died before the trial, as Papadakis feared, Norcross's ruling might emerge as a major blunder. It was impossible to know at the moment whether he'd done the right thing.

Chief Judge Broadwater's self-deprecating description of himself in situations like this was "sometimes in error, but never in doubt." As he'd told Norcross: read the memos, listen to the lawyers until they start repeating themselves, make your ruling, and don't look back. It never helped to dillydally.

The first of the remaining motions was Tarbell's effort to increase his number of peremptory challenges. So-called peremptories allowed an attorney to request dismissal of a potential juror without stating any reason. The rules gave a defendant in a federal criminal trial ten such free shots and the government six. Tarbell twisted himself into the shape of a pretzel and ran through practically every authority back to the Magna Carta trying to get Norcross to give him an extra five challenges, citing extreme prejudicial pretrial publicity. Norcross ended up denying his motion without even hearing Papadakis in response. Ten was plenty.

This time, Tarbell threw himself back into his chair with more pique and less effort to hide it. It was impossible to know whether this display was just theatrics or real frustration. If the performance was an effort to impress his client, it didn't work. O'Connell's face, turned to the side, was a mixture of embarrassment and contempt.

The final topic that morning fell under the quaintly phrased heading of "promises, rewards, and inducements." The rules required government attorneys to reveal, well before trial, all the details of any promises they'd made, or rewards they'd offered, in return for a witness's helpful testimony. The most common promise, reward, or inducement was the government's agreement to drop, or lower, a criminal charge their witness was facing. Defense attorneys had a right to know all about the government's bargain, so they could argue that the witness was not being truthful, just lying to get the benefit of the deal.

O'Connell presented a rare version of the promises-and-rewards scenario, the first time Norcross had faced it. Tarbell's strongly worded written memorandum attacked Papadakis personally and at length for failing to cough up the full details of the government's unusual arrangement with Shaughnessy.

"What's going on here, Your Honor, is cynical and disgusting. There are probably some better words, but those are the best I can come up with. Brian Shaughnessy will not be offering his false testimony against my client to get anything for *himself*, the way this song and dance usually works. Brian will be in his grave too soon for that. Rather, after finishing up thirty-some years in prison for three other murders—on parole now and on his last legs—he's suddenly confessed to a fourth murder, the killing of Officer Scanlon, and he's concocted this outrageous lie about Dominic O'Connell being involved in it. Shaughnessy is doing this to help his *nephew*, James Shaughnessy, a murderous Philadelphia drug kingpin and the son of his sister Brenda—who, by the way, Brian is living with these days and completely dependent on. As a reward for Brian Shaughnessy's lie, the Philadelphia prosecutors have agreed to back off the mandatory life term for Jimmy and recommend only twenty years. This contrivance is so slimy that many people down there, especially in the law enforcement community, are outraged. Who can blame them?"

While Norcross was not astonished by the unusual three-way deal—he knew it was an occasional device used by prosecutors—he found the public outrage understandable. The whole setup certainly looked terrible. But a policeman had been murdered—some of Officer Scanlon's children were sitting in the gallery at that moment—and that outrage cried out for justice. The prosecution needed Shaughnessy to get that. The criminal process worked in a complex moral landscape, barely comprehensible to people unfamiliar with its crisscrossing pathways and was sometimes offensive even to him.

Tarbell pushed on. "So, here's where we are, Judge. The prison door is about to close behind Jimmy Shaughnessy and never, ever open again. Then, out of the blue, up pops dear uncle Brian, who has seen his last Christmas, fabricating this mound of lies against Dominic O'Connell to help rescue his sister's boy. I don't want to be crude, but the smell is overpowering.

"Ms. Papadakis has failed to provide details, but we know Jimmy has a long and complicated relationship with his lying uncle Brian. We're pretty sure that Jimmy was involved in one or two uncharged murders in Philly, which the government seems to be giving him a pass on. As you say, Judge, we're on the eve of trial here. I'm entitled to everything the government has on this kid and on Brian's sister, too, every scrap, to prepare. Instead, she's gaming me. New material comes in almost every day, very disorganized and hard to work through. With every new disclosure, I have to adjust my trial strategy. It's outrageous, and more importantly it's just not fair." He gestured over at the government's table. "I know Ms. Papadakis is a nice person, Judge. She can put a pleasant expression on her face as well as anyone I know. But her misconduct—her repeated failure to follow the rules and give me what I'm entitled to—is brazen and intolerable. All I can do is make a record of her behavior and ask for help from the court. I'm moving for a dismissal."

During most of Tarbell's speech, Papadakis sat without moving, looking unconcerned. The only exception was when Tarbell mentioned her pleasant face, at which point she looked over at Patterson, and the two of them exchanged the minutest of smiles.

It was actually a dangerous moment for her. The vast majority of the criminal defendants in federal court ended up either pleading guilty or going to trial and getting found guilty. This did not bother

Judge Norcross much, since the evidence against them was almost always overwhelming. Truly innocent defendants in his courtroom were as rare as buffalo nickels. Facing these odds, Tarbell was adopting the tactic of going after the assistant U.S. attorney, hoping to get the charges thrown out based on prosecutorial misconduct. With an unethical, lazy, or incompetent prosecutor this sometimes worked.

Papadakis waited for Tarbell to sit down, then stepped slowly to the podium and set her yellow pad in position. "Well, excuse me for being pleasant, Judge. I'll have to work on that." She smiled briefly, and Norcross had to force himself not to smile back. "We are aware, Your Honor, that this situation presents a lot of trip wires for the government, so everyone on my side is being extra careful."

Papadakis proceeded to summarize everything she'd turned over regarding Brian and James Shaughnessy, including their written plea agreements, Presentence Reports, rap sheets, biographies, and marital, medical, and work history.

"Four banker's boxes of documents, Judge. Everything our office has, everything our Philadelphia office has, and everything else I can lay my hands on." She pointed at Tarbell. "He has it all. I flew down to Philadelphia personally last weekend—missed my son's peewee soccer game, for which he will never forgive me—and spent two days going over everything, just to be sure nothing was missing. At the risk of repetition, let me take you again through exactly what the defense has."

Papadakis went back over everything in detail, moving item by item, before concluding. "That's it. Mr. Tarbell has everything about Brian Shaughnessy and his nephew James except their shoe sizes and elementary-school report cards, and I'll get him those if he wants them. There's not much on Brenda Shaughnessy, Brian's sister, since she has no criminal record or other law enforcement contact, but I've turned over what we have. This complaint about not getting what he's entitled to is a magic act, pure and simple, trying to conjure something out of thin air. Mr. Tarbell is reaching into his top hat, but there's no rabbit inside."

This last phrase had the reporters bobbing again. Tarbell, looking flushed, jumped up and started to speak, but Norcross waved both attorneys down.

"Okay, enough." He nodded down at the defense table. "I understand your concerns, Mr. Tarbell, but for now I am persuaded that the government has complied with its obligation to provide you with everything you are entitled to. You can raise the issue again, of course, if necessary. For now, it's time to wrap this up."

Dominic O'Connell had sat, barely moving, during the hearing, but his face had grown increasingly lost and angry. By the time Angie Phipps called the recess and Norcross stood to leave, O'Connell's eyes radiated something approaching real hatred. This did not worry Norcross much. Defendants often knew little about the rough-and-tumble of court proceedings and took every contrary ruling as a personal slight. They tended to settle down once the trial got underway. Whatever was happening might be horrible, but it was certainly not personal. O'Connell had to realize that.

19

Dominic O'Connell rode down with his lawyer after the hearing, the two of them alone in the elevator. Rafferty and Aidan had gone ahead to get the car. He stared at the floor angrily, imagining his body on a cold slab in some Bureau of Prisons morgue. After all he'd been through, there was no way he was ending up like that. No way he was going to allow them to do that to Julie.

Tarbell as usual had to start talking. "Well, that was—"

O'Connell interrupted immediately. "That was a goddamn disaster."

He had eight inches and fifty well-muscled pounds on his lawyer, and in the close confines of the elevator, the difference stood out. He could wad Tarbell up and stuff him into a trash can, and right now that was exactly what he wanted to do.

"Not entirely, Dom. It—"

"The judge loves that Greek chippie, but he sure doesn't think much of Sandy Tarbell."

"Well, I had to push him a little."

"Norcross can be worked, but not by you."

"The hearing really didn't go that badly."

"How badly could it have gone?" O'Connell tipped his head back and looked up at the ceiling. "I never should have listened to Julie. I should've stuck with Sam Newbury and taken the goddamn deal. Do the time and have it over with."

Tarbell's voice rose. "Papadakis made a bad mistake in there. If we'd gotten that deposition, I would have twisted Shaughnessy until his bones cracked. But Norcross had to go and rescue her. Judge Helms would never have done that, and she would have given us the extra peremptories too."

"Can we appeal?"

"No. Norcross's rulings were discretionary." Tarbell set his brief-case down and wiped his hand over the back of his neck. "An appeal would only piss off the court of appeals, and we may need them later."

"Well, it's too late for me to change lawyers. Maybe we can change something else." He paused. "Who was the Black guy with Papadakis?"

"That's Patterson, the FBI case agent. He's got his hands full these days, heading up the investigation of the Harvard thing."

"Hmm." O'Connell took a breath. "Are they making any progress? Wasn't the bomber some Muslim or something?"

"Right. The information isn't public, but I heard the person who handed off the bomb to Khan was a guy who'd dressed up like an old lady."

"Is that so?"

"Yes, and the bomb was some kind of modified U.S. military grenade."

"Really. How'd you find this out?"

"With this many people on an investigation, there are always one or two little birdies."

Rafferty was waiting with the car idling in front of the court-house when they emerged, ready to ferry him back to his home confinement. Aidan sat in the back. Tarbell hesitated on the side-walk, angling for a lift, but O'Connell did not offer one. He'd had more than enough of his lawyer for one day, and he wanted to talk to Rafferty privately. He watched as Tarbell walked off, shoulders slumped. That guy dated Julie?

When he opened the passenger-side door, Rafferty leaned over and gave him a sharp look. "I'm seeing you, and I'm guessing things didn't go too good."

"Tarbell is a punk." O'Connell slipped in and slammed the door. "Papadakis is eating his lunch, and he's too stupid to know it."

"Want us to have a talk with him?"

"Nah, he'll just panic, and that'll make things worse." He took a deep breath. "I'm stuck with him. What I really need is for somebody to get rid of this smart-ass judge for me."

Aidan spoke from the back. "We paid for Helms."

"Exactly. Have we heard anything from Newbury?"

Rafferty shook his head. "Not a peep."

O'Connell muttered, "That kid's going to find himself in the soup real soon."

As they made their way back to Beacon Hill, O'Connell kept an eye out the window. The streets were crowded, and they spent a lot of time sitting at stoplights, but he enjoyed the ride. For all these months now, court appearances and doctors' appointments were the only times he was allowed out of the house. It was nice to see that the world was carrying on.

"How are things going with the dinner?" O'Connell and Julie's tenth anniversary was around the corner, and he was determined not to let his trial mess up the occasion.

Rafferty frowned. "The caterer's being a little bit of a problem, but I'll straighten it out."

"Keep me up to date. I don't want any . . ."

"I know. I know."

He rolled his shoulders and tried, not very successfully, to force himself to relax. Let Raff handle it. After a while, he recalled what Tarbell had said in the elevator and began to smile. Rafferty immediately noticed.

"Something funny, Dom?"

"Listen to this. Tarbell tells me that the guy who set up the thing at Harvard, not the Muslim janitor, but the one who gave him the bag, they think he dressed up like an old woman first."

"Oh boy, that sounds like . . ."

"Yeah. And the bomb was a modified U.S. military grenade."

"You're kidding me."

A silence of two or three minutes went by. Rafferty was unusually silent, obviously chewing on the same thing O'Connell was—some people they'd both known, or at least known about, a while back.

As they were passing in front of the State House, O'Connell spoke. "So what do you think? I'm wondering if the Doyle brothers may have come out of retirement. Their father was a good friend of Uncle Tommy's."

"I remember." Rafferty shook his head, sounding awed. "If it was them, somebody must've coughed up an ice-cold shitload of money. They're both psychos, but the younger brother, Dennis . . ."

"I know. Short, skinny kid. They called him 'The Razor,' right?" O'Connell cast his mind back. "Don't know why he always liked to dress up like a woman to do his business."

Aidan stirred. "Pumps him up."

"Sick."

Rafferty spoke. "I heard they were in Kosovo a while back, free-lancing. Then in Belarus or one of those goddamn countries."

"I don't know how they impressed the Serbs," O'Connell said. "But, by God, they frighten me. Once they get rolling, they don't care about anything."

Rafferty eased his way around a double-parked van. "Not for me to say, Dom, but I could have a word with Mike Patterson. If you helped the feds find their bomber, they might cut you a—"

"I can beat this without going that route, Raff. The Doyles move in a very ugly crowd, and they have friends who wouldn't think twice about coming after Julie and the girls."

"Your call." Rafferty looked out the window, musing. "The older brother—I forget his name—became a real technician, a master at his work. You had to give him that."

"Gerald. Always took pride in a job well done."

"Scary." Rafferty nodded. "Really scary guys."

20

Meeting with Godfrey Mungai was against Judge Norcross's better judgment, but he decided that sooner or later he was going to have to hear what the man had to say.

"Before we get started, Mr. Mungai, you must understand that I can't discuss any cases currently before me, or any cases or legal issues that might come before me in the future."

"I know that, of course. That is not why I'm here." Like Kamau, Mungai had a British accent, though more Americanized.

"Good. Okay. One other thing, if you don't mind. Before we get started, can you tell me something about yourself?"

The question provoked a suspicious look. "About myself?"

"Yes, what you do, how you came to the United States, that sort of thing."

"All right, I suppose." Mungai leaned forward and pushed his glasses up on his nose. "Well. I am a journalist. I've been living in Boston for seven years now. I teach courses on political and economic development in so-called third-world countries, particularly in Africa, at the Kennedy School. I also write occasional articles for the *East African Standard* in Nairobi, where I used to work."

"I see."

"I live with my wife and daughter in Somerville. Is that the sort of thing you wanted to know?"

"More or less." Norcross tried a smile but got no reaction. "I don't mean to pry."

"David Kamau is my best friend. We spent time in the same village, and we were at school together." Mungai glanced around the room, as though he thought someone might be hiding in the shadows. He was an odd man.

"I remember Mwi Muto. A lovely spot."

"Yes, I know you visited. David and I heard the village gossip."

Norcross paused, giving his guest an opening. Nothing happened. Mungai interlaced fingers, then untangled them and set his hands on his knees. He looked around again, knitting his brows.

"So. I don't mean to push, but can you tell me why you're here? I got your note of course, but I've been pretty busy." He broke off, but Mungai still remained silent. "To tell the truth, Mr. Mungai, I'm not sure what you're looking for from me."

Mungai nodded. "It's not complicated." He extended his hands toward Norcross, as though he were holding something precious in them. "I want you to know who David Kamau is, Your Honor." He dropped his hands and leaned back. "I want you to know the danger he faces, especially after this terrible incident at Harvard."

"I see."

"I am hoping you can help him." Mungai seemed to think of something, and an irritated look passed over his face. "Before I go further, I have to say something, for my own comfort. What I am about to tell you is not intended as some sort of criticism of my home country. Every nation has its good and bad people, including Kenya and including the United States. The proportion of bad people in Kenya is no higher than here." He paused and pushed his glasses up on his nose again. "I'm perhaps biased, but I think we may have somewhat fewer in Kenya."

"Okay."

"Before he came here, David said, and sometimes wrote, things that offended a few very dangerous, very corrupt people in Kenya. Twice, he narrowly escaped attempts on his life. The situation became so risky that friends in the Anglican Church of Kenya arranged for the fellowship at Harvard to get him out of the country."

"I see. May I insert a question here?"

Mungai looked at Norcross without saying anything.

"I've had several conversations with Reverend Kamau now. He hasn't mentioned any of this. And he hasn't asked for any help from me."

"He wouldn't." Mungai shook his head. "He would never do that."

"So how does a young, recently ordained minister like Reverend Kamau attract this kind of animosity? I do know Kenya a little. It is a large, diverse country. People have many different opinions about things. They argue all the time, just like Americans. Reverend Kamau is obviously an impressive man. I like him very much, but he seems hardly a—"

"Do you really not know who David is?"

"I don't know what you mean."

"A few facts, sir, if you don't mind. David Kamau is the grandson of a former cabinet minister, Daniel Kamau, a deeply revered figure in Kenya."

"Yes, he told me. His grandfather was the minister of education."

"Daniel Kamau was, and still is, much more than that—but put that aside. David was a brilliant student and eventually attended Oxford. Not many of us Kenyans do that, and it was noticed, I can tell you. He is, as you can see, a handsome charismatic man, and he is also a powerful speaker. He moves people. His integrity is above suspicion. He has the potential to be our future president."

"I certainly can't disagree."

"But along with other members of the Anglican Church of Kenya, he has regularly spoken out, and written articles, condemning corruption very specifically. He has, as you say, named names."

"Okay."

"Because of who he is, people listen. You see?"

"Yes, I think I do." Mungai was beginning to get through, and this was making Norcross uncomfortable. He disliked the notion of Kamau being in any danger, but what did Mungai want from him? What was he supposed to do?

"Has David mentioned his success at sport?"

"He said that he played cricket a bit."

"Played cricket a bit?" Mungai almost laughed. "Your Honor, he was a star, in America you might say a superstar, famous from Kisumu to Mombasa. His name was in the *Standard* almost every week, often with his picture. Hundreds of people would come to his matches just to see him. If he hadn't gone to Oxford, he would have been a dead cert for the Simbas, our national team."

"He said." Norcross cleared his throat. "He said that Hannah Nyeri would come to watch him sometimes."

"That's true. I remember her there. We all came."

"Hannah and I were good friends."

"Yes, I know." Mungai broke eye contact and looked at the carpeting. "I know that. Her death was . . ."

"Yes, it must have been . . ."

He looked up at Norcross, his eyes widening. "It was something terrible for all of us."

Mungai had been inching forward on the sofa, as though he were trying to get closer to Norcross. Now, he abruptly threw himself against the cushions, tipped his head back, and closed his eyes. A silence followed for two or three breaths.

Finally, Mungai took off his glasses, wiped his face, and sat up. "Ever since David came to the United States, certain people have been working very hard to force him back to Kenya. Some of these people have positions in our government, even, I suspect, in our embassy in Washington. If David is forced to return now, it is virtually certain that he will be murdered." Without the glasses, Mungai's face looked younger and more vulnerable.

"Really." Norcross shook his head, then added with greater emphasis. "Really?"

"Yes. He will be shot dead on a street corner or beaten to death in his home. Or he will just disappear." Mungai replaced his glasses and looked intently at Norcross. "Others in his position, including people in the church, have already died. Now, with this terrible thing at Harvard, certain elements have seen an opportunity. I was present this morning when Reverend Kamau was accosted by one of your investigators." Mungai shook his head. "It was very frightening, at least to me."

"The problem, Mr. Mungai, is that it would be improper for me to—"

"You." Mungai started to point at Norcross but withdrew his finger and looked embarrassed. His voice cracked. "You have this connection to David. You are the only strong friend he has in this country. The U.S. immigration system—you'll forgive my saying so—is impenetrably stupid and arbitrary. If you have an entry point into this system and could offer Mr. Kamau any protection, many people would be very grateful. Many people."

"Well . . ." Norcross began.

"That's what I came to say." Mungai stood up abruptly, took off his glasses again, and wiped his face with his forearm. "I do not ask for any promises, or any commitments, only your good offices if you can offer them."

"Well, of course. I appreciate your coming here."

"I have to go now, or I will say too much. Thank you for your time. Goodbye."

Mungai turned and walked out, leaving Norcross sitting in his wingback, wondering what exactly had just happened and how on earth he should, or could, respond.

A shadow moved in the hallway outside the door. Angie Phipps was waiting there to remind him that the lawyers were in the courtroom, ready for his next hearing.

21

Jack Taylor was number one on the list of people Sam Newbury had hoped never to see again, and his heart dropped as he approached him. Taylor was seated with his knees spread on a bench in the Public Garden next to the "Make Way for Ducklings" statues, right where they'd agreed. He was very large, and his round face and apple cheeks made him look like a well-dressed pig. When he noticed Newbury, Taylor's version of a smile turned his eyes into slits, as though he'd just spotted something tasty to eat.

Back when Newbury picked up the O'Connell case, Bill Treadwell had amazed him by calling him into his office, closing the door, and handing him Taylor's card—saying he'd heard that Taylor "might be of some help" in the case. When their short conversation ended, Treadwell put his hand on Newbury's shoulder and, in his godlike way, made it clear that this was a private chat, never to be mentioned again. Treadwell had always been a kindly mentor, but it was clear that if word ever got out, the consequences for Newbury would not be good.

The maddening thing was that, until recently, Newbury's life had been on the upswing. He had more money in the bank now than he'd ever dreamed. He'd been down to his girlfriend's family compound in Chatham twice, first for dinner and then for a sunset sail and an overnight. The Coolidges had apparently been summering on the Cape since the 1960s. Cynthia Coolidge was beautiful, and Newbury was fairly sure he was falling in love. They'd had some serious talks.

Then, Margaret Helms's husband went downhill, *O'Connell* got transferred to Judge Norcross, and Sam Newbury learned what it felt like to be really scared. After the scene in O'Connell's office with the glass paperweight, he'd texted Taylor immediately, and then several more times, trying to set up a meeting. He'd gotten no response. Finally, he'd been forced to leave a voice-mail message on Taylor's phone, hinting that he was about to pay a visit to his friends in the U.S. Attorney's Office and share what they'd been up to. That got action.

Newbury took a seat on the bench as far away from Taylor as he could get, while still within range of a muttered conversation. He hoped that anyone looking on from a distance would assume they didn't even know each other. Their first few sentences made it clear that the news was not good.

"Oh God, Sammy. The money's long gone." Taylor shook his head. "I couldn't get it back even if I wanted to." He twitched his shoulders. "And, frankly, I don't want to."

"Bullshit."

"It's not bullshit. You think I don't have people on my end who need to be paid?" Taylor glared at Newbury. "My commission's only a sliver. Besides, we made a bet. I won. Your case was drawn to Helms."

Newbury set his hands on the edge of the bench and boosted himself up, straightening his back. "Listen to me, Jack. We gave you two and a half million bucks to get the O'Connell trial to Helms and keep it there. That was the deal. My firm had to go through seven levels of hell to find an untraceable way to get the cash to you. We practically had to . . ."

Taylor didn't seem to be listening. "What's the problem with Norcross? I heard he's—"

"Norcross is a disaster. He could not be worse."

Taylor was unconvinced. "Oh, come on."

"We need to straighten this out, Jack. If we don't, I guarantee you things will start happening you won't like." He leaned toward Taylor and put as much low menace into his voice as he could muster. "Do you hear me?"

"O'Connell's bluffing."

"You weren't there."

"Got to be bluffing."

"I've got a week, Jack."

Newbury's options were limited, and it was maddeningly clear that Taylor knew this. Handing over the entire payment as soon as the case was drawn to Helms was, in retrospect, monumentally stupid. Newbury recognized his mistake now, right in the pit of his stomach. As far as the "things" that would supposedly start happening if Taylor didn't fix the problem, Newbury had only the dimmest idea of what they might be. Despite his threat, he certainly had no intention of going to the U.S. Attorney, which would not only end his legal career but probably land him in prison. Worse, it would bring down the rage of Treadwell and certain even scarier higher-ups at his firm. The thought of having to sit down with those alligators and spill what had happened literally made him sick.

Taylor was refusing to stay on topic. "So really, Sam, I don't get it. What's your problem with Norcross? My sources tell me he's not that bad. Is he, like, Mr. Rogers on the outside and Godzilla on the inside?"

"No, inside he's Mr. Rogers too. In fact, . . ." Newbury glanced at his watch. "In fact, I'm meeting him for a drink in about three hours."

"You're meeting Norcross for a drink?" Taylor's expression was half disbelieving, half impressed.

"Yes. Me and my girlfriend. I'm sure it will be a very pleasant experience. That's how he always is."

"Why the hell would he meet you for a drink?"

"Long story. I sort of rescued his wife at the Harvard thing and gave her a ride home. He probably thinks he owes me."

"So he's a nice guy. What's the problem?"

"The problem is that in the courtroom Norcross nices you to death. A couple years back, one of my partners had a tax evasion case in front of him, and her guy got convicted. At the sentencing, Norcross gave the client eight years—the very top of the guideline range—never raising his voice or saying a mean word. Then, after they took the poor schmuck off, the judge went out of his way, in open court, to say what a terrific job the partner did, even though she lost. That's his reputation. Once he starts being extra nice to you, you know you're screwed."

"Did the client deserve it? Just curious."

"Who cares?" Newbury looked down at his shoes, trying to remember. "Probably. Nobody liked him." This was turning from a confrontation into a conversation, and Newbury could feel himself losing leverage.

"But Norcross will give you a fair trial, right?

"We don't want a fucking fair trial. We didn't pay for a fair trial."

"Come on, Sam."

"The only people who want fair trials are the people who aren't on trial. Nobody who has anything important at stake wants a fair trial. They want to win." Newbury waved his hand in the vague direction of Louisburg Square. "O'Connell needs to win. This is not a civics class. It's life or death for him."

Taylor sighed. "Look, Sam, I want to make you happy. Tell the truth, I've got bigger problems than you right now. All sorts of alarm bells going off."

"Yeah, well, guess what? I don't care." Newbury worked hard to make his voice sound as threatening as he could. "Norcross has to go."

Taylor snorted. "So what are you saying? You want me to have him whacked?" He leaned back against the bench and laid his arm across the top. "Is that what we're talking about?"

"Violence is always the last resort."

Taylor looked scornful and blew out a half laugh. "Because if you want to go that route, I know just the guys."

"At the moment, we're not talking about that, Jack."

"Professionals." He sniffed. "Problem is, they're insane. Start up with them, and you're riding the frigging tiger."

"Just get Norcross off the case, Jack, or give me my goddamn money back." Newbury hesitated. "Please." He could feel himself getting desperate, and this scared him more than anything.

Taylor made a softening gesture with his hand. "Take it easy, Sam. I'm already working on this, actually. I'm talking to my person."

A couple of undergraduates walked by within earshot, laughing at the duckling statues, and the two men lapsed into silence.

"I don't want to know who this person of yours is, Jack, and I don't want him to know my name."

"He's very solid, and he doesn't know you from Abraham Lincoln."

Taylor still sounded way too blasé, and Newbury impulsively played his ace.

"We need to do this, and we need to do it soon." He tried putting his hand on Taylor's forearm, which was so bizarre it made Taylor jerk away and give Newbury a look, partly startled, partly offended. Newbury went on, "I've protected you up to now, right? O'Connell has no idea who you are. But I'm not facing the firing squad alone here. I could give him your name, and you could find out for yourself if he's bluffing." Newbury glanced around, making sure no one was nearby. He was almost whispering. "I could do that, you know."

Taylor had been shifting around, getting increasingly uncomfortable with his oversize bulk on the hard bench. He reached slowly down now and pulled his shin up, crossing his legs, not hurrying. "You don't want to do that, Sam." He looked at Newbury levelly, not raising his voice. "You really don't."

"Well, then tell this person of yours to get *O'Connell* back to Helms."

Taylor shook his head. "No can do. But we'll push Norcross out of the way, all right? And we'll get you Ramos, who's basically Helms with a jock strap."

"How will you—"

"Leave that to me."

"Okay, but—"

"And I'll kick back two fifty. It's the most I can get my hands on."

"A million."

"Five hundred. And I promise you, if Norcross goes—"

Newbury raised his voice. "When he goes."

"Right, when he goes. The case will stay with Ramos. You can put two fifty in your own pocket and kick back the other two fifty to O'Connell as his discount. Your partners never need to know."

"I don't play that way, Jack. I never have."

"You do now, Sammy."

22

David had resisted dragging Claire along for his obligatory drink with Sam Newbury, but there was no way she was letting him go without her. The reservation was at a trendy bistro with the irresistible name of Il Gallo Pazzo—The Crazy Rooster. She'd been dying to check it out. Plus, David had told her, with a weary look, that Newbury planned to bring his girlfriend along, a big-firm lawyer who specialized in trusts and estates. Claire pointed out that it would be awkward for him to be a third wheel with these two highfliers, and that she could use the opportunity to thank Newbury properly for his kindness.

As they were getting ready to leave, David had to help her on with her sweater. She twisted around to look at him. "If we order appetizers, remind me to get something I can manage with one hand, okay?"

She had abandoned the Velcro brace too early and overused her sprained wrist. It had started hurting again, and she was back struggling with clothes. David was being a little impatient with her about it.

"I imagine you'll remember on your own." He helped pull her sleeve up, then bent over. "Let me button you up here."

"I don't want you having to cut up my meat."

Il Gallo Pazzo was only a few blocks from the condo. Claire felt a wave of sweetness when David took her uninjured hand as they walked along the leafy sidewalks of the Back Bay. She loved being out again, enjoying how comfortably their hands fit together. The early evening traffic was light. The air was warm. A flowering tree somewhere was flavoring the summer breeze with an unidentifiable sweetness.

Boston, and to some extent the country generally, was still absorbing the Harvard terrorist attack. No further incidents had occurred so far, and at least one of the perpetrators—perhaps the only perpetrator—was in custody. The urban heartbeat was beginning to return to normal, but a pall of wariness hung on, as noticeable as the scent of the blossoming trees. Ugly graffiti was still being scrubbed off local mosques, and the Boston police were continuing to make heavy use of overtime. A squad car at the corner of Dartmouth and Boylston sat parked sideways, its blue lights flashing.

David released Claire's hand as they got closer to the restaurant. "I should probably mention a couple things."

She gave a short laugh. "Uh-oh."

"Newbury is okay, but he may try to worm some court scuttlebutt out of me. Don't be surprised if you see me clamming up."

"Scuttlebutt?"

"Things like which judge has the longest list of stale motions, who's butting heads with who and over what, who's angling for a court of appeals appointment. Things like that. I'll need to be a little careful about what I say."

"I see, and you're worried I'll say something that will create a problem." By this time, she had absorbed many of the court's secrets. She squeezed his hand. "Again."

"Yep." David smiled down at her.

"And you're hoping I'll clam up a little too."

"Yep."

The restaurant was a handsome brick building with several tables arranged in a courtyard in front and a flight of granite stairs leading up inside. It had a big sign next to the door with a brightly colored painting of a bug-eyed rooster and the words *Cucina Toscana* splashed underneath. Sam Newbury was framed in the bow window above them, sitting with a very well-dressed, very blond woman. Newbury noticed them right away and waved.

Claire followed David into the bustling interior. The salon in front, where Newbury waited, featured a long, brightly lit bar and small informal tables with upholstered chairs. Toward the back, a generous doorway opened onto a formal dining area, where white tablecloths and soft lighting offered a more sedate atmosphere.

Newbury and the young woman stood up as Claire and David approached. A hasty survey told Claire that the aggregate cost of the girlfriend's champagne-colored cocktail dress, gold choker, shoes, leather handbag, nails, and haircut probably exceeded the value of Claire's entire wardrobe. The elegant garnet bracelet on her wrist, just by itself, must have tripled the price tag of the total ensemble.

Newbury flashed a gleaming smile at them. "Hello! Thanks for doing this, David." He held out his hand. "Or should I call you 'Judge'?"

"'David' will be fine." The two men shook. "We can save 'Your Honor' for when you're indicted."

This was an embarrassing joke of David's, regularly rolled out in these situations. Newbury produced the mandatory chuckle. "I'll keep that in mind." He picked up his martini glass, realized it was empty, and set it back down.

Claire held out her hand to the young woman. "Hi, I'm Claire Lindemann."

Newbury's girlfriend bobbed her knees, looking shy, and took Claire's hand. "I'm Cynthia." She hesitated. "Cynthia Coolidge. Very nice to meet you." Claire decided immediately that she was going to like Cynthia despite her pricy getup. Her eyebrows, darker than her hair, were exquisitely shaped and symmetrical, and they somehow gave her a wistful look. Claire had the impression that this young woman had been through a rocky time not too long ago. The death of a sibling? Some painful breakup?

Newbury looked down at her affectionately. "Cindy's great-grandfather was the mayor of Northampton, out your way, David."

Cynthia sighed. "Sam . . ."

"Wow. Silent Cal." David nodded. "We've visited his former house, on Massasoit Street."

"Calvin Coolidge?" Claire was tickled. "Did you ever meet him?"

Cynthia's mouth tightened a little, and Claire instantly regretted her stupid question. This topic must come up a lot for her.

"No, he died quite a few years before I was born. My grandfather John used to tell us stories about him, though." She gave a half-hearted smile. "I guess he wasn't so silent around the dinner table."

When they sat down, Claire slipped into the seat next to Cynthia, determined to change the subject and rehabilitate herself. "I hear you specialize in trusts and estates. David tells me that very few women do this kind of work."

Newbury put his hand on Cynthia's shoulder. "She'd never reveal it, but in March she was named Boston's top estates lawyer. Number one."

The compliment, and perhaps Newbury's touch, brought the light into Cynthia's eyes. "It's low-profile work, but I like getting to know the families."

"Including Tom Brady's family." Newbury continued to gaze at his girlfriend with admiration. "Pre-Tampa, of course."

It was time for Claire to get her thank-yous out of the way. "Before we go any further, Sam, I want to tell you again how grateful I am for the way you helped me Friday. I was pretty shattered."

David leaned in. "We're both *very* grateful, Sam."

Memories of the blood and chaos in front of the library began to play in Claire's mind again. "I don't think I've ever been so . . ."

At this moment, a nearby voice piped out, "Judge Norcross! Oh my God!"

David turned. "Angie Phipps! Well, hello."

A young woman with reddish-blond hair and an enormous smile was making her way past their table, holding hands with a handsome dark-haired man.

Phipps looked down at David. "You know Carl, right?"

"Mr. Alberti and I are well acquainted." David stood, using his judge voice. "You've handled—what?—five or six gun cases out in Springfield, I think?" They shook hands.

"Something like that, Your Honor."

Claire saw how Alberti's face had closed down and become opaquely professional as soon as he saw her husband. She let her eyes linger on him. With his quiet eyes and pale skin, he really was delicious.

David gestured at the couple. "Everyone, this is my excellent courtroom deputy, Angela Phipps, and this is Carl Alberti from the ATF." Everyone beamed and nodded. Claire noted that Phipps's dress, while it wasn't inappropriate, had a definite come-and-get-me quality. Good for her.

"We have reservations in there." Phipps nodded into the interior. Her obvious state of romantic intoxication reminded Claire of her early phase with David. Even today, she still felt the same about him amazingly often, though perhaps not with quite the same raging fizz.

A waiter strolled up to the table, pad and pencil in hand.

David spoke to Alberti, lowering his voice. "You two go ahead. We don't want to spoil your fun."

Angie said, "Great to see you, Judge."

Alberti nodded, and they went on their way. The waiter took their drinks order and slipped off, and Claire picked up again. "Anyway, as I was saying, Sam, you were a real lifesaver. I can't thank you enough."

Newbury was staring into the air, a little hollow-eyed, as though he was recalling the scene too. "You did very well. Really. When I got home that afternoon, I just wanted to curl into a ball."

Cynthia looked at Newbury admiringly. "Sam's been on the phone nonstop fielding questions from classmates. Trying to help out and keep people together."

"We finally got some good news this morning," Newbury said. "Looks like they're going to be able to save George Thomas's leg. He'll need a cane, but he'll walk."

David dropped his voice, the way he did when he wanted to be serious. "You're doing good work, Sam. I'm proud of you."

He continued on, after this, to emphasize his gratitude to Newbury for Claire's ride home. There was no risk that the message wasn't getting across. From there, the conversation wandered off to what was happening at David's old law firm, where Newbury was now a partner, lingering on names Claire only dimly recognized. She let her eyes wander around the room. Il Gallo Pazzo gradually grew noisier as the place filled up. When there was a break in the flow, Claire jumped in to widen the conversation.

"So, I'm curious, with different firms and different specialties, how did you two meet?" She looked at Newbury and then Cynthia.

David shifted a little, giving a nervous cough. "Well, we don't want to stick our noses in." He was so stuffy sometimes. Fortunately, at this point, the waiter turned up with their drinks, and after they sorted out who had what, Claire pushed ahead. "So?"

Cynthia glanced self-consciously at Newbury. "Actually, we bonded over a jigsaw puzzle."

"I love them," Newbury said.

Cynthia gave a delicate snort. "You do not."

"I did that day."

"Sam was visiting at the Cape with some friends, and I was doing this jigsaw puzzle on the sun porch."

"Huge," Newbury interjected. "And very hard. Mostly blue and white."

"No one wanted to help, which was okay—it's kind of a weird thing with me—but then Sam came over." Cynthia fingered her necklace, musing. "And we just, you know, sat there for maybe an hour and a half while everyone else was out on the boat." She looked at Newbury. "Filling in the pieces. Not saying much."

"There's a wetland on the edge of the woods below the house." Sam took a sip of his freshened martini. "And two pileated wood-peckers were down there. I'd never seen even one before."

"It was amazing." Cynthia nodded her head. "They usually stay way back in the trees."

"I just sat there, looking for edge pieces, watching those birds, and looking at Cindy." Newbury hesitated and looked awkward. "I wish it could have gone on forever."

"How long ago was this?" Claire asked.

Newbury smiled. "Four-month anniversary tomorrow."

Cynthia fished the cherry out of her drink and nibbled as she spoke. "It's my birthday, and he's taking me to dinner."

The conversation inched along for another twenty minutes with reasonably good cheer, everyone making an effort. Before long, to Claire's relief, the mood around the table began sliding toward thanks and goodbye. She and David had done what they'd set out to do. She was just locating her purse, when a shadow fell over the table, and a large, veiny hand appeared on David's shoulder. A deep bass voice said, "Hello, Your Honor," and Claire found herself looking up into one of the most striking faces she'd ever seen.

It had deep furrows across the forehead, sharply etched folds extending down from the edges of the nostrils, and blue eyes set way back behind bushy white eyebrows. The man's head was large, with thick gray and silver hair combed straight back in waves. Claire's first impression was that he looked like Zeus.

David half rose. "Bill. How nice to see you!"

"Good to see you, too, Judge."

"Claire, this is Bill Treadwell, from my old law firm." The two men shook hands. "He took me in hand when I was just a new associate, barely a pup."

Treadwell's face contracted into a web of delighted wrinkles, and his eyes twinkled. "Professor Lindemann, finally! I've been wanting to meet you." He frowned down at David good-humoredly. "My invitation to your wedding must have gotten lost in the mail."

David sounded abashed. "Well, Bill, we were trying to keep it—"

"I read the professor's piece in *The Atlantic* on *The Second Shepherds' Play*. Fascinating!" Treadwell looked up at the ceiling. "Let me see. What was the title? 'The Exuberance of Medieval Religious Sensibility'—something like that?"

"Good for you!" Claire was sincerely pleased. "'The Wakefield Master and the Exuberance of Fifteen-Century Religious Sensibility.'" Even some of her English Department colleagues hadn't gotten around to it yet.

Treadwell reached out a hand to Newbury. "Hello, Sam. How are you doing? Getting more of our clients out of the slammer, I hope."

Newbury shook hands. "More every day. Bless their felonious hearts." He glanced at Treadwell's cuff. "See you've got your cuff links on."

Treadwell was wearing bright silver cuff links with some ceramic design.

"Always. Sandra got me these for Christmas, and it hurts her feelings when I don't wear them."

David spoke to Claire, smiling. "Bill is famous for his cuff links."

"They're old-fashioned but kind of fun. May I join you for a minute?" Treadwell looked around. "We could pull one of those chairs over."

"Of course." David's voice had a youthful edge. Treadwell seemed to be bringing out a remnant of the eager young protégé in her husband. David shoved a chair up to the table, and Treadwell sat down.

"I'm meeting my wife and a couple friends for dinner inside, but they won't mind waiting five minutes." Treadwell leaned toward David and dropped his voice confidentially. "Actually, Judge, I wanted to get your advice about something." He smiled and held up a hand. "Not case-related, I promise." He nodded over at Newbury. "Sam and I were discussing it just the other day."

Newbury's face made it clear that he had no idea what Treadwell was talking about but was happy to play along.

Treadwell folded his hands in front of him. "As you know, I'm chairing Harvard's Board of Overseers at the moment."

David tipped toward Claire. "Sort of equivalent to a board of directors."

Claire had no interest in Harvard's crimson-tinted hierarchy. It occurred to her that, before the conversation got too dreary, she might need to escape to the ladies' room.

Treadwell picked up on her vibe right away. "Don't worry, my dear." He touched her shoulder quickly. "I won't be going on for long here, I promise." He returned to David. "As you must know, the Widener incident has triggered some disturbing outbursts targeting Muslims, and immigrants generally. I've convinced the firm to make a sizable contribution to the law school's Immigration and Refugee Clinic." He gave David a full blast of eye contact. "It would be a big morale booster if we could entice someone of your stature to sit down with the students some afternoon."

"Ah. I'd love to help, Bill."

"Just a general discussion. How these cases evolve from a judge's point of view. Examples of effective advocacy. Nothing about any particular case."

"Ordinarily, I enjoy talking to students, and this would be right up my alley." Norcross pulled on his nose and sniffed. "But you're hitting me at a tough moment. I've got this big trial coming up."

"Ah, of course. That's right. My old friend Dominic O'Connell." Treadwell nodded over at Newbury. "That was your case, wasn't it, Sam?"

"Yes." Newbury looked uncomfortable. "I took care of the preliminaries before Judge Helms. Sandy Tarbell has it now."

"Right." David's voice was like a key turning in a lock. No more about that.

Treadwell continued, unfazed. "Anyway, listen, Sandra and I are grabbing a bite in there with a couple potential donors." He tipped his enormous head toward the dining room. "We'd love it if you and Professor Lindemann could join us for coffee when Sam and Cindy are done with you." He smiled. "I'd like to twist your arm a little more. There's so much energy right now. The students are really cranked up."

Nothing too obvious had changed about David—nothing in his face or posture—but it was obvious to Claire that Treadwell was backing him into a corner and that David didn't like it.

"Oh, what a shame!" She spoke just a little louder than necessary and leaned toward David. "My leg of lamb, remember? It will be inedible if we aren't back in half an hour."

Treadwell turned his head toward her with something sharp lurking behind his eyebrows. Three or four seconds passed before he spoke. "Pity. Some other occasion then." He stood up. "I'd better go or I'll be in trouble with Sandra." He smiled at Claire and wagged a finger at her. "But let's talk about that article next time. I have lots of questions." He nodded at David. "I'll be giving you a call."

As he moved off toward the dining room, people seemed, just naturally, to give way and let him pass.

Not long after this, Claire and David were on their way. Outside, the sunlight was softer and the air cooler. Well down the street, David checked over his shoulder, then reached around and squeezed Claire close to him. He kissed her on the top of the head.

"Darlin', you are a ministering angel."

"I could see you were having a hard time saying no to Bill Treadwell. Anyone would. He's like a—"

"Freight train. Ordinarily, I'd enjoy meeting with the students, but not right now." David's face looked tired. "Not at the moment."

Arriving back, they discovered a manila envelope with their names neatly typed, slipped under the door of the condo. After they settled up with Brandy and saw her off, David lowered himself onto the sofa, holding the envelope in his hand. He looked doubtful.

"So," Claire said. "Let's open it." The evening had taken a lot out of her. She was surprised at how tired she was.

"I'm trying to decide whether to take this thing to work tomorrow and have the CSOs give it a scan."

"Oh pooh. It's probably something silly from Monica."

"I'm thinking white powder."

"Your call." Claire shrugged. "But I have to admit I'm curious."

David reluctantly opened the envelope, peeling back the seal carefully. Inside were three glossy eight-by-ten photographs. The top one showed Brandy Kim sitting on the bench with her hand on Charlie's stroller, reading. The next showed David and Charlie, mouths open, looking up—rather stupidly—at the statue of William Lloyd Garrison. In the final photograph, Claire was pushing Charlie, smiling down at him and holding the muffin bag. Tucked in the bottom of the envelope was a file card with a message, all in caps: IT WOULD BE SO EASY! STEP AWAY FROM O'CONNELL, OR YOU WILL BE SORRY.

23

Norcross and Claire went together to the meeting the next morning with Chief Judge Broadwater and Mike Patterson. As they sat around Broadwater's desk, Patterson examined the photographs, holding them up one at a time with a pair of tweezers.

"How much did you touch these?"

Norcross sighed. "Probably too much."

Patterson looked at Claire. "I doubt we'll find anything, but would you mind giving us a set of prints for comparison? We already have the judge's."

"Of course." Claire was using her classroom voice, not sharp but quick and in control. "Anytime."

Broadwater gave her a sympathetic look. "How are you managing, Claire? You've been through a lot this week."

The chief judge looked tired. The death of Armstrong had clearly hit him very hard. His woolly eyebrows, the tufts over his ears, and the heavy bags under his eyes were making Broadwater look even more like an elderly, grieving bird. The resemblance was somehow accentuated by his half glasses. He peered over them at

Claire, blinking at her as though he were uncomfortable in the daylight.

"Fine. I'm fine. I just don't like it that someone is trying to push David around." She paused. "And using Charlie to do it."

Claire's reaction to the envelope had surprised Norcross—though, when he thought about it, he realized it shouldn't have. His assumption had been that she'd want him to recuse himself from *O'Connell* immediately, to protect her and the baby, and he'd been preparing for a wrestling match.

"They're trying to push all of you around." Patterson tipped his head at Norcross. "In fact, they may think it's easier to push you than the judge."

Claire nodded. "I understand that, but they're wrong."

Norcross had observed, over the years, how Claire used her outfits to manage crises. Today, she was in what she called her Eileen-Fisher-goes-to-war battle gear: black linen cardigan, white silk shell, and midcalf charcoal skirt—clothes she usually reserved for trustees' meetings. She gave Broadwater a hard look. "When you guys dumped this case on David, it really pissed me off. I thought it was incredibly inconsiderate to drag him east, with our new baby and all. But this is different. Someone's trying to scare us." She flicked something off her knee. "In a way, it's working too. All this frightens the hell out of me, I won't kid you. But I'm not going to dive into a tailspin here. Just tell us what we should be on the lookout for."

"Probably nothing," Patterson said. "Whoever did this probably doesn't plan to do anything. They probably just want to see if they can spook you." He paused and repeated, "Probably."

"Well, they've succeeded." Claire shook her head and looked into the distance. "To know there's been someone out there, shadowing Charlie, makes me murderous. Part of me just wants you to find whoever it is and kill him." She looked at Patterson. "In fact, part of me wants to kill him myself."

Broadwater nodded. "Nobody blames you for that."

"Well, I'm a little shocked at the person this is making me. I'm not used to having thoughts like these."

Norcross wanted to take Claire's hand but held back, knowing she wouldn't like it. He turned to Patterson. "It helps a lot to have you with us on this, Mike. Nine chances out of ten, this is probably nothing—just some idiot stunt. Still . . ."

Broadwater was looking out his window. "I've always hated the word 'probably.'" His chambers, like Norcross's borrowed suite, had a view out over the harbor. After a couple of seconds, he continued. "You'll have to disclose all this to counsel, I suppose, Dave?"

Norcross nodded. "Yep. They're entitled to know."

"Tarbell, of course, will be all over you to pull out. I can hear him already: you've been threatened, you can't preside properly, you'll be looking over your shoulder, you'll blame his client, and so on, ad infinitum."

For some reason, perhaps because of Claire's strong reaction, Norcross felt calm. They'd both been through some tough times. The way to handle this situation, at least in court, was clear to him.

"I'll disclose the contact to the lawyers, on the record but privately in chambers, with a stenographer taking everything down. Let them look at the pictures and the note. I'll seal the transcript. If either of them wants to make an oral or written motion to recuse or whatever, I'll keep those filings under seal too. Nobody wants this on the internet. It will complicate jury selection. If they want me to step away from the trial, I'll hear their arguments, and I'll decide what I'm doing."

Patterson asked, "What do you think your decision will be?"

"Speaking officially? I don't know. I'll have to keep an open mind and wait to hear what Tarbell and Papadakis have to say." Norcross pulled on his nose and sniffed. "Speaking unofficially, I can tell you that if one of them asks me to pull out, they're going to have an uphill climb. What if the next judge gets some pictures? Where does it stop?"

Patterson leaned back in his chair. "Tarbell could be the one behind this, trying to frighten you off the case. Postpone the trial. Get a new judge."

Broadwater added, "Or manufacture an issue for appeal if you stay on."

"All very true," Norcross said. "Tarbell's a loose cannon, and he'd only need to throw out a hint to O'Connell to set him or one of his buddies in motion. O'Connell could be doing this on his own, or it could be a friend, thinking he's helping. Who knows?"

"So. What are you going to do now?" Broadwater looked worried. He was a good chief judge and a very good friend.

"We're driving to Amherst this afternoon, and I'll be back in my own courtroom in Springfield tomorrow. I'll take the day Friday to clean up some things there. We'll be home over the weekend, and I'll be back in Boston Monday to meet with counsel, inform them about the photographs, and hear what they have to say. I'm giving a talk that evening at the Harvard Divinity School. Tuesday, if I'm still on the case, we'll start picking the jury. I figure that may take a day or two, so I doubt we'll start taking evidence before Wednesday or Thursday. It will be tight, but I'll manage. I promised Peggy I'd do my best to get started more or less on time."

Claire smoothed her skirt, keeping her voice casual. "I don't plan to come back to Boston with David. My research is done, and I need to get to work on my syllabi and course outlines for the fall semester."

Broadwater gave a skeptical "Hmm."

Norcross looked at Claire. "We're still negotiating that."

"I see." Patterson looked from one to the other. "I spoke to the marshal. He'll be sending a couple deputies from their judicial security division to check out your alarm system." He leaned toward them, putting his elbows on his knees. "I don't like to bring this up, Judge, but do you happen to have a firearm in your house?"

Norcross started to shake his head, but Claire interrupted, holding up a finger.

"There's the shotgun you got from your dad, remember? I think it's in a trunk in the basement."

"Do you recall what type?"

Norcross responded, "Twelve-gauge. Browning, I think."

Patterson nodded slowly. "I'd bring it up."

David and Claire's trip back to Amherst was a disaster. The traffic going west on the Mass Pike was heavy, and the stop-and-go driving enraged Charlie. As they jerked along, he waved his fists, spat out his pacifier, and howled. By Framingham, after nearly an hour of this, they were so frazzled that David had to pull over onto the shoulder so Claire could climb into the back and give Charlie a bottle. This tactic helped, but only intermittently. It wasn't until they'd passed the I-84 exit, when the turnpike shrank down from three lanes to two and the traffic thinned, that their prayers to the Nap Gods were answered. The boy dropped off to sleep, and Claire and David could breathe again.

In his many commutes to and from Boston, David had come to love this shift in the feel of the Pike, as though it had turned into a different road: up a long hill, with three-quarters of the cars veering off south for Connecticut or New York, then down the far slope, with the sky softening toward sunset—a magical crossing into a less congested, saner, and prettier world. The shadowy conifers came down to the narrower road, the high-summer birches shimmered in their bright greens, and the blue-gray hills rolled soothingly into the distance.

He heard Claire, in the back seat, sigh and mutter, "Thank God. Home ground."

"Yes."

For a long time, neither of them spoke, relishing the silence and giving Charlie time to take a deep dive. When they swung off the Pike at Palmer, David, keeping his voice low, asked, "As an Oklahoma girl, did you ever handle a shotgun?"

Claire leaned forward. "Once, when I was, like, nine, I made them let me shoot one." She gave a short laugh. "I hurt my shoulder and sat down hard. My aunt Gracie nearly split a gut."

"Dad and I would go out for pheasant in the fall sometimes, when I was in high school. I liked walking the fields. It took a while, but eventually I got to be a reasonable shot." They pulled up to a stoplight, and David quickly looked over his shoulder to check on Charlie. He was still conked out. "Dad always checked me out on the gun first: how to load and unload it, how to carry it when I was walking or climbing over a fence, how to aim—typical Midwestern father-son things. I liked that a lot."

"I got the same lecture when Hank took me to Baxter Springs to plink cans with his .22. It made me feel like I was growing up."

David was fond of Hank, Claire's older brother, who still lived outside Tulsa.

Charlie barely squirmed when they pulled into the garage and lifted him out of his car seat. They decided to let him keep sleeping, even knowing that when he woke up, he'd be ready to socialize for hours. For now, his meltdown had exhausted them all. David and Claire were relieved to find a note on the kitchen counter from Lindsay, informing them that she'd taken Marlene home for the night and would be back in the morning. They needed a break from everything.

While Claire went upstairs to get Charlie settled, David went down to the basement and, after a little fumbling around, located the shotgun and a box of shells. As he returned to the living room, he got a text.

He called out to Claire as she came down the stairs. "Mike Patterson says that when the marshals come tomorrow, they're going to install motion detectors on our outdoor lights."

Claire sat down on the sofa next to David. "Great. Every time a squirrel crosses the driveway, the house will light up like a Christmas tree. Very reassuring."

"I know, but I think it's a good idea." David put the shells on the coffee table and zipped the gun out of its heavy canvas carrier. "Anyway, here she is. Let me take the trigger lock off."

"Okay." Claire leaned back into the sofa wearily. "Maybe five minutes? I love you, dear, but I'm fading."

The shotgun was, as David remembered it, an impressive object, with a smooth, beautifully contoured wooden stock, a barrel decorated with engraved filigree, and a cameo of a man's head etched onto the side of the shell chamber over the words *Browning Trademark*.

"If you stay here by yourself, I'm going to leave the gun for you, already loaded. That's something I was taught you should never, ever do, so we'll have to go over that."

"We can talk, but I really don't like having a loaded gun in the house."

"You could always just fire it out the window if you hear something. It makes a tremendous bang." David lifted the gun and set the butt on his knee. "I need to show you this one thing, okay? See this little lever inside the trigger guard?" He pointed. "That's the safety. You slide it back like this, and it's on. The gun's not supposed to shoot, but you never rely on it."

"Right. Hank drilled that into me. Never count on the safety."

"Exactly, but you always use it. Now, it's on." He eased the safety forward. "Now, it's off." He slid it back and then forward again. "On. Off."

"I'll never in a million years remember which is which."

"Yes, you will, because there's an easy mnemonic." He pointed. "See this red dot? It's visible when the safety is off. When you pull it back, like this, the safety is on, and the red dot disappears. There's a wise old adage my dad liked to quote, to help remember when the safety's off and the gun is ready to fire."

"Uh-huh. And that is?"

"Red, you're dead."

"Very pithy." Claire grunted as she pushed herself onto her feet. "Here's another bit of ancient wisdom: Chinese takeout. Your turn to go get it." She walked toward the stairs. "I'm climbing into the tub. See you in an hour."

24

That same evening, Newbury and Cynthia were in a private dining room at the Sheraton Commander in Cambridge, celebrating Cynthia's birthday. They were in the middle of a stupid-joke contest with two other couples, and it was Newbury's turn.

"Okay. Okay." He waved his hands, and everyone around the table fell silent, until Ashley, Cynthia's best friend, hiccuped loudly. Newbury raised his eyebrows. "You done?"

"For now." She poured herself some more wine. "Maybe."

"Okay. So, my cousin Elmer goes into a drugstore. He's very nervous, right? Because he's there to buy condoms for the first time."

Ashley rolled her eyes and started to say something. Cynthia put a hand on her arm and gave her a look.

"He's fifteen, he's a Boy Scout, and he wants to be prepared, right? And the druggist is a kindly sort, and he says . . ." Newbury dropped his voice. "'Well, young man, you're a little young, but I'm glad you're being responsible.' So, the druggist puts the condoms in a bag and says 'Okay, that'll be $7.93 with the tax.' And Elmer sort of gets this look on his face, like . . ." Newbury made a horrible face, mouth open, eyes wide. "And he says, 'Tacks! I thought they stayed on by themselves!'"

The immediate outburst was extremely satisfying. Ashley's husband, Rob, beat on the table with the palm of his hand, and, best of all, Cynthia tipped her head back with outright, sustained laughter, putting her hand on Newbury's shoulder and looking at him with her wonderful smile. "That was really, really dumb, Sam."

"Well told too," Ashley chimed in. "Gotta admit."

At this moment, Newbury's victory was crowned by the entry of a waiter bearing the gourmet birthday cake he'd special-ordered, blazing with a full thirty-four candles. A second waiter followed with a tray of champagne glasses and a bottle of Dom Perignon. After a particularly robust rendition of the traditional birthday song, Cynthia asked for Sam's help blowing out the candles. They managed all of them with one happy, simultaneous breath.

As the smoke cleared, Cynthia held up her glass. "Now, I want to give a toast to Sam, partly for organizing this great dinner, but mostly for all the work he's done the past few days giving families support after the bombing, finding places for people to stay, and all that." She patted his hand. "You're a good man, Sam Newbury. Here's to you."

For once in his life, Newbury could think of nothing to say. "I, um, well, that's . . ."

Fortunately, Rob rescued him. "Actually, he's a total jerk, Cindy. He just hides it really well."

Twenty minutes later, the other couple peeled off to rescue their babysitter. It was Thursday, a weeknight, and people had started glancing at their watches. Rob and Ashley took a few minutes with their coffee, while Newbury settled up the bill. As the four of them were going out the door, the maître d' hurried over to give Cynthia a white cardboard box containing the last third of her cake. He lifted the lid, smiling, to show them that he'd slipped in two nip bottles of Rémy Martin. Everyone laughed. Newbury had given him and the waitstaff a massive tip.

It was a warm summer night, and the foursome made its way down Garden Street toward Harvard Square. Newbury and Rob followed the women, not far behind but comfortably out of earshot. On the far side of the street, the Cambridge Common was a maze of shadows.

Rob spoke confidentially. "You could do a lot worse than Cindy Coolidge, brother."

"I know. She's amazing."

"Pretty. Successful. Great family. Can't imagine what she sees in an ugly sodomite like you."

"Makes absolutely no sense."

"How the fuck did you get so lucky?" Rob broke off as they swerved to make room for a clump of tourists coming up from the Square. "Don't get me wrong. I'm crazy about Ashley, but . . ."

The tourists were speaking Italian and looked lost. Everyone smiled as they worked their way around each other. A tall man with slick dark hair pointed out the Civil War Memorial, pooled in spotlights.

"Turns out Cindy was in some long relationship with an older man. We're just getting to where we can talk about that."

Rob rolled his eyes. "Oh God, and the guy was married, right?"

"I don't think so. But her parents sure didn't think much of him. First time she introduced me, they were grinning so hard I almost got a sunburn."

Rob laughed. "She's on the quiet side. That must be a relief after Barbara."

"I love it." Newbury's first wife had turned out to be a very unhappy, and sometimes very loud—publicly loud—alcoholic. "I absolutely love it. Cindy's really sweet, but she's her own person."

Rob stubbed his toe on a dip in the bumpy sidewalk and grabbed Newbury's arm to steady himself. "Could you stand hooking up with a woman who's got so much more money than you do?" This would have been a pushy question, except for their long friendship. They'd both had a lot to drink.

It was Newbury's turn to laugh. "I could adjust."

"Ya think?"

The women had stopped to wait for them up at the corner of Massachusetts Avenue, ready to go their separate ways. Newbury and Cynthia were parked in a garage three blocks down toward

Brattle Street. Rob and Ashley were grabbing the subway to head back to their condo in Somerville.

As the group rejoined, Newbury had a sudden thought and began slapping his pockets. "Dammit."

"What's the problem?" Cynthia did not sound cross, but Newbury could see she was tired. He was doing these stupid things constantly nowadays.

"I must have left my American Express card back at the restaurant." This was really embarrassing. He'd been distracted by the cake.

Cynthia made an effort to look sympathetic. The dinner reservation had been for 8:00, and now it was pushing 11:00. Both of them had early mornings. "It's okay. We'll just . . ." She nodded toward the Sheraton.

"So stupid. I'm sorry." He reached into his pocket. "Here, take my keys. You go wait in the car. I'll trot back, real quick."

Cynthia looked uncertain, and Ashley broke in. "You and Rob go back. I'll hang out here with Cindy."

"No, no, no." Cynthia took the keys. "You need to catch your subway. It'll be ten minutes, at the most. I'll get comfortable and knock off a few emails." She widened her eyes at Newbury, feigning tartness. "Mr. Magoo here will be back before I know it."

"Exactly." He nodded down at her cake box. "But don't drink all the cognac." This got another smile.

As Newbury hurried down the sidewalk toward the Sheraton, the evening's effervescence wore off, and his mind drifted into its current default mode of deep anxiety. It had occurred to him to share his situation with Rob, but he'd realized it was impossible. Rob wouldn't know what to think and might be disgusted with him.

That afternoon, he had been in touch again with Taylor, who still seemed unimpressed with his problem, only telling him curtly that "things were in motion." Taylor had seemed more interested in cross-examining him about his drink with Norcross. Tomorrow would mark a week since the bombing and his ride with Norcross's wife.

When he'd passed on the latest update to O'Connell, O'Connell had been as brusque as Taylor, just saying: "A week, Sam. Like I said. You have until Monday." Then he'd hung up without saying goodbye. Newbury was praying that, despite his growl, O'Connell would give him an extension if he could credibly report progress. The man had to realize that things like this took time. His circling thoughts rotated around to their usual terminus: all this misery was just because he'd negotiated a small bend in the rules to help out a deserving client. It wasn't fair.

The maître d' smiled brightly when he saw Newbury and held up the credit card before he could even ask for it. After a minute or so of banter, Newbury was on his way back, walking fast.

He consoled himself on the return trip by focusing on Cynthia, remembering Rob's approval and envy. Sam was a few years older than Cynthia, and this actually seemed right. Her last lover had apparently been from a whole different generation. He liked that she was really bright and, as Rob pointed out, not uncomfortable being quiet. It also pleased Sam deeply that, once in a while, she seemed to think he was handsome and funny.

He climbed the stairs up to the fourth level in the garage and spotted his Mercedes waiting in a shadowy corner. The top of Cindy's blond head was just poking over the passenger seat. His heart rate was up a little from the quick walk and the climb up the stairway, and as he approached the car, he was recovering his breath. The overhead fixture above the car was not working. Why couldn't they keep these places properly lighted?

As he bent to get into the car, he saw that Cindy was turned away from him. She did not move as he opened the door and slid in. This was strange. Was she angry? Asleep? Her hair had fallen across her face. The cake box was tipped on its side at her feet, spilling out the two cognac nips. He pulled on her shoulder and felt a stab of horror as her head slumped toward him, her blue eyes staring blankly and her white blouse splashed bright red. Then he sensed a shadow rising up, uncoiling from behind him.

25

At his meeting the next day with Schwartz and Alberti, Patterson pulled in Jeff Ackerman, the task force rep from Homeland Security.

Alberti bustled into the room, still in the middle of a conversation with Ackerman. "Well, we know he lied about his supposed contact with the Kenyan embassy. There's nobody on their staff with a name even close to . . ." He held out a scrap of paper and spelled it out. "O-t-i-e-n-o." He took a seat. "Which means Kamau had some other motive for speaking to Kahlil Khan. Even if he wasn't involved, he has to know something."

Jeff Ackerman took his time getting into his chair. He was a heavy, slow-moving, slow-talking man, with a round face and a sparse gray combover. He scratched his jaw, looked dubious, and said, "Hmm."

When Schwartz came in, Patterson could see that he was bothered about something. His face sagged, and he made no eye contact.

"You okay, Bob? You look like somebody backed over your dog."

"Sorry." Schwartz slowly took a seat. "I'm still on my ass about Sam Newbury. He worked in our office before he went into private practice, and we did a couple cases together. That was a bad way to go."

"Newbury?" Alberti asked. "The guy they found in the parking garage?"

"Yeah, Palmer Street in Cambridge, double homicide, with his girlfriend. He was the blond preppy type, but you couldn't help liking him." He sniffed. "At least I couldn't. They tell us it was a robbery gone wrong, but I don't see it. The whole thing makes no sense." He leaned over the table and squeezed his hands together. "I didn't get much sleep last night."

Patterson was pleased that Schwartz's instincts were lining up with his. "I crossed paths with Newbury a couple years ago. He was an easy guy to work with. The way he and his girlfriend were killed doesn't fit the usual robbery profile. Muggers don't slash throats. It's a state investigation right now, but I'm making some calls."

"Let me know if you find anything out."

Ackerman broke in. "Getting back to David Kamau. What are you guys looking for here?"

"Like I say, Kamau must know something." Alberti sat back in his chair. "We need to find a way to scoop him."

"I could speak to my people and get his student visa revoked," Ackerman said. "That's not hard."

Alberti nodded. "If it helps, my person at the embassy mentioned that the Kenyan Ministry of Interior has been looking into possible criminal charges against Kamau. They're very unhappy with a talk he gave last year in Mombasa."

"Sounds like he's got someone at home on his butt." Ackerman scratched the top of his head. "We've had problems with that sort of thing in the past. These embassy contacts are not always reliable."

Schwartz looked at Alberti. "So you're sure you're comfortable moving on this now, Carl? This soon?"

Patterson laughed. "He's full of beans these days, Bob. He has a new honey."

"Really? Who?"

"Never mind."

Schwartz looked at Ackerman. "An immigration warrant would be ideal, Jeff. It's a civil proceeding, so Kamau wouldn't be entitled to an appointed lawyer. That could really simplify things for us."

"I know. That bothers me sometimes." Ackerman sighed and

rubbed the back of his neck, speaking slowly. "Seems unfair. Anyway, the system has a lot of play in the joints. We could grab him and probably hold him in immigration custody for at least a few days, maybe longer. That depends, of course, on the immigration judge, and whether Kamau manages to dig up some volunteer lawyer. If the IJ doesn't think Kamau's going to run, they could end up sending him back to Cambridge to wait for his deportation order, or just let him go back to Kenya voluntarily."

"We don't want that," Alberti interjected. "We want him here, and we want him on ice."

"Well, it's hard to predict."

"So we can't count on him being detained?" Alberti asked.

"No, not necessarily, and I'll tell you another thing. I'm not sending my people into Harvard Divinity School to snatch Kamau out of class. Can you imagine the press? I could end up getting fired."

Alberti smiled. "They'd beat you to death with their hymnals."

"I don't think it's that kind of divinity school," Patterson said.

Ackerman nodded slowly. "If I can persuade an immigration judge to issue the warrant, which I think I can, we'll find a way to grab him off the street."

"Can you do it sometime today?" Alberti was pushing.

"I think Monday. I need to put my team together and get them up to speed."

"Maybe over the weekend?"

"Monday."

26

Late Saturday morning, Sandy Tarbell visited Dominic O'Connell's sisters, Colleen and Mary, to go over their testimony. They were his key alibi witnesses, and they were both fluttering around like scalded chickens. He had to do a lot of talking, mostly about things that had nothing to do with the trial, and let them feed him boiled ham and potatoes for lunch before they got comfortable and began to focus. After they'd cleared the dishes, he sat Colleen down on the floral club chair in Mary's living room and stood facing her.

"Okay. Let's pretend we're in court."

"Sure." Colleen had never married and had a thin, alert face with dark brown eyes and chrome white hair. She'd taught statistics for thirty-four years at UMass Boston before retiring. Tarbell's concern was that her intelligence and her tendency to see the big picture would get in the way of her testimony. As she sat in the chair, her eyes darted from side to side, over to her sister and out the window, not looking at him.

"And let's say I ask you, like this: 'Ms. O'Connell, do you remember the evening of June 8, 1968?'"

"Okay. Sure. Sort of. It's a long time ago. I can clearly remember hearing the news that Bobby Kennedy had been shot, which was

June fifth, I think—was it a Wednesday?—we were having breakfast and it came on the radio—and then praying that he would pull
through, but then we heard the next day, June sixth, that we'd lost him.
It was terrible. But June eighth, I'm not so sure."

Mary, seated across the room, put her hand over her eyes, sighed,
and shook her head. "For heaven's sake, Colleen, do you want to
help Dom, or not?" She was plumper than her sister and a widow.
The youngest of her five children, a very pretty daughter, still lived
with her. The daughter had greeted Tarbell when he'd arrived, but
she'd zipped off shortly afterward in her green MINI Cooper. Very
cool, but too tall for him, Tarbell decided, and probably too young.

"Well, of course, but . . ."

"Look at me, Colleen." When Colleen kept staring straight
ahead, Mary repeated herself. "Would you look at me for the love of
God? We went to the six p.m. Mass at Saint Brigid. It was Saturday,
June eighth, and Dominic came along. We went out to dinner at the
Regency afterward."

"Uh-huh."

"Take a second to think about Dom's daughters, will you please,
dear? Your nieces. Especially Chloe."

"I know," Colleen said. "Heaven knows I do."

"It's okay," Tarbell said. "I don't want to put words in your mouth.
You'll both be sworn to tell the truth."

Mary gave an emphatic nod. "Right, and so we shall."

"But, in telling the truth, it is usually best to keep it simple. Your
responses should be just enough to answer the question."

"Okay." Colleen's eyes wandered toward her sister again nervously.

"So, when I ask you if you remember the evening of June eighth,
your best answer—but only if it is true—would just be yes. Because
it's the simplest. It's the easiest for you to remember, and it's the easiest for the jury to understand. You see what I'm saying? Then I'll
follow up from there."

"Okay."

"And try to keep your hands away from your mouth when you
answer."

"Oh goodness. Okay."

"It will keep you from distracting the jury, that's all."

Mary shook her head. "People don't believe people who jiggle around like . . ."

This sort of thing went on right through the afternoon. When the two sisters had clearly taken all they could take, Tarbell broke off and drove over to the Regency restaurant. The place was still going strong, and he wanted to get a feel for it. He talked to the restaurant manager and had an early dinner. Not surprisingly, nobody could remember anything helpful going back to 1968.

The next day, Sunday, Sandy met Dominic and Julie at their Louisburg Square palace. He needed to let Dom know that he would be calling Julie as a witness, but he was worried about Dom's response and stalled before bringing it up. The three of them were sitting in the same front room where they'd waited for the marshals' dawn visit. The days were rushing by.

"You saw the news about Sam Newbury?"

O'Connell's expression did not change. "Yeah, too bad."

"Really."

Julie shook her head. "I never liked how Sam handled Dom's case, but this was just terrible. And his girlfriend too."

"Shouldn't have been in a public garage that late," O'Connell said.

Not long after this, Tarbell revealed that he planned to call Julie as a witness, and Dom hit the roof, leaping up from his chair and coming at Tarbell as though he were going to knock his teeth out. It took Julie half an hour to calm him down. The substance of what Tarbell wanted Julie to testify about—Dominic's strong reputation in the community for honesty—was a pretext. Tarbell would put her on the stand to read from *iPads for Idiots* if Judge Norcross would let him. What he wanted was for the jury to see Julie, to imagine what Dominic's imprisonment would mean to her, and to ask themselves how a man who'd married such a beautiful and intelligent woman could be capable of murder. All he needed was to weave into the mind of one juror a strand of sufficiently stubborn doubt, and he'd be home. He knew he'd never get an outright acquittal. All he needed was a hung jury.

When Tarbell returned to the courtroom on Monday morning with Dom and Julie, the place was crowded with reporters and spectators, curious to see the attorneys' last dance steps before jury selection, which was scheduled for the next day. Rafferty and Aidan came along as usual, taking seats in the gallery next to Julie, and keeping an eye on who came and went in the courtroom.

Tarbell had deliberately waited to file a raft of motions *in limine* at the last minute, requesting the issuance of summonses, looking to sequester witnesses, and seeking permission to conduct individual cross-examination of potential jurors. He'd also refiled his motion for extra peremptory challenges, arguing that the murder of Newbury had kicked off a renewed surge of publicity that was prejudicial to his client. All this paperwork would distract Papadakis, he hoped, and complicate her final preparations.

As he settled into his chair at the defense table, Tarbell experienced the usual sensation at the approach of a big trial—a black tornado on the horizon, getting closer, about to hit. Pieces of barn flying into the air. He loved it.

Angie Phipps bawled out the opening as Norcross came in, walking in his usual stooped, hurried way, like a man being pursued by something and wanting to reach the bench as quickly as possible. After a couple of pleasantries, Norcross dropped his bomb.

"Good morning. We have a number of things to work through today in preparation for tomorrow's trial jury selection." He looked down, making eye contact with Tarbell and Papadakis. "Once we've finished up, I have a minor matter that I want to discuss with counsel in chambers."

Tarbell had no idea what the hell this could be about, and he worked hard to keep his face neutral. As he was fond of saying, he didn't even like surprises on his birthday. O'Connell glanced over at him with an inquisitive, irritated expression, and Tarbell shrugged, feigning indifference. In the corner of his eye, he could see Patterson and Papadakis sitting inscrutably. Did they know something that he didn't?

The hearing after that went well. Norcross allowed his renewed motion for additional peremptories—both sides got two extra—and he agreed with Tarbell's request to keep the witnesses out of the courtroom until it was time for them to testify. Norcross's questions to the potential jurors would, as Tarbell asked, include an inquiry about their exposure to the news of Newbury's murder. The one disappointment was Norcross's denial of his request to conduct individual *voir dire* of the jurors, but this was not surprising. Federal judges rarely allowed this. They liked to do it themselves.

As the clock on the side wall ground slowly forward, he could sense O'Connell, and probably everyone else in the courtroom, getting bored. Norcross was droning from point to point, ticking things off his yellow pad and obviously enjoying the tedium. The last thing most judges wanted was for things to get interesting. That was always when the problems arose.

After an hour and a half, Norcross summarized his rulings and looked down. "Okay. Anything else?"

Papadakis stood. "No, Your Honor, the government will be ready to begin jury selection tomorrow." Tarbell stayed seated and only shook his head. Now what?

"As I mentioned, I have a brief matter to take up with counsel in chambers." Judge Norcross looked down at the court stenographer. "It will be on the record, so I'll ask Ms. Walsh to join us with her machine." Walsh glanced up at the judge with a quick smile, fingers dancing. "Ms. Phipps, would you please escort counsel back to chambers?"

A few minutes later, when they gathered in the judge's library, Tarbell found Norcross waiting for them, seated at the head of a long oak table. The walls of the room were lined floor to ceiling with bookshelves, except for the area directly behind Norcross, which was plastered with bright crayoned drawings.

Papadakis looked at them as she and Patterson took their seats. "One of your kids, Judge?"

Norcross glanced over his shoulder. "Judge Conti's granddaughter, I think." He didn't change expression. Something serious was up. On the table next to him, there were two folders. "For the record, we are in the conference room I'm using here at the Boston courthouse. Present in addition to the stenographer are Mr. Tarbell, counsel for the defendant; Assistant U.S. Attorney Papadakis for the government; Special Agent Patterson; and my courtroom deputy, Ms. Phipps. The transcript of this proceeding will be sealed, and I am ordering everyone present to make no public statements regarding what we're about to discuss. Mr. Tarbell, I see you are by yourself. Your client is welcome to join us, if he wishes."

"I prefer to meet without my client, Your Honor, until I know what this is about."

"You've spoken to him?"

"Yes. He's okay with it."

The last thing Tarbell wanted was to risk was having O'Connell erupt at the judge if things went in a direction he didn't like. Back in the courtroom, when Tarbell suggested that he go in alone, O'Connell had not protested, muttering only, "No more goddamn postponements, Sandy. I want this show on the road." He was at his limit.

"Very well. For the record, I'm handing Mr. Tarbell and Ms. Papadakis copies of three photographs and a note that my wife and I found tucked under our door. I'm directing Ms. Phipps to mark the originals, which the court has retained, as Court Exhibits Roman numerals I to IV. I'll give you a moment." He slid the folders to Tarbell and Papadakis.

It took less than five seconds for Tarbell to absorb the significance of what was in his folder.

"How long have you had these, Judge?"

"We found them on Wednesday evening."

Tarbell's reaction was immediate and indignant. "And this is the first you're telling me?" He held up a hand and shook his head apologetically. "Excuse me, Your Honor, did you consider informing me of this earlier?"

Norcross nodded over at Patterson. "There were some preliminary inquiries . . ."

"So Agent Patterson has also known about these photographs since last week?"

Patterson nodded.

Tarbell gestured toward Papadakis. "So, Judge, respectfully, I just need to ask, I'm assuming Ms. Papadakis has also known about these photographs since then?"

Papadakis set down the photograph she'd been looking at and shook her head. "This is the first I'm hearing about this, Sandy. I'm in the same boat you are."

Tarbell raised his voice. "Really." He pointed at Patterson. "You're telling me Agent Patterson hasn't said one word to you about this?" He was positive Papadakis was lying. Patterson had to have slipped something to her.

"That's what I'm telling you." Papadakis's face had gone stony.

Patterson was staring at Tarbell intently. "It's true. We maintain a very strict wall between—"

"Okay, fine." Tarbell was thanking whatever lucky star hovered over criminal defense attorneys that he hadn't brought O'Connell with him. "You see where this puts me, Judge? If I'd known about this last week, I might have had the weekend to investigate. I might have had time to do some research. Respectfully, Your Honor, I might have had time to draft a motion to recuse." He pointed at the photos. "Because, honestly, I don't see any way this side of the moon that you can preside at the trial now, after these."

"Would you like a continuance, Mr. Tarbell? I'd consider giving you a few days, perhaps up to a week."

"A few days won't change the facts. The only remedy here, respectfully, is for you to step away from the case. I can be ready as soon as we have a new judge on board."

As he said this, Tarbell felt a very slight movement to his left and looked over to see Patterson staring at him even more intently. The meaning was obvious: Patterson suspected he was the one behind the photographs. This made Tarbell angry, but also scared. The last thing he wanted was a team of FBI agents scouring his office with a search warrant. He wasn't worried so much about the O'Connell case as he was about some other, sketchier clients and their files. Was O'Connell or one of his crew behind this brain-dead photography stunt? Could they be that stupid?

"Mm-hmm." Norcross folded his hands on the table. "Let me say a couple things—"

"Respectfully, I'm putting myself in your shoes, Judge." Tarbell picked up the photo of Norcross and Charlie in front of the Garrison statue. "They're threatening your son here. I don't see how—"

"Well, let me finish, Mr. Tarbell. I have some things to say, and then I'm going to want to hear from the government. First, I find

Ms. Papadakis credible when she says that she has not spoken to Agent Patterson about these materials. That would be against protocol. Second, I have absolutely no subjective bias for or against either side as a result of the photographs or the note. In fact, it's impossible to tell if the person who delivered them favors the government or the defense. Nothing about the photographs or the note will affect my ability to conduct a fair trial."

"Judge—again, respectfully—somebody followed your wife and son around to take these pictures? They got up pretty close. Are you saying that doesn't bother you?"

"For heaven's sake, of course it bothers me, but it doesn't make me biased. If judges recused themselves every time they got a threat, Mr. Tarbell, things would grind to a halt pretty quickly." Norcross dropped his voice. "But we aren't here so you can cross-examine me. What are you asking the court to do?"

"I'd like the record to reflect that I am making an oral motion for you to recuse yourself, Judge, and I'd like—I guess I'd like—a one-day postponement to put it in writing." He could use more time, but if he asked for a longer delay, O'Connell would break his neck. "I don't have a choice here."

"May I have a turn?" Assistant U.S. Attorney Papadakis broke in, tapping her fingers on the table.

"And I'll be submitting an affidavit to make the record clear about the position this puts me in. I mean, really . . ." Tarbell gestured again at the photographs. "This is nuclear."

Papadakis's voice pressed in, more emphatic. "Okay, Sandy, my turn now."

Norcross turned to her. "I'll hear you."

"Okay, first, Your Honor is absolutely right. We can't tell what the motives are here, progovernment or antigovernment, prodefense or antidefense. Second, Your Honor has stated that you have no subjective bias one way or the other, and there is no appearance of bias at all in these circumstances. Short answer: there's no basis for recusal. Getting our witnesses lined up was not easy. Brian Shaughnessy is very ill. We're ready to go. There's no reason for recusal or any extended delay. End of story."

The back-and-forth after this did not take long. There was little more Tarbell could say, and he was concerned about pushing too hard. Patterson was still sitting there doing his eyeballing, and Tarbell wasn't sure what O'Connell or his goons might have been up to.

Norcross wrapped up. "Okay, Mr. Tarbell, you've got your extra day. I'll give the government and the defense until two p.m. tomorrow to make their submissions. You'll have my ruling on any motion to recuse by five. The record will reflect that I offered the defense up to a week's continuance if they wanted one, but I understand, Mr. Tarbell, that you are not asking for that."

"No, Judge, but I do hope you will carefully consider—"

"I certainly will do that. As I say, you'll have my ruling, under seal, by the end of the day tomorrow. I don't want anything that we discussed in this conference to be mentioned publicly. I'll consider your arguments for recusal, but my advice is to proceed with your trial preparation as though I will be staying on the case. Assuming I do, I plan to commence jury selection Wednesday morning."

Afterward, Tarbell found Julie and O'Connell sitting by themselves in the courtroom. Rafferty and Aidan had already left to get the car. To his surprise, when he gave them a summary of what had happened in the chambers conference, O'Connell looked grave but not volcanic.

"Norcross or whoever, I want this over. A day I can manage, but that's it. I want this goddamn ankle bracelet off."

Julie put a hand on her husband's shoulder. "You should talk to Raff, Dom. We need to be sure that someone didn't—"

"I know." O'Connell cut her off. "I'll be doing that." He looked grim. "Don't worry."

27

Judge Norcross was jotting down an outline of his memorandum on Tarbell's expected motion to recuse, when his law clerk, Mossy, stuck her head in to let him know Agent Patterson was outside.

"Really?" He tore off a page of his yellow pad. "Take this and put together a draft memo denying the motion to recuse in *O'Connell*. Fill in a couple of the controlling First Circuit precedents." He could imagine no convincing argument in favor of recusal, and he was ninety percent certain what his ruling would be. "We can buff it up tomorrow once we have the attorneys' submissions, but I want to get a head start on this."

"No problem. I can have a draft for you in an hour."

"Good. Thank you." He handed her the sheet of paper. "Tell Agent Patterson I'm ready to see him."

When he entered, Patterson closed the door behind him and took a seat. He looked uncomfortable.

"So are your wife and boy all settled in Amherst now?"

"Yes. Unfortunately, I couldn't persuade Claire to come back with me." Norcross sighed. "She can be a toughie."

Patterson smiled briefly. "I noticed that. She and Charlie are out there by themselves then?"

"Why are you asking?" The judge's reaction had more snap than he'd intended, and he softened his tone. "She has a friend staying with her, actually. What's up?"

Norcross had worked hard to convince Claire to return to Boston with him, and they'd had something close to a fight when she'd refused. The trial was going forward, she pointed out, and there'd been no further threats. The photographs had to have been a bluff. She was sick of dealing with Charlie in the borrowed condo, and she wanted to be in her own house, near her office at the college. She and the baby would be safer in Amherst, anyway. In the end, their compromise was that her friend Monica would come out and spend a few days while David was away.

Judge Norcross noticed that Patterson was gazing out the window at the harbor, clearly weighing how much he could say in response to the judge's question. Norcross did not like this. If Patterson was worried, he needed to know why.

"Come on, Mike. Talk to me. What's going on?"

"Maybe nothing." Patterson turned away from the window and looked at him. "You heard about what happened to Sam Newbury and his girlfriend last week?"

"Yes. I saw it in the paper. Horrible. We had drinks with them just a few days ago. A really frightening, terrible tragedy."

"He'd represented O'Connell earlier on."

"I know. Judge Helms allowed his motion to withdraw."

"There might be no connection, but—"

"The reports said it was a robbery that turned ugly. Something like that. I keep thinking of them in that garage, and it makes me sick."

"The thing is . . ." Patterson stopped and then pushed forward, speaking more quickly.

"There is a separate ongoing state investigation, and I'm bending the rules by disclosing any details here, Judge, but I think you deserve to know. The murders were probably not random. They were more likely something else, something worse."

Any distracting background noise in Judge Norcross's brain ceased, and his mind went blank. He just listened.

"Some homeless man—I have his name written down somewhere—tried to pawn Coolidge's garnet bracelet, and the broker had the sense to call the Boston PD. It took them a while, but they found the guy at a shelter this morning. After a little friendly persuasion, he told them he dug it out of a trash bin right down the street from where Sam Newbury and Cynthia Coolidge were killed."

"So taking it was a ruse."

"Exactly." Patterson sounded almost relieved to be talking. "Tell the truth, the entire situation has never made sense to me. Whoever killed Newbury didn't bother to strip his Rolex . . ."

"I didn't know that."

"Then, an hour ago, I got a more detailed copy of the forensics report. Stains with Coolidge's blood type were on the back of Newbury's pants, which means her blood was already on the driver's seat when Newbury entered the car. They can't be sure, but from the smears it looks as though the blood had begun to dry before Newbury sat in it. This would mean that he entered the car ten to fifteen minutes after Cynthia Coolidge was already dead."

"I see." A chill deepened over Norcross as he listened. He remembered Sam and Cynthia at the restaurant, their story about the jigsaw puzzle, and Cynthia's endearing shyness. Their deaths were sickening enough, but this new information was making his skin crawl.

"Plus, the whole thing appears to have been planned, not spur of the moment. The killer, or killers, disabled the ceiling fixture near their car, not by smashing the bulb, which someone might have noticed, but by using a tool like a knife or screwdriver to disconnect it."

"I really hate this, Mike."

"This was almost certainly a deliberate hit, by people who knew what they were doing, and Sam Newbury was the target. Whoever it was stayed hidden, probably behind the seat, after he'd killed Cynthia Coolidge, waiting for him. She was just . . ." Patterson shook his head.

"In the wrong place at the wrong time."

"Right. I don't have anything concrete yet, but I'm worried there is some connection between Newbury's death and your trial."

"Really." Norcross had a sudden vision of his isolated house, back in the trees. In his imagination, he was standing outside in the shadows, looking in through the brightly lit windows, seeing Claire bent over Charlie in his high chair, smiling. Oblivious.

"I'm just going on instinct, Judge. Newbury was O'Connell's lawyer. We don't know why O'Connell fired him, or what exactly was going on between them. Then, with the trial coming up, you got that threat. Somebody had his eye on you and your family. I'm not a big fan of Sandy Tarbell. He's been on our list for—"

"Tarbell's not a big fan of me either. I noticed you keeping an eye on him during our conference."

"We know he has certain connections, Judge. Figuratively speaking—or maybe not so figuratively speaking—he knows where a lot of bodies are buried. O'Connell has had a bad smell, too, for many years now. I wouldn't put anything past him. What we're learning from the Palmer Street murders has upped the ante a lot. Somebody's circling around out there, and now we know what he's capable of."

"Judge Helms told me she had a funny feeling about the case."

Patterson nodded. "She was right—something is off. I'll be honest with you, Judge. I'm a little worried about Claire out there in Amherst by herself."

"Me too, very worried. I'll call her the minute we finish here." Norcross paused for a moment to think. "I'd drive home to Amherst right now, but I've got this darned talk at the Harvard Divinity School tonight. I can't really pull out this late."

"I'll ask the Amherst PD to keep an eye on your house this evening. They could also swing by from time to time over the next couple weeks while you're tied up here. Would you mind?"

"For heaven's sake, Mike, of course not. I appreciate it."

"Could you let Claire know? The Amherst cops are on the ball. I wouldn't want her getting worried when she sees their cruisers nosing around."

"I'll call her the minute we finish here." Norcross paused to think. "I'll drive back to Amherst after my talk tonight, which should have me home by around ten thirty or eleven. Ask the police to make one of their passes sometime around then, okay? I want to talk to whoever is on nights, in person." Norcross pushed his pad away. "Let me know immediately if there are other developments. You have my cell number."

"Absolutely."

"And listen." Norcross lifted a finger. "If anyone takes a jab at you for disclosing this information, tell them to come see me. If I hadn't been informed, and then learned about this afterward, I guarantee you somebody would have been very sorry."

28

That same day, Monday, was Julie and Dominic's tenth anniversary. Always before, these had been joyful occasions, but Julie was not looking forward to this one at all. She knew Dominic would want to do something super extraordinary to mark the milestone, and she was worried that, because of his home confinement, he wouldn't be able to organize anything grand enough to satisfy his high standards. This would put him into a deep funk, and his bad mood would drive her crazy. He was not an easy man to be trapped in a house with.

Julie made a quick decision to pull Rafferty aside when he dropped by that afternoon to see Dom. She needed to find out what she might be in for. Rafferty had had a crush on her going back forever, though he'd never in the world say or do anything about it. Julie felt bad taking advantage of him, but this was an emergency.

Rafferty and Dominic conferred behind closed doors for an hour or so before breaking up, and Julie managed to catch Rafferty in the entryway as he was leaving. Dominic was upstairs in the bathroom.

At first, Rafferty seemed as grateful as she was for a sympathetic ear. "Yeah, Jesus, he's been impossible for, like, a month now." Rafferty glanced up nervously as the toilet flushed in the distance. "He just fried my ass because he thought I might have been out taking snapshots of Norcross. He's nuts."

"And you didn't—"

"No, for Christ's sake, how dumb do you guys think I am?"

"Sorry. And what about our dinner?"

"I think we're in the clear." Rafferty sighed and shook his head. "Finally. We had a breakthrough with the caterer yesterday." His eyes were darting back and forth anxiously, and his voice dropped down to a whisper. "Also, he has this big surprise for you, which almost got screwed up. Aidan had to pay the poor guy a visit."

"He didn't hurt him, did he?"

"Nah. Just chitchat, God help him. Aidan's good at that."

"So you think everything's okay?"

"Yes, yes, yes. Just, please don't mention I told you about any surprise. He'd—"

"Never." She put her hand on his arm. "Let me walk you to your car. I wanted to ask you about something else." She opened the door.

Rafferty looked apprehensive and glanced up again at the second floor.

"It's okay," Julie said. "He'll be going straight to his office. Listen." The two of them stood frozen together, mouths open, with the breeze rippling in through the doorway and her hand still on his arm. After a few seconds they heard the clunk of an upstairs door closing. Julie patted his arm and gave him a conspiratorial look. "It's just a walk to the car, Raff. It's not like we're going away for the weekend."

He actually blushed, which was so sweet. "Yeah, well . . ."

The two of them made their way down the steps. "This weird thing happened." The sun was strong, and the heat was radiating off the sidewalk. "Dom usually never makes a sound when he's sleeping. He'll toss and turn a little sometimes, but once he's gone, he's gone. Then, out of the blue, two nights in a row now, he's said a name in his sleep I've never heard before."

"Yeah?"

"Doyle. Doyle something, or something Doyle."

"Oh man." Rafferty looked troubled.

"Who's Doyle?"

Rafferty was on the bottom step. He looked up at the tops of the trees in the little park across the street. "Oh boy. I don't know, Jules . . ."

Rafferty was not saying he didn't know who this Doyle was. He was saying he didn't know whether he should tell Julie who he was.

"It's okay. If it's a problem, you don't have to—"

"Couple guys from way back. Not very nice people."

"I see." She followed him down the steps to the sidewalk, staying close.

"Dom would never fool around with them. You don't have to worry about that."

"Then why do you think he'd—"

"We were talking about the Harvard thing the other day, and the MO sort of reminded us of these guys, that's all."

"Uh-huh."

Julie and Rafferty looked into each other's eyes. Julie was not naive, and no words were necessary. In her work as an event planner, before she'd met Dominic, she'd spent a lot of time dodging around the Boston quicksand, handling contractors, negotiating with unions, and making her world work. She realized immediately that if these Doyle people had anything to do with the Harvard bombing, even if they just *maybe* did, that information would be very valuable. It could be bartered, though Julie didn't know with whom yet, or exactly how.

"Did you talk to Dom about using the Doyle thing for—"

"Oh jeez, Julie, I shouldn't even be talking about this."

"Did you?"

Rafferty glanced up at the second floor of the house. "Dom doesn't want to go that route."

"Why not?"

"He thinks he can beat the case in court."

"Maybe, but I don't see why we can't—"

"And he has other reasons I'm not going to get into. You know I'd do anything for you, Jules. Please don't push me on this."

"Okay, but I won't pretend I'm happy."

"My advice? Don't even bring it up." As he walked to his car, he continued talking, not looking at her. "Dom has his reasons. Let it be."

It turned out that Julie needn't have worried about the anniversary dinner. Rafferty and Aidan had been performing their usual miracles. The catering crew had been persuaded to get the shopping done locally, very early, so that everything would be fresh. At 6:00 p.m. on the button, Dominic appeared in the door of the dining room, smelling of Brut and wearing a blue open-neck shirt, gray slacks, and a navy blazer—very handsome and elegant with his silver hair.

The appetizers the caterers served were melt-in-your-mouth scallops in wine sauce, accompanied by a two-hundred-dollar bottle of champagne and a violinist from the Boston Symphony Orchestra, who performed a heartbreakingly beautiful solo version of the opening segment of Sibelius's Concerto in D Minor, Julie's favorite piece of classical music.

Over the entrée, a beef tenderloin she could cut with her fork, the topic of Newbury's death somehow came up. Newbury had always struck Julie as a phony, and she'd worked hard to get him fired, especially after she talked to her old boyfriend Sandy Tarbell. She could see that Newbury would be happy to take a big check from Dom and let him go off to prison to die. Still, she'd been shocked to hear about the murders.

"If they got Sam's wallet and so on, why would they kill him? And that poor girl?"

Dominic frowned and shook his head. "Newbury was okay, but he was a punk." He took a sip of his champagne. "He crossed somebody. Guys like him do that sometimes. It's a shame."

"I know you were not happy with him."

"Yeah, but I'd never . . ." Dominic broke off and gave Julie a close look. "You worry about me sometimes, don't you, sweetheart? Worry about what I'm up to."

"Well, Dom, you grew up rough, and you've made your money in a rough world. I love you beyond the beyond, but, you're right, I do worry sometimes . . ." She trailed off.

He gazed at her, taking his time. "You love me for the scary things I do, and I love you because you worry about them."

"You're right, babe, but—"

"I don't hurt people." He spoke a little louder, cutting a bite of steak and talking down to his plate. "But sometimes I have to make people think I can hurt them." He looked up. "They need to know they can't muscle me. Otherwise, I couldn't do business."

"But what makes you think the Newbury thing wasn't a robbery?"

"The way it happened. Whoever did it wanted to impress somebody, so they made sure it was messy." He started to say more but stopped himself. "I don't want to get into details, okay? It's not a pleasant topic." He lifted the champagne bottle. "Here. Let me top you up."

"I feel so bad about the girl."

"She may have been part of the plan." Dom shook his head. "But let's leave it, okay?" He slipped an envelope out of his jacket. "I got something for you, or to be honest, I got something for both of us."

Inside the envelope, Julie found tickets for a ten-day Viking cruise, Athens to Venice, scheduled for October. An adventure like this was something she'd been talking to Dom about for years, but he had always been too busy. The booking was for the top-scale suite, two full rooms, twelve hundred square feet, with its own balcony, priority onshore dinner reservations, and everything she'd dreamed of. When she looked up, Dom was smiling at her.

"Oh, babe." She stood and gave him a long kiss. "You are such a sweetheart."

"Once we're past all the garbage with this court case, we'll both deserve a good break."

"I can't wait." They both knew that the outcome of the trial was uncertain, but she loved that he'd put on this confident face for her.

Later on, after the caterers had cleaned up and gone, and the house was empty, Dom—looking especially pleased with himself—said that he had one more thing for her. Julie realized this had to be the big surprise Rafferty had been talking about, and she prepared herself to look astonished. He led her into his office, where she found a large framed painting perched on an easel with a green cloth over it.

When he slipped the cloth off, Julie didn't have to act. She was bowled over. It was a painting of the two of them, done from a favorite photograph, sitting in the window seat in their front room, with Louisburg Square in the background. Julie was looking over her shoulder out the window with the sun on her face in a very flattering profile, and Dominic was gazing at her with an adoring expression. It was spectacular. Julie had trouble finding words to describe how very touched she was, but in the end her floundering probably got the point across better than any well-turned phrase ever could have.

After a long embrace, Dominic stepped back and nodded at the painting, looking satisfied. "The framer, a local guy, called the day before yesterday and had the gall to tell me he'd need another week to get it finished."

"Oh, Dom, I hope you didn't . . ."

He couldn't suppress a smile. "After Aidan talked to him, he decided to stay up late and get it done for us. It was very nice of him." Dom must have seen something in Julie's face, because he softened and added, "I paid him a couple bucks extra."

"Well, it's beautiful, just beautiful. It's the most beautiful thing I've ever gotten." She kissed him again. "Thank you."

Dominic nodded at the painting. "We'll always be sitting there, the two of us. I like that."

"Yes." She took his hand.

"It wasn't easy getting it up here either." He cleared his throat. "That's why—I can tell you now—I made the run down to New York and got my spanking from the judge."

"That was why you went to New York?" She was aghast. "Dom, for God's sake, why didn't you just send Rafferty to get it?"

Dominic shook his head. "The only taste Raff's got is in his mouth. There was no way I was shelling out that kind of dough unless I saw it myself, in person." He looked at the painting and nodded. "Sometimes you have to take risks, you know, just do what you have to do, and take what comes."

29

Divinity Hall rested comfortably on a placid, tree-lined street in Cambridge next to the University Herbaria, not far from Harvard Square. The early evening had softened, and as Judge Norcross walked from his car, he enjoyed how calm the midsummer air was. The disturbing conversation with Patterson was still on his mind, and the quiet neighborhood was a relief after his day in court. He'd be home tonight, his denial of Tarbell's motion to recuse would enter tomorrow, and the day after that they'd begin jury selection. A couple more weeks, and all this would be behind him.

Inside, the building was cool, and Norcross hesitated at first, unsure where to go, until Reverend Kamau came hurrying around a corner in conversation with a young woman with blond, spiky hair. The moment he noticed Norcross, Kamau burst into a smile, then touched his upper lip and rearranged his face, as though he didn't want to be too exuberant. The gesture might have reflected just youthful awkwardness, but Norcross felt his own features going through the same transition. It was hard not to overdo how pleased it made him to see this young man. Kamau's flash of smile had released a memory of Hannah Nyeri hurrying past the purple bougainvillea, a vision so quick and sharp it was almost painful.

Kamau approached and bowed slightly. "Your Honor, how very generous of you to join us. We are all so pleased." His voice was welcoming, but dignified.

"Delighted to be here."

"Permit me to introduce my excellent friend, Helena Toivonen from Finland." He looked down at her. "Helena is an orthodox Lutheran agnostic." Kamau smiled, and Toivonen rolled her eyes. "But we are doing our best to forgive each other."

Norcross nodded. "Hello."

"The root of my name means 'hope' in Finnish." Toivonen looked up at Kamau. "So, we'll be seeing." She had a charming Nordic accent.

A few steps took them to Divinity Chapel, where the event was taking place, and where several students were already standing around talking. Kamau excused himself to check some detail, and Judge Norcross strolled to the lectern at the far end to get the feel of the room. As people filtered in, he saw Godfrey Mungai enter and begin talking to a couple of Asian women and a man in a turban. Mungai nodded at Norcross, but he did not approach. It seemed as though Mungai was done with him. He'd said what he wanted.

The judge took a seat off to the side, and within a few minutes an audience of about thirty people had gathered, with a broad spectrum of races and nationalities. Soon after that, Reverend Kamau stepped to the lectern to make his introduction, and the room fell silent.

"It is a great deal more than merely a pleasure for me to introduce our speaker tonight, David S. Norcross. As you can see, Judge Norcross's presence has inspired me to do something I almost never do . . ." He paused and tugged at his throat. "Wear this dog collar on a weekday." This produced a good-humored murmur. Most of the audience apparently knew Kamau and were fond of him. "Although I only met Judge Norcross in person recently, I have known about him, and wondered about him, from my early childhood." He nodded at Norcross. "To be standing here with you this evening, Your Honor, feels almost like a miracle to me."

Kamau dropped his voice and leaned over the lectern, speaking confidentially. "This should not be surprising, you know. Here we all are . . ." He spread out his hands, as though he were bestowing a blessing on the room. "From the farthest corners of the world—at the Harvard Divinity School, on Divinity Avenue, in Divinity Hall, within the Divinity Chapel. What more appropriate occasion could there be, I ask you, for an instance of divine intervention?"

A more pronounced wave of chuckles and murmuring passed over the room.

"His Honor and I are both children, in a sense, of one small village in the Highlands of Kenya, near where Judge Norcross taught and where I spent much time as a small boy. Not too far, in fact, from the very spot in East Africa where, we are told, human beings, the ancestors of us all, first began to fan out all over this earth. A tiny, tiny dot in our vast universe, and only a quickly passing thought, I sometimes fear, in the busy mind of the Almighty."

He paused and dipped his head to let this idea pass before continuing.

"Judge Norcross taught at the Kenya Institute of Administration, a prestigious institution in my country, with handsome brick classroom buildings originally funded by the USAID, a sports field, and well-manicured lawns." Kamau lifted his hands and fluttered his fingers. "Lanes of Nandi flame trees and jacaranda with lavender blossoms." He glanced over at Norcross.

"But, after his workday, His Honor would walk to my little village and teach English to the older men, our elders." He wagged a finger. "This was before I was born, of course, but stories were handed down, and I listened to them eagerly. I remember one story in particular, and tonight I want to ask our guest if it is indeed true."

Kamau rubbed his hands together. "Years after young Bwana David left Kenya and began his journey to become the Honorable United States District Judge David S. Norcross, back when I was a schoolboy, my older cousins told me that they, too, had wanted to attend his afternoon classes. But they were just children then, you see." Kamau looked over at the judge and smiled. "They were too quick with their English, and they put the older men to shame. So they were forbidden. Do you remember what these boys did then, Your Honor?"

"Oh yes, I remember very well." A sweetness dropped over Norcross at the recollection of those warm afternoons, the high blue sky, the deep green maize fields, and the round huts. "When the men chased them away, the boys retaliated by standing at a distance and chucking rocks onto the tin roof of the school building." This produced an immediate burst of laughter. "The racket drove us crazy." Two African men in the front row tipped their heads back and slapped their thighs, nodding to each other.

"And what happened then, Your Honor?"

"Well, we let them into the class, of course. We had to." This got an even louder laugh. Norcross enjoyed playing the straight man in this routine. Kamau & Norcross seemed like a hit.

As things quieted down, Reverend Kamau's face lapsed into gravity. "Bwana David is still remembered for his kindness in our village. Now, he is here tonight, in a different sort of village, with all of us. Let me share with you a few details about His Honor's career and what we will be discussing this evening."

Kamau quickly summarized the formal details of Norcross's curriculum vitae, and a polite spatter of applause greeted him as he stepped to the lectern. After Kamau's masterful warm-up, Norcross was nervous that he might let the young man down.

In the end, the description of his death penalty case, *United States v. Hudson*, provided enough melodrama to keep the audience awake. His remarks focused on the nature of the charges, a double homicide, and described, step-by-step, the stress of a court proceeding where someone's life was at stake. He then expanded to an overview of capital punishment in the United States generally, its suspension by the Supreme Court for several years, its reinstatement in 1976, and its gradual decline since 2000, as more than half the states discontinued its use.

After about forty minutes, he stopped, perhaps too abruptly, and opened things up for questions. At first, there was an awkward silence with everyone just staring at him, not saying anything. Reverend Kamau, off to the side, shifted in his chair getting ready to rescue him, when Helena Toivonen waved her hand and called out

"Please?" She was at the back of the room and had to stand to be seen. Her resolute expression made her face quite pretty.

"I have a question for Judge Norcross." Toivonen's lightly accented voice carried well, and she spoke to the room, not just to the judge. "We know certain things, okay? We know innocent people, many innocent people, have been sentenced to death here in the United States who then, while they were waiting to be executed, turned out to be not guilty. More than one hundred fifty, I have read. They were exor . . ." She hesitated, wrestling with the word. "Exoron . . . I can't pronounce the word."

A voice called out, "Exonerated."

"Thank you, Paul." Toivonen nodded to a man near the front. "Yes. In many cases they were released. But these people only barely avoided a very unjust death. It seems to me some others, some other innocent people, must not have escaped. Tell me, Your Honor, do you think your country, your court system, has executed people who in fact have committed no crime?"

Norcross took a breath. "Recently?"

His question was mostly intended to provide space for him to frame his response. He knew what he wanted to say, basically, but the actual words were important.

"Let us say since 1976."

"It's a very good question, Ms. Toivonen." He looked down at the lectern briefly, then back at her. "And my answer, my personal answer, is that, yes, I think that has probably happened. If I am honest, I find it hard to imagine that so many dozens of innocent people could have been taken off death row, without at least one innocent person going to his or her death improperly in the past forty-five or fifty years."

"Perhaps more than one? People quite innocent, who committed no crime?"

"Very possibly."

"Okay, one more thing. Also, we know that, even if they are not innocent, the people who face execution are chosen . . ." Toivonen hesitated, carefully pronouncing the word. "Inequitably. Unfairly. Yes? Black people, brown people, poor people, people with mental illness are all more likely to die by execution. We know that is true.

Far more likely to go to prison in your country, also. And to go to prison for longer. We certainly know that. So, tell me, Judge Norcross, I don't wish to offend, but how do you sleep?"

The question was so provocative that it made some audience members shift around uncomfortably. The issue she raised was basic, and one Norcross had struggled with, in one form or another, throughout his time on the bench. Reverend Kamau, seated under a window off to the side, smiled at Toivonen with grateful affection. Then, as the judge searched for words, Kamau turned his face to him, raising his eyebrows expectantly. His expression seemed to say: *So, Bwana David, how are you going to handle this stone on your tin roof?*

Norcross had what he considered a decent answer, one that satisfied him, but he was aware of how weak and disappointing it might sound—especially, perhaps, in front of this audience.

"I have no good answer for you, Ms. Toivonen, except to say that I try in my daily work to do as much good as I can, more good than harm I hope. A strong, independent judiciary, charged with the responsibility to protect people's rights, is absolutely essential. It represents the difference between a free country and a tyranny. But that judicial system—our system, perhaps any system—will inevitably have flaws." Toivonen put her hands on her hips, ready to argue, and Norcross pushed on. "One job we judges have is to try to identify those flaws and moderate or eliminate them. I cannot keep bad things from happening. I don't have that power. My task sometimes is just to do as much good as I can, and to try to make sure the bad things, when they do happen, happen in an orderly way, following the rules. I tell myself that is something. Something important."

The man in the turban spoke up. "Even God cannot keep bad things from happening." He lifted his hands and dropped them wearily.

A Black woman in a brightly colored dress leaned forward to respond. "God is a very busy woman, you know. She has many, many children to keep track of." There was a soft ripple of approving laughter, which diminished the tension.

"Any legal system can be twisted." Kamau's deep voice broke in.

"In my country, as you know, Your Honor, we had a very violent time, sixty or seventy years ago, when we Kenyans were fighting to obtain our freedom from the British colonial regime." His remark prompted murmurs of sympathy and agreement. "I can understand the British, you know. They enjoyed our beautiful land and wanted to keep it for as long as they could." He leaned forward and put his elbows on his knees. "During what we call the 'Emergency,' and what they liked to call the 'Mau-Mau Revolt,' they executed, formally executed through their laws, many of our freedom fighters, more than one thousand, in a short period, for what they supposedly did. The documents are not clear, so we do not know the precise number, but we do know one number quite exactly, the number of British colonials who were executed for what they did, which was often much, much worse. That number was zero."

"It was the same in my country," a voice called out. "In Algeria. They murdered my father and my uncle, and they called it the law."

A woman in a headscarf spoke up. "Yes, but in a democracy, is it not proper to allow the people, the people themselves, to decide that certain terrible crimes, the murder of children for example, might require the most terrible punishments?"

The discussion after this, mostly among the members of the audience, got quite lively. Someone pointed out that, long after independence, Kenya still had capital punishment and that executions had been carried out, though rarely. As the conversation stretched on, Norcross resisted the temptation to check his watch. He was dying to get back to Amherst to check on Claire. Kamau somehow picked up on this and intervened before too long to bring the evening to a close. The applause at the end was satisfyingly warm. It seemed the talk had been worth everyone's time.

Kamau, at any rate, seemed very pleased, which delighted Norcross. He accompanied the judge as he headed out the building back to his car. The two men were similar in height and build, and as they moved in step down the hallway, Norcross remembered how in Kenya men who were close friends often held hands when they walked together. He couldn't do this, of course, but as they dodged around a clump of students, he allowed his hand to linger on Kamau's shoulder. Mungai trailed along behind them.

"I loved remembering how your cousins used to throw stones." Norcross dropped his hand as they approached the outer door. "Thank you for taking me back to that."

"Good." Kamau smiled. "I was afraid I'd told the story incorrectly."

"Oh no. You got it exactly right. They were smart, high-spirited kids, your cousins." Norcross had a sudden impulse. "Listen. Claire and I are having my niece Lindsay over for dinner this coming Saturday. She's taking a course on Third World development."

Kamau sighed. "Third World, yes. That's what they like to call us."

"I'm sorry. The actual title of the class is probably something else."

His lips tightened. "I imagine it would be."

"Anyway, I'd love to introduce you to my wife, Claire, and our son, Charlie."

"Ah, your son. You must be very proud."

"Yes. And I know Lindsay would enjoy meeting you. Are you free by any chance?"

"Well . . ." A pensive expression came over Kamau's face.

"I realize it's last minute, so if you're busy, we'll do it some other time."

They walked in silence, while Kamau pondered something. After a few steps, he made his decision. "Yes. Of course. This coming Saturday." He nodded. "It would be a great pleasure, Your Honor."

"Wonderful."

Kamau laughed and touched the judge's arm. "Perhaps, you know, I could bring some ugali."

"Terrific." Ugali was a traditional Kenyan dish made with maize or cassava flour. Norcross smiled, thinking back. "I still remember the flavor."

As they emerged from the building into the warm night, Mungai drew up with them, looking less grumpy than usual. Perhaps he'd enjoyed the evening too. The streetlights were making apricot pools on the darkened sidewalks, and a rhythmic scritch of insects was keeping up a delicate beat. Norcross hesitated on the portico, needing to be on his way, but reluctant to rush off.

He began to say something but was interrupted when a black

SUV suddenly jerked up in front of them with a sharp skid. The vehicle lurched as its front left tire bounced up onto the curb. A woman stepped quickly out, and a tall man in a black T-shirt exited the passenger side and slammed the door. The woman strode toward them, speaking in a voice louder than necessary.

"David Kamau?" She was wearing blue jeans and a rugby shirt, loose at the waist, with some kind of plastic ID on a lanyard around her neck. Her hair was pulled back in a tight ponytail. Norcross saw two more figures, trotting quickly up the sidewalk from opposite ends of the building, closing in on them. One of them wore an open yellow raid jacket with the initials "ICE."

"What is this?" Norcross felt his body going tense. "Who are you?" They did not wear uniforms, and the SUV was unmarked.

"Step back, please, sir." The woman with the ponytail turned toward Kamau. "Reverend Kamau?"

The man in the black T-shirt came up and took a position near the judge, closer than necessary, pressing into his space.

Kamau spoke calmly. "Yes, I am David Kamau."

"Brenda McNair." She produced a badge from her back pocket. "Immigration and Customs Enforcement. We have a warrant for your arrest."

The agent running up from the farther end of the block had a blond crew cut and very broad shoulders. As he approached, he shouted, "On the ground. Get him on the ground."

Kamau sounded puzzled. "A warrant? For me?"

McNair was already putting her badge back, too fast for them to check it. Judge Norcross remembered Mungai's warning that Kamau might be in danger.

"Wait a minute here." Norcross broke in. "Let's see that badge again."

Mungai came closer. "What is this? What's going on? What's going on?"

"On the ground!" The blond agent closed in, reaching out to grab Kamau's shoulder. Everything was happening very quickly.

The fourth agent, the one in the raid jacket, came in from the nearer corner and inserted himself in front of Mungai. "Step back, please. Step back."

"Sir." McNair continued. "We need you to come with us right now."

"Get the cuffs on him, for Christ's sake. Cuff him."

The blond agent tried to shove in, and Norcross stepped between him and Kamau, rotating his back to block him. He spoke to McNair, raising his voice. "Reverend Kamau is not going anywhere until I see that warrant." Norcross felt the blond agent crowding into him, grunting into his ear, and, without thinking, he gave the man a fierce hip and elbow. "Back off." There was a satisfying sound of a sharp intake of breath. The guy was going to have a bruise.

Immediately, a hand was back snatching at Norcross's shoulder. "Hey, pal, don't fucking . . ."

Judge Norcross leaned down into Agent McNair's face. "Your paperwork, Ms. McNair, before we go one step further here."

A fifth agent walked up, grunting as he stepped up over the curb—a gray-haired man, older and heavyset. His voice was authoritative.

"And who, if I might ask, are you, sir?"

The judge's heart was pounding, and there was a ferocious anger inside him. David Kamau was not going to suffer the indignity of being forced down onto the sidewalk. Mungai, meanwhile, was pressing in at the edge of the group, calling out. "Reverend Kamau has a valid . . ."

Norcross caught a glimpse of the agent in the yellow jacket putting a hand on Mungai's chest and pushing him roughly. Mungai shot backward, arms pinwheeling. His glasses flew off, and he staggered two or three steps, falling heavily onto his back on the pavement.

Kamau was the calmest one in the group. "Please," he said. "There must be some mistake. I have my visa right here." He began to reach into his jacket pocket. When he did this, the blond agent immediately reached in and grabbed his wrist, hard. Norcross saw McNair sliding her hand up under the tail of her shirt, presumably reaching for her gun.

Norcross spoke urgently into Kamau's ear. "For God's sake, David, keep your hands visible."

"But I only wanted to—"

"Hold them up." Norcross demonstrated. "Like this."

The older agent came closer and spoke again, louder and directly to Norcross. "I'm going to ask you again, sir. Who are you and—"

Mungai called out hoarsely, "Reverend Kamau has a valid . . ." He was sitting on the sidewalk, propping himself with one hand and wiping the corner of his mouth. His face without his glasses looked pinched and vulnerable.

"My name is David Norcross. Not that it matters, but I happen to be a federal judge." He was breathing hard. "This man is a close friend of mine. If you have a warrant for him, I want to see it immediately."

The older agent stopped in his tracks and stared for a second. "Christ, you are Judge Norcross. I had a case before you a couple years ago in Springfield." He sighed and shook his head. "Oh boy. Show him the warrant, Brenda. Dan, let go of Mr. Kamau's arm."

Agent McNair pulled a wad of folded papers out from under her rugby shirt and reluctantly handed them to Norcross.

Mungai was getting onto his feet. "Reverend Kamau has a valid student visa. You have no right to interfere with his—"

The older agent looked irritated. "Well, sir, the State Department revoked that visa as of this morning. We need Mr. Kamau to come with us, right now." He dropped his voice. "Let's keep this friendly, okay?"

McNair resumed, machinelike, talking to Kamau. "Hold your arms straight out, please. A little higher. Do you have any weapons on you? Fingers spread, please."

A quick review of the papers told Norcross that the agents had authority. He would not be able to keep them from taking Kamau into custody.

Mungai spoke indignantly. "Weapons! Where is he supposed to have—"

Kamau looked over at him. "It's okay, Godfrey. They have to do this." A cluster of people was gathered in the doorway of Divinity Hall, looking on.

Mungai bent to retrieve his glasses from the sidewalk. He moved his mouth in a circle and spat on the grass. He must have bitten his tongue. Blood was running down his chin onto his shirt front.

McNair was feeling the front of Kamau's pants. "What's this in your pocket, sir?"

"Peppermints." Kamau's tone was calm but condescending. "Help yourself." It occurred to Norcross that he must have been through something like this before.

"Right. Arms out, just like that. Good. Don't move." McNair patted inside Kamau's jacket, retrieved his wallet, and handed it over her shoulder to the older agent, who began looking through it. She ran her hands over Kamau's chest area and around his waist.

Kamau stayed still, holding his arms out. "May I ask why they have revoked my visa?"

The older agent spoke absently. "We have no idea." He was rifling through Kamau's wallet.

There was a metallic sound as McNair retrieved a pair of handcuffs from around her waist. "I'm going to have to cuff you, sir. Standard procedure. Place your hands behind your back, please." Kamau complied, and a clicking noise followed. "Good. Thank you." McNair turned to Norcross. "May I have my papers back now, Judge?"

The blond agent was rubbing his side and glaring angrily at Norcross. Norcross ignored him. He handed the papers back to McNair and looked over at the older agent, clearly the supervisor. "I have a few questions."

"Gimme a sec here." The agent pulled a piece of paper out of Kamau's wallet, unfolded it, and took his time looking it over. Eventually, he refolded the document and put it back in the wallet. He shoved Kamau's wallet into his back pocket and reached out his hand to Norcross.

"Jeff Ackerman, Homeland Security Investigations Unit." Norcross shook his hand briefly. He knew it didn't hurt to be civil, but he noticed Godfrey Mungai giving him an ugly look, as though even talking to these people was an act of betrayal.

Ackerman slowly scratched the back of his neck. "Sorry to spoil everyone's evening here, Judge."

"Can you tell me more about what's going on?"

"Not really. All I know is that we have an administrative warrant to pull your friend in. That's it."

"Reverend Kamau has a valid visa. He's been at the Divinity School for months."

"Well, Judge, I'm afraid he doesn't have a valid visa anymore." He pulled out a very wrinkled handkerchief and blew his nose. "Just doing my job here."

"How are we supposed to find out what this is about?"

"Kamau's details will be on his NTA when he . . ."

"NTA?"

"Notice to Appear. The paperwork we use in a civil removal case." Ackerman looked around. "So this is Harvard." He frowned glumly. "And you're a federal judge. I suppose that means we're all going to get our asses sued."

"Where will you be taking him?"

"Enforcement and Removal Operations field office in Burlington. North of here, about a half hour—"

"I know where the field office is. Will Reverend Kamau be released after he is processed?" Norcross's hand brushed something, and he looked down to see that his suit jacket pocket, torn half off, was hanging down limply. How did that happen? His heart was beginning to slow down, but he still hadn't quite caught his breath.

"Maybe, but I doubt it. They'll probably keep him for now and bring him before an immigration judge in a few days. He can make his pitch for release then. Tell the truth, I have no idea how that works."

"I'm coming to Burlington."

"I'll let them know you're on the way." Ackerman looked on as McNair led Kamau over to the SUV. "I doubt it will make any difference, but if you really want to help this fella, Judge, I'd get him a good lawyer ASAP. Things can happen real fast in these situations."

"Easy does it, sir." McNair was placing her hand on top of Kamau's head as he ducked to enter the SUV.

He'd call Bill Treadwell from his car on the way to Burlington. Get him out of bed if necessary. Thank heaven they'd reconnected at Il Gallo Pazzo. Treadwell would rally his myrmidons at Harvard, and they would bury these people in lawyers, hopefully in the next twenty-four hours. Somebody, besides him, was going to rue this day.

Mungai called over to Ackerman. "Will he be safe?" His voice was almost pleading. "Excuse me, sir. Will he be safe?"

"Of course, he'll be safe." Ackerman sounded annoyed. "Why wouldn't he be safe?'

Norcross watched as Kamau settled into the back of the SUV, his white clerical collar standing out against the dark interior. He leaned forward to give Norcross a last look. Kamau's expression might have been frightened or angry or something else—Norcross couldn't tell—but then he fell back, dropped his chin, and closed his eyes. He was praying.

PART TWO

30

The clincher was when Uncle Tommy told Dominic they'd be taking the Fleetwood. Tommy and this buddy of his, a guy Dominic never saw before, had a little errand, and Tommy's usual driver was sick or something. It would be two, three hours at the most, an easy hundred bucks and maybe a chance to get in on something big.

Uncle Tommy's pal was skinny, had a goatee, and walked with a limp. He looked like a weasel. The guy didn't say anything, but when he glanced at Dominic, he took a drag on his cigarette and made a face. In return, Dominic shot him his best go-fuck-yourself look. Dominic was only nineteen, but six foot four and in shape. Sometimes, when Tommy needed to talk to people, he liked his nephew standing off to the side, out of earshot but close.

As he slid into the driver's seat, he heard Tommy say, "Toss the butt, okay? I don't want my car stunk up."

The heavy silence after the doors closed told Dominic that this wasn't going to be just another chin-wag. Something was up. Fine with him.

As he eased away from the curb, Dominic savored how sweetly the Cadillac moved. The giant V-8 engine, 390-horsepower, was pure brawn, and the car's two-and-a-half-ton frame rolled along like it was made out of Styrofoam. There might be one or two cars on the road he couldn't outrun, but not many.

He pushed the button to lower the driver's-side window, and the spring air touched his face. It was around eight thirty, just dusk, and people were out on the sidewalks of South Boston. The breeze along Dorchester Street carried the aroma of french fries. Dominic looked around, elbow out the window, hoping someone would notice him at the wheel. This was living.

Uncle Tommy and the weasel sat in back, which was how it usually worked. After a couple of blocks, Tommy tapped Dominic on the shoulder. "Close the window, please, Dom."

"How come? It's nice."

"Because it's bothering me." Tommy leaned back in his seat. "And we're going to want some privacy."

Dominic buzzed his window up. "Where to?"

"Take a right up ahead. I'll tell you where to stop."

A few minutes later, waiting for the light at East Broadway, he got another tap on the shoulder. His uncle's voice was behind his ear, soft but with an edge. "Gonna keep this simple, okay? In a little while now, we'll be meeting someone. He'll sit next to you. You don't say a word. Can you find the Pike?"

"Sure, it's—"

"Good. Once we do the pickup, take it west toward Framingham. Understand?"

"Sure, but—"

"Whatever happens, you just drive, eyes on the road."

"Okay, but—"

"It's green. Let's go."

In the decades that followed, Dominic recalled how people were standing around on the steps of Saint Brigid that evening, wiping their eyes and looking lost. The death of Bobby Kennedy, a few days earlier, had hit people hard; the churches were laying on extra services. Even the trees bending over the side streets looked mournful. The flag by the VFW drooped at half-staff. The scene darkened Dominic's mood. It should have been a warning.

Tommy pointed. "Pull over there at the Regency."

The street was nose-to-bumper with parked cars, but Dominic slipped in by a fireplug, and Tommy's pal jumped out. The Regency was a family restaurant, cafeteria-style for breakfast and lunch, sit-down for dinner, not pricey. Birthdays, his mom would take Dominic and his sisters there to celebrate.

When Uncle Tommy's friend came hobbling back, it was like he was a whole different person. He had a hand on this new guy's shoulder, and he was practically doubled over laughing. Dominic recognized their passenger right away, a Boston cop he'd seen cruising around City Point. He didn't know his real name, but he was heavyset and everyone called him Chunk. Chunk was grinning, and his face was glowing pink. He'd obviously just cracked a good joke and was feeling proud of himself.

The weasel gestured, still laughing. "Take the front, my friend. You need the legroom more than me."

When Chunk got in, he looked over at Dominic and gave him a light punch in the shoulder. "Hey there, buddy boy. How they hanging?"

From the back, the weasel snorted. "High and tight."

A new, very strong odor of beer wafted over Dominic's face. He didn't say anything.

Chunk swiveled to take Uncle Tommy's hand. "Mr. Gallagher. And how are you, my good sir?"

Tommy leaned forward and shook. "Couldn't be better. Glad we're getting all this straightened out."

"Bah. Simple misunderstanding." Chunk turned and settled into his seat as Dominic pulled out into the traffic. Two high school girls in halter tops standing on the corner brought the conversation to a stop. One of them looked familiar.

In the rearview, Dominic saw his uncle twisting around to stare back at them and heard him mutter under his breath, "Jesus, Joseph, and Mary, give me the strength to say no."

Everyone, even Dominic, laughed.

After a pause, Chunk began. "So, like I was telling Brian, I know how to keep my mouth shut, Mr. Gallagher. This BS about . . ."

Tommy leaned forward, gripping the back of Chunk's seat. "I'm going to interrupt, if you don't mind. We've got my nephew Dominic's virgin ears here. I promised my sister we'd keep them that way."

"Oh, oh, fine. Fine." Chunk waved his hands. The weasel gave another chuckle.

Dominic felt himself starting to blush, something he hated but couldn't control. He realized with disappointment that he was not riding tonight as muscle, but mostly as an excuse to shut Chunk up. The cop must know some things Tommy didn't want the weasel to hear.

"We can talk better when we get there, if that's all right with you."

"Fine. Fine." Shifting uncomfortably, Chunk looked over at Dominic. "So. Where'd you get a name like Dominic? Makes you sound like a wop."

Against orders, Dominic began to speak, "Hey, I don't need—"

"Must have taken a load of crap in high school." Chunk laughed, and the weasel started to say something.

Tommy broke in, not happy. "Nobody gets smart with Dominic more than once, Chunk." He leaned forward, putting his hand on the seat back. "His great-grandma, my grandmother, was half Italian. We all loved her." Tommy dropped his voice. "I assume that's all right with you?"

"Sure. No offense." He paused. "Didn't mean anything."

The atmosphere in the car took a minute to recover, then drifted toward the usual Red Sox gossip, and the miracle—or near miracle—year of 1967. Nineteen sixty-eight, in comparison, was shaping up to be a fizzle. Yastrzemski's production was way down and so on and so forth. Unlike most Bostonians, Dominic was not particularly a Red Sox fan. His sport was hockey, and his team was the Bruins.

The traffic thinned out after they got on the Pike and passed the Newton exit.

"Stay in the right lane, okay?" Tommy's voice was calm.

A silence fell over the group for several minutes, and it occurred to Dominic that maybe Chunk, who was slumped slightly forward and not moving, had either fallen asleep or passed out. Then, very suddenly, the man was thrashing around like a hooked tuna, twisting from side to side, arching his back, and kicking hard against the dash. His left arm lashed out and caught Dominic a ringing smack in the ear. Was the guy having a seizure? It was happening so fast and was so frightening that Dominic, his heart slamming away, lost control of the Caddy for a moment and veered onto the shoulder. Immediately, Dominic felt Tommy's warm hand on the side of his neck. "Just drive now, Dom. Eyes straight ahead."

Before long, Chunk stopped moving, and everything went quiet again. Uncle Tommy's hand withdrew, leaving a cool patch on the skin. Dominic heard the weasel grunt and say, "There." Glancing back, Dominic saw him sticking a piece of cord or wire into his pocket.

Chunk lay crumpled against the passenger door, eyes bulging horribly, mouth open, his face a sickening shade of bluish white. Dark blood ran down his chin and along his neck. Once more, the car drifted onto the verge. Dominic felt like he might black out or be sick.

Tommy's hand was on his shoulder again. "Deep breaths, Dom, okay? Deep breaths. Eyes on the road." Dominic heard his uncle expel a breath of his own. "It's all over now. Everything's okay."

Dominic kept his eyes fastened on the median strip. His heart would not stop hammering. After a while, he heard his uncle's voice in the back, talking to the weasel, low enough that he had to strain to hear it.

"I said to wait until we pulled over, for Christ's sake. If the kid hadn't kept his head—"

"I don't tell you how to do your business, Tommy. Don't tell me how to do mine."

"Big shot from Philly." There was a grunt as his uncle shifted position. "Should have handled this with my own crew."

The silence from the back seat after that was so heavy Dominic could feel it pressing against the back of his head.

Ten blurred minutes passed before they exited the Pike. Dominic followed his uncle's directions through several shadowy turns to a dark landfill, mounded with garbage. Night had settled in, and the headlights swept over a couple of beat-up warehouses. Tommy pointed Dominic down a winding gravel drive ending after several hundred yards at the foot of one of the trash piles, where Dominic could make out a grave-size hole already dug. Chunk was so heavy it took all three of them to tumble the corpse out and roll it into the hole. By then, Dominic was shaking so badly he had to go sit in the car while Tommy and the weasel took shovels out of the trunk to fill in the grave and spread trash over it.

When his uncle returned, he held out his hand. "Give me the keys, Dom. You can get in back now."

Dominic stepped out of the driver's seat into the warm night air unsteadily. "Was he . . . was he blabbing?"

Standing nearby, the weasel made a disgusted noise. His face glowed orange as he lit a cigarette.

"A lesson, Dom." Uncle Tommy held up a finger. "You don't give a man the push because he's talked. You do it because he might talk. You stay ahead of your problems."

The weasel limped up to Dominic. "Remember that, pally. You aren't going to see me again, ever, so I'm gonna give you another little bit of advice."

"Brian." Tommy sounded irritated. "The kid did fine."

"Let me say my piece, Tommy. You owe me that." He came close, leaning up into Dominic's space. "People also get smacked for making smart-ass faces. If it wasn't for my respect for your uncle, you'd be sucking dirt right now too." He nodded over at the hump of trash. "Plenty of room for two in there, and one less yap to worry about."

"Okay," Uncle Tommy said. "Time to go."

"Count your blessings, asshole."

Forty minutes later, Tommy dropped Dominic off at his mom's double-decker in Southie. Neither of them ever uttered another word about that evening. In 1996, after helping Dominic get his contracting business off the ground, Tommy Gallagher dropped dead from a heart attack during a birthday dinner at the Union Oyster House. If his uncle's support had been payback for the Framingham errand, Dominic never knew. Except as it reappeared in nightmares, that whole terrible evening just vanished, for more than fifty years.

PART THREE

31

The metallic snap of the opening door was like a starter's pistol, and Angie Phipps leaped up.

"All rise!" A hundred or more people rumbled to their feet. "All persons having anything to do before the Honorable David S. Norcross may draw near, give their attendance, and they shall be heard . . ."

When she'd first started as a fill-in courtroom deputy, Phipps had had to force herself to speak up. Now, banging it out came naturally, and she'd gotten to enjoy it. For thirty seconds, she was the woman in charge.

"God save the United States of America and this Honorable Court. The court is now in session. You may be seated."

The courtroom was crowded with potential jurors, reporters, and spectators—including friends and family of the victim. Two sketch artists sat squeezed into the front row of the gallery, working with their easels and chalk. Once, in a prior trial, a botched profile of Phipps, with a pointy nose and bad hair, had made it onto the six p.m. news. She'd looked like a witch.

The artists wouldn't miss Dominic O'Connell. He sat fifteen feet away, wearing a charcoal suit with a bright white, open-collared shirt—a big, silver-haired, broad-shouldered dude who towered over his attorney. The Dom's biggest problem at the moment was his face. The newspaper photos always showed him with a grin, but here in real life his expression was a lot different. He looked like he'd just come from shooting someone in the back of the head and was pondering his next victim. Most of the jurors would be ready to find him guilty just for looking like such a badass. Bye-bye, Dom.

In the pew directly behind the defendant, O'Connell's celebrity wife, Julie, stood out. She was only about medium height, but she held herself in a way that Phipps envied and admired, very elegant without looking snooty. Her outfit must have cost a ton, but it was not flashy, and her hair was perfect.

Two guys, one dark and one with coppery hair, sat on either side of her. The red-haired guy muttered something, and Julie gave a quick, distracted nod. The other man looked like Dracula on steroids. A couple of days ago, he'd intercepted Phipps coming out the clerk's office. He liked cars, he said, and he'd seen her driving her X-5. Was he trying—really badly—to flirt, or what? Now, his beady eyes were darting around the courtroom, watching everything.

"Good morning." The judge's chair squeaked as he took his seat.

Claudia Papadakis produced her automatic smile. "Good morning, Your Honor." Then she smoothed her hands over her butt and sat. With her American flag pin in her lapel, she wasn't exactly Phipps's type, but she was okay. Mike Patterson was with her. Tarbell, scribbling something, barely looked up.

"Call the case please, Ms. Phipps."

"Now before the court: *United States of America versus Dominic O'Connell*, criminal action number 21-10231-DSN."

Norcross launched into his standard preliminary instructions to the potential jurors. Phipps had heard it all many times now, and soon her mind was wandering. A call from her uncle Jack the night before had seriously pissed her off. Somehow, he'd found out that she was seeing Carl—the ATF guy, Jack called him—and he'd pretty much ordered her to dump him. When she'd asked him how he knew about Carl, he'd only answered, "I just know."

Too much was happening. The day before, Mike Patterson had hit her with some sharp questions about a call she'd made just before the Harvard bombing. She'd been freaking out about the IT jocks maybe coming up from D.C. to check out the Case Assignment Program, and she'd called Jack, which was dumb. It turned out Norcross had noticed her looking upset, but she'd told Patterson that she had no memory of any particular call. Her stonewalling wouldn't protect her for long. All Patterson had to do was pull her phone log.

Then there was the horrible murder of Sam Newbury and his girlfriend. The *Globe* said it was a robbery gone wrong, but it felt like something very bad was out there, coming closer. The different parts of her life, locked in their private rooms, were pushing to get out.

As Judge Norcross described the trial's daily schedule, Phipps tried to shove these thoughts down. She pulled the Jury List over and reviewed it again. Before court, she'd practiced pronouncing the names.

When Jack had demanded that she ditch Carl, she'd followed her new life strategy, stayed calm, and said okay. Plenty of alphas were always sniffing around her door, she said, ready for fun. She'd just latch on to someone else. This was not exactly true, of course—she liked Carl a lot, and she wasn't giving him up without a fight—but in her life she'd had to learn how to shave the truth sometimes. For better or worse, she'd gotten good at it.

Norcross was reaching the final segment of his remarks, emphasizing that the pool members, if selected as jurors, would not be able to discuss the case with anyone and would have to avoid reading or watching anything relating to it. In a couple of minutes, they would begin selecting the actual jury members from the pool, and Phipps would be stepping back into the spotlight. She took a sip of water and cleared her throat.

Phipps liked jurors. They tended to be decent folks, like her, just trying to get from one day to the next without stepping into a dog pile. Part of her job was to be the jurors' mother hen, and she was good at it. She was sympathetic when someone wanted to slip outside for a cigarette, needed a couple of Tylenol, or had an embarrassing problem with the toilet. Soon she'd be moving from being a floater into a permanent courtroom deputy slot, regularly assigned to one of the Boston judges. It would mean the end of her little arrangement with Uncle Jack, but it was time to bring that curtain down. Carl, she hoped, was going to be the new man in her life.

Judge Norcross came to a stop and leaned over her. She could almost feel his shadow on the back of her head.

"All right, Ms. Phipps, we'll begin now. Call our first juror please."

Phipps checked the list. "In seat number one, Carlos Torruella."

Judge Norcross took a swallow of water as Torruella crossed over to the far end of the jury box. A bout of vertigo had come over him as he'd bounded up the stairs onto the bench. It had passed quickly, but its lingering effect was making the room seem slightly off-kilter. He'd settle down in a minute.

Phipps rolled on. "In seat number two, Geoffrey Zaft." Zaft was a retired Smith College professor with wire-rim glasses and tufts of white hair over his temples. Papadakis leaned toward Patterson and muttered something. The government shed academics whenever possible, and Papadakis would definitely be using one of her peremptory challenges to shuffle this one out.

The past forty-eight hours had been rough on Norcross: the first night up late in Burlington trying to get Reverend Kamau out of detention, and the second with the Amherst police swarming around his house until nearly dawn. The lack of sleep was making his eyes feel grainy. It helped that, as Phipps rolled out the names of the jurors in seats three, four, and five, all he had to do was sit on his perch looking wise. His heart rate slowed down, and the room continued to return to normal.

Memories of the night at Burlington played around the edges of the judge's mind. The ICE officials had made him wait an hour and a half for only a few minutes with Kamau in the visitors' pen. They'd been instructed, they said, to hold their detainee until his hearing at the end of the week. Kamau had been grim-faced but calm. There was a toughness about his Kenyan friend that Norcross hadn't appreciated before. Everything was all right, Kamau said. He would be fine.

The attempt at reassurance was brave but unconvincing. People in immigration custody regularly got marched onto planes and flown off to remote locations with very little notice. Bill Treadwell, when

Norcross reached him, had immediately agreed to represent Kamau and try to head this off. Treadwell was disturbed at the detention of this perfectly innocent clergyman, but absolutely furious at ICE's violation of the hallowed grounds of Harvard University, particularly the Divinity School. His legal team was already in gear, sharpening their knives for the Friday hearing.

Norcross sighed and rubbed his left eye. Phipps continued to reel off names.

"In seat number six, Rita Novak."

Reviewing the Jury List, the judge noticed a problem with Ms. Novak. When she'd taken her seat, he addressed her.

"Ms. Novak, I'm sorry, the list we have indicates that you are married, but it does not give the employment status of your husband. May I ask what sort of work he does, if any?"

Novak was a nurse practitioner in her midthirties with curly brown hair, professionally dressed in black slacks and a green silk blouse. Now, Norcross saw her pleasant face close down. She looked tired and irritated.

"I don't have a husband, Your Honor."

This was a stupid error, the first time Norcross had ever bungled this.

"I'm sorry. I should have asked what sort of work your spouse does."

"She's an architect."

"Thank you. That is the last time I will make that mistake, I promise you."

Ms. Novak looked at him without changing expression.

Tomorrow, Norcross hoped, he would be more on his game. Last night, he had gotten to bed early, hoping to catch up on his sleep, but around two a.m. there'd been an urgent knock on the bedroom door. Monica was apologetic but very worked up, telling them she was sure she had seen a man down in the trees outside her window. Claire called 911, and Norcross took the trigger lock off the shotgun. An Amherst cruiser pulled up in less than three minutes, blue lights flashing, and called for backup. After a delay, the canine unit finally arrived and spent a long time combing the woods, finding no one.

Fate dealt gently with Judge Norcross after the Novak blunder, and the remaining jurors filed into the box smoothly. To his delight, only two asked to be excused. Even more surprisingly, neither Papadakis nor Tarbell exercised all their peremptory challenges. Both lawyers appeared satisfied after a few fill-ins with the group they'd ended up with: seven women and five men, and two males as alternates in case one of the main jurors was unable to sit through the trial. By midafternoon, Norcross had excused the rest of the jury pool, the courtroom was less crowded, and he instructed Phipps to place the panel under oath.

Phipps spoke up firmly. "Stand please and raise your right hand."

Even in his exhaustion Norcross found himself moved, as he always was, at this pivotal moment—these awkward strangers standing and holding up their hands, promising to do their best. All the books, all the struggles through the centuries, and this was what it came down to: twelve people ready to listen and decide, and him on the bench to help them. Justice in the flesh.

Phipps peeped down at a piece of paper in her hand and looked up, continuing in the same clear, steady tone.

"Do you and each of you solemnly swear that you will well and truly try the issues presented in the case between the government and the defendant, and render a true verdict therein, according to the law and the evidence, so help you God?"

The response was an ambiguous mumbling. Five or six managed to say something resembling the words *I do*. Others, holding their hands up, just looked to the side as though they weren't sure what they were supposed to say, nodding or shrugging uncertainly. This didn't matter. However they'd responded, the jurors were now under oath, and tomorrow *United States of America v. Dominic O'Connell* would be getting underway.

32

The next morning, Claudia Papadakis was seated at her table, waiting while Judge Norcross polled the jurors to confirm that they hadn't read anything about the case. Every media outlet had been bursting with coverage of the imminent trial—much of it distorted, biased, or wildly speculative. As Papadakis observed Norcross putting his questions to each of the jurors in turn, she noticed how firm he was, but also how steady and reassuring. She was relieved that he'd denied Tarbell's motion to recuse and glad to have him up there.

Judge Norcross was not brilliant, thank heaven, just good. Too much intellectual wattage could make a judge pushy and arrogant, constantly butting in to make sure everyone knew he or she was the smartest, most important person in the room. What she wanted in a judge, what most lawyers wanted, was something more modest, like Norcross: reasonably intelligent, well prepared, and not crazy.

When Norcross was satisfied with the jurors' answers, he emphasized the transition by folding his hands on the bench, smiling, and leaning toward the jury box.

"Before we get started here, I have one piece of good news for you. Tomorrow, as you know, is Friday and you can sleep late." The jurors looked at one another, exchanging happy looks. "I have another matter to attend to, and so we will not be getting started until eleven. No need to speculate about that, but please don't forget. If you show up at nine, bring a book because you'll have a bit of a wait."

Norcross raised his voice. "Okay. We are ready now to move to the first stage of the proceeding. As I told you, this is the time for the government to present its opening. Feel free to raise your hand if you have trouble hearing or if you are having any other problem." He nodded. "Ms. Papadakis, the floor is yours."

Papadakis walked over to the portable lectern she'd placed in front of the jury box, not hurrying, giving the jurors plenty of time to shift their attention to her. She carefully set her yellow pad and a file of photographs in place and stepped to the side of the lectern to present herself face-on—creating, she hoped, an image of unguarded candor. Then she clasped her hands in front of her and began.

"May it please the court, Madam Foreperson, ladies and gentlemen of the jury. They say that the wheels of justice grind slowly. In this case, as you will learn, the wheels of justice have taken more than fifty years to finally catch up with a cold-blooded murderer." She held up an enlarged black-and-white photograph of a man in a police uniform surrounded by children. Next to him was a slender woman with long dark hair, obviously the officer's wife, beaming and holding an infant.

"On June 8, 1968, this man . . ." She stepped toward the jury, pointed to the photograph, and pivoted slowly, making sure everyone could see the victim's face. "Officer Charles Scanlon, a nineteen-year veteran of the Boston Police Department and the father of eight, stepped into a white Cadillac outside the Regency restaurant on East Broadway in South Boston and was never seen alive again." She turned and gestured toward a group of men and women seated in the front two rows of the gallery. "Officer Scanlon's children, his brothers and sisters, all his loved ones spent the following five decades with that awful mystery hanging over them. His wife, Bernadette, the woman here in the picture with the baby"—she pointed again—"died four years ago never knowing what happened to her husband."

Papadakis took a moment to put the photograph back on the lectern. During the preparations for trial, she'd grown close to the

Scanlon family and could name every child in the picture. She paused now to let the jury take them in. The silence in the courtroom had an eloquence beyond words.

"About a year ago, Charles Scanlon's surviving family members finally learned the terrible truth. Shortly after Officer Scanlon stepped into that white Cadillac on that June night, he was strangled to death. Yes . . ." She responded to the disturbed expressions of several jurors. "Yes, horrible. This act of murder was so violent, in fact, that Officer Scanlon's windpipe was crushed like an egg, and two of his cervical vertebrae—these are the small bones in your neck, right here . . ."—Papadakis reached around to the base of her skull—"cracked. Afterward, his murderers drove the body to Framingham and dumped it into a hole they'd dug ahead of time. They filled up the hole, covered their tracks, and went on with their lives, confident that nobody would ever know of Officer Scanlon's fate."

Papadakis paused again and gazed down at the floor. Then she looked up and spoke, carefully emphasizing each word.

"In this trial, the government will prove to each and every one of you beyond a reasonable doubt, beyond any doubt, who Charles Scanlon's murderers were. You will learn that the driver of that white Cadillac, one of the architects of Charles Scanlon's murder, the man who helped dig the hole and fill it up, is sitting right here in this courtroom, at this very moment. And that man . . ." She took a step back, turned, and pointed, raising her voice. "That man is the defendant, Dominic O'Connell." She drove her point home with a second jab. "There he sits."

O'Connell reacted just as Papadakis hoped he would. He pulled in his chin, bless his heart, and glowered at her, looking like a B-movie gangster. His two flunkies, sitting behind him, heightened the effect, mirroring his expression. She sniffed contemptuously and turned her back on them, dropping in a pause before shifting from her preamble.

"Ladies and gentlemen, good morning." Four jurors nodded and murmured in return; others were flicking nervous glances over at the defendant. No mistakes so far. She hadn't overdone it. "As the judge has told you, my name is Claudia Papadakis, and it is my honor and privilege to represent the United States of America this morning in the trial of the defendant, Dominic O'Connell."

Her outline for the next portion of her opening was routine. Although the heart of her case was Scanlon's murder, the technical charge arose under the federal Racketeer Influenced and Corrupt Organizations Act, known as RICO, and she needed to explain what that meant. She kept it simple: Tommy Gallagher ran an illegal racketeering organization, concentrating on gambling, extortion, loan sharking, and bribery. An FBI expert would describe the structure and operation of Gallagher's mob in detail. Two other witnesses would testify that Dominic O'Connell, Gallagher's nephew, had worked during the sixties and seventies as one of his uncle's enforcers. The government, Papadakis told the jury, would prove, first, that Gallagher ordered Scanlon's murder to further and protect the interests of his corrupt organization and, second, that O'Connell helped carry out that order—just like in the Mafia movies everyone had seen.

These intense minutes were what Papadakis had trained for, what she'd wanted to do since college—perhaps, in some ways, what she'd wanted to do for her whole life. Her mind was entirely focused on the sequence of her words and their impact on the jurors.

"I will be calling as the government's primary witness a man by the name of Brian Shaughnessy. As you will learn, Mr. Shaughnessy is suffering from terminal cancer. He is nearing the end of his life. You will also learn that this life, Mr. Shaughnessy's life, has been utterly despicable. He will admit to you that he lived a substantial portion of his years as a professional murderer." Again, the eyes of several jurors widened. "That's right, a man who killed people for money. A year and a half ago, he was released on parole after serving a long prison sentence for murders he committed in Pennsylvania and New Jersey."

Papadakis took a moment to look down at her yellow pad and collect herself. Brian Shaughnessy was a decrepit old man, a convict, coming to court to describe events occurring more than fifty years ago. She knew very well that he had a motive to embroider his story. Despite this, after many hours debriefing him, she was convinced that the core of what Shaughnessy said was true. She was aware that certain details—to her, minor details—were shaky, but she'd made her peace with that. Shaughnessy was what she had. If there was to be justice for Charles Scanlon and for the Scanlon family, she had to convince the jury to believe him. She squared her shoulders, lifted her chin, and pushed off confidently.

"Brian Shaughnessy was the man Dominic O'Connell and Tommy Gallagher brought up from Philadelphia in 1968 to help them with the murder of Officer Scanlon. Mr. Shaughnessy will tell you frankly that he hopes his truthful testimony in this courtroom will benefit his nephew James, who is facing certain separate criminal charges. I submit to you that there is nothing unusual or sinister about this, especially when the government's evidence includes strong corroboration for everything Brian Shaughnessy will say."

Papadakis folded her hands on the lectern and let her eyes travel over the faces of the jurors. "Let me outline for you exactly what Mr. Shaughnessy's testimony will be. He will tell you that sometime in late May of 1968 he was contacted by Tommy Gallagher, who said he had a job for him. Gallagher told him that he was worried about a certain Boston police officer, nicknamed 'Chunk,' who was what Gallagher called 'a talker.' Gallagher was afraid that federal investigators might sniff Chunk Scanlon out and, if they pressured him, Scanlon might reveal certain damaging information about Gallagher's criminal enterprise. Gallagher wanted this potential problem eliminated. A few days after their phone call, Shaughnessy came to Boston to meet with Gallagher and"—she turned and pointed—"that man, the defendant Dominic O'Connell."

Papadakis was pleased to see that O'Connell had spread his big arms forward onto the table and was still wearing his surly face. Sandy Tarbell was leaning back in his chair, hands clasped behind his head, staring at the ceiling with a bored expression. This pleased Papadakis too. Tarbell's ho-hum performance was an obvious act. The jury would never buy it.

"The defendant arranged a get-together with Officer Scanlon in a South Boston bar to introduce Shaughnessy to his target. Everyone had a few beers and a few laughs. Shaughnessy worked hard, he will tell you, to gain Scanlon's confidence. After their pub night, Brian Shaughnessy went back to Philadelphia. He will tell you that a week later, he got a call from . . ." She gestured over her shoulder. "Once more, the defendant Dominic O'Connell. He described to Shaughnessy how he and his uncle had found a spot to dispose of the body. They'd dug the hole. The trap was set. It was time."

Papadakis stopped to take a sip of water from the plastic cup on the edge of the podium. She needed to clear her throat, and she wanted the tension to build. The courtroom had fallen into a deep silence. The jury was with her.

"On June 8, 1968, Tommy Gallagher, Brian Shaughnessy, and the defendant picked up Scanlon at the Regency restaurant in South Boston, supposedly to take him to a dinner with some associates in Framingham. O'Connell was behind the wheel as they drove west on the Pike, with Scanlon in the front passenger seat and Shaughnessy directly behind him in the back next to Gallagher. Not long after they cleared Route 128, Shaughnessy slipped a wire cord over Scanlon's head and wrenched it back. Scanlon was a big man, and Shaughnessy will describe how his victim resisted, grabbing back with both hands, fighting for his life, like this." Papadakis bent her head down reached up behind her head. "Shaughnessy, who you will see is rather small, will tell you how he was yanked off balance and was losing his grip until Dominic O'Connell grabbed a wrench at his feet and struck Scanlon in the forehead, swinging his arm like this . . ." Papadakis demonstrated. "Stunning him, so that Shaughnessy could finish the job. After that, the trip to the abandoned landfill and the disposal of the body did not take long. Officer Scanlon's grave was waiting. Dominic O'Connell had made sure of that. He helped roll Scanlon's body out of the car, dump it into the hole, and fill the ugly grave, using shovels he'd stored in the trunk."

O'Connell was seated behind Papadakis, so of course she could not see him. What she could see were the faces of the jurors as their eyes darted over her shoulder toward the defendant. Their expressions were everything she could hope for. It was a good moment for a short detour into the applicable law.

"Now, as you just heard, Brian Shaughnessy will not be testifying that the defendant was the one who put the wire around Officer Scanlon's throat. The government is not required to show that. Judge Norcross will instruct you that if Dominic O'Connell joined the conspiracy to murder Charles Scanlon and knowingly performed some act in furtherance of it—such as driving the car, striking the victim, or helping dispose of the body—then he is as guilty of Officer Scanlon's murder as he would be if he'd physically strangled him."

Papadakis flipped a page of her yellow pad over and cleared her throat, marking a transition. "Of course, Brian Shaughnessy will not be the government's only witness. As I told you a few minutes ago, other witnesses will corroborate his testimony in every detail. I know I've gone on for a while, but I'm hoping you will be patient with me for just a little longer while I summarize this powerful additional evidence." She smiled and held up a finger, raising her eyebrows. "Then I promise to shut up." Almost all the jurors returned her smile in some way—by nodding, smiling back, or shifting their posture.

"The first corroborating witness is special. Her name is Loreen Laplante, and I suggest that you will find her an open, honest, entirely credible person. On June 8, 1968, Loreen was seventeen, and she had a giant crush on Dominic O'Connell, who was two years older. She will testify that she saw her idol driving down East Broadway that night behind the wheel of a big white Cadillac with two men in the back seat. She saw him stop at the Regency. She witnessed Brian Shaughnessy going in and bringing Officer Scanlon out, and she recounted what she saw in her teenage diary later that night. By great good fortune, she kept that diary, and we will be placing it into evidence for your review. Two other eyewitnesses at the restaurant will also back up Brian Shaughnessy and Ms. Laplante, and a forensic pathologist will confirm that the victim's injuries were exactly consistent with Brian Shaughnessy's description of the murder. Let me give you a preview of what these folks will say."

Compared to the earlier fireworks, this portion of Papadakis's opening was rather flat. Not far along, she noticed Jurors Two and Six glancing up at the clock and Juror Nine crossing her legs and sighing. Not wanting to risk losing the panel's attention, she skipped two sections of her outline and quickly summarized the most important details in the pathologist's report. Norcross had given counsel a half hour for their openings, a short time given all she'd had to cover, and it was time to wrap up. To emphasize the shift to her conclusion, Papadakis braced her hands on the lectern and leaned toward the jury.

"At the end of this trial, after you have heard all the evidence, I will have an opportunity to speak to you again. I submit to you that when I do, the story of what happened to Charles Scanlon, and exactly what this defendant did, will be clear to you. All the pieces will fit. You will have no reasonable doubt, no doubt of any kind, about Dominic O'Connell's responsibility for the terrible crime he is charged with. At that time, I will ask you to give the Scanlon family what they have been waiting for, for over fifty years: justice. I will be asking you to return a verdict of guilty against the defendant Dominic O'Connell on the charge of murdering Officer Charles Scanlon in aid of a racketeering enterprise. Thank you."

When Papadakis turned to resume her seat, she noticed one of O'Connell's stooges, the dark-haired one, giving her a look. Mike Patterson had shifted his chair around and was giving it right back at him.

33

Tarbell had been seething all through the final portion of Papadakis's opening. As soon as Phipps escorted the jury out of the
courtroom, he leaped up and exploded with a ferocious attack on her
reference to the Laplante diary, which he said was clearly inadmis-
sible. Even mentioning it, he argued, constituted gross prosecutorial
misconduct and grounds for a dismissal or mistrial.

Judge Norcross seemed unimpressed. "Really, Mr. Tarbell, I don't
follow you."

"Well, Your Honor, let me see if I can make myself clear." Tarbell's performance after that was the sort of aggressive courtroom
oratory he loved. The two overlapping evidentiary rules—Rule 803,
which governed "past recollection recorded" and Rule 801, which
defined "prior consistent statements"—formed a doctrinal labyrinth,
with reversible error lurking at every bend. He was about a minute
into his argument, weaving it together pretty well he thought, when
Norcross began shaking his head. Half a minute later, he interrupted.

"Nope. Nope. Nope." Norcross wrote something on his pad. "I'm
pretty familiar with these rules, Mr. Tarbell, and I see no problem
at this point. If something comes up during the trial, you can raise

your objection again. If at that time you persuade me, which frankly seems unlikely, I can instruct the jury to disregard the reference to the diary. Your client will suffer no prejudice. For now, your motion's denied."

"But by then, Your Honor, it will be too late. The jury will have . . ."

Ms. Papadakis stood and broke in. "May I be . . ."

"Not necessary. You have my ruling. Let's keep things in motion, okay?" The side door, the one used by the jury, opened and Phipps leaned in. Norcross looked over at her, and she nodded her head. "I see that the jury is about ready to get back to work. Unless someone needs a break, I'd like to move right on to the defense opening. Any problem with that?"

"If I can't change your mind . . ." Tarbell shook his head. "I suppose not. I'm ready to go." He sat down and took a breath to steady himself. Norcross's ruling was disappointing, but it had a positive side. The Laplante diary presented just the sort of law-schoolish evidentiary conundrum that might catch hold of the fussy mind of an appellate judge. A year from now, if O'Connell were found guilty, Norcross's decision to let the diary in just might get the conviction reversed and give O'Connell a new trial. The same was true of Norcross's decision not to recuse himself. Planting firecrackers like these in the trial record was crucial, and banging heads with Norcross had gotten him pumped up for his opening. He noticed his knee was jiggling again, and he placed his hand on it. He had to stay calm.

Julie's voice wafted in from behind Tarbell. "Dom." She was leaning over the railing. "I need to slip away for a minute." Her voice was a stage whisper.

O'Connell glanced around and looked irritated. "Couldn't you have gone ten minutes ago, when he . . ."

Julie eyes widened, and she responded tartly, "I didn't need to go then." As she made her way out of the courtroom, Tarbell noticed two women behind her sharing a smile.

The delay after this, while they waited for the jury to be herded in, was torture for Tarbell. Distractions he really didn't need kept creeping into his mind. He was still sure that something backhanded was going on with his trial. Newbury, the luckless bastard, had more than hinted at some big-firm black magic when he gave him the news about Tony Helms's terminal cancer and then handed him Jack Taylor's card. One of Tarbell's sources had recently passed on some disturbing rumors about Taylor. The guy was definitely someone to stay away from. It had been a mistake to connect Graham to Taylor, a stupid impulse to stop his brother's whining. The filing date for *Cimarron* must be getting close, and he hadn't heard a peep from Graham about any lunch.

Julie returned before long and slipped into her seat behind them. She and O'Connell exchanged brief nods. O'Connell apparently was too on edge to smile. Tarbell reminded himself to do something about that. His client looked guilty as hell.

"All rise."

The sound of the courtroom door opening and the rustling reentry of the jurors was a relief. Tarbell rocked forward on his toes, getting ready. Showtime.

Norcross gazed down, smiling as though he didn't have a care in the world. "Okay, welcome back. We're ready to resume." His eyes swept from Papadakis to Tarbell. "If you recall, before we broke, you heard the opening statement for the government from Ms. Papadakis. Now, it is the defense's turn. Mr. Tarbell, the floor is yours."

As Tarbell walked to the podium, he recited to himself Aaron Burr's famous axiom: "Law is whatever is boldly asserted and plausibly maintained." The statement was only sort of true, but its cynicism inspired him, and it had become his ritual incantation and secret motto.

He glanced back over his shoulder and nodded curtly to Judge Norcross. "If it please the court . . ." Then he turned to the jury. "Ladies and gentlemen of the jury, I am standing before you right now in a very uncomfortable position. It's discourteous to call people names, and we all try to avoid it." Tarbell looked up at the ceiling for two beats before resuming with a lowered voice. "But, at this important moment—you might say, sacred moment—when so much is at stake, I have no choice, so I am going to ask you to forgive my discourtesy. If you remember only one thing, one word, from what I say in this next half hour, please remember this." His volume increased. "The government's entire case rests on one witness, a professional

killer named Brian Shaughnessy, and Brian Shaughnessy is a liar."
He paused to let his eyes brush over the jurors' faces before repeating. "A bone-deep, shameless liar." Three long seconds passed before
Tarbell nodded, as though confirming the fact to himself. "A lifelong, *habitual* liar.

"No one knows how many people Brian Shaughnessy has killed—
certainly not Ms. Papadakis, and maybe not even Brian Shaughnessy
himself anymore—but what we *do* know, and what Ms. Papadakis
can't dispute, is that Brian Shaughnessy's whole life, except when
he's been in prison, has been nothing but nonstop violence and nonstop lies. Just one lie after another. Now, he's come to this court to
offer you the biggest lie of all, bent on destroying an innocent man to
help his drug-dealing nephew." He looked at the ground for a beat
of two, to let this sink in.

"In this trial, Brian Shaughnessy's lying will enter a whole new
dimension, because Brian Shaughnessy will be sitting in that witness
box . . ." Tarbell pointed to the oak enclosure on the other side of the
courtroom. "Knowing that he can lie with *complete* impunity, getting
an absolute free ride. He will know that he runs no risk whatsoever
of any consequences for his lies. And this fact requires me to touch
on another difficult topic. The fact is, Brian Shaughnessy is very
close to death, ladies and gentlemen. The evidence will show that by
the end of this year, or earlier, it is likely that Brian Shaughnessy will
no longer be with us on this earth. The wheels of justice that Ms.
Papadakis talked so much about are never going to catch up to Brian
Shaughnessy for his murder of Charles Scanlon or for the perjury he
will be committing in this very courtroom. In this trial, he literally
has nothing, not one single thing, to lose by lying."

A faint, liquid noise broke in from behind Tarbell. The eyes
of several of the jurors twitched up toward it, and Tarbell glanced
around to see what it was. Judge Norcross was up on the bench
blandly pouring himself a cup of water. Tarbell knew that Norcross
wasn't doing this on purpose. He wasn't the shithead type of judge
who would deliberately puncture a lawyer's attempt at a moment
of drama. Norcross was probably just thirsty and, like most judges,
intermittently oblivious to the huge impact on a jury of every little
thing he did.

The minor distraction was maddening, but Tarbell quickly found a way to take advantage of it. He turned to face the jury, raised his voice, and, smiling a little, gestured over his shoulder toward Norcross. "And, as Judge Norcross will instruct you, in order to obtain a conviction, the government at this trial has to convince you, beyond a reasonable doubt—*beyond* a reasonable doubt—that Brian Shaughnessy is telling the truth, the whole truth, and nothing but the truth before you here in this courtroom." Tarbell looked back again, and to his delight, Norcross set his pitcher down and rewarded him with a slight affirming nod—not much, but enough for the jurors to notice.

Turning back to the podium, Tarbell leaned forward and raised his voice. "Beyond a reasonable doubt, ladies and gentlemen. Not maybe. Not likely. Not even probably, but *beyond* a reasonable doubt, as Judge Norcross himself will tell you. If the government doesn't carry that burden, if you don't absolutely and entirely believe the lifelong liar and professional hit man Brian Shaughnessy, then your verdict must be not guilty." Tarbell paused and dropped into a conversational tone, taking a half step back. "Just those *two* facts . . ." He held up two fingers and surveyed the jurors. "Brian Shaughnessy's complete lack of credibility—his lifelong career as a murderer and liar—and the government's burden to prove my client's guilt *beyond* a reasonable doubt will make your job in this trial very, very easy. You must acquit Dominic O'Connell of the false charge against him. You must find him not guilty, which is exactly what he is."

Tarbell stepped to the side of the podium and ran his hand through his hair. "As you know, my name is Sandy Tarbell." He bowed slightly and placed his hand on his chest. "And I represent, proudly represent . . ." He turned and nodded toward his client. "The defendant Dominic O'Connell. Dominic had to sit there, pinned in his chair, while Ms. Papadakis had such a good time wagging her fingers at him, so let's give you a good look at him. Stand up, please, Dom."

This was a risky move—Tarbell deliberately hadn't warned his client—but it worked. Surprised in the sudden, full glare of the jurors' eyes, O'Connell rose awkwardly, and his arrogant expression broke. For a few seconds, he just looked like an elderly man getting stared at, uncertain how to arrange his face, vulnerable. For all his charisma—his height, his silver hair, and his well-tailored suit—he briefly became an ordinary human being that at least some of the jurors might identify with.

"Sitting behind Dominic is his wife, Julie, who will be testifying. Would you stand, too, please, Julie?"

Julie, of course, nailed it. She'd always managed to be beautiful in the best way, which was by never trying too hard. In a flicker of memory, Tarbell recalled how it felt to hold Julie's hand, long ago, when they were teenagers. Standing there in the courtroom, without over-smiling, Julie O'Connell looked deeply sympathetic, and her quick, loving glance at her husband was the perfect capper. It was still a long shot, but they might just have a chance here.

"Thanks. You guys can sit down now." He paused to let the moment sink in, and then he picked up with the next segment of his opening.

"Okay, before I get to Mr. Shaughnessy, the totally unreliable murderer the government will be basing its whole case on, let me tick off for you the evidence that you'd typically expect in a case like this, but which the government *won't* be presenting, because it doesn't exist. First, there will be no forensic evidence: no fingerprints, no photographs, no bloodstains, no DNA—nothing at all of that kind. Second, despite Ms. Papadakis's statement about Dominic being his uncle's so-called enforcer . . ." Tarbell held up air quotes. "A scary-sounding word that in this case means exactly nothing, there will be no evidence that Dominic, even way back more than fifty years ago, at age nineteen, ever enforced *anything*. No one will be testifying that he ever actually hurt *anyone* or ever actually said *anything* to threaten *anyone* in this fantasy role the government has dreamed up for him. You'd think that Dominic O'Connell would have gotten into trouble at least once over the past fifty years if he were the heartless killer Ms. Papadakis says he was. He's the opposite. We will bring in a slew of witnesses—and I apologize for this ahead of time, because it will be a little boring and repetitious—who will corroborate Dominic's reputation for honesty in his community. Yes, he was a tough kid, who grew up in a tough neighborhood and worked hard in a tough business, becoming successful and giving so much back to Boston, the city he loves. He can be gruff, he has a temper, and he has a salty way of talking sometimes. But that's all—and that, ladies and gentlemen, is no crime."

Tarbell moved on, covering the next section of his opening, the slicing and dicing of Brian Shaughnessy, more quickly than he would have preferred. Recounting the man's record—including the uncharged crime he'd now confessed to—and unwrapping the cynical plea bargain the government was giving Shaughnessy's nephew took time. Norcross's insistence that the lawyers keep their openings to thirty minutes, in a high-stakes trial like this, was a travesty. Judge Helms would have given them at least an hour, and she would have been tolerant if they'd run over.

As compressed as his remarks were, Tarbell could see from the jurors' faces that he had gotten at least some of them thinking. That was the best he could hope for at this stage. It only took one holdout to hang the jury, and, with Shaughnessy so sick, a mistrial was as good as an acquittal. Shaughnessy would be deep in his grave before Papadakis got a second shot.

Running his hand through his hair again, Tarbell moved on to the final portion of his opening.

"Now, last of all, let me talk for just a minute about this so-called corroborating evidence, this snake oil that the government is trying to sell you." He nodded back at Papadakis. "The government says that they have witnesses who will corroborate Shaughnessy's fairy tale, supposedly in every detail. Well, I'll let you in on something. What they really have, and *all* they have, is three people who will say that they saw Dominic O'Connell some evening over fifty years ago, maybe June eighth, maybe some other day, at the Regency restaurant or its immediate area.

"There's a simple explanation for this. Dominic in fact *was* at the Regency around then. The evidence will show that he was there pretty regularly in those days. It isn't surprising in the least that people saw him at that restaurant, and it proves exactly nothing.

"Let's start by reviewing the timeline. Robert Kennedy was shot in the kitchen of the Ambassador Hotel in Los Angeles, California, a little after midnight on June 5, 1968, and he died on June sixth, breaking the hearts of just about everyone in Boston. Two days later, on June eighth, there were Catholic masses all over the country in remembrance of him. Some of you may be old enough to recall, or may have heard from your parents or grandparents, how traumatic this assassination was for the country.

"I will call two witnesses, Colleen O'Connell and Mary Conroy, who will take that witness stand . . ." Tarbell pointed. "Right there. And testify that the two of them, along with their now deceased mother and their brother, the defendant Dominic O'Connell, attended an evening mass at Saint Brigid's in South Boston on June eighth to offer prayers for the Kennedy family. Afterward, they went to the Regency for dinner. They were at the restaurant for a little over an hour, returned home, and spent the rest of the evening together in their mother's living room, watching television and grieving with the rest of the nation. The notion that Dominic, who was nineteen years old . . ." He paused and tapped the syllables out on the podium. "*Nineteen years old.* Was off somewhere during this time helping strangle a Boston police officer, is—excuse me—a revolting lie, a total fabrication straight out of the Brian Shaughnessy playbook. In fact, Dominic O'Connell didn't know Brian Shaughnessy from the man in the moon. He's never even met him."

Tarbell took two steps to the side of the podium and folded his hands in front of him. "Now, it is true, and I'm sure you will be hearing from the government not once, not twice, but over and over, that Colleen and Mary are Dominic's sisters and that they love their brother very much. They certainly won't deny that. That's not a sin. But the government, I expect, will argue based on this that these two women are not credible, that you should just reject, just throw away, what they say.

"All I can ask you to do is listen to them. Observe them. Weigh their credibility. Ask yourselves whether they would come here and perjure themselves. Ask yourselves whether that is likely. Please remember that after fifty years it would be virtually impossible for anyone in Dominic's position to locate witnesses other than people, like family, who've been close to him continuously, all this time. Colleen and Mary are all Dominic has, and all *anyone* facing a false charge like this today would have to show their innocence."

Tarbell moved back to the podium and held out his hands. "And, as you listen to their testimony, please ask yourself this. Is it more likely that Mary and Colleen are coming to this court and deliberately lying, committing a felony where, unlike Brian Shaughnessy, they could end up in prison? Or is it more likely that the government's supposedly corroborating witnesses are simply misremembering, getting mixed up, about something that happened over five decades ago?" Tarbell paused and grabbed a clump of hair at the side of his head. "When I'd barely started kindergarten and this hair was a glossy black. Back before many of us . . ." He looked over his shoulder. "Back even before His Honor himself, I believe, had been born."

This was another risky move, but it paid off. Norcross raised his eyebrows and nodded, agreeing with him, unoffended. It gave him a good moment to wrap up.

"In conclusion, I ask you to remember what I said a few minutes ago about the government's burden. I submit that you will find Mary's and Colleen's testimony perfectly truthful. But . . ." Tarbell held up a finger. "You don't need to. If you find yourself even *wondering* about Mary's and Colleen's testimony, if you're not *sure* whether it's true or not true, if you think that perhaps it *might* be true, if you think it could *possibly* be true, then that's a reasonable doubt, ladies and gentlemen, and you must return a verdict of not guilty.

"At the end of the trial, as Ms. Papadakis said, we will both be returning to speak to you again. At that time, I submit, it will be crystal clear to all of you that the government has failed to carry its burden. It has failed to prove Dominic O'Connell guilty *beyond* a reasonable doubt. Following His Honor's instructions, you will have no choice but to put an end to the nightmare that Dominic and Julie O'Connell have been living through for so long now. You will, with complete confidence in the justice of your decision, vindicate an innocent man and return a verdict of not guilty. Thank you."

34

Angie Phipps slipped out of bed early, leaving Carl Alberti sleeping, and moved as quietly as she could into the hallway, closing the door behind her. As she crossed the living room, she noticed a light rain speckling the windows. Through the trees, on the far side of Memorial Drive, the Charles River lay dead still under the silver morning light. A single car whispered by.

Phipps went into the half bath off the apartment's foyer, where she could talk without disturbing Carl, and called in a recorded message for the *O'Connell* jurors, reminding them that the trial would be starting today at eleven instead of nine. Judge Norcross had mentioned in court that he would be tied up this morning, but it never hurt to pound the nail home. The extra two hours were a treasured gift for her. She could make French toast for Carl, and they could have a relaxed morning. Just the thought of watching him chew made her smile.

She washed her face, slipped on her bathrobe, and was moving toward the kitchen when her phone gave a muted hum. The caller ID told her it was her uncle Jack, and Phipps's stomach plunged. Had Jack somehow learned that she was enjoying a forbidden sleepover with Carl? He always seemed to know everything.

She let the phone ring four times, working hard to fabricate a convincing lie, then answered, half whispering. "H-Hello?"

"It's Jack. Speak up, for Christ's sake. I can barely hear you."

"You woke me up. What's going on?" She faked a yawn. "I'm still in bed."

"Sorry. I wanted to catch you before work. Give you some good news."

"'Kay."

"We've got a new client."

Phipps didn't say anything. She'd been dreading this moment, but she'd assumed she'd have more time to prepare herself. The realization of where she was now—suddenly on the edge of a cliff, looking way, way down, with no warning—made her almost woozy. She took a seat on one of the tall chairs at her kitchen island. The rain was coming on a little harder, making shiny rivulets down the glass. She had to be a warrior. She had to be absolutely clear.

Jack was going on. "So, write this down, the case is *Danforth v. Cimarron Systems*. Plaintiffs' lawyers are out of California. It's being filed today or tomorrow, and they want it drawn to Helms, which is why I'm calling you this early."

"Judge Helms? Again?"

"You'll be getting another bank transfer next week. Congratulations."

"We just used Helms for *O'Connell*."

"It's only the second time this year. Nobody will—"

"It's too risky, Jack, with everything that's happening. It's—"

"Come on. Don't go all virginal on me." Jack waited and when she remained silent, he added, "After this one, we'll take a nice long break."

There was only one way to do this. Phipps blurted out, louder than necessary. "Jack, no."

"Excuse me?"

"I'm done. I-I don't want to do this anymore." She set the phone on the counter, faceup, and wiped the palm of her hand on her thigh. Jack's tinny voice rose up to her—not a person. A Martian.

"The fuck you talking about?"

Phipps leaned over the counter, not touching the phone. "I said I'm not doing this anymore. I'm all done."

"You sound funny. Are you recording me?"

"No, what I'm saying is—"

"You better not be."

She picked up. "I set the phone down. I'm putting on my bathrobe, okay?" She nodded, encouraging herself. "What I'm telling you is I'm not doing this anymore. I'm finished."

"That's not an option, Angie." Jack's voice went quiet. "It really isn't."

"I don't care. I'm done." A heavy blank followed on the other end of the line. "Okay. I'm hanging up now, Jack. I really have nothing else to say."

"Listen to me, Angie."

"I'm just not going to—"

"Goddammit, Angie!" He burst out so loud that she held the phone away from her ear. "Just listen to me for a second, will you?"

"A second, Jack, and that's it."

"You remember what happened to your pal Armstrong? And Newbury? Just the other night?"

"What about them?" This was everything she feared. She'd struggled so hard to keep herself convinced that what happened to Warren had nothing to do with any of this.

"I'm just telling you that we've got a dangerous situation here."

"Bullshit. What are you talking about? Harvard was a terrorist attack. A Muslim." In the Panic Room of Phipps's mind, the ghost of Warren Armstrong rose up, very large and scary. Jack had to be bluffing. Harvard was bad luck, a lightning strike.

"What I'm saying is, you need to be careful here. This isn't just you and me."

"But—"

"And what I'm also saying is, don't be stupid. There are people keeping tabs on you."

This frightened Phipps and made her even angrier. "Don't try to scare me, Uncle Jack. I'm a big girl now. *O'Connell* was a giant mistake, like I told you. We never should've—"

"Lot of heavy hitters in the background, and if things go south . . ." He paused.

"I've made up my mind. *Cimarron* goes wherever it goes. I'm through."

The wind had come up, blowing hard, and the rain was increasing. It sounded like gusts of Cheerios pattering against the windows. Phipps could sense Jack changing gears, the way he always did.

"Look. I understand you've got the jitters. But I'm thinking about Ronnie. Did I mention that I took him out for some ice cream again last week? He's doing great. The place is perfect for him." Ronnie worshipped Jack for some reason, and the boy tended to be relatively calm around him. Phipps had filed a form with the facility so Jack could visit and take Ronnie out any time. Jack's voice dropped to the edge of a murmur. "Something happens to you, where will he be, Angie?"

"Uh-huh, so now you're bringing Ronnie into this? You're a pathetic asshole, Jack, you know that?"

"Listen to me! I'm not kidding. You could get hurt, Angie. The guys I'm working with don't mess around."

"Oh, please. You sound like—"

"I know them. You don't. They're brutal motherfuckers."

"What is this?" She was raising her voice. "Our Mickey Mouse magic act, shifting a few cases, is suddenly a *Sopranos* episode? Complete with bombs going off? Gimme a break."

"I'm going to let you in on something, Angie. Newbury got in the line of fire. It was out of my hands. I'm telling you the truth here."

"Sure." She tried to sound dismissive, but she could hear the weakness in her voice, and she knew that Jack would be picking up on it. The ground was sliding out from under her. Jack cleared his throat and came at her from another angle.

"Okay, listen, Angie. I hear you. I can tell you're upset."

"You can tell that, huh?"

"So, here's the—"

"Very perceptive, Uncle Jack. Very, you know . . ."

She put the phone down on the counter and wiped her sweaty hand off on her robe again. Jack's voice floated up, small and inhuman.

"Listen to me, please. Here's the deal. We'll do just one more. Just *Cimarron*, okay? You shoot it to Helms, and—"

She picked up the phone, shaking her head. "Jack, I'm sorry. This is so hard, and I'm just so—"

"You know what's hard, Angie? Always getting the short end of the stick. This has been our chance to get a little slice of the pie, that's all." He paused, and when she said nothing, he continued, almost in a whisper. "Come on, Angie. It's for both of us. Once it's done, I'll stick my neck out to protect you." He raised his voice a little. "You should've given me some warning if you wanted to fold. I've got people counting on me now. Please, please just meet me halfway here. That's all I'm asking."

"I don't think I can, Jack. I've been going round and round about this." She closed her eyes and shook her head. She had to be strong.

"And you'll get your hundred. Fact, I'll bump it to one twenty-five, more than half. Don't make me beg."

"I don't know, Jack. I can't, I don't—"

"Hey, I may retire too. Take a trip somewhere." He made a snorting noise. "I've got a little pile stashed away in the islands. You can come visit. We'll drink margaritas on the beach. Come on."

"One more, and that's it? Just one?"

"One and done."

A movement on the other side of the room caused Phipps to look up. In the mouth of the hallway, Carl was staring at her. He was leaning against the doorframe, naked except for his boxers. For a second, she wondered how much he'd heard, but as she looked closer, his face told her. He'd heard everything. When their eyes met, Carl folded his arms. His nostrils flared, and a deep in breath lifted his shoulders. Then he turned and disappeared down the hallway. She needed to get off the phone. She needed to talk to him right away.

"Okay. Fine." She didn't know, or care, if she was lying. Carl's face had been awful. She'd never seen him looking like that before.

"That's my girl." Jack sighed into the phone. "You had me shitting my sweatpants here. By the end of the day, right?"

"Okay. Or first thing tomorrow. Soon as they file."

"Call me. Just to—"

"I will. I'll do it." She looked at the empty doorway. "I have to go. I have to get ready for court."

Phipps hung up and hurried into the bedroom. Carl had pulled on his jeans and was buttoning up his shirt. When she started to talk, he raised his hand.

"Please." He punctuated his words. "Don't. Say. Anything."

"But—"

"Don't say anything, okay?"

"Carl, it's—"

"Just listen to me, Angie. I know what I just heard, and I'm going to have to hand it all over to Mike Patterson. Then I'm going to have to put it into a report. You know that?" He shook his head. "Unbelievable." He wiped his hand over his face. "I can't believe it. A written report."

"Couldn't you just—"

"No, I couldn't." His face was flushed. "I'm not going to kid you. I still have all these feelings . . ." He dropped his eyes to the floor, breathed, then looked back up at her. "I'm a real mess right now, Angie. I feel like . . . I don't know, like the floor just disappeared or something. I thought I loved you, I guess, but I won't join your rat pack. I won't help you get out of whatever garbage can you and this uncle Jack of yours have been rooting around in. It wouldn't work for long anyway." He gave her a wondering look. "My God. I actually do love you. At least, I thought I loved you. I never—"

"Carl, Jesus, all I wanted to say was . . ."

Alberti almost shouted. "Angie, please don't say anything. Every single word that comes out of your mouth now is going to Patterson and Schwartz. Not long after that, it will go to ten other people I could name. I'm going to have to tell them about us, right? About us. It's unbelievable. As of this second, we're not just talking to each other anymore." He lifted his head to the ceiling and raised his hands. "We're talking to the whole damned world. So please do me a favor and just shut the fuck up. Don't make it worse."

He sat down on the bed and began putting on his shoes. His voice was lower.

"Patterson will want to talk with you right away, probably this morning. You'll need to make up your mind what to do, so I'll give you a piece of advice, and then I'm out of here." He nodded to himself. "Bob Schwartz is going to unpeel this banana real fast now. If you want a deal, you'll have to get to him soon and put everything you've got on the table. If you wait, he won't need you. I know him. He'll just toss you to the wolves." He finished tying his shoes and stood up. "He won't care."

"I'm, I'm really sorry. I'm . . ."

"Sure. Whatever." Alberti grabbed his windbreaker off the chair. "Tell me one thing, Angie."

"Okay."

"Was I crazy? Was I ever anything to you but an insurance policy?"

Phipps felt her chest tighten, and her voice go cold. "You're really asking me that, Carl? Really?" She looked over at the windows, breathing hard. The wind had let up, but it was pouring buckets now. They both stood there silently for several seconds, in the drumming of the rain.

So . . . this was it. This was who he was and what he thought of her.

"I need to get to work, Carl. *O'Connell* will be . . ."

"Yeah, I know. *O'Connell.*" He nodded at her. "Your big case. Busy day."

Alberti stepped around Phipps, being careful not to touch her, and left the bedroom. As he walked through the living room, he called out, "Nice furniture. Top of the line."

The sharp snap of the outer door was like a circuit breaker cutting out. Phipps stood in the bedroom doorway, listening to the rain. After a while, she wandered back into the kitchen. More robot than human, she made herself French toast, whisking the eggs ferociously and tossing in a little cinnamon. She ate three bites—not tasting anything—and scraped the rest into the garbage disposal.

She showered and made sure to get her hair right, took a little extra time with her makeup, and selected her top outfit, the one she'd worn to Il Gallo Pazzo. Standing in front of the full-length mirror, she could see she looked good. Sophia Antelope, whoever she was, would be proud of her.

In the corner of her bedroom, there was a small teak desk that Phipps used to pay bills. Ronnie's residential program gave a five percent discount when the tuition, room, and board were paid in advance. With a few taps on her iPad, Angie transferred everything in her money market and savings accounts into her checking account, and then wrote out a check large enough to cover Ronnie's expenses for the next five years. The withdrawal would pretty much take her down to zero. She addressed and stamped an envelope and slipped the check inside, with a note explaining what she was doing. She'd drop the envelope into the mailbox downstairs.

Then she put on her raincoat, shifting it onto her shoulders as though she were putting on a backpack for a long uphill climb. She checked herself out in the mirror one last time. She still looked good. Carl was gone, her last, best chance for happiness. If she was going down, she was going to do it with all flags flying. They could all go to hell. She would not cry.

35

A prickle of rage was running up the back of Mike Patterson's neck and fingering its way into his scalp. He fisted his hands under the table, digging his fingernails into his palms, keeping his voice casual.

"So, Angie, first of all, we need you to tell us how you pulled this off."

Patterson, Bob Schwartz, and the federal public defender, Tom Redpath, were sitting in a conference room in the U.S. Attorney's suite, all looking at Phipps. From her end of the table, she seemed, to Patterson's eyes, pale and frightened but ready to fight. She was dressed to the nines, which was usually just a sign of bravado. In her case, he wasn't so sure.

As soon as he'd talked to Carl Alberti that morning, Patterson had gone into high gear. He and Schwartz confronted Angie Phipps when she arrived at court and escorted her, more or less voluntarily, up to the conference room. She didn't seem surprised to see them. Schwartz cashed in a couple of favors he'd given Tom Redpath to persuade him to come and represent Phipps, solely for purposes of the conference. She needed a lawyer present if they were going to use anything she said.

While Phipps and Redpath talked privately, Patterson got the acting Clerk of Court, Warren Armstrong's temporary replacement, to dig up a fill-in for Phipps as Norcross's courtroom deputy in *O'Connell*. He quickly concluded that Angie's "Uncle Jack" had to be Jack Taylor, and he collared two FBI colleagues to put together the paperwork for an emergency intercept on Taylor's cell. Alberti, at his own request, was off the case. He was a witness now, and Patterson would have punted him anyway. Finally, pursuing an inspired impulse, Patterson made a couple of quick calls to check out what was going on with Phipps's son, Ronald.

What they really needed now was for Angie Phipps to talk.

She looked over at Tom Redpath. "So you're telling me I should answer his question?"

Redpath shook his head. "No, I'm absolutely not telling you that, Angie. Like I said, whether you say anything is your call." Tom Redpath was a big man, about Patterson's height, but heavier. His intelligence and long experience as a public defender were conventional strengths, but his shaved head and diamond ear stud gave him a powerful, almost thuglike, physical presence in the small conference room. No defendant was going to suffer abuse while he was around, but no defendant was going to get away with bullshitting anybody either.

Patterson liked Tom Redpath, and he watched as Redpath gave Angie a steady look. "What I said was, if you *are* going to talk, do it now and do it all. Don't go halfway. That's my advice."

"I don't know." Angie shook her head. "What's going to happen to me? I have a son. I don't . . ." Her mouth tightened. "I'm not leaving him all on his own."

"No promises, Angie." Patterson leaned back in his chair. "If I could make any, believe me I would."

"He's telling the truth." Redpath nodded. "The proffer letter you signed means that anything you say during this session cannot be used against you. You're getting a kind of free ride right now. But they can still charge you, using other evidence they have. My guess is they probably will, and it's going to be pretty soon."

"We haven't decided." Schwartz shrugged. "All I can say is that if it comes to that, and you plead guilty, we promise to tell the judge you cooperated, early on. That may help you. It may not." Schwartz gave a half smile, acknowledging the irony. "Probably depends on which judge you draw."

Schwartz was sitting opposite Phipps, with his elbows on the table, his large silver head catching the light. "Carl told us pretty much everything we need anyway. We're just looking for help cleaning up a few details."

Redpath broke in bluntly. "Don't listen to that, Angie. They want the whole tuna here." He nodded at Schwartz. "Sorry, Bob, but let's be honest, okay?"

Patterson leaned in. "Carl was pretty broken up when I talked to him. He's worried about you." He paused. "I'm sure you know that."

Patterson and Schwartz had agreed ahead of time that Patterson would be the Questioner and Schwartz would be the Nudger. Schwartz would stare at Phipps constantly—transmitting what he called the "Bob Schwartz piercing look"—and toss in offhand, innocent-sounding questions, while Patterson took the lead. Later, if necessary, Schwartz could pretend to lose his patience and come down on her harder. Get disgusted. Throw his pencil. He and Patterson had done this routine a few times.

Patterson and Schwartz knew that Carl Alberti's report of the overheard phone conversation was not, in fact, nearly enough to give them what they needed. It was hearsay and maybe too vague to give them probable cause even for the wiretap application, let alone an arrest warrant. And the clock was ticking. A thick complaint out of California involving Cimarron Systems had hit the clerk's office that morning and was waiting to be drawn. If it didn't go to Helms, Taylor might realize his scheme was collapsing and take off. They needed Angie to talk, and they needed her to do it very soon, preferably in the next hour.

Patterson raised his voice very slightly. "We're not blaming you for any of this, Angie. In a way, you're sort of the victim here. We know that. All this was your uncle Jack's idea, right? Jack Taylor?" His tone conveyed contempt for Taylor. "That's what Carl told me anyway."

This was sort of a lie. Carl hadn't actually said anything about whose idea it was, but Patterson wanted Phipps to think that Carl had not named her as the primary villain. Expressing sympathy to loosen up a target was a textbook interrogation technique, and with his years as a public defender, Tom Redpath clearly recognized it. He gave Patterson a glare but remained silent. Redpath had to know that Phipps's only hope was to cough up everything right now. All the men in the room, for different reasons, wanted the same thing from her.

Angie swallowed and wiped the corner of her mouth. "Uh-huh."

Uh-huh wouldn't do. Patterson sat up in his chair. "So Carl was right. Jack was paying you. Can you just tell us how that one part of it worked?"

During their brief contacts, Patterson had never much liked, or disliked, Phipps. He'd noticed, of course, how hard she worked to make males light up around her. He'd even wondered if she'd had something going on with Warren Armstrong. They'd been awfully good friends. Then, recently, he'd learned that Phipps was an excellent liar. She'd lied to his face about the phone call Norcross mentioned, and it had gotten past him. That wasn't going to happen again.

"I don't know." Phipps looked around the table at them. "What about my boy?"

"It's Ronald, right? How old is he?" Patterson knew how old Ronald was.

"Eleven. He has problems. He's in a . . ."

Patterson nodded. "I have two, one in college." He paused. "So you wanted something better for him. I'd probably do the same thing. Anyone might."

Phipps still didn't say anything.

Patterson looked at Schwartz. "How many do you have, Bob?"

Schwartz held up three fingers. "All boys. Hell on earth."

Patterson set his hand on the conference room table about a foot from Angie's hand and leaned closer. "Listen, we know your son's program charges a pretty penny. And Jack must have been helping you out with the tuition. Do I have that right?" Patterson's question was like one of those ordinary-looking flowers that lures a bumblebee in and then closes up. "That's what Carl tells us, anyway."

"Right." Phipps's voice was barely audible. "He was."

Patterson followed up, also keeping his voice low. "He was what, Angie?"

Phipps shot a glance at Redpath, who remained expressionless. "Jack was paying me to, like, make sure certain cases went to certain judges."

And, right there, they had her. Patterson nodded and glanced over at Schwartz.

It would take patience to fill in the details, but they were basically home. They could ease, tease, or squeeze every drop out of her now.

"Well," Patterson said. "We all do things for our children."

"Right." Phipps breathed in shakily. "Jack set up the deals, and when he got paid, he gave some to me." She darted a glance over at Tom Redpath. "Half."

"Do you know the names of any of the lawyers he worked with?"

Phipps shook her head and spoke down to the table. "No. He never told me."

Schwartz broke in—just inquiring, not accusing. "Is that really true, Angie?"

Redpath gave Phipps a worried look. There was a silence until Patterson continued, deliberately changing the subject.

"We can get back to that. My question a minute ago was this. How did you go about it? How did it work?"

Tom Redpath spoke up. "I'd like a few minutes to speak to Angie privately."

Patterson sat up. "You want us to leave?"

"Yeah."

Patterson nodded to Phipps. "Would you remind Angie that, if she decides not to speak to us, that's her choice. But it's a five-year felony to lie. She's already got a problem there."

"No, she hasn't." Redpath appeared unimpressed. "And if she has, it's covered by the letter."

Schwartz was already walking to the door. "I think you're wrong on that one, Tom."

"I think I'm not, Bob."

The three men made grunting noises, resembling laughs. They'd been around on this one in other cases. Phipps just looked confused.

"Is it okay if I go to the bathroom?"

Out in the hallway, Patterson spoke to Schwartz. "I need to feed this new information to my guys for the Title III application. What we have now should be enough. Can you brief Broadwater?"

"Yeah. I'll call him now. We'll need to pause the Khan prosecution. Looks like we may have the wrong guy." Schwartz scratched the back of his neck. "And I'll want Broadwater's approval to do a shell assignment of *Cimarron* to Helms to keep our pal Jack sleeping. I want Taylor, but I want the sons of bitches who've been hiring him a lot more."

36

Judge Norcross hurried into his chambers with only ten minutes to spare before he was due to resume *O'Connell*. He'd been up in Burlington, observing Reverend Kamau's immigration hearing, and he'd stayed long enough to learn that the IJ would be releasing Kamau on various standard conditions. Deportation proceedings were still moving ahead, and Kamau could be expelled any day. He could return to Kenya voluntarily if he wished, but for now he would be returning to his apartment in Cambridge. Their Saturday dinner in Amherst was still on.

Treadwell and his team were still finishing up the release paperwork when Norcross had to leave, so he did not have a chance to speak to Kamau privately. He'd already postponed the resumption of the trial that day for two hours, and he could not stand the thought of being any later.

Unfortunately, Godfrey Mungai had run up to him in the parking lot as he was leaving. He still had some bruising around his mouth, and a bandage on one of his hands, which must have come from when he lit on the sidewalk. Trotting alongside Norcross, Mungai had told him that he'd managed a visit to Kamau the day before and had learned that—against Treadwell's recommendation—Kamau was refusing even to consider applying for asylum in the United States. Kenya was his home, Kamau had said, and the Kenyan people were his people. He did not need the United States to protect him from them. With his student visa revoked, deportation was probably inevitable, and Kamau was considering breaking off his program at Harvard and just going home. Mungai was terrified of this. His contacts had informed him that Kamau's enemies were already making plans for him on his return. Norcross had to do something.

Norcross had told Mungai, perhaps a little tersely, that he couldn't think of all that now. One step at a time. They'd get Kamau out of detention and see where things went from there. Now, as he hurried to put on his robe, the memory of Mungai in the rearview mirror, standing by himself on the blacktop, utterly desolate, was still haunting him.

His phone rang. He considered leaving it, but it was Broadwater.

"Got some sad news I need to pass on, Dave. Tony Helms died at three a.m. this morning."

"Oh, I'm so sorry." Norcross glanced up at the clock. Five minutes until court. "How is Peggy doing?"

"Not great. She'll be out for at least two weeks. Going to stay with her daughter, I guess."

"That's really terrible. Listen, can I . . ."

"One other thing. Bob Schwartz just called me and said he was going to be asking me to slow things down with the Kahlil Khan prosecution. New developments, he said."

"Wow, that's interesting." The news kindled a flicker of hope in Norcross.

"Yes, they—"

"I wonder if they've gotten some information about who handed that bag to Khan and whether Khan knew what was in it. If he didn't, then the whole Kenyan connection could be out the window."

"Right, just what I was thinking. I'm going to see Schwartz and Redpath in chambers this morning to try to keep a lid on this. We'll probably postpone Khan's pretrial conference."

"The news is bound to leak out pretty soon, Skip. Somehow these things always do."

"Yes. But if Schwartz has somebody in his crosshairs, God help them. He's good, and when his blood is up, he's darn near unstoppable. The entire Boston bar has learned that."

"I only have a minute here. Sorry. We're getting a late start this morning."

"Oh, that's right, *O'Connell*. How's it going?"

"Not too badly. Got the openings out of the way yesterday. The government has scheduled a couple of its expert witnesses today. They're bringing in their fact witnesses, including this guy Shaughnessy, next week, I guess. I may wrap up early today. Let the jurors jump-start their weekends."

"That will make them happy. We've assigned you a new courtroom deputy, by the way. Phipps isn't available."

"Okay, listen—"

"Seems like things are moving along smartly."

"So far." Norcross hesitated, feeling awkward. "To be honest, Skip, I've got court in three minutes, and, as usual, I have to hit the bathroom."

Broadwater laughed. "Most important part of trial preparation. We can talk more later."

37

Okay." Phipps settled herself and scratched at the top of her shoulder. "Here's how it worked."

Patterson interrupted. "Let's have the truth, please. You burned me last time, and I didn't appreciate it."

Phipps nodded. "I'm really sorry, Mike, but . . ."

"Yeah, well . . ."

Tom Redpath spoke with an edge. "Leave her alone and let her talk, okay? We can walk out of here any time."

"Feel free." Schwartz leaned forward and cupped his hands together, as though he had something small trapped inside. "We can manage without her."

Redpath snorted. "Sure."

"Okay, boys? Can I start?" Phipps looked around the table. When nobody said anything, she began. "Okay then. Here's how I did it." She pulled her chair forward. Patterson noticed that she'd regained some of her poise. She'd made her decision, and her voice was stronger than it had been before the break.

"When, let's say, a new civil case arrives, one of the clerks will do the case opening, making sure everything is filled out right. A different clerk handles this job every day, which helps. Once the intake is complete, the clerk sends the Case Assignment Request to me. If I'm sick or tied up, another person will take care of it, so there's no delay."

Patterson broke in. "So you don't always do the assignments?"

"Not always, but most of the time, if I'm not busy. Or I can step in sometimes, if . . ." She cleared her throat. "If, you know, there's some special reason."

"Okay. And then?"

"Right. So then, I'll input the Nature of Suit from the filing docs—civil rights, diversity tort, employment discrimination, patent, or whatever."

"Okay."

"And I'll also put the case into one of three categories based on the number of parties and the likely length of the trial. This makes sure no judge gets randomly stuck with a bunch of the same kind of cases—like patent cases, which a lot of judges don't like—or gets loaded up with too many monsters, a bunch of four-month trials or whatever."

This description of standard clerk's office procedure was the typical tiptoeing. Patterson had often had to sit through this sort of thing. Cooperators would come in agreeing to take all their clothes off, but then go on forever removing a glove one finger at a time. Usually he was patient with this, but this time he couldn't keep himself from breaking in.

"We know all this, Angie. Could you—"

Redpath stifled a smile. "If you just let her talk, Mike, I promise you this will go a lot faster."

Schwartz patted the table. "It's okay." He nodded at Phipps. "Keep going, Angie."

Phipps pushed ahead, happy to stay on safe ground. "Some judges are automatically excluded from certain categories of cases. Like, our senior judges don't draw *pro se* cases, and the habeas petitions don't usually go to magistrate judges. I also look over the parties to be sure the case belongs in Boston and not Worcester or Springfield. Then, after I go through all this, I input the case, let the computer randomly pick out one of the judges, and issue a formal Notice of

Case Assignment, so the lawyer can send out the summonses. That's how the draw usually works."

"Okay." Patterson forced himself to speak conversationally. "So what happens when things don't go as usual?"

Phipps dabbed at the hair on the back of her head. "Some cases are what we call direct assignments, meaning that they are drawn out-of-random. For example, an MDL case . . ."

"MDL?"

"Multi-District Litigation, which is where one judge is assigned nationally to handle all of a certain group of cases, like the old asbestos cases, or the opioid cases, where there were thousands of plaintiffs, or some huge product liability litigation, or a plane crash, with maybe two or three hundred cases filed all over the country. You have to catch them when they're filed, because they're always drawn to the same judge. We call these assignments out-of-random."

Phipps paused and chewed on her lip. She was bringing herself up to the brink.

"I see," Schwartz said. "Interesting. And so . . ."

"So." She took a breath. "There's another type of direct assignment, which is called a related case. When a case is filed that is closely related to an earlier case some judge already has—let's say, the exact same auto accident but a different injured passenger—the new attorney will note in his filing papers that his case is *related* to the earlier one. When this happens, the second case, the related case, will go to the same judge as the first case, automatically, out-of-random."

As he listened to her, Patterson began to feel a new respect for Phipps. She was a lot smarter than he'd taken her for, which was part of the reason she'd fooled him with her earlier lie. Dumb mistake on his part.

Phipps continued, explaining. "This way, you don't have two or three judges duplicating the same work, and you also avoid any risk of inconsistency. It makes sense."

"Fine. So . . ."

"But the new attorney filing the second case has to specifically ask for the relatedness designation on the filing form—there's a section to fill out for that—and the judges' docket clerks, and even the judges themselves, look this over to make sure that the relatedness thing is not being abused—that it's not a camouflage for what they call forum shopping, meaning fiddling with the system to get a judge tailor-made for your case. That was my crack in the system."

Patterson leaned forward. "You have me on the edge of my seat here, Angie."

Redpath looked at Patterson. "What did I tell you?"

Phipps continued, sounding almost eager now. "Okay. Let's say a certain case comes in, right? One we have our eye on."

Patterson said, "Like, say, this *Danforth v. Cimarron* case?"

"Like that. And let's say I want it to go to a particular judge."

"Like, say, Judge Helms."

"Like her. The e-filing, or the paper doc, won't say that *Cimarron* is related to any of Helms's cases. If the plaintiffs' lawyer did that, it would be an obvious con, and they'd be in a shitload of trouble. But I can enter the new case—let's say, *Cimarron*—into the system electronically, on my own, as related. I can pick out one of Helms's cases already on her docket that's sort of similar. Like, *Cimarron* is a securities fraud case, and Judge Helms has four or five of those already. Every judge does. So, even though the plaintiffs never asked for *Cimarron* to be drawn to Helms as a related case, I can just put it into the system as related to this earlier securities fraud case, and the system will enter it as an out-of-random draw to Judge Helms. To anybody going over the docket, it just looks like an ordinary random draw, but the little electronic brain inside the system thinks the case is related." She wiggled up her fingers in the air like a magician pulling off a trick. "Because, abracadabra, that's what I secretly told it. And nobody can see it, unless they get way down in the weeds and open up my input sequence."

"But suppose somebody did check the system, got inside, and saw what you did?"

Phipps gave a quick shrug. "Well, first of all, nobody has so far. Boston's got thousands of cases a year coming in, and I was only doing this, like, once every three or four months at the most. Also, within a day or two, I'd cover my tracks."

"How's that?"

"I'd just go back into the system once the case was drawn, let's say, to Helms, and the case was entered onto her docket, and I would edit out the relatedness designation I snuck into the system earlier. In other words, I would just sort of scrub out the system's little brain. There's a tool to do that—not many people know where it is, but I stumbled onto it—so my fingerprints will only be visible for a day or two. Our quality control people are really good, but they're not on top of things that close. You could still catch me if you really looked, but it takes a lot more work, and remember there are, like, hundreds of cases rolling in every month."

"But it's not totally foolproof."

"Right, but I told myself, if they ever caught me, I'd just say the relatedness entry was an accident. I'd apologize, say I was distracted, having a crisis with Ronnie, or whatever. Worst-case scenario, the relatedness designation would be deleted, the case would be redrawn randomly, and I'd get a slap on the wrist. If the new draw didn't go to Helms, which it probably wouldn't, we'd piss off the client, but that's all."

"But that never happened . . ."

"Right. Because I never got caught." Phipps looked almost smug.

"And how much did Jack pay you for this, Angie?"

"We split fifty-fifty. I got a hundred thousand dollars a pop, tax-free. Maybe three, four hundred thousand a year, give or take."

Schwartz, who had been scribbling furiously on his yellow pad, broke in at this point. "So you're looking at tax evasion as well as conspiracy to obstruct."

"Hope not. All the payments were reported right on my tax returns as gifts from Jack into Ronnie's trust fund."

Schwartz kept writing. "Just a loving gesture from a generous uncle."

"Exactly. I have a good accountant. The terms of Ronnie's trust are loose enough that I can pretty much spend the money however I want as long as it helps him in some way. A big part of it goes for his residential program and into his Fidelity trust account to support him when I'm gone. I have the account indexed to the S and P, and it's done pretty well. It's got, like, almost a . . ." She caught herself. "It's got a lot built up in it now."

Schwartz made a note. "We're going to want those investment records."

Phipps glanced over at Redpath. He nodded, and Phipps said, rather weakly, "I guess."

"They'll be subject to forfeiture as the proceeds of the illegal conspiracy."

Redpath sniffed. "Not my area, but I wouldn't be so sure. I'm betting the terms of Ronnie's trust will make it hard to pry that money loose."

Schwartz pushed. "Any funds in your name?"

"There were for a while, but there's not much in that account anymore."

Patterson picked up again. "So how long has this been going on?"

"Maybe four, four and a half, years."

"For how many cases?"

"Twelve, fifteen, sixteen, around there. I haven't kept track."

"And you never worked directly with the attorneys, just with Jack Taylor?"

"Right."

Patterson dropped his voice. "Don't lie, please, Angie. You never did any freelancing?"

"Never."

"And you really didn't know who the lawyers were, your so-called clients?"

"Not really. Most of the time, I just looked at the case name and the docket number."

"You knew Sam Newbury's name, though, didn't you?"

"Right." Phipps glanced nervously at Redpath. "Jack knew him from before somehow, and his name did come up."

"So, when you told me before the break that you didn't know any of the lawyers, you weren't telling the truth, am I right?"

"Leave it, Mike," Redpath said. "She needed to consult with her lawyer. Nothing unusual about that."

Patterson pushed. "Did Jack mention the names of any other lawyers, even in passing?"

Redpath shook his head. "Leave that too. She can't remember any other names at this point in time. If she thinks of any, we'll be in touch."

Phipps broke in, raising her voice. "*O'Connell*, which was New-bury's case at first, was our only criminal case. It was all over the *Boston Globe*. I told Jack I didn't want to do it. And, sure enough, it blew up in our faces."

"Can you at least tell us the names of the cases you worked on?"

"We'll get back to you on that," Redpath said.

"I'd need to think about it. Like I say, I never kept track. Never even wrote them down. It was just, every three or four months, I'd get a phone call from Jack: Here's the case, here's the docket num-ber, and here's the judge we want. I'd do my magic, the case would get drawn, and sometime later, not too long, the electronic transfer would hit the trust account. I didn't even see Jack face-to-face most of the time. Except for a couple of times when we visited Ronnie together, it was just phone calls. Even on the drives out to Lenox, we never mentioned our little deal. It was, like, in a separate world."

"Lenox?"

"Ronnie's residential program."

Schwartz stopped writing and tossed down his pen. "So you knew what you were doing was illegal?"

This drew a spark. "Of course. I'm not stupid." Phipps frowned and shook her head. "But, to be honest, I never thought it was all that illegal. The Honorables didn't know anything about it. The judges just went on doing whatever they did. The law is the law, and one judge is supposed to be the same as any other, right? It was just, at the most, making some big-shot lawyer think he was getting an edge once in a while. BFD."

"Excuse me?"

"Big Fucking Deal."

Schwartz pushed. "Pretty serious money for such a tiny thing, Angie." He was down in his yellow pad again and didn't bother to look up.

Phipps shook her head impatiently. "Except for *O'Connell*, these were all fat-cat corporations. The amount I was getting was less than chump change to them. It wouldn't even show up on their annual reports. Basically, it was zero. But it was everything to Ronnie and me."

Patterson sighed. "So that's how you justified it."

"I was a single mom, Mike, with nothing but a cute butt, an associate's degree, and an autistic child—fighting it out in Boston. Try it some time."

"Uh-huh, but you—"

"And I got the degree before my mom died, when she could still help out with Ronnie. Once she was gone, I was sailing solo."

"Until Jack called."

"Actually, he didn't call. He came by for Ronnie's, like, sixth or seventh birthday. We were struggling like hell back then, and he brought us this big chocolate cake. Jack's a jerk, okay, but he's not just a jerk. I don't know why, but he really took to Ronnie. Once Ronnie went to bed, I started bragging to Jack about what I'd stumbled onto. I'd had a couple glasses of wine, and I was telling him how easy it would be, that sort of thing. The Honorables think they're gods, but us girls and boys downstairs can take the whole system and turn it on its head if we want to." Phipps gave a short laugh. "Well, Jack's law practice was going nowhere, and he lit up like the Fourth of July. A few months later, we were in business. It was like something fell straight from heaven. In his new residential program, I'd never seen my little guy so happy. He was making friends, he'd gotten to where he'd actually let me hug him once in a while, and I was finally living like a human being."

"But then something happened, right?" Patterson had been waiting pretty much the whole time to turn this corner.

Phipps ducked the question. "Jack was taking Ronnie out for little sightseeing adventures sometimes, just the two of them. I gave the school permission to let him go. They'd get ice cream. Ronnie was loving it. The staff thought Jack was a prince."

"Sounds very nice, Angie." Patterson deliberately repeated his words. "But then something happened, right?"

There was a pause. The conference room had no windows, but it felt as though a cloud had come over the sun. Patterson watched Phipps carefully and waited.

Finally, she said, "Yes."

"And that was what?"

Phipps looked up at the ceiling, breathed in, and closed her eyes. "The CAP, the Case Assignment Program, started going wonky." She dropped her head and looked at Patterson. "The system is weird sometimes. You fiddle around with something on one end, and you start getting problems on the other. Somehow, what I was doing, probably when I reentered the system to do my scrubbing, started to mess up the draw."

"And Warren began to suspect something wasn't right?"

"Yeah. Judges were getting repeats. Judge Ramos drew three giant patent cases in one week and went bananas. Other judges started complaining too. Warren Armstrong told me if I couldn't untangle the problem, he'd have to bring in an IT team from Washington."

"And could you untangle the problem?"

"No way." Phipps sighed. "Even if I could have, the correction would have showed Warren what I'd been up to. The jocks from Washington would definitely have seen it once they were on-site."

"So what did you do?"

"Well, for a while . . ." She gave an exhausted laugh. "For a while, I basically went back and forth between stalling and freaking out."

"And then you called your uncle Jack."

"Yes. It was stupid, but Warren was all over me, and I got upset."

Patterson pressed. "And that was the Wednesday before the Harvard bombing."

"Yes." Her voice was losing its bounce.

"And you told Jack that Warren was getting ready to bring in the IT people from Washington, right?"

The room went silent. Patterson was trained to observe body language, and he was naturally good at it, but it wouldn't have taken many seminars or much skill to observe the transformation Phipps was undergoing. She was motionless, staring down at the table. It was like watching air go out of a balloon.

"Yes. I did that." She drew in a trembling breath and wiped her eye. "But I swear, I never, never—"

"Okay." Tom Redpath broke in. He slapped his palm on the table. "That's all we're doing for today."

Patterson pressed. "And you told Taylor that Warren Armstrong would be going to his Harvard reunion."

"Yes, but—"

"Hey, hey, hey!" Redpath slapped the table several times, drowning out Phipps. He glared at Patterson. "Angie's playing ball, Mike.

She's given you a ton of useful stuff here, plenty of probable cause for your Title III application. But I'm telling you we're done for now. She and I need to talk more before we go any further. She may need to retain a private lawyer. We'll be checking into that."

Phipps looked up. "I could just—"

"Uh-uh, Angie." Redpath shook his head. "No. This time, it's my call. You're not going down this road any further until you and I talk more." Redpath looked at his watch and glanced at Schwartz. "Besides, you and I have a conference in *U.S. v. Khan* before Judge Broadwater in fifteen minutes, and he'll rip the shit out of us if we're one minute late." He pointed at Phipps as she continued to squirm. "No, Angie. Trust me." Then, louder, as she started to protest: "I'm not kidding. No." Redpath looked at Schwartz and Patterson. "That's it for now. We're agreeing, right? No more questions for Angie without contacting me first." When he got no response, he leaned into the table and pointed at them. "Right?"

Patterson shrugged, pretending indifference. "Sure." He would have given up Christmas for just four more questions. "Fine."

"And we also agree that you're not going public with Angie's cooperation, right? She's taking a big risk coming in here."

Phipps broke in, looking alarmed. "Yeah, I'm wondering if I should . . ."

Redpath nodded at Phipps. "We'll talk about that." He looked again at Schwartz and Patterson. "So this is all under wraps for now, do we agree?"

Patterson nodded. "Except for the folks I have putting together the intercept paperwork, no one will know Angie is anywhere near this. My affidavit will only refer to an anonymous confidential informant, a CI, without even mentioning the gender."

"Okay. People will eventually figure things out, but let's keep all this on ice as long as we can." Redpath frowned and stood up. "Time to go, Angie. We're done for today."

Patterson's eye followed Phipps as she left the room with Tom Redpath. He hoped Redpath would be suggesting that she find a friend or relative she could stay with for a couple of weeks—someplace off somewhere, far out of the way.

38

Claire, bending over the sink, decided for the fifth time that she needed a dinner party like· a hole in the head. David did not cook for company, she had no idea what an African clergyman ate, and Charlie had a tooth coming in, which meant he'd been up half the night. Plus, the book she was coauthoring was due at the publisher in four weeks. Monica was back in Boston, but her nonstop texts were driving Claire batty.

Somehow, she'd get through this. It was a help that their niece Lindsay would be joining them and had promised to bring a salad. Also, after a hot afternoon, the evening was cooling off. The breeze coming in through the screens was pleasant and sweet. To get in the mood for Reverend Kamau, David had dug out some of his old African CDs, and the effervescent highlife rhythms, happy but not too loud, were giving a cheerful animation to the house. Their yellow Lab, Marlene, was circling around Claire's feet, toenails clicking on the tiles, restless with the sense that something was up.

She was dredging the chicken when David bounced into the kitchen, holding Charlie and dancing around to the irresistible African harmonies. He'd wrapped up his trial day early on Friday and was enjoying being home for the weekend. Somehow, his ridiculous rhumba had finally put their son to sleep. Charlie was lolling back, flopping gently in time with the music, his mouth wide open. They just might be able to get him into bed on time. The potatoes were on the boil, and the green beans were blanching. Tomorrow was Sunday, and they had nothing on the calendar. They might even get a little playtime. All might yet be well.

She shoved the dog out of the way with her calf. "Marlene, go lie down." Marlene sat, right in the way, looking up at her with her tongue hanging out. She'd gotten a little deaf.

Claire turned on the faucet and rinsed the flour off her hands. Family life. She'd wanted it so much.

David boogied over to the window and peeked out. "Here's Lindsay."

Claire had grown very fond of her niece. The girl was still mostly a sphinx in company—speaking little, but always worth listening to when she did say something. Her grades at Amherst College put her in the top ten percent of her class.

Kenya's former president, Uhuru Kenyatta, had attended Amherst College during the eighties. This was a source of pride for the administration, and despite some controversies he was remembered by one or two of Claire's emeritus colleagues with respect. Lindsay was taking a course called "African History Post-1900." Who knew where this sophomore-year caprice would lead? Lindsay's real passion remained softball. Claire and David had gone to watch the Amherst College women clobber Wesleyan and Williams that spring. Lindsay, the team's catcher, had thrown out two runners against Williams and knocked in four runs over the two games.

Typical of Lindsay, she did not say hello as she entered the kitchen, just raised her eyebrows with a self-conscious smile. She was carrying a large plastic bowl.

"Salad?" Claire pointed.

Lindsay set the bowl on the island. "Waldorf."

"Fabulous. It'll be perfect with the chicken."

"Carmen had me fold in her secret ingredient." Lindsay looked pleased.

"What's that?" David was still by the window bouncing Charlie.

"Whipped cream."

"Whipped cream improves everything." David orchestrated a slow jigging spin.

Carmen was Lindsay's roommate. Claire speculated to herself about the nature of their relationship, but she asked no questions.

There was the sound of a car door slamming. She turned off the music and went over to the window to watch as Reverend Kamau came up the front walk, looking formal in gray slacks, a navy blazer, and a yellow dress shirt, open at the throat. Claire, in green capris and a linen top, wondered if she should have stepped up her outfit.

Kamau was taller and handsomer than she'd expected, and there was something striking about how he carried himself as he crossed the lawn. The way he moved, rolling fluidly on his long legs, reminded her of a giraffe, and she recalled David telling her that *twiga*—the Swahili word for "giraffe"—had been David's nickname in Africa. Kamau was carrying something in his hand. The trees behind him rocked in a sudden gust, scattering the shadows.

David turned to Lindsay and held out the baby. "Would you mind putting Charlie down?"

Lindsay had babysat numerous times, and Charlie allowed himself to be transferred into her arms without stirring. She headed upstairs, while David hurried to the front door, followed by Marlene, who gave a couple of elderly woofs. Soon, Claire heard David's voice in the distance.

"Karibu!"

Pronounced "car-*ree*-boo," this was one of the handful of Swahili words David had taught Claire. It meant, among other things, "welcome." Her limited vocabulary also included *Asante sana*—thank you very much—which she heard David and Kamau exchanging as they approached the kitchen. This was easy to remember. Now and then, she liked to use it as a silly compliment to David as they were dozing off after sex. The only other word Claire had managed to remember was *mzee*—pronounced "mm-zay"—which David said was a term of respect for an older man.

"It's just terrific that you've come." David was sounding almost boyishly happy. "Was the drive a problem?"

"Not really. I hope I'm not late. I had a meeting and left straight-away after that." As they entered the kitchen, Kamau smiled uncertainly at Claire. There was something in his eyes, some vulner-ability that surprised her.

"Not at all. This is my wife, Claire."

Claire wiped her hands on a dish towel, and they shook. "Rever-end Kamau. Lovely to meet you at last."

"It is my pleasure, but please call me David. Otherwise, I might have to call you Memsahib." He laughed shyly. "That would be quite old-fashioned, not to mention a trifle colonial for me."

Claire smiled back. "Sure." She pointed at the container he was carrying. "What is that?"

He held it up. "This, I'm afraid, is my attempt at ugali. I tasted it before coming, and it is a disaster. Nothing like my mother made. But I told His Honor that I would bring some, so . . ." He set it on the counter. "I'll set it here, where I hope it will be forgotten."

"Not at all." Claire picked it up. "I'll put it in the micro, and we'll have it with dinner."

David put his hand on Kamau's shoulder. "Please call me David. 'His Honor' is too judicial."

Kamau shook his head. "I cannot do that, I'm afraid. It would feel, to me, somehow . . . I don't know. I-I can't do that."

"Then I will have to call you Reverend Kamau."

Claire broke in, half joking, "How about if we call Reverend Kamau 'David,' and Reverend Kamau calls you 'Mzee'?"

"Yes, yes." Kamau broke into a smile. "That would suit very well."

David laughed. "Good grief, have I gotten that old?"

Kamau's smile broadened. "I am afraid, Mzee, that you qualify, both in your age and your position."

"Okay." David nodded at the floor, pondering the idea. "I think I like it." He looked up. "It's coming a little earlier than I'd planned, but it's all right I guess." He walked over to their liquor cabinet. "Still, you've had a long drive. Can I get you something to drink?"

"The journey was longer than I expected, I must confess, and with some traffic." Kamau gave a sigh. "If possible, what I would like most, if you have it, would be an inch of scotch whiskey, neat."

"I'll have the same." David never drank scotch. "What can I get you, Claire?"

Claire needed to focus on the dinner. With the ugali, the potatoes might be too much. She'd have to consider some improvising.

"Nothing for me at the moment."

As David was getting the Glenfiddich down and wiping the dust off it, Kamau noticed one of the CD sleeves on the counter.

"My goodness, Papa Franco and L'OK Jazz?" He picked the CD up and began reading the titles. "You have some genuine Congolese oldies here." His voice went up. "Oh my heavens, 'Matinda'?" He ran his finger down the song list. "Dr. Nico. I love these songs. Versions of them are still sometimes played in the clubs in Nairobi."

"Why don't you two take your music and go out in the living room while I get things ready, okay? It won't be long."

They moved off, talking over each other in inscrutable Swahili phrases, presumably the titles of songs. Soon, the melodies were floating in from the Bose at the front of the house. Claire found herself responding without thinking, moving in time to the music as she steered the dinner into its final phase. After a few minutes, Lindsay returned from putting Charlie down and joined her uncle and their guest in the living room. She heard David indistinctly, introducing her. No sound from the baby monitor on the counter. Perhaps Charlie was going to let them have their evening.

After a few minutes, the various components of the meal were well along, and Claire took a break to see how things were going in the living room. The music was louder in there, and when she arrived David was standing by the coffee table, looking at Lindsay and swaying his shoulders.

"It's kind of like this." He moved his hips, bobbing his elbows out to the side.

Lindsay was sitting on the sofa, watching her uncle with a closed-mouth smile. Kamau stood by the fireplace. He'd put his jacket over a chair and had his arms folded.

"Forgive me, Mzee." Kamau shook his head. "But you are hopeless."

Lindsay leaned back against the cushions. Her eyes brightened.

"No, it's just . . ." David gave a slow pivot. It wasn't bad.

"Here." Kamau came over and held out his hand to Lindsay. "Come. Let me show you. It's easier with two people."

Lindsay got up and stood in front of Kamau, shrugging her shoulders expectantly. She was only about an inch shorter than he was, and she had the same straight athletic build.

"What should I . . ." She looked willing but uncertain.

"Start by letting the rhythm take hold of you." Kamau began moving his shoulders and hips in time to the music. "It's about feelings as much as movements." He smiled as Lindsay went into motion, matching his cadence. "See? It's happy."

Claire hadn't realized her niece was such a natural dancer.

Kamau beamed. "Perfect. Now, your arms to the side, like this." Lindsay, watching, followed along. The music had taken off into a lighthearted guitar riff, repetitive but with subtle, addictive variations.

As they continued, Lindsay let herself relax more, moving easily and smiling with pleasure. Kamau exaggerated the swaying of his shoulders, moving more stiffly than Lindsay but conveying the idea. "Now, to the side—like this. And step back." The music lifted into a refrain.

"Yes." Lindsay's smile broadened. "Okay."

"That's right, you've got it." Kamau tossed his head back and took her hand. They both laughed again and did matching twirls— shoulders, elbows, and hips keeping the rhythm.

The dancing was somewhat awkward, particularly on Kamau's part, but the overall effect was magical. David, at the far end of the room, was looking on with delight, mouth open. Their performance continued for perhaps a full minute with Kamau and Lindsay moving in sync. When the music drew to a close, David burst out clapping.

"Bravo!"

Lindsay spoke to no one in particular. "Gotta teach Carmen this."

Claire caught a whiff of her chicken possibly edging toward disaster.

"Sorry to interrupt, but we're just about ready to eat."

David followed her out of the living room. "I'll come set the table."

In the kitchen, nothing had turned black or caught fire. With the music resuming in the background, Claire served up the food while David arranged the silverware and set out water, Lindsay's salad, and the bottle of Glenfiddich. Claire spooned the ugali into a ceramic dish and put it into the micro.

Lindsay and Kamau were still beaming and a little out of breath as they came into the dining room. As Kamau took his seat, Claire noticed how his expression reacquired its hint of caution, as though he was on his guard. Was he concerned about having been too forward with Lindsay? Being careful to mind his manners? It was a little odd.

After everyone was settled, David surprised Claire by looking at Kamau. "Should we say some sort of grace?"

Kamau smiled. "That's very kind, Mzee, but not necessary." He broke off as a thought struck him. "Actually, there is a line by your poet Emily Dickinson that I like very much. It's a sort of prayer." He sat up and took Lindsay's and Claire's hands, while David did the same on the other side of the table. Kamau closed his eyes. Claire was struck by how warm and smooth his palm was.

"Grant me, O Lord, a sunny mind, thy windy will to bear!"

After a silence, Lindsay said, "That's it?" She nodded. "Nice."

"Well, it's short, but it covers a lot." Kamau looked down at his plate and then at Claire, raising his eyebrows. "This looks excellent. Thank you, Claire."

"Very welcome." She nodded at the Glenfiddich. "Please." Kamau replenished his glass and slid the bottle toward David, who had turned to speak to Lindsay.

"Game today?"

"Just a practice. It's an off week."

Kamau looked at her, intrigued. "What do you play?"

"Softball."

"Aha. Which position?"

"Catcher." Lindsay looked down at her plate, pulling herself in.

"Really! In cricket, we would call you the wicketkeeper. It's a very difficult position. You must have very good, very quick hands."

Lindsay, chewing, eyed Kamau warily. Claire could see she was trying to decide where he was coming from. Did he really care about this or was he just making conversation? Lindsay hated being patronized.

Kamau pressed her. "Tell me, please, Lindsay. What is the most difficult delivery for a catcher to handle?"

"Well." She swallowed and put down her fork. "When the pitcher releases the ball too early, you know?"

"Yes. Yes."

"And especially if there is some topspin . . ."

"Yes. Yes." Kamau took a sip of his scotch.

"The ball will come in low and fast and hit in the dirt right at the batter's feet, okay? Or it can even skip off the plate." She sat up and leaned toward Kamau. It was clear he was truly interested. "This can be a big problem, especially if there are runners on base. You don't know where the pitch is going until the last second—you can't anticipate it—and you have to lean in to smother it. Whatever happens, you can't let the ball get past you, but if you stretch forward too early, you can get clocked with the batter's backswing. You have to time it perfectly, sort of absorb the ball, you know, get onto your feet, toss the face mask, and step forward to be ready in case one of the runners takes off."

"Yes. Yes. I see. I see."

"Sometimes the batter will block you out, accidentally or on purpose, and you have to sort of elbow her out of the way to clear your throw line."

Claire looked at David and saw that they were both thinking the same thing. This was one of the longest speeches either one of them had ever heard from Lindsay.

Kamau had been nodding eagerly the whole time. "We call that sort of delivery a Yorker." He took another, deeper sip from his glass.

"A Yorker?"

"Yes. Yes, the ball is bowled so that it strikes the ground directly at the batsman's feet, just at what we call the crease. Very hard for the batsman to handle. It can skip under the bat, and strike the wicket, and the batsman will be, we call it, bowled out. When that happens, we say the batsman's been Yorked."

"In softball, if the batter is completely fooled, sometimes she'll swing at a ball in the dirt. This makes staying on top of it harder, so that you have to really . . ."

At this moment, the baby monitor, now sitting next to Claire's plate, emitted a trailing squeal. Kamau started and looked at it. "My goodness. What a useful device."

Everyone stopped to listen. After a few seconds, there was another, louder bleat, and almost immediately afterward a vigorous howl.

Kamau looked around anxiously. "Have we been talking too loudly?"

Claire started to get up, but David waved her down. "My turn. He probably just needs changing." As he trotted upstairs, the volume of Charlie's cries increased. Marlene hauled herself up and stood at the bottom of the stairs, wagging her tail vaguely.

Kamau continued in a half whisper, leaning toward Lindsay. "If the ball is bowled without bouncing at all, we call that a 'full toss,' which in cricket can be a serious mistake. A good batsman can hit a full toss very far."

Lindsay and Kamau continued for a few minutes in this vein, forking in Claire's chicken thoughtlessly and, from time to time, laughing as they compared their sports. At one point, Kamau poured himself another finger of scotch. The cries from the monitor softened but did not let up. After a while, Lindsay and Kamau seemed to realize that Claire was saying very little and returned to complimenting her food. This reminded her of something.

"Oh hell." Claire hopped up. "I left your ugali in the micro. I'm so sorry. I always do that."

"Please, please, don't trouble yourself with my embarrassing effort." Kamau waved. "My mother would be quite ashamed of me. She had a particular way of making ugali, using some special spices, so that it was so delicious, you know? My aunts always begged her, 'Hannah, teach us your secret.' But she passed on, sad to say, without revealing it even to me."

Claire suffered from mild tinnitus, a soft, high-pitched ringing in her right ear that she rarely noticed. Now, as the anxious chatter in her head ceased and her brain went silent, this slight squeal, like a high dial tone, was all she heard. She stood at the end of the table, feeling her breath coming and going.

"So." She sat back down. "Your mother was Hannah?" The ugali could wait.

"Yes, she liked to . . ."

"Hannah Nyeri, David's friend?"

Kamau stiffened. He set his glass down and put his hand over his mouth as though he wanted to take his words back.

Claire continued. "That was her name, right? Hannah Nyeri? When she and David met at the Institute?"

Kamau dropped his hands into his lap and closed his eyes.

"And your father." Claire picked up her fork and set it down. "David tells me he is a doctor."

"Yes, a professor at our School of Medicine."

"But he would actually be your stepfather."

Claire could see at the edge of her vision that Lindsay was aware of exactly what was happening. She had folded her hands on the table and was watching attentively, her eyes going back and forth between them.

"I think of him as my father."

"Mm-hmm."

"I-I didn't intend to mention my mother in this way. I wish . . ."

"Too late, David." Lindsay broke in. "It's obvious. I've known for the last half hour." She leaned toward Kamau and dropped her voice. "You're not really that great a dancer, you know. You dance like a parson. In fact, you dance just the way Uncle Dave would if . . ."

Claire finished the sentence. "If he hadn't been born in Wisconsin."

"Exactly." Lindsay patted Kamau's hand quickly. "Hello there, cuz." Then, she looked up at the ceiling and broke into a wondering smile. "Holy shit, we have the same grandpa."

Kamau put his hand on his forehead. "This was not . . ."

Lindsay turned to Claire. "And Uncle Dave hasn't figured this out yet, right?" When Claire shook her head, Lindsay added, "I love him, but he's an amazing doofus." Then, she gave Kamau another pat on the hand. "Welcome to the family." Her emotions were clearly beginning to well up. She added, her voice going unsteady, "And good luck, man." She sniffed and blinked. "Seriously. Good luck."

A very awkward silence followed, with Claire at the end of the table unable to move or speak, Kamau staring down into his lap, and

Lindsay beginning to breathe hard. Finally, she stood up. Her face was flushed. "Listen, guys, I think I'm going to skip dessert and head out."

Kamau glanced up. "No. Please. You mustn't . . ."

"Nope, nope, nope. If I hang around, I'm only going to lose it and start bawling my eyes out in front of everybody. Just . . ." She put her hand on her chest and took a deep, steadying breath. "Just tell Uncle Dave something." As she was leaving the room, she stopped in the doorway and looked back at Kamau. "I'll see you, right?"

"Yes."

"You have to . . ." Her voice by this time was shredding. "You have to come to one of my games, okay?"

"Yes, I will come."

"And meet Carmen."

"Yes."

As Lindsay hurried off, Claire heard her mumbling. "Can't believe this. I need to . . ."

Kamau's face was anguished. "I should go too. Will you tell him what has happened, please? And apologize for me. I didn't mean for this to come out in such a clumsy—"

"No. I won't do that. David would never forgive me. It has to be you."

"I can't. It would feel as though I came here because I wanted to claim something from him, when all I was looking for was—"

"I think you wanted this, David, even if you couldn't see it."

"I don't even look like him. I've searched so often for him in my face, but he is not there. I see only my mother."

"You don't look like him, David, but you are like him. You're like him in your bones. Does that make sense? Lindsay saw it right away." Claire picked up her glass and set it down. "Me, too, but I was fighting it for some reason."

"But how can I . . ."

"I don't know, but you have to tell him."

"I-I was afraid something like this would happen. I should not have come."

"Perhaps, David, but you did come." She picked up her napkin and put it down. "So."

There was a sound of clumping on the stairs and David came into the room, stage-whispering. "He's down, but maybe not out." He looked around. "Where's Lindsay?"

"She had something come up."

"Ah." He shook his head and smiled down at Kamau. "Typical, I'm afraid."

Claire looked to the side. Some strength, some spirit she could actually feel, was gathering inside her. This was not going to be easy. This would not be a simple thing. "David, I think you and David— you and Reverend Kamau—need to take Marlene for a walk." Marlene had curled up in a corner. She lifted her head at the sound of her name.

"But—"

"She needs one." Claire gave her husband a look she knew he couldn't miss. "She really does, David."

"Okay," David said uncertainly. "Okay." He nodded at Kamau who was sitting as though he'd been turned to stone. "Shall we?"

David obviously knew something was up. He just didn't know yet how far up that something was.

Charlie resumed his wailing almost as soon as the front door closed behind the two men, and Claire went upstairs. She hoisted the boy up out of his crib and sat down with him in the rocking chair by the window, feeling his precious weight relaxing against her chest. A sense of exhaustion fell over her. How would they ever manage this? Charlie squirmed once or twice and within a few seconds fell back to sleep. The light had faded, but through the window she could make out the two Davids walking down the driveway through the pines, with Marlene trotting ahead. Farther down, there was a light pole. Passing through the pool of amber light, Kamau was gesturing with his hand. David stopped at the edge of the glow, and Kamau, not noticing, continued for a few steps into the shadows before he realized that David was no longer next to him. He turned and looked back. Then, they just stood there, the two of them, staring at each other.

David, her dear, sweet husband, had two sons.

39

The pyramid of Dunkin' Donuts boxes in the war room at FBI headquarters in Boston was leaning precariously to one side. Patterson was slumping in a chair, feet on a table, headset in place, taking his night shift on the Jack Taylor intercept. His coffee was stone-cold. Something was floating in it.

Because Taylor was an attorney, the agents had to work in two teams. One agent—at the moment, Patterson—would monitor the calls for anything relevant to the Harvard bombing investigation, while a second agent would listen simultaneously to screen possible communications between Taylor and any of his legitimate law clients. The attorney general's guidelines dictated that Patterson had to turn off his headset as soon as any even arguable attorney-client communication commenced. The screening agent would then make a record of the communication and keep the transcript separate. This was called maintaining a "Chinese Wall" between properly discoverable evidence and protected communications— an antiquated and dubious term rendered especially ironic by the fact that Patterson's partner this evening was FBI Special Agent Alan Chen.

The double-teaming was turning out to be overkill, for the simple reason that, so far at least, Taylor never engaged in any attorney-client communications. As far as the monitoring agents could tell, Taylor didn't actually practice any law. He was all scam, all the time.

Patterson was flipping through the *Globe* financial pages, when the tap picked up an incoming call. He took his feet off the table, jotted down the time, and adjusted his headset. Taylor's voice was immediately recognizable.

Jack Taylor: Yeah?

[Inaudible.]

JT: You're breaking up, Dennis. Speak up or call me back.

Dennis (Last Name Unknown 1): Can you . . . can you hear me?

Patterson noted that Dennis LNU1 seemed to have an older man's voice.

JT: It's better. What's up.

LNU1: Fuckin' . . . [inaudible] . . . nowhere. Nothing to . . . [inaudible.]

JT: You're breaking up again. Call me back, for Christ's sake.

[Lengthy Static.]

JT: Hello?

LNU1: Hello? Hello? Is that better?

The caller's voice was reasonably clear now, distorted by only occasional bursts of static. Patterson jotted down that he was male and at least middle-aged. Certainly not young.

JT: Yeah, yeah, I hear you. What's up? It's late.

LNU1: Fuckin' power lines.

JT: Yeah.

LNU1: Your girl's not at her place.

JT: That's why you're calling me? Gimme a break. She's probably away for the weekend.

A second voice broke in, older and raspier.

LNU2: We don't like that, Jack. We don't want her going anywhere.

JT: Gerry, is that you? You're on the line too?

LNU2: I'm always on the line. I wouldn't let this idiot . . .

LNU1: We don't want her going any fucking where.

JT: Come on. She has a life, and she just did us another big . . .

LNU1: We don't like not knowing where the fuck she is, know what I mean?

JT: She's okay. Any problem with her, let me handle it. She's not . . .

LNU2: We're concerned she's up to something. She's not . . . she's . . . [inaudible]

JT: She's not up to shit.

LNU1: We're keeping an eye on her, you know?

JT: Feel free. You're wasting your time.

LNU1: And we don't like what's going on with Schwartz these days either. Fuckin' midget. We heard he's . . . [inaudible] . . . dicking around with the Muslim guy's court date. The fuck's up with that? It's making Gerry very fuckin' nervous. And you know how he gets when . . . [inaudible]. I can't sit on him forever.

LNU2: I'm just saying we might need to do something.

JT: Right. I heard about the Khan pretrial too. It could mean anything.

LNU2: We were lucky at the Yard, but . . .

LNU1: Yeah, who knew Armstrong would be sitting right next to the fucking . . .

LNU2: Shut up, Dennis.

JT: And no more pictures, okay? I told you that wouldn't work. Stupid idea.

LNU1: Didn't hurt to try. But that's not what we called about.

JT: Yeah?

LNU1: Your fuckin' buddy, Graham Tarbell . . .

JT: He's not my buddy.

LNU1: Schwartz starts sniffing around, Graham's a fuckin' hamburger.

JT: You might just be right.

LNU1: Take them two minutes to flip him. You need to talk to him.

JT: We got his money, Dennis. You got your slice.

LNU2: Our commission.

JT: Well, I'm not going anywhere near . . . [static, inaudible] . . . condescending asshole.

LNU1: The what?

JT: Never mind.

LNU1: We may need to . . . fuckin' whatever, you know?

The older voice was slower and sounded more educated.

LNU2: We're in the removal business, Jack. Our approach is simple: meet the client, identify the removal, do the removal, get paid, disappear.

LNU1: Once in a while, we remove the fuckin' client, too, on the way out.

LNU2: Pretty solid business model.

JT: Look, Gerry, do what you have to. Graham is not my problem anymore.

LNU1: It's getting fucked up, you know? Really . . . [inaudible] We're thinking we might have to fuckin' do something.

JT: Like I say, not my problem. We delivered, we got paid, we're done.

LNU1: Gotta go. Gotta go.

LNU2: We have to see someone.

JT: Fine. It's late.

LNU1: Tell your fuckin' girl to stay the fuck home.

JT: I'll do that. I'll call her. Don't worry, okay?

LNU1: Yeah. Sure. Fuck.

[Call ended.]

Patterson and Chen took off their headsets, looked at each other, and spoke at the same time.

"Dammit."

LNU's phone would almost certainly not be traceable. Dennis and Gerry would have bought a cheap mobile for cash, and they'd ditch it once the call was over. This was frustrating, but at the moment the two agents had another, more serious problem to solve.

The AG's guidelines created special procedures for situations where a wiretap turned up a credible threat to someone's life. If the risk were imminent and unambiguous, the line assistant U.S. attorney—in this case Bob Schwartz—had an obligation to report it to the higher-ups in D.C., and get guidance. Normally, they'd be instructed to reveal the tap to the man or woman whose life was at risk. The problem was that doing this could capsize the whole investigation. The warned party might contact the target and let him know he was being tapped. A very helpful source of intelligence would immediately dry up. Worst-case scenario, the target would take off.

Here, Patterson could argue that no imminent, unambiguous threat to Graham Tarbell or Angie Phipps had really turned up. It was a stretch, but the intercept might not be reportable.

Chen spoke. "You need to talk to Schwartz."

"Yeah, I know." Patterson took a sip of cold coffee. He spit something off the tip of his tongue. "But I'm not going to be in any hurry about it."

40

Norcross and Kamau walked slowly down the driveway in identical postures, hands clasped behind their backs, looking at the ground.

"It made me so happy, Mzee—I can scarcely find the words—when you mentioned my mother, with no prompting, at our first meeting. I almost revealed everything to you at that moment. Afterward, in the lift—in the elevator—I wept like a small child."

"I have never forgotten Hannah, never, even after more than twenty-five years."

"Yes. You made that obvious." Kamau wiped a hand over his face.

"Does your friend Mungai know? And the young woman from Finland?"

"Helena. Yes, she and Godfrey both know. Godfrey was furious in court before our first meeting. He wanted me to disclose everything straightaway and entreat your help. I refused." Kamau nodded at the ground. "That was not what I was there for."

"He's very worried about you."

"Yes, but still, you know, this was my decision to make, not his."

Norcross leaned forward, trying to look into Kamau's face. "But why did you hold back, David? Why didn't you tell me? You could have written."

Kamau stopped walking and turned toward him. "I did not know you, Mzee. Suppose you thought I was some charlatan looking for a handout? Suppose you demanded a DNA test or some other degrading proof?" He paused. "Plus, to be candid, I suppose I was simply shy. The words froze in my mouth, every time I even thought of uttering them. Some greater force took control this evening." His voice dropped. "God's gifts of mercy take strange forms."

They resumed walking. It was their third circuit down the driveway. The lights in the house had gradually gone off, and now only three remained, one by the front door and another upstairs in the bedroom where Claire waited. The third, the pole lamp at the edge of the lawn, shed its soft light on the shadowy drive. Marlene was staying close, glancing up at them from time to time, confused. Her nightly constitutional never went on this long.

"I wish . . ." Norcross hesitated. "I wish so much that Hannah had told me."

"When I was leaving for the UK, when she knew I would be away for a long time, she sat me down and revealed everything. She told me she regretted that she did not tell you." A tone of intensity came into Kamau's voice. "But she could not do that, you see? She could not let herself be another woman of Africa standing at a white man's door with an infant in her arms. Even at the door of a very honorable white man."

"But . . ."

"And you were gone before she even knew, Mzee, starting your life, far away. What were you going to do?" Kamau lifted his hands and dropped them. "Send her a check every month, as though she were some Oxfam charity case? No."

"I can see that, but . . ." Norcross broke off. "I don't know. I only wish I had known."

Kamau stopped again and turned to Norcross.

"We Kenyans, we are a vigorous, intelligent people, Mzee, and we have learned to be wary of condescending helpers. Assistance is welcome, of course, but not when it comes at the cost of self-respect. She would not take that risk, even with you." Kamau shook his head and expelled a breath. "But I am climbing onto my soapbox here. Forgive me."

He turned, and they continued to walk.

"I know it would have been complicated, but Hannah must have been—"

"My mother had no anger at you, none at all, but when I learned, I certainly did, you know? At first, I was mostly in shock. By the grace of God, and the caprice of genetics, my appearance is one hundred percent African. I never in my wildest dreams looked into the mirror and thought, 'There stands a white man's child.' Then, as I tried to absorb what my mother told me, I must confess, Mzee, I placed you in the role of the villain. Just another Mzungu walking away from an African woman. In time, I realized I was becoming a prey to hatred, which is why I wanted so much to see you, to set my eyes on the real man behind the caricature I had invented." Kamau gave a short, disgusted laugh. "Then, I barely arrive, and your people suspect me of helping to murder one of your cabinet ministers. How our Lord loves His little jokes!"

"It's absurd, I know." Norcross picked up a stick and tossed it into the woods. "But it's also dangerous, David. You must realize that."

Kamau looked up and spoke musingly. "Life is dangerous, Mzee. I have been compelled, for some years now, to make my peace with that."

Part of Norcross's mind was already at work trying to come up with ways to protect Kamau—protect his son—but at the moment his ideas were too vague and floundering to put into words. Vivid scraps of memory continued to bring Hannah back: the long walks they used to take through the coffee fields above the Institute's campus, sharing their dreams. Her musical laugh. Her smart, happy eyes.

"I . . . I could have done something," Norcross stared at the ground. "Hannah must have felt so alone."

"Perhaps, but not for long." Kamau lifted his hands. "She met my father—technically my stepfather, as I know now—barely two months after you left, while she was carrying me. He was a medical student and a very good man, Mzee. She was completely honest about her situation, but it did not matter to him one whit. They fell in love, and that changed everything." Kamau stopped again to look into Norcross's face. "There are many forms of love, of course, but theirs was boundless. They were mad for each other from the beginning, and grateful for every day they were given. Few people are so fortunate."

Kamau looked down at the ground. "I imagine she was concerned at first about what would happen, but I doubt that she was deeply frightened." He leaned toward Norcross and smiled. "My mother was not easily cowed by anything, you know."

"No. I certainly remember that."

"And our family is strong. She was, one might say, a blessed person." Kamau scratched the back of his head. "I do not believe she ever thought of herself as some great tragedy, some Madame Butterfly, or what have you. Many, many people embraced her. She would never have felt abandoned."

The dark pines along the driveway caught the humid breeze, rocked, and whispered. Somewhere in the eastern part of the sky, behind a gauze of cloud, the moon was rising. Its soft light, filtering through, silvered the hemlocks.

"I wish I'd seen her again. Just once."

"I think that would have happened, Mzee, if she had not . . ." Kamau cleared his throat and swallowed. "If she had not been called back."

"When did that happen? I couldn't bring myself to ask before."

Kamau sighed. "Three years ago, after I came down from Oxford. She was working with the UN, and there was a conference in Nakuru to discuss programs for AIDS orphans. On her return, on the escarpment, there was a car crash." Kamau closed his eyes and shook his head. "I don't know if my father, my stepfather, was merely trying to console me, but he said it was very quick. She did not suffer, he said." After a silence, Kamau added, "Those she left behind certainly suffered and still do, to this day. I doubt my stepfather will ever remarry."

Together they dropped into wordlessness, adrift in their mutual loss, walking in unison. Norcross laid his arm over Kamau's shoulders, and Kamau reciprocated, putting his arm around Norcross's back, pulling him close. The stillness that gathered around them felt like a presence.

Kamau spoke softly. "God alone knows why people are taken out of this world. Or brought into it."

When they were turning for the fourth time, the breeze died. The light swelled as the moon threw sharper shadows across the driveway. They dropped their arms, and Norcross shook his head. "I miss her. We could have been such good friends."

"Hannah would certainly have liked Claire. They are both, you know, strong women." Kamau touched Norcross's arm and gave another of his short laughs. "Claire would brook no tiptoeing from me, Mzee, I can tell you that."

"My meeting Claire was like a miracle."

"Yes, they do happen, more than we think." Kamau gazed up into the sky for few moments, exhaled a deep breath, and turned back to Norcross. "I don't wish to impose myself on you, but I would like very much, at a proper time, to meet your son, Charles. I was hoping to see you, but I foolishly never considered that I might have—you remember the phrase?—an *ndugu mdogo*? A baby brother?"

"I've forgotten so much of my Swahili, but that much remains, yes." Norcross touched Kamau's arm, his voice deepening. "You must of course meet the boy. You will . . ."

"I will love him."

They approached the house, and Kamau walked over to his car. "It would be best, I think, for me to go now. Please thank Claire." He smiled. "Thank her for being so fierce."

"I'm so glad you have forgiven me. You understand, Hannah and I were very young and very . . ."

"Yes, and you never dreamed that you were starting a family." He put his hand on Norcross's shoulder. "You must forgive me, too, Mzee. I was very, very determined to be born."

41

Dana and Cameron Schwartz, eleven and eight, were kicking a soccer ball around in the front yard of their home in the village of Waban in Newton, Massachusetts. It was Sunday afternoon, they'd had lunch, and they were killing time waiting for their father to come home to watch the Red Sox game with them. Their little brother was having his nap, and their mother wanted them both outside. The off-and-on drizzle earlier that morning had finally let up.

These Sunday baseball games had become a much-anticipated family ritual to make up for their dad's late nights and weekends. He was going through another one of his typical work blitzes, at the courthouse constantly, so this was about the only time they saw him. Their mom always made her amazing cheese popcorn.

Newton was an upscale suburb, seven miles west of Boston, consistently rated one of the most livable, and safest, small cities in the United States. The Fig Newton was invented here, and the town's boundaries embraced Heartbreak Hill, a famously grueling segment of the Boston Marathon. Waban was one of Newton's most comfortable neighborhoods, a village of large, well-maintained homes and tree-lined streets.

As he passed the ball back to his brother, Dana Schwartz was keeping an eye on Sally Hoffman, who was also eleven and in the same class he was in. She was watching Cameron and him from her front stoop next door. Sally was better at soccer than either of the boys, and Dana knew it, which was why he wasn't asking her to come over. Dana could tell that the clumsy way Cameron was kicking the ball sometimes, using his toe instead of the side of his foot, was driving Sally crazy. Their yard sloped downhill, and the ball kept shooting stupidly off to the side and bouncing into the street. Every time this happened, Sally would slap her knee and look off over her shoulder, as though she were trying to find someone to complain to.

Apart from being a better soccer player, Sally was taller than Dana, and her long legs allowed her to run faster. Her breasts were just beginning to get noticeable too. She was wearing a pink Red Sox hat with her blond ponytail sticking out the back, which—Dana had to admit—made her look, he guessed, sort of hot. This was another reason he was doing his best to ignore her. If he paid the slightest attention to Sally, his gabby, extroverted brother would shower him with taunts.

Twice now, Cameron had fumbled the ball over onto Sally's lawn, and she'd sent it back at Dana with hard, well-aimed kicks that he'd barely managed to handle. Unlike, Cameron, Dana was a quiet boy. The whole situation was beginning to stress him out so much that he was looking for an excuse to go inside and read a book. Dad would be home any minute now, anyway.

At this awkward moment, a white delivery van drew up. It braked with a squeak in front of the Hoffman house, and the driver leaned and called out something from the passenger window. Dana watched as Sally got up and walked over.

It was some lady in a brown uniform. Sally had to speak up. "Excuse me?" She went right up to the van's window.

"Looking for the Schwartz house. Is that you, sweetheart?"

The question didn't surprise Dana. The house number next to their door was obscured by ivy, and his dad had deliberately not put their name on the mailbox out by the road. People got confused all the time.

"You want them." Sally pointed at Dana and Cameron. They'd stopped playing. Cameron, staring at the van with his mouth open, picked up the ball and tucked it under his arm for safekeeping, then walked up the slope toward their front door.

The truck crawled down to the Schwartz driveway, with Sally, looking nonchalant, following across her lawn. The woman called out to Dana.

"Hello, dear, can you help me out?" She had pulled over to the side of the street, two wheels on their grass.

Dana walked over. "What do you want?" He kept his distance, outside her reach. Cameron had seated himself up on the front stoop, watching.

The woman in the uniform checked the address on the package. "Is your dad Robert Schwartz?"

Dana made a noncommittal movement with his shoulder. His father had instructed Cameron and him many times not to touch any packages that came to the house and to keep their distance from delivery trucks. Back during the holidays, Dana had brought a parcel inside once, and he'd lost his computer privileges for an entire weekend.

Cameron yelled out a warning. "Dana!" He stood, dropped the ball onto the grass, and set his hands on his hips.

Dana turned and shouted back in an annoyed voice, "I know, Cameron!" He really didn't need his little brother telling him how to handle this situation, especially with Sally a few yards away on the sidewalk.

The lady got out and came around the front of the van carrying a brown cardboard box with printing on the side. "Okay. I'm just going to set it by your mailbox, all right?" It looked like some medium-sized appliance, like a microwave, not very heavy. "Just let your dad know it's here." She pointed up at the murky sky. "Probably be better if it didn't get soaked."

The lady made her way slowly back around the front of the van, took her time backing off the grass, then picked up speed and turned at the end of the block. Dana walked back toward the house, determined to go in, but keeping one eye on Sally over his shoulder.

She was either bored or nosy, or maybe both, and took a few steps to where the package sat by their mailbox. She didn't touch it but leaned forward, trying to read the printing on the side. As she did this, she reached absently around to rub the back of her neck.

The gesture accentuated the slight curve of her chest, and this momentary distraction meant that Dana did not notice when Cameron took a short run off the porch and drilled the soccer ball extra hard down the slope at him. Dana was only able to deflect the ball at the last second, so that it went bounding toward Sally.

Dana opened his mouth to call out a warning but hesitated because he thought what was about to happen might be funny. The ball glanced off Sally's right knee and hit the box fairly hard. She hadn't seen it coming and, for a split second, looked startled.

Dana was aware of a shattering bang, the sound of breaking glass, and some heavy, rushing blow that knocked him off his feet. He found himself on his back, half stunned. Over the violent ringing in his ears, he could hear Cameron screaming, but he couldn't make out the words.

42

The waiting room of Tarbell & Knight was so spotlessly elegant that it looked as though it had just come back from the dry cleaner. The large, gold-framed watercolors of Faneuil Hall, the Statehouse, and Beacon Hill projected good taste and safe New England values, while the expensive walnut paneling, inlaid coffee tables, thick carpeting, and plush leather chairs were clearly chosen to make the firm's clients feel privileged to pay $700 an hour, or more, for the firm's confidential advice.

It was against protocol for Mike Patterson even to be sitting here, but the Waban bombing the day before had ratcheted everything up. Sally Hoffman was dead, and someone out there was going crazy-homicidal. It was time for some rule bending. Plus, Dana Schwartz was home resting after a night at the Newton-Wellesley Hospital, and Bob Schwartz was spending the day with his family. Patterson was not going to bother Schwartz to get clearance for this interview, especially since he probably wouldn't get it. This was one of those intuitive, high-stakes decisions Patterson was ready to take responsibility for. The O'Connell trial was continuing through its plodding phase—the testimony of the expert witness on the structure of racketeering organizations—and Papadakis had no problem letting him slip away for a couple of hours.

The goal was to convince Graham Tarbell to cooperate, or at least to get him thinking about it. Informing Graham that one of his buddies might be planning to take him out was obviously one way to do that. On the other hand, the situation was tricky. He didn't plan to disclose the wiretap, but if the interview fell apart, Graham might panic and get in touch with Jack Taylor. Taylor would immediately figure out what was going on, toss his cell in a dumpster, and head for Logan Airport. The tap would be blown, and Patterson would be in big trouble.

"Mr. Tarbell will see you."

"Thanks."

The young Latina woman who ushered him down the corridor was a perfect reflection of the waiting room's good taste: smartly dressed in a pale green suit and cream-colored blouse, heels not too high, small gold hoops in her ears, and a poised, competent stride.

"Beautiful day out there, Mr. Patterson." She spoke over her shoulder. Her speech was lightly accented.

"Going to be a hot one."

"Please." She gestured toward the doorway of a corner office and slipped off.

Graham Tarbell was sitting at a spacious oak desk—the size, it seemed, of a Ping-Pong table—positioned at an angle between two walls of glass. Behind him, in the hazy morning air, Patterson could see the Bunker Hill Monument in the distance. Graham had a telescope rigged up on a tripod pointing toward it. On the other side, where the view faced the Old North Church, an enormous ceramic pot holding some sort of flowering tree stood in the sunlight. The draft from the air-conditioning was making its leaves quiver. Against a wall of books, someone had set up an easel with an architectural drawing of a handsome colonial house. The office was meticulously designed to impress, and it succeeded.

Piles of paper fanned out in a semicircle in front of Graham. He was clearly hard at work on something, or at least trying to look as though he was. His laptop was open, his tie was loose, and the sleeves of his white dress shirt were rolled up to his elbows.

The track lighting in the ceiling was bouncing off his shiny bald head.

"Hello." He looked up blankly. "I have no idea what this is all about."

Patterson closed the door behind him. "Mind if I have a seat?"

"I've, uh, got a pretty busy morning here."

"Can I sit down?" Patterson gestured at one of the chairs facing the desk, and Graham nodded. He held out his identification. "Mike Patterson. FBI."

"I know. Marta told me. Should I get a lawyer?" Graham said this in a light tone that might, or might not, be ironical. He gestured toward the door. "Just a shout away."

Patterson put his badge back and sat down, returning Graham's smile. "Up to you." He waved a hand. "But this is no big deal. Just trying to get some routine background."

"Okay. Happy to help, if we can make it quick."

"Ten minutes, max." Patterson looked around. "Beautiful office."

"Thanks. I like it."

"That your house?" He pointed at the easel.

"Place my wife and I are fixing up on the Vineyard, in West Tisbury." Graham folded his hands on the desk, composing himself. "Sorry, um, I don't want to . . ." He gestured down at the papers.

"I understand. We're following up on an informal request for assistance from the federal court here in Boston."

"Uh-huh."

He deliberately let several seconds go by, allowing Graham see that he was eyeballing him and that there might be something extra behind what he was saying. As with most of these encounters, Patterson was communicating as much, or more, with his body as he was with his words. Graham did a reasonable job of maintaining a blank expression. He kept his mouth closed and only blinked twice.

"One of the clerk's office staff was concerned about something to do with case assignments. It's probably nothing, but we noticed that your firm is defending a lawsuit that was recently filed against a local outfit, Cimarron Systems. My supervisor asked me to drop by and see if you noticed anything unusual about that process."

"What do you mean, 'anything unusual'?" Graham made air quotes, sounding unconcerned.

Patterson gave him another long stare. This time, Graham dropped his eyes and rearranged one of his paper piles. Compared to other acts he'd witnessed, Patterson would give Graham's performance maybe a B.

"Don't know, really. The guy I talked to didn't have many details." Keeping his tone offhand, he gave the big push. "Was there anything at all, for example, that seemed out of the ordinary about the process of assigning *Cimarron* to Margaret Helms?"

Graham responded quickly. "No. Nothing as far as I could tell." He turned to look out the window, making a show of recalling the details. "Let's see. The plaintiffs' firm filed the complaint, the case was randomly drawn to Judge Helms, and we accepted service on behalf of Cimarron." He shifted back to Patterson. "I'm told our litigation team will be moving for an extension to put together a motion to dismiss." He leaned back and turned up his palms. "That's it. Nothing at all unusual that I know about."

This was a felony. A person could decline to speak to an FBI agent, but if they did speak and deliberately lied, as Graham just had, then that was a crime carrying a prison term of up to five years. Bob Schwartz would, without any doubt, prosecute Graham for this, and possibly other crimes. Life as he'd known it was over for Graham Tarbell as of that moment. He just didn't know it yet.

Patterson let an even longer silence draw out this time. Finally, he slid forward in his chair and set his hand on the desk.

"If you know anything unusual, Mr. Tarbell, anything at all, about how *Cimarron* ended up before Judge Helms, it would be very much in your interest to speak to me."

It was the trapdoor moment. Graham pulled his chin in, and the color drained from his face as he dropped through. From this point, they would be communicating in two channels: the false channel with words, and the true channel without them.

"I have no idea what you're talking about." Graham's mouth had gone slack.

"I think you do."

"I really don't." Graham licked his lower lip.

It was pathetically obvious that Graham did know—knew in his heart, lungs, and bowels—exactly what Patterson was talking about. He knew, first, that the FBI had found out about *Cimarron*, and, second, that he was in very deep, possibly bottomless, trouble. But Graham's brain was still refusing to acknowledge reality, too frozen to take in what his other terrified organs knew perfectly well.

"Listen." Patterson spoke with sympathy. "I know this is hard. But if you have been dealing with certain people, especially one particular person, I have an obligation to tell you that you may be in danger. We could offer you some protection."

"From what? I don't need any protection." Graham ran a hand over the top of his head. "I'd like you to go now, if you don't mind."

Patterson continued staring at Graham for maybe fifteen seconds, a long time, not saying anything.

Graham blinked back at him, finally pointing at the door. "You need to . . ."

"Sure." Patterson stood up and put his card on Graham's desk. "But I'm going to leave you this. Please think carefully about what you're doing."

"I don't need to think about it." Graham licked his lip again.

Patterson slowly leaned forward and put both hands on the desk. "Remember your family, Mr. Tarbell." From this angle, he towered over Graham, who seemed to shrink. "Remember your kids."

"I really have nothing to say, Mr. Patterson."

"You might consider consulting a lawyer."

"I *am* a lawyer. Jesus Christ." Graham shifted and squared his shoulders. "I haven't done anything, and I have nothing to be afraid of." He nodded again toward the door. "We're done here."

"You might want to talk with your brother."

"Get out."

Patterson straightened. "I really hope you'll reconsider." He took his time walking to the door, turned, looked back at Graham for a count of four, and left.

He spent the drive through the downtown traffic reviewing the interview, running over the sequence of his questions and the substance of Graham's responses. He'd deliberately taken no notes to avoid making his target jumpy. If he'd overplayed his hand, Schwartz was going to kill him.

Back at his desk, Mike Patterson typed out a summary of his report, memorializing the sequence and exact words he'd used in putting the key questions and precisely what Graham had said in response. If it came down to a trial, it might be his testimony against Graham's, and he wanted his report in the system, with the date and time noted only half an hour after the interview, backing him up word for word.

When he was satisfied with the draft, he picked up his phone and called Bob Schwartz. He was hoping to get away with just leaving a message, but Schwartz must have been keeping his cell phone close, and he answered immediately.

"Yeah, Mike. What's up?"

"Wanted to check on how you all were doing."

"Thanks." He could hear the strain in Schwartz's voice. "We're managing, I guess. Dana's okay now, physically okay, but not saying much. All he wants to do is read. I can't get him to talk." He paused. "Cameron's my big worry at the moment, though. He's . . ." There was another pause, while Schwartz seemed to decide not to go into any more details. "Anyway, we're managing. We're okay, but that's about it."

"You all safe there?"

"They've got somebody parked out front. It's a pain, but . . ."

"Good."

"Is that why you called?"

"Not really." Patterson stepped off the high dive. "I just got back from talking to Graham Tarbell." An ominous silence rose up on the other end of the line. "I couldn't just—"

"Goddammit, Mike, you shouldn't have done that. We weren't ready."

"I know, but—"

"Who went with you? Chen?"

"I went by myself."

"You're shitting me."

"Two agents would have spooked him. It had to feel—"

"You're way over the line here, Mike." Patterson winced as Schwartz expelled an angry breath. "I can't deal with this right now. There was no goddamn reason for you to rush this."

"Well . . ."

"No reason at all."

"I don't agree, Bob."

"Disagree all you want, but don't jump the fence on me."

Patterson picked up a pencil and jotted down the time. He might want to include this call in his report.

"Do you want to hear how it went, or should we save it for a better time?"

Someone called out in the background. Patterson couldn't tell whether it was one of the boys or Schwartz's wife.

"Fine. Let's hear." The muddled voice in the background repeated whatever it was saying, still indistinct but closer, and this time Patterson could tell it was one of the boys. Schwartz's voice dropped as he turned away and responded, "Two minutes, Cameron, okay?" Then he came back. "Let's hear."

"Graham's not interested in helping us. Not right now anyway. It's possible he'll—"

"You asked him to cooperate? Just like that?" Schwartz blew out a massive sigh. "Shit, Mike."

"No, no, of course not. But I gave him an opportunity, even offered protection, and he didn't bite."

"Uh-huh. I bet he didn't."

"If we can't bring him around, I'm worried someone will pay him a visit, probably in the next couple days, end of the week at the latest."

Another silence followed that Patterson had to force himself not to interrupt. When Schwartz spoke, his voice was low. "I have a dead child next door, Mike. Graham Tarbell made his choice. He can go to hell."

"Come on. You know we need to report this up the line and get instructions."

"If I make the call to Washington, the assistant AG might instruct me to tell Graham about the tap on Taylor, and it could damage the whole investigation." Schwartz's voice went up. "I'm sick of these Graham Tarbell types. They start with some big-firm hard-ball—that's all they think it is—and they end up killing little girls. I want names."

"I want them as much as you do, Bob. That's why—"

"I want all the names. We need to keep the intercept going."

"I can document in my report that I warned Graham."

"You informed him he was at risk?"

"More or less."

"Did you tell him how we knew? Did you mention the tap?"

"No."

"Then your warning probably wasn't good enough. You know that."

"It buys us time. We're pretty busy, but I can have someone try to keep an eye on his house."

A voice rose again in the background, more drawn out and impatient. "Daaad!"

"I have to go, Mike. Really."

"You'll get in touch with Washington?"

"Yes, but I have my priorities here, including a funeral tomorrow. It may take me a couple days to report this and get my walking orders. Meanwhile, tell your guys to keep those headsets on."

43

It was Monday evening, her second dinner alone at the Red Lion Inn in Stockbridge, and Angie Phipps was going nuts. Tom Redpath had instructed her to stay away from her condo for a while—he didn't say how long—and she'd packed up and left right after Friday's big huddle. She'd negotiated an emergency crash on a friend's couch in Mattapan for Friday and Saturday, but the friend had a small apartment, a baby, and a husband with big eyes.

Sunday, she'd driven out to visit Ronnie at his program and decided to stay on for a while at the Red Lion, a few miles down the road, until she could decide what to do. She hated eating alone—it felt incredibly weird—and she had no idea where things would go, long term. She felt like she was floating alone in outer space with nothing in sight and nothing to hold on to.

The main advantage of Stockbridge, besides the three hours' distance from Boston, was that she could visit Ronnie more often—not every day, since that disrupted his schedule and got him worked up, but at least every two or three days. The Red Lion Inn was four-and-a-half stars on TripAdvisor and not cheap, especially during the summer high season, but a couple of years back the good folks at

Capital One Mastercard had graciously extended Angie a $50,000 credit line. They were going to regret that, by God.

She had the same waiter for this second dinner, a nice kid just out of high school, taking advantage of a summer job to save for college. She was desperate for company, and they'd had some friendly conversation about his future plans. She'd left him a big tip.

He came over. "Another glass of wine?"

Phipps had drunk three glasses of cabernet with dinner the evening before, and he'd obviously remembered, which was sweet.

"Two's enough tonight, thanks. I want to be on my toes."

"Uh-uh. Monday night." He smiled. "Got something special happening?"

This was almost certainly an innocent question, but Phipps in her boredom could not resist some harmless flirting.

"Don't know yet." She lifted her eyebrows at him. "I'm pondering the situation." The boy twitched, and his eyes went wide.

This was ridiculous. He had a clump of hair sticking out the side of his head, and he was heading off in six weeks to study chemical engineering at Worcester Polytechnic Institute. He looked like the captain of the chess team.

"Want to take a look at the dessert menu?"

She was about to respond with, *I wouldn't say no to something sweet,* when Carl Alberti slid into the chair opposite and folded his arms.

Phipps gaped for a several seconds. "Well, shit."

"Back at you, Angie." He did not smile.

She looked up at the waiter. "Just coffee, please. Caffeinated."

After the WPI boy disappeared, she and Carl sat and looked at each other for a long time. Eventually, he cocked his head to one side and raised his eyebrows. He was ready to talk, but he was going to let her take the lead.

"How did you find me?"

Alberti held up three fingers. "Ronnie's program. Red BMW with your tags. High-end place to stay."

"High end?"

"You have good taste, Angie." He looked her in the eyes. "And you don't have a lot to lose right now."

"Guess that's right."

The waiter delivered the coffee and ducked his head to Alberti.

"Get you anything, sir?" All of a sudden, he looked about twelve years old.

"No." Alberti shot him a glance. "Give us some space, though, okay?"

As soon as the waiter was out of earshot, Alberti looked around and spoke, keeping his voice low. "You need to move."

Phipps took her time putting the cream and sweetener in her coffee. "I'm pretty happy where I am, Carl."

"You heard about the bombing in Waban Sunday?"

"I haven't been reading the papers."

"Uh-huh. Listen. You're not hard to find. It took me less than an hour on the phone." He looked around, studying the room. "Couple of old cop friends here in the Berkshires, and if they can find you—"

"Yes," she interrupted. "But you have connections."

"Right. There's a guy in a black Lexus with dealer plates parked across the street." He pointed with his thumb toward the entry. "He's using binoculars, and he's not one of ours."

"Well, if he keeps sitting there, pretty soon somebody's going to—"

"They have a relay vehicle, Angie, a green Malibu."

"Relay?"

"Switching cars so they don't attract attention. It's called handing off the eyeball. They're not kidding around."

Phipps tried not to show it, but this really scared her. She could end up like Newbury's girlfriend or—she could barely let herself think it—like Warren Armstrong. How had her life gotten so messed up? She was not that bad a person.

Carl held her gaze with his eyes. "You need to get out of here right now." He sat back and waited while some people made their way past them. "Give me the key to your room. I'll collect your stuff."

"I thought you were off the case."

"I am." His expression altered slightly, the beginning of a smile perhaps, or a grimace. "I'm taking some personal time here." He looked around the room. "Everyone loves the Berkshires in the summer."

"Carl, you have to know, I never, ever . . ."

"I know. I had a heart-to-heart with Mike Patterson. We'll talk about all that later."

"I never would have . . ."

"I know." He reached across the table, not quite touching her hand. "Give me ten minutes and then go out the back." He nodded toward a hallway at the far end of the room. "I'll swing around. Get in the rear passenger side and lie down on the seat. We'll leave your car here."

"Where will we go?"

"Wherever you want to go."

"I don't—"

"I have a friend with an empty lake house not far from here. It'll do for a day or two."

The waiter eased up, glancing nervously at Alberti. "Check?"

"I'll put it on my room like before." Phipps quickly signed the bill, adding her usual forty percent tip. She smiled up at him. "Thank you, Rickie. You're awesome."

Alberti sighed and scratched the side of his head.

When the boy had left, Phipps looked at Alberti. "The room's a real mess, Carl. It's kind of embarrassing."

"I've spent time in your bedroom, Angie. I won't be shocked." He held out his hand. "Key?"

44

Dominic O'Connell was in his upstairs office, getting ready for court and keeping an ear out for Rafferty and Aidan. The portrait was still standing in the corner on its easel, waiting for Julie to decide where she wanted to hang it. They had made love twice since their very successful anniversary dinner, and O'Connell was reflecting that an occasional happy afternoon was not the worst way to get through home confinement. It beat the hell out of Scrabble.

O'Connell knew it didn't make sense, but as he slipped on his suit jacket, he was feeling more optimistic about the trial. The lies Brian Shaughnessy had told Papadakis to beef up his story were pathetic, and some flickers of eye contact from two or three of the jurors had been encouraging. They seemed to like him. All his life O'Connell had believed that by good luck or brass balls he could get through anything, and the trial was no different. Somehow, he would beat this.

The missing payment he'd made to Sam Newbury was irritating him much more. Someone had screwed him, and he was determined to get his money back. Newbury's death hadn't changed that. The conversation after Rafferty and Aidan arrived went straight to this topic.

"Sam Newbury must have been spreading oil on somebody." He sat down on a leather hassock and began tying his shoe. "And whoever it was must have been working at the courthouse. Or had a pal who did."

Rafferty was leaning against the doorframe with his disapproving frown. "Aidan's come up with an idea." Raff was a good man but kind of an old lady, fussing about the trial into the wee hours. He'd made it clear that, for him, the Newbury money was a dangerous distraction.

"Yeah?" O'Connell looked over at Aidan. "What's your idea?"

Aidan had turned the desk chair around and sat, looking down at the carpet with his usual end-of-the-world expression. Aidan's chronic gloom was his strength. Nobody gets pushy with a guy who really doesn't give a damn about much.

"The girl who calls your case?" Aidan looked up. "The one at the desk up front?"

"Yeah?"

"Turns out she also handles the case assignments. Or most of them."

"Really."

"I got to talking with her during one of the breaks. We both like cars."

"Don't go romantic on me, Aidan."

"She's okay." Aidan hesitated, making O'Connell wonder if Aidan did have something for her. She was certainly a cookie.

Aidan continued. "But I never mix business. Anyway, she drives a brand-new BMW X5. I talked to a couple people, and it turns out she lives in this pricey condo on Memorial Drive. Unless she hit the lottery . . ."

"What's her name again?"

"Phipps. Angela Phipps. Angie."

"Stay on her."

"She's taken off somewhere." Aidan sniffed and swallowed. "I'll find her."

O'Connell leaned forward to tie his shoe. "If she's mixed up in this, I doubt she dreamed up the scheme herself."

"She hasn't been in court since the bombing Sunday."

O'Connell smiled. "You noticed, huh?"

"Or last Friday either."

Rafferty broke in. "The Waban blast has Gerry Doyle's finger-prints all over it. I'm still thinking, Dom, maybe I should have a talk on the side with Patterson. I bet he'd—"

O'Connell shook his head. "I've never played the rat game—Uncle Tommy would turn over in his grave—and I'm not starting with the Doyles. They have long memories." He poked a finger at Aidan. "Find out who this Angela Phipps's friends are. Keep an eye on her, okay? Somebody has my dough, and I want it back."

Rafferty sighed impatiently. "We're in good shape these days, Dom. Even with the Newbury money gone, we're sitting pretty." Among his other duties, Rafferty kept his eye on the books, making sure the accountants had everything squared up and kept their hands out of the cash register. It was complicated, since there were two sets of books.

"Maybe. But, like the man says, every little bit extra is just that much more. Bring up the car, okay? I'm going to find Julie. We don't want to keep our fan club waiting."

Julie was in the kitchen, and as O'Connell entered, she was putting the phone down. When she turned her face to him, he knew that something was wrong.

"Julie?"

"I don't think I can go to court today, Dom. Something has—"

"What's happened, sweetheart? You look—"

"The thing in Waban?" Julie's face was pale, and her lips were trembling. "The papers mentioned a child, but they didn't, you know, they didn't release the name."

"Right. I remember."

"That was my friend Laura Hoffman on the phone. She could hardly talk. It was her granddaughter, Dom. Her granddaughter Sally was the one who—"

"Oh Christ, Julie." He stepped quickly over and put his arms around her. "I'm so sorry."

She spoke into his shoulder. "I held Sally, Dom." Her voice rose up. "I remember I was visiting Laura, and I held her when she was just a little baby." She stepped back and folded her arms in front of her. "You know, the way you, you know . . ."

"Oh, Julie, I'm so sorry. I don't—"

"I remember it like yesterday. She wasn't smiling yet, but she was looking at me as though she was thinking about smiling. That face babies get when they . . ." She pressed her face into his chest and began to sob.

O'Connell pictured his three girls—especially Chloe, his youngest and secret favorite, with the infant on the way—and he felt himself turning to ice. It was a rare but recognizable feeling for him, one he hadn't experienced for a while, when his anger took control. No thoughts, just a still, freezing, dangerous emptiness.

Julie breathed in. "Laura called to ask me to come sit with her. Somehow, it's all come crashing down, I guess, the realization. They'd made plans for Sally's birthday, she'd bought presents, and she's . . . she's out of her mind." Julie looked up at O'Connell. "I have to go to her, but I don't want to . . ."

"No, no, no."

"It's stupid, but I'm worried that Tarbell will be pissed."

"You go, sweetheart. Sandy can say what he wants. He's not the boss."

"If I don't pull myself together, I won't be any use to you at all."

"You'll manage. You always do." He gave her another long hug. "I love you, darling. You go now." As she hurried out the back toward the garage, he added more softly, "You are a dear soul."

O'Connell strode quickly through the house and out the front door. Rafferty and Aidan were waiting in the car, with Rafferty at the wheel and Aidan in back as usual.

He slipped into the front passenger seat and turned to look at them.

"Something's come up you need to know about." His voice was very tight but very calm as he passed on what Julie had told him. When he finished, he said, "Gerry and Dennis have crossed the line. I want you to find them."

Aidan did not change expression. "Give me a day or two."

"They've upset Julie." Rafferty looked over his shoulder checking for traffic. "That's enough for me."

"Fine. Let's get going." O'Connell nodded impatiently at the windshield.

"Let us take care of this, Dom." Rafferty pulled away from the curb. "Might be time for the Doyles to have a little accident."

45

United *States v. O'Connell* was moving more quickly than Judge Norcross had expected. Sandy Tarbell, to the judge's relief, spent only two hours cross-examining the government's RICO expert. He wisely chose not to contest what Papadakis's direct examination had made blatantly clear, which was that Tommy Gallagher had run a classic racketeering organization and that he had been a very bad man. During his questioning, Tarbell was mostly content to have the expert repeat, four or five times, that he had no knowledge of the teenage Dominic O'Connell's role, if any, in Gallagher's mob back in 1968 and had no idea whether he'd ever done anything to further his uncle's corrupt activities.

When he cross-examined the government's second witness, Dr. Ahmed Aziz, a professor at the U.S. Naval Academy who had examined Scanlon's exhumed remains, Tarbell put the first points on the board for the defense. After confirming that the police officer had indeed died many decades before as a result of a violent strangulation, the witness conceded that there was no evidence of a fracture to Scanlon's skull consistent with having received a blow from a heavy object like a wrench prior to his death. Papadakis, her arms folded, maintained a studiously bored expression as this portion of her case threatened to collapse.

It was always remarkable to Judge Norcross how his raised position allowed him to see, immediately, when the jurors were paying attention and when they were glazing over. More than half of the panel members leaned forward, scribbling away in their notebooks, during this segment of Tarbell's cross. They continued to follow the testimony alertly when Papadakis spent much of her redirect of Dr. Aziz prying out a rebuttal. It *was* possible, the witness said, for a person to suffer a concussion, including one that resulted in unconsciousness, without a skull fracture that would be evident during a forensic examination fifty years later. After this, Tarbell's recross laboriously established that *some* evidence of damage to the skull, though not certain, was *likely* if such an incident really had occurred. As this wrestling match dragged on, Norcross saw from his perch how several of the jurors started to squirm and glance up at the clock. The panel seemed relieved when Norcross intervened, repeated his standard end-of-the day instructions, and brought a conclusion to the trial day.

As the jurors made their way out, the judge called after them, "See you tomorrow. It's hot out there, so stay cool."

Muted laughter floated up, and Juror Eight, an Italian woman from the North End, said, "Won't be easy," which got some chuckles. The group was clearly coming together.

Once the door had closed, Norcross looked down at Papadakis. "Okay. Who will the government be leading off with tomorrow?"

Papadakis stood. "Loreen Laplante, Your Honor." She was propping her hands on the table, looking tired. "I will be an hour and a half, two hours, with her, at the most. I expect to have Brian Shaughnessy here tomorrow or the day after."

Tarbell, looking weary, too, got to his feet more slowly than usual. "I may be a while with Ms. Laplante, Judge. I take it your decision on her diary still stands?"

"If your cross-examination is going to suggest that she is either misremembering or fabricating something, then, yes, I will allow the government to put in the relevant portions of the diary as corroboration."

Tarbell frowned. "Well, Judge, you know it won't be possible for me to question Ms. Laplante without suggesting that she is either misremembering or fabricating. I just can't . . ."

"Then the diary's coming in."

"Please note my objection on the record."

"Your objection couldn't be clearer, Mr. Tarbell." Norcross pointed behind him. "I can feel the breath from the court of appeals on my neck right now." He stood up. "See you tomorrow morning. Court's in recess."

As soon as Norcross was out of the courtroom, Tarbell twisted around to confront O'Connell. "The fuck is Julie?"

O'Connell did not look at him. "She had something come up."

"Like what?"

O'Connell shrugged, and from the neighboring table Tarbell noticed Papadakis peering over with a faint smile. He walked around to where O'Connell was sitting and leaned over him, whispering fiercely. "If Julie doesn't give a shit about you, Dom, how do you expect the jury to?"

"Keep your shorts on, Sandy. She'll be here tomorrow." O'Connell closed his eyes, and his face tightened as though he were feeling some pain. "I have to sit for a second."

"You okay?"

"I'm fine." O'Connell looked up. "Go home. Rafferty will be here in a minute."

"I need to talk with you. I have a couple questions about this Laplante person."

"Call me tonight. Go home."

As soon as he was outside in the corridor, Tarbell switched on his cell. Norcross had a strict rule about phones in the courtroom. A forbidden ringtone that interrupted a proceeding meant a contempt citation with a fine of $250.

He had three messages from Colleen O'Connell, obsessing about things she might or might not be sure about, anxious about what Papadakis might ask her. Tarbell had tried to recruit Dom to talk to his sister and settle her down, but he had refused. Tarbell had been planning to ask Julie for help with Colleen, which was part of the reason he was so annoyed that she hadn't shown up today.

After he'd listened to Colleen, Tarbell noticed that he had another message, farther up the queue, from his brother's wife, Alice. This was weird. Alice never called Tarbell. She hated him. From the first words of the recording, it was clear she was working hard to hold herself together. She was very sorry to bother him, she said, but she'd tried everything. It had never happened before, never. Graham had not come home the previous night, and he hadn't called. He wasn't answering his phone. His office was baffled and concerned. Did Sandy have any idea, any idea at all, where he might be?

46

Judge Norcross paused only briefly in his chambers to hang up his robe and retrieve an envelope he needed. Then, he took off into the maze of unfamiliar hallways that would lead him, he hoped, to the other side of the courthouse, where Chief Judge Broadwater kept his nest. The so-called back of the house, the area of the building inaccessible to the public, was a labyrinth of blind turns and keyed doors that wound from one identical corridor to the next. Norcross was soon lost and had to make his way forward more or less by instinct.

The hallways were like his wandering thoughts. He knew what he wanted to discuss with Skip, but he hadn't figured out how he would broach the topic. No matter which angle he came at it from, the conversation he had in mind veered sickeningly close to a breach of the Code of Ethics. If he could form a phrase that would get him going, the rest might follow, but no words came to him. He had nothing to rehearse.

Because Broadwater's position as chief judge carried a load of additional responsibilities, he had a bigger staff and a larger set of chambers than the other judges. His admin, Dorothy, had been with him from before he went on the bench, back when he'd worked for Ted Kennedy on the Senate Judiciary Committee. This was more than thirty years ago now, in the Stone Age, when people in Dorothy's position were called secretaries. She was a white-haired, big-boned, impatient woman, fiercely loyal to Broadwater, with a large desk on guard at the entry to his chambers and a piercing look that intimidated everybody, including Norcross.

"Hi, Dorothy." Norcross put on a cheerful smile as he finally came through the door. "Can I grab the chief for five minutes?"

"Let me check." Dorothy picked up her phone, scrutinizing him suspiciously. "Do you have an appointment?" She knew he didn't.

Fortunately, Broadwater heard this, and he called out from his inner office, "Dave, come in." He paused. "It's okay, Dottie. It's okay." He sounded as though he were calming a Doberman.

When Norcross entered, he saw Broadwater bent over a pile of papers, probably caught up in the complexities of the brutal MS-13 trial.

Peering up over his half glasses, Broadwater gestured at his window. "Been outside? I just ran out to pick up a prescription, and it's hotter than a scalded salamander out there."

"That time of year." Norcross took a seat, not quite ready to get to his real business. "How's *Torres* going?"

"Jury came back this morning, all guilties."

"Wow. You must be glad it's over."

"Yes, in a way." Broadwater sighed. "It's the usual. When these guys were out on the street, you wouldn't want to be within a hundred miles of them. Terrifying, murderous thugs. But when they arrive for sentencing, one by one, I imagine I'll find that at least one or two of them are just hopeless, terrified kids. No dads, no education, ADD, PTSD, ADHD—every acronym in the book. Illiterate in any language. The top ones will probably end up with life sentences without parole, and none of the others will get less than twenty years. Morally, I don't have any qualms about putting them away, but, as a human being . . ." He shook his head. "I can't help wincing a little when I do it."

"It's a heavy load. My feeling is if you don't wince, you shouldn't be on the bench."

The conversation rambled on a while longer. Broadwater wanted to know how Norcross, and especially Claire, were doing after the threats and the photographs. No progress had been made on who'd pushed them under the door. The chief asked a couple of tactful questions about *O'Connell*, and they shared some eyerolling about Sandy Tarbell.

Finally, Broadwater leaned back and asked, "So, what's on your mind, Dave? I can see this is not just a social call. What brings you to my thorny neck of the woods?"

"Tell the truth, I've been struggling with how to raise this. Let me know if I'm out of line."

"Oh, I will." Broadwater smiled. "Don't worry about that."

"There's a young man I know named David Kamau. He has a fellowship at the Harvard Divinity School right now."

"Uh-huh."

"He's here from Kenya. He grew up in a village near where I used to work when I was over there."

"Not a great time to be from that part of the world in Boston at the moment, Dave."

"I know. He's a priest with the Anglican Church of Kenya, and he's facing some visa problems."

"Doesn't surprise me. They're chucking them out thirteen to the dozen, I hear, no matter who they are." Broadwater's phone buzzed, and he picked it up. "Yes?" He paused, making a face. "No, tell him absolutely not."

Broadwater was obviously talking to Dorothy, who was screening a call. Norcross could hear her muffled voice on the other side of the door. The chief's face darkened, and he shook his head. "No earthly way, okay? Tell him I said that." He hesitated. "Right, those exact words, and hold my calls, will you? Thanks." Broadwater hung up and glared as though Norcross were the bad guy. "Some people have a lot of nerve."

"You must get a ton of these . . ."

"Yeah, well, anyway . . ." He flapped his hand. "Where were we? Your Kenyan friend, right?"

"Right, they may be about to deport him, and from what I'm

told, he'll be facing some serious danger back home, maybe life-threatening. He's been involved in anticorruption efforts."

"Does he have a case with us? We've got a bunch of these now, looking for injunctions."

"He hasn't filed anything."

Broadwater took off his glasses and tossed them on his desk.

"Well, you know the drill. He should file an application for asylum, or a petition to withhold removal. Maybe both. Get before an immigration judge and go from there."

"Well, the problem is . . ."

"I can recommend a couple of good Boston immigration lawyers." He pointed a finger at Norcross. "In fact, your old boss Treadwell . . ."

"Reverend Kamau won't file anything, Skip. He won't seek asylum." Norcross sighed. "It's a matter of principle for him. He'd have to demonstrate, as you know, that he has a well-founded fear of persecution back in Kenya. His friends think he could make the case—I guess there was an attempt on his life before he left—but he won't do it. He thinks it would amount to smearing his own country."

"If he's going to be finicky, Dave, there's not much the courts can do for him." Broadwater waved a hand. "His problem is over in the executive branch. We're the judiciary. We can't do anything until somebody files a case."

Norcross took a deep breath and turned to look through the large window beside Broadwater's desk. The Inner Harbor was dead calm, not a ripple under the unblinking sun. A seagull was wheeling slowly near the horizon. The silence while Norcross followed the bird's long swoop went on for too long, and Broadwater picked up his glasses and gave a couple of taps on his desk.

"I have something to say, Skip." Norcross shook his head, defeated. "And I'm failing to find words that will keep this from coming across as melodramatic."

"Okay."

He looked into Broadwater's eyes. "He's my son."

"Excuse me?"

"Reverend Kamau is my son, Skip."

Broadwater pulled in his chin. "Really." He looked down at the floor absorbing this, then looked up again. "When did you . . . I mean, how did you . . ."

"I just learned this Saturday. I didn't know until then."

"I won't insult you by asking if you're sure."

"I'm sure. He's . . ." Norcross took a breath, still getting used to the idea. "He's definitely my son."

"You know he won't qualify as protected family. He's too old."

"I know. He's over eighteen. I've checked into it."

A phone rang in the outer office, and Dorothy's voice answering was audible through the door.

"I'm not sure what I'm supposed to say here, Dave."

"Well, I'm going to ask you for a favor." Norcross pulled on his nose and sniffed. "I wouldn't even talk about this if Reverend Kamau, if David, had a case pending before you, or pending anywhere in our court. I wouldn't do that."

"Right. I know you wouldn't."

"But there isn't a case, and there won't be one, so . . ." He hesitated and plunged. "I was hoping you might know somebody to talk to informally, to try to get ICE to be a little more flexible. I'd really love to find a way to keep David in the country for a while longer."

Now, it was Broadwater's turn to look out the window. After what seemed to Norcross like a very long time, he shook his head as though he'd thought through something and made a decision. "Listen to me, Dave. I'm sorry, but you're asking me to stick my oar into something over there in the Department of Justice. Maybe use my position to get some leverage for you and, um, . . ." He paused. "Your son. I sympathize, but I can't do that. Among other things, it's unethical. Maybe even illegal. You really never should have brought this up." His mouth tightened, and he looked intensely at Norcross. "You must know that."

Norcross felt a wave of embarrassment so intense it verged on despair. He'd realized months ago, with Charlie, that he would die to protect his son. He'd be terrified, but he'd do it. But this kind of humiliating misery he was not prepared for. He couldn't say anything.

Broadwater put his glasses back on, picked up his pen, and looked down at his papers. "What did you say his name was again?" He spoke absently. "Out of curiosity?"

"Kamau. David Kamau. K-A-M-A-U."

"Birth date?"

"This is his information." He took the envelope out of his pocket and placed it on the corner of Broadwater's desk. "Bill Treadwell pried it out of the Divinity School."

"You understand I can't do anything, and I won't be doing anything."

"I understand. I'm, believe me, I'm really sorry I bothered you."

"And I'm going to ask you, as a friend, never to mention this to me again, Dave." Broadwater leaned over his desk and poked a finger. "Never. You're a valued colleague. We'll just agree that this conversation never happened, okay?"

"Yes. I agree."

"Now, I have some things I need to get to here." Broadwater looked down at one of his folders.

Norcross got up quickly and turned to leave. "Well, thanks."

Broadwater, already lost in his paperwork, said nothing. They were done.

47

In the courtroom the next day, Mike Patterson walked over to the defense table, where Sandy Tarbell sat unloading his briefcase. He dropped a hand on Tarbell's shoulder.

Tarbell jerked away and looked offended. "What?"

Patterson bent close, not quite whispering but pitching his voice so only Tarbell could hear. "Talk to your brother."

Tarbell did not bother to lower his voice. "What the hell is that supposed to mean?"

"Tell him I suggested it." As he returned to the government table and was taking his seat next to Claudia Papadakis, Patterson was pleased to notice that Tarbell kept staring angrily at him. The arrow had hit.

Shortly after this, a loud thump and a sudden silence announced the entry of their next witness, Loreen Laplante, into the courtroom. During their prep session the previous evening, Patterson and Papadakis had only barely managed to get Laplante's careening anxiety under control.

Her outfit was not reassuring. She was wearing a zebra-stripe tunic, black tights, large red dangly earrings, bright red lipstick, and bright red high-heeled sandals that she was still getting used to. As she came down the central aisle of the gallery, Patterson noticed with concern that she wobbled. Laplante eventually found a seat and sat, gripping a bright red pocketbook with both hands as though it might fly away. When she noticed Patterson, she broke into a big smile, detached one hand from the pocketbook, and gave him an extravagant wave.

Not long after this, Judge Norcross made his entry, the jurors were ushered in, and the kid who was pinch-hitting for Angie Phipps called the case. Up on the bench, Norcross looked uncharacteristically stone-faced—all business. After a few words to the jurors, he got things going quickly. He nodded at Papadakis.

"Government's next witness, please."

Under her breath, Papadakis whispered to Patterson, "Here goes nothing," and stepped up to the podium. "Thank you, Your Honor. The government calls Loreen Laplante."

Laplante made her way slowly across the well of the court, humped up the two steps into the witness box, and dropped herself heavily down.

The courtroom deputy cleared his throat. "Um, please stand and raise your right hand."

Laplante made an *oops* face, pushed herself back up, and raised her hand.

"Do you solemnly swear that the testimony you are about to give to this court and jury will be the truth, the whole truth, and nothing but the truth, so help you God?"

"I certainly do."

Papadakis waited while Laplante took her time settling into her seat and pouring herself a cup of water. Mike Patterson leaned back and folded his arms, doing his best to exude a sense of complete confidence.

"Okay. Now, Ms. Laplante, for the record would you please state your full name and where you're presently living."

"Well, my name is Loreen Laplante, and I am presently living in Walpole, Massachusetts."

"And how old are you?"

"Oh dear, do I have to tell?" She peeped coyly up at the judge.

Norcross did not look up from his notes. "I'm afraid it's customary, Ms. Laplante."

Tarbell got to his feet. "Well, in this case, Judge, it's also essential. The jury will need to know how old this witness was, when—"

Laplante glanced over at Tarbell, looking prim. "I've been thirty-nine for the past thirty years or so." She took a sip of water.

There were a few chuckles at this old joke, and Tarbell sat down, giving a contemptuous snort.

Papadakis smiled. "That's good enough, Ms. Laplante. We can do the math. And are you married?"

"Oh boy. Am I ever!" She grimaced and looked up at the ceiling. "Third time, fifteen years now. My personal best."

It wasn't clear whether Laplante intended this remark to be funny, but it garnered smiles from several jurors and a burst of outright laughter from the gallery. A spirit of fun was beginning to contaminate the proceeding. Laplante's uncertain expression made it hard to tell whether she was embarrassed or pleased.

Norcross tapped lightly on his microphone with his pen and said, not too loudly, "Okay, let's move on." Things quieted down immediately.

Papadakis pushed forward. "In June of 1968, would you tell the jury, please, where you were living?"

"Well, my family had moved to Southie—South Boston—three years earlier, when I was thirteen. My father was an ironworker, and he'd been having an awful time trying to find a job. He'd been sick, and we were really struggling, you know, and then he finally found a spot at . . ."

Papadakis broke in, "Thank you."

Tarbell was on his feet again. "Objection! The witness hasn't completed her answer."

It was a classic strategy. Tarbell wanted Laplante to have as much rope as possible. Every word could trip her up on his cross-examination.

"Sustained. Go ahead, Ms. Laplante."

"Well, Dad finally found a job, and we, you know, moved to Southie." She glanced at Papadakis, looking abashed. "Then, you know, he got sick again, but that's another story." She took a quick swallow of water.

Loreen Laplante's performance was an example of something Patterson had often seen at trials. He knew from speaking to her that, although gabby, she was basically an intelligent, reliable person. She'd worked for many years as the office manager for a high-end tech company in Brookline, not an easy job. But the pressure of this public situation was making her look like a ditz. Other witnesses sometimes reacted in the opposite way: they were evil and stupid, but in the witness box they sounded like a blend of Tom Hanks and the Dalai Lama. Fortunately, in Patterson's experience, jurors could usually see through these surfaces.

As Papadakis took a breath to move on to her next question, Norcross broke in.

"Excuse me. Let me have a word here, please." The judge swiveled toward the witness box. "We have strange rules in our courtroom world, Ms. Laplante. When we talk in our everyday lives, it's natural to go from one thing to another. In court, though, we ask witnesses just to listen carefully to the question put by the attorney and answer that question, as concisely as possible, without adding too many details. Would you do that, please? It will help move things along."

"Yes, Your Honor. I'm sorry. I guess I'm nervous."

"It's not unusual. Just take your time."

Tarbell stood, mumbled, "Note my objection," and sat down again.

Papadakis resumed. "Okay, just to pick up: Where were you living in 1968?"

"South Boston."

"Thank you. And who were you living with."

"Um, my mom, my dad, and my, you know, my younger brother, Danny."

Things after this went more smoothly. Laplante described how she had known Dominic O'Connell in high school, mostly from afar since she was two classes below him.

"And did you develop, let's call it a little bit of a crush on Mr. O'Connell?"

"Well, yes, maybe even more than a little bit. Most of the girls thought he was . . ." She stopped herself. "Yes, I did have a sort of crush on him. Still do. Maybe." Laplante darted a glance at O'Connell. "I mean, I've read all the articles about him, and I still think, you know . . ."

Tarbell started to get up to object, but as another amused murmuring ran through the courtroom, he sat down, giving O'Connell a tolerant glance. O'Connell looked back at Julie, who raised her eyebrows good-naturedly, as though they were sharing a private joke. It wasn't a bad moment for the defense.

Papadakis moved on, establishing how old Laplante was in June 1968, working up to the key moment when she saw O'Connell at the Regency on East Broadway that night in South Boston. Laplante did not remember the specific date, but she definitely recalled that it was the Saturday after Robert Kennedy was shot. She'd been out with friends. Everyone was still really upset.

"Other than your memory, Ms. Laplante, is there anything else that helped you pin down the exact date that you saw the defendant at the Regency?"

Tarbell was on his feet again. "Objection."

His voice this time was more muted, almost bored. The diary issue had been fought out during the earlier hearings outside the presence of the jury, but Tarbell had to make a formal record of his objection at the trial itself.

"Overruled."

"Can I answer?"

Norcross nodded. "Go ahead, Ms. Laplante."

"Yes, I had my diary."

"Objection. Move to strike."

"Overruled."

"And do you have it with you now?"

"Yes." Laplante reached into her red purse and extracted a pink volume about the size of a deck of playing cards. "Right here."

"And what period did the diary cover?"

"Objection."

"Overruled."

Tarbell continued. "Your Honor, may I have a standing objection to any questioning of this witness regarding her diary? I hate to keep interrupting Ms. Papadakis."

Patterson had to stifle an eye roll at this. Tarbell loved interrupting people.

"Yes, Mr. Tarbell, your rights are saved regarding any testimony related to the diary."

"Thank you."

Papadakis turned back to the witness. "I'll ask my question again. What period did the diary cover?"

"End of school 1968 until that fall."

"And did you write in it every night?"

"Not really. Just sometimes."

"And do you have an entry for the first Saturday in June 1968?"

"Yes."

"Would you read it to the jury, please?"

"Yes, it says . . ." She opened the diary and flipped a couple of pages. "'Out with Kathleen. Saw Dom driving a giant white limo by the Regency. Total stud as usual. Don't think he saw me.'" She looked up. "And then I drew a frowny face."

"Objection." Tarbell stood and leaned with his hand on the table.

Norcross looked down at Tarbell, not happy. "You have your standing objection, Mr. Tarbell. What's the problem?"

"This is different, Your Honor. That was not the entire entry. If Ms. Laplante is going to read this, I'm entitled to have her read the whole segment."

Laplante looked again at the diary. "But that's what it says."

Tarbell raised his voice. "The day and date, please, Ms. Laplante, just before the passage you read."

"Okay. It says Saturday, June 7."

"Saturday, June *seventh*. Thank you very much, Ms. Laplante."

"Oh, for heaven's sake," Papadakis muttered just loud enough for the jury to hear. "Ms. Laplante, did you sometimes get the dates wrong when you wrote in your diary?"

"Yes, sometimes, I guess. Days of the week, too, sometimes."

"Okay, let's talk about what you saw that evening."

Laplante went on to testify that she'd seen Dominic O'Connell at the wheel of a big white Cadillac that Saturday with two men in the back seat. Laplante had seen one of the men in the back get out, go into the Regency, and return a little while later with another man, a big man, almost as big as Dom. Then all four had driven off. She had no idea who the other three men were.

"Okay. What did Mr. O'Connell do while the man from the back seat was in the Regency?"

"Just, you know, sat there in the driver's seat." She finished her water.

"I see, and . . ."

"With his elbow out the window, sort of. Like this." Laplante demonstrated.

"And the time?"

"Eight or eight thirty. It was just getting dark."

Papadakis clasped her hands at her waist and looked down at the carpeting for a count of three.

"Ms. Laplante . . ." She looked up. Her voice was grave, and her words came out slowly. "Is there any doubt in your mind that the man you saw at approximately eight or eight thirty on the Saturday after Robert Kennedy's assassination, at the Regency restaurant on East Broadway in South Boston, was in fact the defendant, Dominic O'Connell?"

"Oh no."

"Driving what model of car?"

"Big white Caddie."

"And doing what?"

"Sitting, you know, in the driver's seat, by a fireplug. With a guy in the back."

"Was there anyone else there at the time?"

"Yes, like I said, another guy in the back who went into the Regency and came out with a fourth guy a little bit later."

"Any doubt at all in your mind that the man sitting right there" — Papadakis pointed at the defense table—"was the man you saw that night waiting outside the Regency restaurant?"

"Oh no, no doubt at all." Laplante looked at the defendant, her expression regretful. "I'm sorry, Dom. That was you."

"Thank you." Papadakis looked up at the bench. "No further questions."

Judge Norcross stopped writing, sighed, and nodded down.

"Mr. Tarbell, your witness."

Mike Patterson felt a trickle of something like dread run through him. He'd seen Tarbell in action before. There was very little either he or Papadakis could do to protect Laplante once Tarbell started tearing into her. They were just going to have to sit there, watch, and hope.

Tarbell walked briskly up to the podium. "Good morning, Ms. Laplante. My name is Sandy Tarbell, and I'm here representing Dom O'Connell. You understand that?"

"Yes."

"Good." He paused. "By the way, I see you've taken some trouble with your outfit here this morning. Isn't that right? It's very striking."

"Thank you."

"You're welcome, but would you answer the question, please? You took some trouble with your outfit before coming here today. Isn't that right?

This line of questioning was surprising. Ordinarily, an attorney, especially a male attorney, would never touch the topic of a witness's clothing for fear of offending some of the jurors. The subject seemed too personal, a low blow. Patterson saw that Tarbell wouldn't care if he lost eight or nine of the twelve jurors. He wasn't going for an outright acquittal, a not guilty, which would require a unanimous defense verdict. He was aiming for a mistrial—a hung jury. For that, he needed only three, two, or even one juror if that juror were stubborn enough. A couple of the male jurors already looked as though they thought Laplante might be a kook, and one of the females, an ER nurse, was giving her a superior look. With Shaughnessy at death's door, the government would never get a second chance to retry this case. A hung jury, a single holdout, would probably be enough to set Dominic O'Connell free.

Laplante hesitated, looking uncomfortable, as Tarbell obviously intended. He wanted this witness off-balance from the get-go.

"Would you like me to repeat the question? Did you make a special effort in selecting what to wear this morning when you—"

"I-I guess. Yes."

"Of course, you did. And did Ms. Papadakis, or any government agent, advise you as to the best sort of clothing to wear to court today to make a good impression?"

Laplante nodded at Patterson. "The FBI guy said to try to keep it, you know, conservative."

Several of the jurors exchanged skeptical glances. This was her idea of "conservative"? Patterson gave a bored sigh and folded his arms.

"Really? Special Agent Patterson told you that?"

"Something like that. Nothing over the top, he said. So I toned it down." She picked up her cup, realized it was empty, and set it down.

"But you still wanted to look nice, even though you toned it down, to make a good impression, right?"

"I suppose."

"So that the ladies and gentlemen on the jury would find you a credible witness, isn't that right?"

"I don't know about that."

"Well, you take pride in looking good, right?"

"I think everyone does."

"That may be true, but you take particular pride, correct? You like being noticed."

"Well, I don't, you know . . . I don't know about that."

Papadakis deliberately turned to Patterson, frowned, and shook her head, as though she couldn't believe how stupid and inappropriate this line of questioning was. Several jurors clearly noticed this. Papadakis couldn't formally object without looking defensive, but she could telegraph her opinion of Tarbell's tactic with her facial expression.

"You knew you'd be particularly noticed with what you're wearing today, isn't that right?"

"I didn't think about it."

"Really? You didn't think at all about whether that outfit would be especially noticeable today, maybe a little over the top in Agent Patterson's words?"

"I don't understand."

"Let me try it this way. We've established that, like everyone, you enjoy making a good impression, getting attention, and so forth, am I right?"

"I guess."

"And you hope to do that here? I mean this is your moment in the spotlight, isn't it?"

"I don't know what you mean by 'spotlight.'"

"Well, you told us you've read the papers all along about Dom O'Connell—with your little crush and everything—and you know that this morning *you* got in the papers, right? You yourself? You saw that, right?"

"I may have glanced at the paper, I guess."

"You looked at the front page of the *Boston Globe* this morning and there you were, right?"

"Yes."

"You held the paper in your hand and you saw the article, your name, your picture, didn't you?"

"For a minute or two."

"And you read the article, right?"

"I guess."

"Fine, you guess you read the article. Right to the end. Am I correct?"

"Okay."

"And that was kind of exciting for you, wasn't it? Making that impression? Getting that attention?"

"Well, yes, sort of."

"And you checked out the *Herald*, too, didn't you?"

"Not really."

"You didn't look at the *Boston Herald* and see that you were on the front page there too? You never did that?"

"My cousin called me about it. I looked at it online."

"Okay, online. So you're getting a lot of attention here, right?"

"I guess."

"Uh-huh. And you find that exciting."

"I guess."

"You guess? Come on. Being in this trial, getting advice from Agent Patterson about how to dress, coming here to testify, being in the papers and on the internet—all that, surely, is the most exciting thing that has happened to you in the past, let's say, three years. We can be crystal clear about that, right? Can't we?"

"Yes, I guess."

"And you bought that outfit, the one you have on, especially for this trial, didn't you?"

This had to have been a blind swipe, but it hit pay dirt.

"Yes, I did."

"Because you wanted to make an especially good impression, didn't you?"

"I guess."

Tarbell folded his hands on the podium for two breaths.

"Okay, let's drop the guessing. One thing you know for sure, no guessing, is that if you didn't have something damaging to say about Dominic O'Connell in this courtroom, you wouldn't be here, right? You wouldn't be getting this attention."

"Something damaging?"

"Something helpful to the government's case, right?"

"I don't know about that."

"Something that will make it more likely that this jury will find Dom O'Connell guilty, isn't that right?"

"I don't know about that."

"Well, you do know that you wouldn't be sitting in that witness box if the government hadn't called you as a witness? That's crystal clear, right?"

"I suppose so."

"You wouldn't be wearing that outfit?"

"No, obviously."

"Obviously. You wouldn't even have bought it, right?"

"No, I wouldn't have bought it."

"By the way, how much did it cost? The whole outfit."

Laplante looked uncertain. She glanced up at Norcross and around the courtroom, perhaps hoping for help. None came. "I'm not sure. Maybe four hundred dollars with the shoes and the pocketbook." She held the purse up.

"Lot of money for you, right? To spend on one outfit?"

"Yes. That's a lot for me."

"Okay. And you wouldn't have bought that outfit, if Ms. Papadakis hadn't called you as a witness. And you wouldn't be in all the newspapers, the *Globe* and the *Herald* and so forth, either, would you? Getting this attention."

"I guess not."

"You're here because the government called you as a witness, and they wouldn't have called you as a witness if you hadn't told them that you knew something that might help their case. I mean, you agree with that, right?"

"Yes, I suppose so."

"And you find all this a little bit exciting, right? We've established that."

"A little bit, maybe."

"Maybe, sometimes, more than a little bit?"

"Okay. I guess."

On it went. As it did, Patterson noticed the faces of several jurors falling into expressions of amused condescension, almost smirking. Sandy Tarbell deserved his reputation.

Laplante, with a shaky hand, began refilling her water cup, and Tarbell looked up at the bench.

"Judge, I'm about to move into a new area, so, if you'd like, this might be a good moment for the morning recess. I'm going to be a while on this cockamamie diary."

"About how far are you into your cross?"

"Maybe ten percent. I have a lot to get through."

Laplante's face fell. She set the pitcher down and picked up her water cup, downing it in one gulp.

During the recess, Tarbell fielded another phone call from Graham's wife, Alice. The message the day before hadn't bothered him much. Tarbell had his hands full with the trial, and he hadn't really cared what his brother was up to. Maybe Graham was off on a frolic with some cheery paralegal. Good for him.

This new call from Alice, however, hit him hard. Afterward, he spotted Patterson and waved him over to a deserted area down the corridor.

"The fuck's going on with Graham, Mike?"

Patterson shrugged. "Like I said, ask him."

"I can't. I just talked to his wife." Tarbell ran a hand through his hair. "The idiot's disappeared. Nobody knows where he is."

Patterson shook his head. "I'm really sorry to hear that, Sandy."

"Day and a half, two days, now. It's not like him."

"I'd be worried if I were you."

"Yeah, and Alice just told me that a bottle of high-dose Seconal has gone missing from their medicine cabinet."

"Shit." Patterson shook his head, looking truly disturbed.

"She didn't mention the pills before—because she was embarrassed, she said. I called her a stupid cow, which I probably shouldn't have."

"Probably not."

"Look, I know you can't talk to me, Mike, but can you tell me the size of Graham's problem? Is it, like, small, medium, or large?"

"Jumbo."

"Like going-away-for-years size, or . . ."

"Hard to say, but the clock is ticking if he wants to help himself."

"I'm thinking this involves a certain party with the initials JT? If I'm correct, don't say anything."

Patterson just looked at him, lips sealed.

Tarbell dropped his eyes and muttered. "Goddammit."

He'd told Graham to call him before he took any handouts from Jack Taylor. He should have known Graham might not pay attention to warnings from his asshole older brother. They were both idiots, but now Graham was paying the price. He might do anything now.

Papadakis came hurrying up to them, back from the ladies' room and just turning off her phone.

"Sorry to interrupt, but I need to talk to you, Mike." She looked unhappy.

It destroyed Tarbell to do it, but he had no choice, and he blurted. "Listen, Claudia, I have to ask a favor."

Papadakis looked at him, eyes widening, and pointed with her thumb at the harbor. "When will the tsunami hit?"

"I know, I know." Tarbell held up his hands, surrendering. "I hate this, but I've got a family emergency. I need to ask Norcross to give me the rest of the day off. And I was hoping—"

"That I'd assent to a motion for an immediate recess?" She started to smile. "Give me a break."

"Yeah, I know. Exactly. It's very serious, or I wouldn't ask."

"The Scanlon family is burnt to a crisp in there . . ." She pointed
at the courtroom. "Really ready for this to be over. And if I agree to
take the afternoon off, I'll have to deal with another eruption from
my boss. Buddy Hogan will have a—"

"Buddy will be nothing compared to Dom, Claudia, believe me.
If I ask for any sort of postponement, he'll be ready to cut off my—"

"Right. So what's up? I need details."

"Okay." Tarbell dropped his voice. "Bottom line is my brother,
Graham, is in trouble, and now he's disappeared with a big bottle of
sleeping pills." Tarbell wiped a hand over his face. "Mike can fill you
in. The short of it is I'm worried he'll . . ." He paused. "Worried he
might do something if I don't move fast."

Patterson looked uncomfortable. "I can't say much at this stage,
even to you, Claudia."

"Graham won't have the stomach to do anything right off, but if
he's left alone for very long, things could go south fast."

Tarbell could picture it. Graham would pace around whatever
room he was holed up in, dawdling and agonizing. Every hour that
went by, it would be harder for him to imagine crawling home to
Alice and breaking the news that he'd made a total fucking mess
of their lives. Graham would also be thinking about having to tell
his kids, and about his kids having to cook up some story to tell the
grandchildren. He'd sink lower and lower, and before long, it would
just seem a lot easier to lie down on the Big Soft Pillow. Tarbell had
a pretty good idea where Graham was, but it was a three-hour drive,
longer if there was traffic, and he needed to move fast.

"Well, Sandy . . ." Papadakis looked troubled, which was wonderful. "I've got some good news, and I've got some better news."
She waited while a flock of lawyers fluttered past.

"Uh-huh. Cute. Give me the good news first."

"Well, first, I just learned Brian Shaughnessy has had some kind
of episode, and the marshals have taken him to Mass General for
observation. The docs want to keep him overnight, at least."

"Really sorry to hear that, Claudia."

"Yeah." Patterson snorted. "Bullshit."

"Mm-hmm. Now, the better news. I had Shaughnessy slated to
take the stand tomorrow or the next day, once you finish chewing

Laplante up, but the doctors say they'll need a day or two to check him out. I was bracing myself to ask if you'd agree to take tomorrow off."

"And you knew there was no way I'd get on board with you."

"Right. I kept picturing you laughing in my face."

"I'd never laugh at you, Claudia." Tarbell didn't let himself look pleased, but this news felt like a miracle.

"Sure. So now, here's our deal. I give you the rest of the day today, you give me tomorrow and the next day if Shaughnessy needs it, and that gets us to the weekend."

Tarbell did not hesitate. "You got it, Claudia. We can file a joint motion, but we'll still have to convince His Holiness . . ." He gestured over his shoulder toward the courtroom.

"We can ask for a conference in chambers and pitch it to Norcross there. And, Sandy, please . . ." Papadakis raised her eyebrows. "Let me do the talking, okay? You just nod."

Julie was waiting out the morning recess with Dom and Rafferty in the small attorneys' conference room just off the courtroom. Aidan had disappeared to go sniff around somewhere. Dom looked tired, which was worrying her. He'd gone very quiet ever since she'd told him about Sally Hoffman.

The door opened, and Sandy Tarbell bustled in. "Bad news. Brian Shaughnessy has some kind of medical issue . . ."

Rafferty gave a short laugh. "Call that bad news?"

"Well, okay, but it means that Papadakis wants to ask Norcross to recess the trial for a day, maybe two days, so they can figure out what's up with him. We might not resume until Friday, or maybe even Monday."

"Forget it, Sandy." O'Connell lifted his hands and dropped them in his lap. "We're not making life easy for Brian Shaughnessy. We need to keep the pressure on."

Tarbell shook his head. "Bad idea, Dom."

"I want this over, Sandy."

"I know, but Norcross is probably going to give Papadakis the time—"

Rafferty broke in. "Oh Christ, he'd give her his left—"

"I know, but we'll just piss him off by getting starchy about this." Tarbell hesitated. "And I told Papadakis that if I agreed to her motion, I'd want the rest of today off in return."

O'Connell's eyes widened dangerously. "What the hell . . ."

"I could use more time to put together the next section of my cross of Laplante. This is a godsend, frankly. It's going pretty well so far, but . . ."

"Damn well, Sandy. I feel like I'm finally getting my money's worth."

Julie patted Dom's hand. "Hey, couple Scrabble games, couple early nights. Little break. Sounds pretty nice to me." She shot him a sly look.

Dom sighed. A silence followed while everyone gave him time to think. Finally, he looked over at Julie. "What's another day or two, I guess." He pointed at Tarbell. "But that's it. We're going to win this. We need to keep hammering."

"Thanks." Tarbell sat down and looked around the table. "I've got one other thing to talk to you about, Dom." He glanced at Rafferty and her. "This should probably be between us. If you guys could . . ."

Dom shook his head. "Raff knows everything, and Julie will pry whatever you say out of me anyway. Let's hear."

"You sure?"

"Very sure. Talk."

"Well, a little bird told me that Bob Schwartz is hot after some conspiracy involving the assignment of cases—what we call 'the draw.' Conspiracy to obstruct justice, conspiracy to commit bribery, all that fun stuff. You need to know that if Sam Newbury roped you into something, you might have a problem."

"Sam Newbury?" Julie was unimpressed. "He was a complete flop. Dom canned him."

Rafferty shrugged. "If Newbury was up to something, he was playing his own hand. Nothing to do with us."

"Well, just so you know. We don't want any more dawn raids." Tarbell stood up. "Okay. I have to go talk to His Lordship."

48

By late afternoon, David was pulling up his driveway, pleased to be home but uncertain what sort of state he'd find Claire in. They had not had time since the Kamau earthquake to get their feet under them. Around the house, the trees were dead still in the suffocating heat of the midsummer pall.

He found Claire by the kitchen counter—looking, somehow, especially pretty.

"Your hair's different."

"I had it cut this morning." She was pulling the cork on a bottle of wine. "It came out all right."

He touched her cheek and gave her a quick kiss. "You look terrific." She had a faint, wonderfully fresh scent. "How's Charlie?"

Some bug had hit the boy Saturday evening after Kamau had left. It turned out to be another one of his ear infections, combined with something intestinal, and he'd been miserable the whole weekend. The stress had put them both in bad moods and left them with no real time to talk.

"He's better." She filled two glasses and gave him a sharp look. "I'm really glad we're getting a break from this trial of yours, David."

"We've suspended until Friday at the earliest, maybe Monday. Then we'll pick up with the current witness, Loreen something. I forget her last name."

"Boon from heaven."

"I can work from home until then. I have a pile of . . ."

Claire suddenly set the wine bottle down with a clunk and put her arms around him. He ran his hands up her back, pressing her against him, feeling as though something delicious was being squeezed back into the marrow of his bones.

"I'm sorry I was so snappish Sunday." She pressed her head into his shoulder. "This is a lot for both of us. It's like—"

"You weren't snappish."

"This is not your fault." She spoke, muffled, into his shirt.

"I know."

"Well." She lifted her head and looked up at him. "It sort of is, actually."

"I know." He kissed her. "We need to talk."

She shook her head. "I don't want to talk."

"You don't want to talk?" He peered into her face. "You always want to talk."

"Business first." Claire slid her hand into his jacket, took his cell phone, and turned it off. "I've muted the landline." She gave him a swift, fiercely sexual kiss, holding the sides of his head before abruptly breaking off. "And my cell too."

"Uh-huh." He put the emphasis on the second syllable. The lingering taste of her mouth was blotting out sequential thought. He ran his hands down her back onto her butt.

"Charlie just went down." She looked guilty. "I-I gave him a little Benadryl. It was—"

"Brilliant." He picked up the glasses. "We can take the wine."

In the bedroom, they began kissing and trying to get undressed at the same time, which became so complicated that they both started to laugh. Toward the end, he had to pull his tie off over his head. Soon, they were sliding under the sheets, and the feeling of Claire's skin against him was like the resumption of life itself.

An hour later, David and Claire were dozing in each other's arms and for the moment entirely content with their world. Everything would be manageable. Then, as David raised himself to reach for his wineglass, he heard the distant sound of Charlie banging his crib against the wall.

"Damn." Claire squirmed and murmured. "I was hoping he'd be out longer."

"Let me go check on him." David grabbed a robe, hurried down the hallway, and peeked into Charlie's room. To his puzzlement and delight, he saw that the boy was still sleeping soundly. But then, the knocking continued, uncertain but more distinct, coming from the front door. After taking a quick look out the window, he took off at a trot back to the bedroom.

"Oh gosh."

"What?" Claire had propped herself up on the pillows and was holding her wineglass. "What is it?"

"It's David Kamau."

"What?" She set the glass down.

"It's Kamau. It's David. He's at the front door."

Claire scrambled up out of the sheets. "For God's sake, David, first you don't even want children." She was snatching up her clothes. "Now, we have them coming out our ears."

Claire let David throw on his clothes and dash down to deal with Reverend Kamau. She took her time, dressing slowly, washing her face, and putting on a little makeup. Downstairs, she found the two men sitting in the living room in an atmosphere that felt as though someone had died. They didn't even look at her.

"So, it's definite," David was saying. "You're really sure?"

"Yes, I'll be leaving very shortly. As soon as Godfrey and I can arrange a flight."

"But why so sudden? Why now?"

Kamau noticed Claire and stood up. "Claire, hello. I am very sorry to be disturbing you. It was . . ." He paused, searching for the right word. "An impulsive act on my part, coming here, I'm afraid. I tried to ring you several times en route."

"No problem. It's wonderful to see you."

David was sitting on the hassock, staring straight ahead. Now, he looked at Claire. "He says he's leaving. Going back to Kenya." He turned to Kamau, who was lowering himself back onto the couch. "I don't understand. I'm sure Bill Treadwell and his people could drag out the immigration proceedings until the end of the year, at least."

"But, Mzee . . ." Kamau leaned forward and held out his hands. "He also says that without my student visa, deportation is inevitable, unless I apply for asylum. The expulsion could happen tomorrow or some months from now. At any time. Or they could change their minds and decide to detain me again."

"Then just apply for asylum."

"I will not do that." Kamau shook his head. "A student visa is one thing. I was given leave to come here as a student, and I have been honored to attend the Divinity School. But now, that is no longer possible. Even the university says so."

"But the application for asylum will buy you time. That's all. And we could have you here for the holidays. I . . ." David's hand fluttered over his eye. "I was counting on that." There was the beginning of a crack in his voice.

Kamau closed his eyes and nodded, as though he were reciting words to himself. "I will not ask for protection from my own people, and I will not wait to be expelled." He raised his hand as David started to speak. "No, Mzee, please. I have spent many hours now in prayer about this. It is perhaps pride, or some other failing, I admit, but I am determined to leave freely. That is my decision."

"Godfrey told me what you were thinking, and I respect your feelings, of course, but you shouldn't—"

"I will not risk being escorted again. It would be too degrading."

Claire interrupted. "Didn't I hear that there would be some danger to you in Kenya?"

Kamau turned to her, smiling gently. "Godfrey exaggerates these things, Claire. Yes, there have been a few stray comments, an article or two attacking me, and some wild accusations from one particular government minister who hated my grandfather. For the present, that's the lot. Everyone in public life faces these things, even in your country."

David broke in. "And what about your Finnish friend—was it Helena?"

"She understands perfectly. Perfectly. We are making plans for her to visit Kenya soon."

"And your father, your other father, your stepfather . . ." David waved his hand, almost spluttering. "Professor Kamau. What does he think?"

Kamau sighed. "He—I must confess—he would prefer if I applied for asylum."

"See?"

"Fathers are the same everywhere." Kamau's dark eyes, as he smiled at David, were tender and sad.

"And Hannah? Your mother? What would she say if she were here?"

Kamau tipped his head back and laughed. "I can tell you, Mzee, if my mother were on this earth right now, and I came home, she would kill me herself, with her bare hands."

David, still looking numb, shook his head. "I don't understand."

"Don't try." Kamau held up a finger. "All good fathers and all good sons have these times. They have to, do they not?"

"Yes, but this is a matter of . . ."

"Listen now, please." Kamau spoke a little louder. "I didn't come to debate my decision. I came to say goodbye . . ." He held up his finger again. "Only temporarily, only temporarily, and to tell you how much it has meant to me to see you, to meet you, to talk to you. It is more than I ever dreamed."

Claire saw David slump, surrendering. He spoke haltingly, still in a daze. "For me, it's . . . it's not only more than I dreamed. It's more than I even knew." He shook his head. "I'm not sure I can bear having you go. I will be worrying about you every single day."

"Yes. That is, I think, what all this means. Mzee."

At this point, as if on cue, Charlie let out a couple of soft bleats. Kamau looked up at the ceiling and said something in Swahili that meant, as Claire learned later, "little brother." After a pause of three or four seconds while they waited in silence, Charlie let out a piercing, insistent howl.

David stood up, looking confused, but Claire rose quickly. "My turn."

Upstairs, she found that the boy's diaper was a record-breaking disaster, needing an extended cleanup that included the inside of the crib and part of the wall. It took a several minutes, and by the time she came back downstairs, David Kamau was gone.

49

Thanks to Claudia Papadakis's maddeningly effective job persuading Judge Norcross to give them the recess, Tarbell was able to spend Wednesday afternoon finding out if his brother was still alive. It was a long drive down to the Cape, but once he'd turned up Route 6, his search did not take long.

Graham's silver Volvo was sitting in the weedy parking lot of a semicircle of cabins near Eastham, not far from the Nauset Lighthouse, where the brothers used to spend two weeks every summer with their parents. The place was crumbling even back then, but the weekly rental was affordable, and the kitchenette allowed them to bring their own food and save money. Tarbell remembered how he and Graham would walk the sandy, windblown cliffs above Nauset Beach, watching the rollers crashing in from Europe.

The sun was low when he pulled in, but the stifling heat still hit Tarbell hard as he stepped out of his car, slammed the door, and walked to the manager's office. The imminence of some obliterating horror loomed over him: the crushing loss of his brother, his oldest life companion—brought on by his own inexcusable, bungling idiocy—and the sight perhaps very soon of Graham's waxy body, his eyes staring. Tarbell had seen dead people, mostly in morgues, one or two on sidewalks, and he was remembering the odor of the corpses, the gluey, sickening feel of death coming off them.

The white-haired man in the office pointed out Graham's cabin and mentioned that he'd spotted Graham walking out some time earlier. The man was not sure exactly when Graham had left, where he'd gone, or even which direction he'd taken. After knocking on the door and peeking through the window into the empty room, Tarbell took a seat in the seagull-spotted wooden chair on the deck of number six to wait. The time passed like a sort of illness. Graham could easily just tell him to fuck off. What would he do then? Then again, his brother may have already walked into the surf, lost forever.

Sometime later—he couldn't have said how long—Tarbell saw Graham, dark against the orange horizon, walking across the far end of the parking lot, clutching a paper bag to his chest. Details came into focus as Graham got closer. His clothes looked slept in, he obviously hadn't shaved for days, and the crown of his bald head was badly sunburned. When Graham came up to the cabin and noticed his brother sitting on the porch, he stopped.

Tarbell did not get up. "Bad news, Graham. You're going to have to stick around." He kept his voice sharp. In charge.

Graham was about ten feet away, swaying slightly. After a long pause, he dropped his head, prodded the gravel with his toe, and looked up. "What's going to happen to me, Sandy?"

Graham's dead voice was painful to hear, but Tarbell kept his tone upbeat.

"Well, for starters, we're going back to Boston, and I'm going to introduce you to a friend of mine named Mike Patterson."

"I already met him."

"Fine." Tarbell stood. "Now, you're going to get to know him even better."

After another pause, Graham pointed at the cabin. "Okay if I get my . . ."

Tarbell stood in the doorway while Graham entered and looked unsteadily around. The bed was unmade, and the room smelled strongly of bourbon and body odor. Graham put the liquor store bag on the pine dresser next to a pill container and a Jack Daniel's bottle that was down to an inch. Graham seemed to notice but did not say anything when Tarbell strode across the room and pocketed the pills. Another bourbon bottle, empty, was poking out of the wastebasket.

Graham sat down slowly on the edge of the bed, groping with his hand at the wadded bedspread. "Am I going to prison, Sandy?"

"Maybe." He definitely was.

Graham gazed down at the floor and nodded his head. "Okay." After a minute, he looked up. "Will we take both cars?"

"It was a long drive down here. I'd really prefer to go back together."

"But . . ."

"I'll send somebody down to collect your car in a day or two."

"You don't have to . . ."

"It's not a problem. Really."

Graham rubbed the top of his peeling pink skull. "How was the traffic?"

"Weekday. Not too bad." Graham was not Graham. "Want some help collecting your stuff?"

Graham blinked but did not say anything. Tarbell took a seat on the creaky wicker chair next to the dresser and let some more time pass.

After a while, Graham spoke. "Remember our walks above the beach?"

"Yes, we loved that, didn't we? It was so beautiful."

"What you really loved was grabbing my shoulders and pretending you were going to throw me over the cliff."

Tarbell sighed. "Sorry."

"You were such an jerk, Sandy."

"I'm sorry." Tarbell leaned forward and put his elbows on his knees. "I'm sorry."

Graham didn't seem to hear. He inhaled deeply and dropped his shoulders, giving up. "And yet, it turns out that of all the people in this wide, wide world, you are the only one who knew where to find me."

"Well, after all, Crack, I am your brother."

50

She should have known it was a setup. They had a simple plan, relying on her stupidity, and it worked.

The cabin that Alberti took Phipps to was off the main highway, down a mile and a half of unpaved road, with widely dispersed cottages nestled around a lake. Their nearest neighbor was fifty yards through the trees. A rusty pickup and an elderly basset hound that emitted occasional weary woofs let them know that somebody must be over there, but otherwise they were on their own.

The first evening went well. They got in late from the Red Lion, both exhausted, and went to sleep pretty much right away. Phipps slept in the bigger bedroom, with Alberti at his insistence across the hall, folded into the bottom of what had to be the kids' bunk bed. There were clean towels in the bathroom, and her queen-size had fresh sheets, which was heavenly. Phipps woke up a couple of times that night to the patter of rain, but by morning a mild sun was already shining, and the breeze through the window smelled piney and fresh. Alberti got a dish towel and dried off the pair of Adirondack chairs on the front porch. They took their coffee outside and began a very long talk—relating, among many other things, Phipps's long struggle with Ronnie and Alberti's painful marriage.

Alberti stayed with Phipps the whole day, leaving her only once for a jog around the lake—his morning run, never omitted, rain or shine—and again when he dashed into town to pick up a few groceries. Other than that, their conversation tumbled along at a sometimes painful level of intensity, with Phipps pouring out what she'd been up to with her uncle Jack, and Alberti describing what he'd felt when he'd overheard her phone call.

The second night, the two of them slept in her big bed, but chastely, just holding hands. Phipps thought it was silly, but she did not push it. Things were moving in the right direction. No sign appeared of any car hovering nearby, and no strangers were revealed lurking in the woods.

The weather continued to cooperate the second day. Temperatures cooled down, and they had another, shorter overnight rain, but at dawn the sun appeared again, fanning out over the still surface of the lake. Alberti cooked up a cheese omelet, and they had breakfast again on the porch. Phipps allowed herself to relax, which was her big mistake.

Ten minutes after Alberti took off for his daily run, Phipps was sitting on the porch reading a book when her phone chimed, signaling she had a text. It was Uncle Jack. She'd ignored a cheery text three days before, when she was at the Red Lion, asking how she was doing. This text was terrifyingly different. It read: *On my way to pick up Ronnie. Not sure when I'll be bringing him back. Where are you? Call me. Now.*

Her pulse surged so forcefully that she could feel the throbbing in the tips of her fingers. How had she not thought of this? Jack had always been sweet to Ronnie. Ronnie loved him. But now, as she reread the text, she was overwhelmed by a sickening sense of what Jack might be capable of. She had always sensed an ugliness in him, but she'd tucked the knowledge away to keep everything convenient. Now, he was taking her son.

Or maybe he hadn't, yet. Her hands were shaking so badly that she had to punch in the number for Ronnie's residence three times before she got it right. The person who answered sounded very young. She confirmed that, as far as she knew, Ronnie was still there. There was no record of anyone picking him up. She'd have to check to make sure.

Phipps worked to keep her voice calm. She told the girl they should not let anyone, and specifically not Jack Taylor, take Ronnie anywhere. She was on her way. The girl responded, apologetically, saying that she was a new hire, and it would take some time for her to find out where the permission forms were kept. Her supervisor was out, but she was sure Ronnie was fine. He was probably in a class somewhere, or on an outing.

Foolishly, it never ever occurred to Phipps to call 911. Maybe her reeling brain thought it would take too long. Maybe she was afraid it would make Carl angry, or get him in trouble. Instead, she decided to make a dash for Ronnie herself, just as they must have known she would. The cabin was not far from Lenox, and she might be able to intercept Jack, or collect Ronnie and be gone before Jack even arrived. She jotted Alberti a quick note, grabbed his car keys, and dashed out the door. He wouldn't approve of what she was doing, but with any luck she'd be back before he returned. She hopped in the car, adjusted the seat quickly, and shot a little gravel as she took off.

Two minutes into the drive, coming around a curve, Phipps saw an elderly woman walking in the grass at the margin of the road, holding walking sticks and pushing herself along energetically. She was wearing faded jeans, a plaid top, and a red feed cap over her white hair.

As Phipps was coming up beside her, the woman glanced over her shoulder. She started to smile and wave one of her sticks, but at that moment, she must have stepped on a rock or something. She fell heavily into the swale along the side of the road, almost disappearing into the tall weeds.

Phipps couldn't bring herself to stop completely—her entire being was focused on getting to Ronnie—but she slowed down and shouted out the window. "Are you okay?"

"Oh God." There was a floundering in the brush and a groan. "Please . . ." The woman sounded hurt.

Phipps stopped the car and shouted again. "Are you all right?"

From the weeds, the voice called out, "I'm sorry. Could you just . . ." The woman's face appeared briefly, blood on her forehead, and flopped back down. "I-I can't seem to . . ."

Sighing heavily, Phipps turned off the car, got out, and walked quickly over.

"I'm in sort of a rush, ma'am." She hadn't used the word *ma'am* since she was a teenager. "What should I do? Are you . . ."

The woman was below her, facedown, working her way awkwardly onto her hands and knees. She spoke in gasps. "So clumsy. My house is just two minutes . . ." She lifted her head and nodded down the road. "My husband will be . . ." She worked one leg up under her. "Oh golly . . ."

"Can you make it to the car?"

"I think . . ."

The woman got slowly to her feet and stood up, very shaky. She put a foot on the side of the swale, and Phipps helped pull her up. Very flustered, Phipps hurried over to open the passenger door.

"Okay, here we go. Like I said, I'm in kind of a rush."

"Thank you. I . . ." She put a hand on her chest to catch her breath. "I'm just down the road. Not, not two minutes."

Phipps trotted around to the driver's side, while the woman lowered herself gingerly into the passenger seat. Sliding in, Phipps reached to push the ignition button.

The passenger-side door slammed, and the old lady was suddenly leaning against her, pressing a box cutter against the side of her throat. Her humid breath moistened Phipps's cheek.

"Don't fucking move, okay?" The lady reached up with her free hand, pulled the feed cap and the white wig off her head, and flung it behind her in a swift, annoyed movement. "Fucking hot."

"Who . . ." Phipps was frozen, her finger still hovering over the starter.

"Listen to me, right?" The voice was deep and male. "Do what I say, and you won't get hurt."

Out of the corner of her eye, Phipps could see the deep creases etched in the makeup on the imposter's face. He kept the cutter pressed against the side of her throat, just enough so that she could feel it.

"Okay."

"I only want the car, and I don't want any fucking blood in it. You understand?" When she didn't say anything, he prodded a little harder. "You understand?"

"Yes, yes, I understand. I understand."

"Good girl. Now, I'm going to take you down that little side road up there. Once we're out of sight, I'm going to let you out. If you don't do anything stupid, you'll be fine, but if you try anything, I'm going to cut you, and we'll have a mess. You understand?"

"Yes."

He was lying. He was going to kill her, somewhere down there in the woods, and she would never see Ronnie again. This was clear from the way the man's words sounded so rehearsed, but she couldn't think of anything to do, could barely think at all.

"You see that big rock down there?"

"Uh, no. I'm sorry . . ."

"The big fucking rock, right there, for fuck's sake." He took the cutter away from her throat and pointed, then quickly put it back against the side of her neck. She could feel he'd nicked her, sense the warm, tickling dribble of blood. "Shit. You see it? It's right fucking there."

"Yes. That big rock. Okay." She started driving as slowly as she could. It was all she could think of to do.

He mumbled to himself. "Told me not to get blood on the seats."

"You have blood on your forehead, you know."

He jerked the visor down and looked in the vanity mirror. "Oh, fucking fuck."

He was a skinny man, shorter than Phipps, and with all the makeup he looked like something out of a horror movie. It was obvious that he was very wired—probably on meth or something—and that in a few minutes he was going to kill her. Behind her terror, she sensed a deadly, corroding resignation threatening to capture her, pushing her to let whatever was going to happen just happen. She gritted her teeth, squeezed the steering wheel, and fought it. Maybe she would die but, by God, she was not just going to give in and go along with it.

The man wiped his forehead with his free hand and pointed. "Turn here. We'll go into the woods a ways and do our thing." He quickly added, "Everything is going to be fine. I may need to tie you up, though. We'll see."

Phipps's mind was dancing around. She realized now that of course her uncle's text was a decoy. It should have been obvious. Jack didn't have the stomach for dirty work like kidnapping, and he couldn't manage Ronnie, anyway. After the first couple of hours, he'd have no idea what to do with him. Jack must have had a very good idea, though, what this guy was going to do with her.

She slowly took the turn, inching around the rock, and headed down what looked like an old dirt logging road. The grass began swishing against the fenders.

The man had let his knife hand drop when he'd been distracted by his cut. Now, he leaned into her and placed the box cutter against her throat again. "Speed up, sister. I'll tell you when to stop. Let's do this."

In the distance, Phipps heard a sound like a high-pitched explosion, not a boom but a sort of echoing bang. "What was that?"

The man snorted. "Fraid that was probably your swank friend." He pressed his free hand against his forehead again, looked at it, and wiped it on his jeans. "Lucky for you I'm a nicer guy than my brother."

Phipps swallowed but didn't say anything, looking hard for an opportunity of some sort. She could run the car into a tree but they were going so slow, and if she sped up too abruptly or didn't hit the tree hard enough, he'd finish her fast. All it would take was a flick of his hand.

She continued driving as slowly as she could, dragging it out, pretending to be worried about the road. It was all she could think of to do. The weedy path dropped off steeply at one point into a dip, and she stopped before a crude bridge made of logs arranged across a stream. After the overnight rains, the stream had a vigorous current.

"Come on, for fuck's sake."

"What if the bridge collapses? We'll go right into the—"

"It's not going to fucking collapse."

"I don't know." Phipps managed to sound uncertain. "Your forehead's still bleeding, by the way. It's about to run into your eye."

"Fuck." He looked in the mirror. "Do you have a Kleenex?"

"I don't think so."

"I thought girls always had Kleenexes."

"There might be one in my purse in the back. I could . . ."

He dug his fingers into her arm. "Don't do anything stupid." He nodded toward the log bridge. "Move." The blood trickled down into the makeup. "Fuck." He squeezed his eye shut and scuffed at the area with his upper arm.

She bumped over the bridge, sensing the pressure of the man's impatience in his grip on her shoulder and going just fast enough to keep him from flipping out, but no faster.

After the bridge, at the top of the rise on the far side, the road smoothed out. Not far beyond that, he told her to hold up.

"Okay. This'll do. We're getting out."

"Okay." She started out the driver's-side door, bracing her legs to run.

"Not that way." His hand gripped her arm fiercely, jerking her back, and he pressed the blade into the soft depression at the side of her throat. "You're almost done with me, okay? Let's not be stupid." His face was so close she could see brown stains between his teeth. "I'm just going to take your car, and you won't ever see me again. Won't that be nice?"

He dragged her over the center console, never loosening his grip. As soon as she was outside, he twisted her arm around behind her, wrenching it so hard she cried out in pain.

"Sorry," he said. "We've come this far. I'm not taking any . . ." He shoved her ahead of him so hard that she stumbled through a puddle, soaking her feet. The pain in her arm and shoulder was intense. If she tried to squirm free, and it took any time at all, he'd just kill her on the spot.

An old sugar maple stood uphill through some weeds, fifteen or twenty yards back from the gravel road. He dragged her over to it and pushed her face-first against the trunk, using his body and left hand to press her into it, holding the cutter in his right.

"Okay." He spread his legs to set himself. "Another couple seconds, and we're done."

Using all her strength, Phipps twisted to the side and kicked up backward trying to get her heel into his groin. It wasn't as good as she'd practiced in her Saturday classes, but she was taller than he was, and it knocked him off-balance. In the struggle, she managed to break his grip and shift around to face him. He shoved himself up against her and pressed her into the tree, setting his legs farther apart to steady himself.

"Come on. Let's not make this . . ."

She kneed him hard, this time right in the sweet spot. He fell back a step and bent to the side, holding his groin with his free hand. "Oh fuck, you fucking . . ."

She shoved him in the chest with both hands and dashed down-hill toward the car, screaming as loud as she could, "Leave me alone!" But as she reached the bottom of the slope, the ground sank sud-denly and she stepped into sticky mud. One of her sandals came off, and she stumbled, falling onto her knees. She could hear him behind her, and she grabbed a baseball-size rock, pulled herself onto her feet, and threw it at his head, yelling "Get away from me!" Four steps away, hobbling, he ducked just in time, and the rock flew over his shoulder. She snatched a stick off the ground and swung at his face. He dodged backward, the cutter waving in his hand, and the branch, wet and rotten, broke off in midswing.

Things stopped momentarily. They were both panting hard, looking at each other. Phipps's breath was coming out in ragged, high-pitched squeaks, but her voice when she managed to form words was a growl.

"You get—you get away from me, you fucker!"

"Okay, now we . . ."

He took a step toward her, and Phipps thrust out with the stub of her stick, trying for his eye. He swatted it away. As she turned to run, he grabbed her by the hair, jerking her backward. She braced herself for the slash.

A loud voice, coming from somewhere, called out, "Hey!"

The man coiled his arm around her, squeezing hard. His other hand, dancing in front of her face, still held the cutter.

"The fuck are you?"

"You don't want to know." A dark-haired man was coming toward them with long strides. He looked at her. "You're a real pain, Angie."

It took Phipps a few seconds to recognize who it was. She'd seen Aidan in the courtroom, but only spoken to him once, outside in the corridor. They'd talked about her car and where she lived. She could hear herself now, breathing in loud gulps that sounded like sobs. What was he doing here? Nothing made sense.

As Aidan got closer, the man held up the box cutter and yelled out, "You see this, asshole? Back off, or I'll . . ."

Eight feet away, Aidan stopped and shook his head. Then he reached behind him and pulled something black out of his waistband. There was an earsplitting bang, and the arm around Angie suddenly jerked away, knocking her off-balance. She staggered two steps and fell on her side into the weeds. When she managed to scramble up, she saw her attacker sprawled on his back with a mess of something bloody where the top of his head had been.

"Jesus Christ!" Phipps's ears were ringing. "You could have . . ."

"Right. But I didn't."

"I can barely hear." She gaped at Aidan. "You can't just . . ."

"I saved your life, Angie. Is that okay?" Aidan gestured at the body. "And the world is a little less of a shithole now."

Phipps twisted to the side and held up a hand to block out the sight of all the blood. "My God." It was horrible.

"We need to get going."

She straightened up, closed her eyes, and took a deep breath through her mouth. "Okay." Something had happened to Carl. She needed to pull herself together. "Okay." She picked up her sandal and stepped toward the car, holding it in one hand. She would not let herself go zombie.

Aidan tapped her shoulder. "I've got a Jeep. There's a shortcut back there." He pulled a cloth of some sort out of his back pocket and held it out to her. "You've got blood on your face."

"How did you . . ."

"Just got here. Good thing you put up a fight."

Rafferty was too late to save Carl Alberti from the ambush, but not too late to help.

He had been barreling down the road from the far side of the lake, when he rounded a bend and saw Alberti jogging toward him at a steady pace. He slammed on his brakes and blew the horn in time to get Alberti to stop seconds before the bomb detonated. The blast flung Alberti onto his back, sent a tree crashing over, and threw a hail of stones into Rafferty's SUV, cracking the windshield.

Up the hill, he saw a tall figure legging it through the trees. Whoever it was must have stuck around to hand-trigger the bomb. Rafferty immediately floored the accelerator and took off uphill after him, straight through the brush, dodging stumps and boulders. The guy saw him and ran for a few steps up the incline, but he was past his prime and not in the best shape. After a bit, Rafferty abandoned the car and overtook him on foot easily.

The man was leaning against a tree, gasping for breath. It was Gerry Doyle, older but still recognizable. "Okay, okay." Doyle held up a hand. "Little old for this kind of thing. You youngsters . . ."

"Who hired you for this, Gerry?"

"It's Rafferty, right? One of Dom's guys?"

"Who paid you to set this up?"

Doyle's face turned impatient. "You know I'm not gonna tell you that. We have a business, and we can't just—"

"I understand." Rafferty pulled out his automatic and shot Doyle in the thigh. "That's for upsetting my friend."

Doyle screamed and grabbed his leg. "Come on! For the love of . . ."

Rafferty took two steps closer and shot Doyle through the heart. "And that's for Sally Hoffman."

Doyle's eyes widened in a brief, wondering look, and he flopped backward like a sack of rocks.

Rafferty worked quickly. He slipped on a pair of plastic gloves, then pulled a second, smaller handgun out of his fanny pack, and wiped it off with a rag he'd brought. He fired two quick shots from the new gun into a big birch tree behind him, smeared Doyle's bloody hand over it, and set it next to the body. The gun was a cheap .38 caliber with its serial numbers ground off, picked up from a street dealer—just the kind of thing Gerry Doyle would pack. It would do for a throw-down. Then Rafferty removed the gloves, stuck them in his pocket, and headed back down the slope.

When he reached the road, he found two people already at work on Alberti. Alberti's right side, the side toward the bomb, was badly torn up, but he was still alive. One of the men kneeling over him looked like he knew what he was doing. He was working with quick, efficient movements.

Rafferty trotted over. "Is he going to make it?"

"Don't know." The man spoke without looking up. "Saw a lot of this in Iraq." He leaned toward the second man. "Keep pressing down hard, okay?" He jerked out one of his bootlaces and began tying it around Alberti's arm.

Aidan came skidding up in his Jeep with Angie Phipps. Phipps had bloody scratches on her face and arms, but when the ambulance showed up a few minutes later, she immediately crawled in the back with Alberti. It still wasn't clear if he was going to make it. The EMTs looked grim.

A squad car pulled up just as the ambulance was leaving, and Rafferty took Aidan aside.

"You all set?"

Aidan nodded. "I can tell the truth for once. Angie will back me up."

Rafferty wasn't too worried either. No one was going to mourn the Doyles, and no one was going to look very carefully into the details of how they'd left this world.

51

When David Kamau said he was thinking of going back to Kenya, Godfrey Mungai did everything he could to change his mind. This included pointing out that if Kamau went, Mungai would feel compelled to disrupt, and possibly risk, his own life to go with him. Even after it became clear that Kamau was adamant, and starting to get angry, Mungai kept bombarding his friend with emails, texts, late-night phone calls, and passionate in-person speeches. Nothing worked. The upshot was that, the Sunday after the Lenox bombing, Mungai found himself seated very unhappily next to his friend on Delta Flight 9585 nonstop to Amsterdam with a connection to Nairobi.

Mungai was quite frightened at what they were doing, and this was making him more peevish than usual. As he groped for his seat belt, he muttered, "This is mad. Judge Norcross deserved more than a half-hour visit."

What he had wanted to say—what he had almost said—was: *You should have said goodbye to your father properly*, but he stopped himself. The word *father*, referring to Norcross, still felt strange, and Kamau would have resented it as a manipulative jab.

"I did the best I could, Godfrey. He knows how I feel, even if he does not understand." Kamau put his hand on Mungai's shoulder. "Please drop it, will you? It's going to be a long flight."

"And Lindsay?"

"I did speak to her, and she respects my decision."

"They will be watching for us at the airport when we land. You know that."

Kamau leaned back and closed his eyes, ending the conversation.

Kamau's stepfather and a group from the Anglican Church of Kenya would be waiting when they arrived. They would notify airport security, and this would give them some protection, at least initially. The office of the president had been contacted as well, and they would provide what assistance they could. Everything possible had been done, Mungai told himself, in the short time they'd had. Based on what he'd heard, though, he was very afraid that what they'd done would not be enough, or not for very long.

Mungai had managed to book a pair of seats, a double, on the port side of the Airbus, seats 23A and B. Kamau preferred the window, where he could lean against the fuselage to sleep. Mungai was happy to take the aisle, which would allow him to stretch his legs a little.

The middle section across the aisle had four seats, and this arrangement was causing a kerfuffle one row up, at 22.

An obese man had stopped in the aisle and was waving his boarding pass over a woman—possibly African, possibly African American—who was wearing a brightly colored headscarf and was seated in the aisle seat.

"I specifically told them I could not manage a middle seat." He was speaking indignantly and louder than necessary. "I mean, look at me."

"Yes?" The woman had been reading and looked up from her book.

"Well, you can see that I'm pretty big, right?" The heavy man seemed to be suggesting that the lady had somehow overlooked this. "I'm going to have a hell of a time squeezing in over there."

"What does your boarding pass say?"

"22D."

She gestured to her right. "Then that's your seat."

"We could switch places. That would—"

"Excuse me." The lady set her book on her lap and looked up at him, smiling. "What planet do you come from? It's a seven-hour flight."

"I know, but it would be a lot easier for both of us, if—"

"You would not like it, believe me." She spoke firmly and shook her head. "I make frequent use of the bathroom." She returned to her book.

As the man steamed, a female flight attendant walked up. "Can I help you?"

By this time, people were peeking over the tops of their seats to see what was going on. Mungai began to worry that they might be about to experience one of those dreadful airplane incidents the newspapers regularly described. A restless line of people was waiting to get past, most of them lugging carry-ons.

The man spoke aggressively. "They assigned me the wrong god-damn seat."

The attendant looked at his boarding pass. "You have 22D, right there."

"Yes, but I told them I needed an aisle seat."

"When did you make your reservation?"

"I bought the ticket an hour ago, for Christ's sake, right here at the airport." His voice was increasing in volume.

"Well, I'm sorry." The attendant pointed. "That's your assigned spot. If you're unhappy, you can deplane and make other arrange-ments. We need to get everyone seated before we can close the doors. I'm afraid we're full."

Kamau opened his eyes and turned to Mungai. "What's going on?"

"Travel melodrama."

The man did not budge. He looked down at the woman, who was determinedly keeping her nose in her book. "Look, I'll pay you five hundred bucks to switch seats with me."

She looked up. "May I see the money, please?"

"I don't have it on me." His voice rose in pitch, as though he thought she was being stupid. "I don't carry that kind of cash . . ."

The woman went back to her reading.

A high voice from back in the clogged line said, "Oh, for heaven's *sake*," and a deeper, male voice called out wearily, "Come on, clear the aisle up there." A young woman seated behind them said, just loud enough to be heard, "Try cutting down on the milkshakes, Big Guy." This got some laughs.

"Sir." The attendant pointed at 22D. "You can take that seat or get off. Those are your options."

The woman with the headscarf stood and stepped into the aisle. The man squeezed past her into the inner seat, frowning and huffing, and the line of passengers flowed again. Disaster averted.

Not long after this, the main cabin door closed, and they began taxiing down the runway. Their die was cast. Mungai thought of his wife and daughter in Somerville. The pilot came on, reminding everyone to make sure their seat belts were fastened, their tray tables were in the full upright and locked position, and so forth. They were number three for takeoff, looking forward to an on-time arrival at Schiphol Airport in Amsterdam. A smooth flight was expected.

The conversation in which Mungai had told Barbara and Taisha that he would be returning to Kenya for a few weeks had been very emotional, and he was still not over it. The fact was that he did not really know how long he would be away, and there was some chance he would never return. They were his treasures, and he missed them already, very much. The plane rolled forward relentlessly.

When they were just about lined up for takeoff, the pilot came on again.

"Well, folks, I'm afraid I've got a little bad news. Something's come up, and we're going to have to return to the gate." This was greeted with groans. "I know. I hear you. But we don't expect the delay will be long, so sit tight. We'll be doing everything we can to get in the air and on the way just as soon as possible."

The plane crept slowly back to the gate and stopped. There was some bumping as the gangway was reattached, and then, for a couple of minutes, nothing happened. Kamau, looking resigned, wedged a pillow under his head and settled down to sleep. He looked exhausted.

Soon, Mungai saw a broad-shouldered Black man with a commanding presence striding down the aisle. Another man was behind him, and Mungai noticed two others moving purposefully up the far aisle on the starboard side of the plane. They seemed to be there on some sort of official business. Mungai was relieved when they stopped just short of his seat, blocking the two ends of the central section of row 22.

The Black supervisor leaned across the woman with the headscarf and spoke to the oversize man next to her. His voice was easily audible.

"Jack Taylor?"

The man looked up with his mouth open, not saying anything.

"Mike Patterson, FBI. Please come with us."

"I refuse. I'm not coming."

The woman in the headscarf spoke up immediately. "Oh yes, you certainly are." She stood and stepped into the aisle, still holding her book.

Taylor said, "You can't just come on here—"

"We have a warrant, sir. You're going to have to come with us."

The lady chimed in cheerfully. "Move along, dear, move along." She turned to Patterson, touching his forearm and beaming. "Bless your heart. You've made me *such* a happy woman!" As they escorted Taylor down the aisle, she tossed her book on the vacated seat and settled herself contentedly, lifting the armrest to make more space. Several people clapped as the group departed.

Five more minutes went by, and the plane was beginning to get stuffy, when another new man, middle-aged and white, began working his way ponderously down the aisle toward them. At first, Mungai thought he might be a lucky standby grabbing the vacated seat. Then he recognized the ICE agent who had overseen Kamau's arrest at the Harvard Divinity School. Remembering how he'd been knocked down, Mungai swallowed, and his mouth went dry. What now? Kamau was sitting up, awake and watching.

The man progressed slowly toward them, shifting his weight from side to side. He puffed his cheeks, blowing out a breath, stopped, and spoke.

"Reverend Kamau?"

"Yes."

"Remember me?"

"Yes, Mr. Ackerman, I remember you quite well." Kamau sighed. "How may I help you?"

"I had to run to catch you."

Mungai could see that Ackerman was a little winded.

Kamau said, "You need to take better care of yourself, Mr. Ackerman."

"You're right. You might want to know that your student visa has been reinstated." He looked at his watch. "As of an hour ago." Ackerman bent his knees to peer out the porthole, not looking at them. "We're dropping the deportation proceedings. You're free to continue your flight, of course, but there is no longer any . . ."

Mungai immediately grabbed the seat back and pulled himself up. "No, we'd prefer to, uh . . ." He looked down at Kamau, gripped by a fear that, for some reason, his friend would still insist on continuing their flight. To his relief, Kamau began to stand up too.

"Thank you, Mr. Ackerman." Kamau bent to collect some papers out of the pocket in the chair back. "I think my friend here would like to postpone our departure." He set his hand on the back of Mungai's neck, smiling. "He'll be getting off, and I will be accompanying him."

Ackerman took the lead down the aisle, with Kamau and Mungai behind. Ackerman looked over his shoulder. "I entered the reinstatement into the system. You shouldn't have any more trouble."

"Thank you." Kamau continued, his voice lower, speaking to Mungai. "A tiny erasure on an invisible chalkboard, Godfrey, and we are still alive. Providence works in mysterious ways."

"By the way," Ackerman continued. "Check with us if you get any more calls from your embassy. Someone there might be playing games."

As they emerged from the gangway, Mungai saw Jack Taylor in the distance, cuffed in back, being escorted down the concourse. Mike Patterson was walking next to him with his hand on Taylor's elbow.

As Ackerman started to drift toward the Dunkin' Donuts, Kamau called after him. "Excuse me, sir." Ackerman turned. "Can you inform me, or give me any information at all, as to why my visa has been restored?"

Ackerman shook his head. "I have no idea."

52

Judge Norcross hurried up to Chief Judge Broadwater's chambers Monday morning before court, barging past Dorothy with a wave of his hand and poking his head into Broadwater's office. The chief was peering into his computer screen and looked up distractedly.

"Hi, sorry. Won't be a minute." Norcross stepped in and quickly closed the door behind him. "I got the news that David's student visa was reinstated. I wanted . . ." He put his hand on his heart and bowed slightly.

"Congratulations. Wonderful news."

"We've been very worried. It's actually been . . ."

"Well, that's life, isn't it? You want a pearl, you have to get a little sand in your oyster."

Norcross put a hand on his heart and tipped his head. "I wanted to thank you, privately."

"What for?"

"Well, it meant—it means—a lot to me."

Broadwater tossed his glasses onto his desk and scrubbed his eyes. "What makes you think I had anything to do with this, Dave?" He was looking at Norcross sharply. "I told you I couldn't help."

"Well, something happened somehow." He nodded at Broadwater. "I thought—"

"Yes, and I thought we agreed you would never bring this up again."

The news of his son's last-minute rescue had hit Norcross like a blast of sunshine and rose petals, and he had been looking forward to expressing his gratitude to Broadwater—maybe even giving the dear man a hug, or something ridiculous like that. The chief's reaction now was deflating, to put it mildly. Broadwater seemed annoyed.

"Well, Skip, I'm sorry if . . ."

Broadwater's expression softened, but not much. "I'm happy for you, of course, but look . . ." He waved a hand. "Things just happen. Nobody knows how or why. It's usually best to leave them that way." He took a breath and patted his desk. "So how is Claire doing these days? She must have the start of the semester roaring down on her."

The conversation after that fell into familiar channels and stayed put, leaving Norcross feeling as though he'd showed up a day late for the party. Before long, he looked at his watch, made his excuses, and wrapped up. *O'Connell*, he said, would be resuming in a few minutes.

As he reached the doorway, Norcross turned. "These past few days, Skip, it's like my world turned upside down. I never imagined . . ."

Broadwater was already bent over his computer, tapping the keyboard. He spoke without looking up. "My advice, Dave. Enjoy your good fortune." He shot Norcross a quick glance. "Just enjoy it. And don't talk too much about it."

53

As Judge Norcross was hurrying back to his chambers, Mike Patterson was upstairs in the U.S. Attorney's suite, meeting with Bob Schwartz and Alex Chen.

Schwartz was sitting at the head of the table like a small stone Buddha, staring straight forward with his hands folded in front of him. He gave off an almost scary energy—something remote and dead calm. Patterson had seen it before at this stage of a case, but never this strong—a smoldering rage, only half buried.

Schwartz shifted his eyes to Patterson. "I don't like admitting this, Mike, but your visit to Graham Tarbell paid off. He and his lawyers are coming in this morning. He's ready to talk." Schwartz picked up a pencil and tapped on the table top softly. "Down." He gave a couple of taps. "He." Another *tap-tap*. "Goes."

Chen glanced over at Patterson, smiling. "Does he always get like this?"

"Only when he smells blood."

Schwartz put the pencil down. "The whole house of cards is teetering." He made a fist. "I can feel it. I'm going to bag them all."

"Well then, you'll be interested in this." Chen opened a folder. "I went with the search team to the Doyles' house yesterday. They found an impressive bomb factory in the basement. Here's the warrant return with the details." He pushed a sheaf of papers over to Schwartz.

"Bingo." Schwartz began flipping the pages, running his eyes over the summary of items seized. "It's a shame Dennis and Gerry won't be around for the fun."

Chen nodded. "O'Connell's leg-breakers must have been tracking them."

"Or tracking Angie Phipps." Patterson had been very worried that someone would catch up with her. The turn of events, ugly as it had turned out, was a relief.

Schwartz waved his hand. "The Doyles are a state court matter, a straight double homicide. Let the Berkshire County D.A. deal with it, if she wants to. We've got enough on our plates."

"I looked into it," Patterson said. "O'Connell's guys have a pretty good defense. They probably saved a couple lives. I doubt she'll be bringing charges. We'll see."

Agent Chen continued. "We have a forensic team flying up this afternoon from Alabama. They'll give us a clearer picture, but it's a definite that it was the Doyles who planted the Harvard and Waban bombs." Chen hesitated and glanced over at Schwartz, who was staring forward, miles away. "You okay there?"

Patterson realized that Schwartz was probably recalling Sally Hoffman and re-living what his boys were going through, thinking it was his fault.

Chen pointed over at the sheet of paper. "Same components, same materials, same triggering device. Probably Lenox too."

"Buddy Hogan will be holding a press conference this afternoon, announcing that he's solved the Harvard bombing." Patterson sighed. "He's getting his hair cut as we speak."

"How about Kahlil Khan?" Chen leaned back and folded his arms.

Schwartz spoke distractedly, almost mumbling. "Tom Redpath has filed a motion to dismiss, which I won't be opposing. Broadwater lifted the detention order this morning. Khan's out."

"Good news for him," Chen said.

"Yeah," Patterson said. "And I heard Harvard's giving him his old job back, with a little bonus and a raise."

Chen sniffed. "Ivy League guilt."

"Okay, listen to me." Schwartz lifted his hands off the table. "Jack Taylor was obviously paying the Doyles." His voice went eerily low. "Now, I want the names of every single person who paid Taylor. I want to know what they did, when they did it, and what they knew."

Patterson shook his head. "I doubt that any of Taylor's clients—if you can call them clients—were aware of what the Doyles were up to. Gerry and Dennis were a force unto themselves, and they were out of control. Can't say it breaks my heart that they're gone."

"Maybe." Schwartz shook his head. "Maybe. But I'm not ready to buy that yet. Some of the Big Boys may have known and not cared. Or they might have guessed and worked hard to keep themselves in the dark. Willful blindness can be a form of intent. I'm hoping we'll have enough to charge at least some of these guys with the conspiracy to murder. That way, I can crowbar them into pleading to the counts for obstruction of justice and bribery."

Patterson asked, "Can we pull Sandy Tarbell in? He was all around this."

Schwartz frowned. "I doubt it. He knows the terrain, and he's good at staying in the underbrush."

"Jack Taylor could help us a lot, but he isn't talking."

"He might eventually." Schwartz shrugged. "We'll manage without him if we need to."

"You should have seen his face on the plane." Patterson chuckled as he remembered. "Thank heaven we got help from the woman sitting next to him. I thought I was going to have to snatch him up by the ears."

"His trying to take off was a gift. He's shown that he's a risk of flight." Schwartz nodded with satisfaction. "No judge will release him before trial, and that won't be six or eight months, minimum, assuming he doesn't plead."

"Do you really think he might cooperate?" Chen asked.

"If he doesn't, he's spent his last day on this earth as a free man." Schwartz pushed the search paperwork away. "We're putting together an indictment against him for conspiracy to murder under the RICO statute, along with the obstruction and bribery charges. It's a life sentence at least for Jacko unless he comes on board."

Chen said, "Can't say my heart bleeds much for him either."

"Taylor deserves whatever he gets." Schwartz leaned into the table, moving his eyes from Chen to Patterson. "But I want the money guys, the ones who greased the machine—the virtuous untouchables."

"We have a team up from Washington combing the dockets right now," Patterson said. "Only a few big firms could afford Taylor, and we've already discovered two or three who got miraculously lucky draws. Some top lawyers."

Schwartz's face went hard. "There's going to be some very bad news, in some very expensive houses, very soon."

Patterson broke in. "Do we know how Carl's doing, Alex?" He'd been trying Angie Phipps's mobile, but she wasn't picking up.

Chen shook his head. "The news is mixed. Bad news is he lost two fingers off his right hand, and he may never recover full use of that arm. Good news is that it looks like he's going to make it. Angie Phipps has a cot set up in his hospital room. She never leaves."

"Good for her." Patterson's phone chimed. He glanced down at it and nodded to Schwartz. "Showtime. Let's go see what Graham Tarbell has to tell us."

"No deals today." Schwartz stood up. "This is just a proffer session. I want this guy twisting in the wind for a while."

Patterson put his arm on Schwartz's shoulder. "Bob, I've done this before, you know."

"I don't care if Graham gives us the moon. He's going down for a good, long time."

"He's not a bad guy, actually."

"Oh, I'm sure he's not a bad guy, Mike—just evil. That's our world."

54

Norcross had finally gotten used to Judge Conti's courtroom and was feeling pleased to have *O'Connell* back on course. The only way to reach the finish line was to keep going forward. As he took his chair and did his customary survey of the courtroom, he noticed a small, bent man in the gallery, seated right behind Assistant U.S. Attorney Papadakis.

The man resembled a gnome, or some other very old creature out of folklore. His wrinkled face was small and triangular, with a pointed chin accentuated by a wispy white goatee. One shoulder dipped below the other giving him a gnarled look. This had to be the government's big witness, the informant Brian Shaughnessy, but what was going on? Shaughnessy wasn't scheduled to take the stand today, and Norcross had barred witnesses from the courtroom until they were called to testify.

His new courtroom deputy looked up from his seat below the bench, inquiring wordlessly if he should bring the jury in. The judge noticed Papadakis getting onto her feet and shook his head.

Very composed, Papadakis stood with her hands behind her

back. "Before we get started, we have a little problem, Your Honor, that we're going to need your help with."

"Okay."

Tarbell glared first at Papadakis and then up at the judge.

"The government is requesting to call a witness out of order."

"Really. And you're telling me now?"

Papadakis swiveled and nodded behind her. "Brian Shaughnessy signed himself out of Mass General this morning, against his doctors' advice. He's in critical condition, Judge, and every minute he's away from medical monitoring puts him at greater risk."

"What about Mr. Tarbell's cross of Loreen Laplante? He's barely started."

Tarbell jumped up. "Exactly, Judge."

Papadakis gestured toward the gallery. "I've spoken to Ms. Laplante. She is available tomorrow or any time at Mr. Tarbell's convenience."

A voice piped up from the back of the courtroom. "It's okay." Laplante bobbed up and waved a hand. "It's okay. It's no problem."

Tarbell looked back at her and snorted. "Oh, I bet it's no problem."

Papadakis continued as though Tarbell had not spoken. "The government is prepared to accommodate any reasonable adjustment of the schedule—"

"Accommodate, my foot." Tarbell ran a hand back over his hair, his voice rising. "Judge, this guy right here . . ." He took two steps toward Shaughnessy, leaned over, and gestured at him. "Is their key witness, right? They don't have a case, they don't have squat, without him." His voice went up another notch. "I was up most of last night outlining my continued cross of Ms. Laplante. I'm not *ready* to tackle Brian Shaughnessy today. You can't let Ms. Papadakis put me in this position, Judge. It's just wrong. I strenuously object."

As Tarbell spoke, the judge couldn't help noticing O'Connell and Shaughnessy. The two men were tracking the debate with exactly the same blank expressions, heads mechanically turning from one lawyer to the other and up to the bench. Shaughnessy's face in particular had remained impressively indifferent while Tarbell kept pointing at him.

Papadakis moved from behind her table and stepped up to the podium, placing herself closer to the bench and increasing the punch of her words.

"Judge, let me remind you that you made the decision a few days ago, over both our objections, not to permit Mr. Shaughnessy's deposition. Respectfully, but for that ruling, we wouldn't be in this pickle. The deposition transcript would have preserved Mr. Shaughnessy's testimony in the event of a sudden decline in his condition, which has now unfortunately occurred." She gave the judge a full blast of eye contact. "Just as I told you I feared."

"Well, Ms. Papadakis, you waited until right before trial to file your motion."

"We had our reasons for that, Your Honor, good or bad, but the fact is: here we are."

Tarbell broke in, pointing at Papadakis. "She has no evidence whatsoever that a delay of a day or two is going to make any difference. I repeat: this is their do-or-die witness. You can't allow this."

Papadakis continued to ignore Tarbell. "I don't want to go all operatic here, Your Honor, but I spoke to Brian Shaughnessy's doctor an hour ago, and I can represent to you, as an officer of the court, that Brian's condition is dire. It's taking a lot of courage for him to even be here."

At this, Shaughnessy nodded and gave a pinched, leprechaun smile, as though he were resigned but amused at the situation. Then his face contracted into a wincing twist of pain. Was this for real or for show? Judge Norcross had no idea.

"Oh, pass me a hankie." Tarbell pointed again at the defendant. "What's at stake, Judge, is whether Brian Shaughnessy's drug-dealing thug of a nephew gets a break. That's why he wants to be sure to get his evidence in."

Norcross noticed Shaughnessy raise his eyebrows and nod. He didn't disagree.

"Thank you, Mr. Tarbell." This was going on too long. The jury would be wondering what the holdup was. "What you say may be true, but it's irrelevant. The jurors are entitled to hear and weigh Mr. Shaughnessy's testimony, whatever his motives."

Tarbell's argument was weak, which was why he was peppering it with a lot of snarl. The interruption of his Laplante cross would not hurt him, and the claim that he wasn't prepared to question Shaughnessy was pure foam. He must have been planning his cross of this witness since the day he took the case. The manifest, macabre fact was that Tarbell was stalling, hoping that Shaughnessy would die.

"We'll get started with Mr. Shaughnessy and hold Ms. Laplante for now."

Tarbell groaned. "Your Honor, this is . . ."

Norcross looked at Papadakis. "How long do you think you'll be?"

She walked slowly back to her table, following every good lawyer's basic rule: never keep fighting after you've won. "I expect my direct will take most of the day, certainly into the afternoon." She looked over at the defense table. "Mr. Tarbell will have all this evening to buff up his cross-examination, if he really needs to."

Tarbell shook his head. "Judge, this is an outrage, pure and simple."

Norcross shook his head. "Well, I'd agree with you, Mr. Tarbell, but then we'd both be wrong." Papadakis produced a twitch of smile. "I think Winston Churchill or somebody said that. Anyway, let's bring the jurors in."

A few minutes later, after the jury was seated, Norcross explained that he was suspending the testimony of Loreen Laplante to allow the government to call a witness out of order. This sometimes happened, he said, and they should not concern themselves with the reason. He did not tell the jurors who the witness was or mention Shaughnessy's medical condition. The panel members looked intrigued but not particularly bothered.

Norcross nodded at Papadakis. "Government's next witness?"

"Your Honor, the government calls Brian Shaughnessy."

Shaughnessy closed his eyes and grimaced as he pushed himself onto his feet and then worked his lopsided way slowly across the well of the court to the witness stand. His use of a knobbly wooden cane added to the sense that he'd arrived from a different world.

Papadakis looked on as Shaughnessy struggled to hoist himself up the two steps into the witness box.

"Can I give you a hand there, Mr. Shaughnessy?"

"I can manage." He set the cane against the box and pushed himself up with both hands, then pulled the cane up with him, waving it at the jurors and muttering, "Gotta have my magic wand." He managed to remain upright as he was placed under oath, and then, with a grunt, lowered himself into the seat.

"All set?"

"Yes, my dear." He paused, closing his eyes and clenching his teeth. "Have at me."

Papadakis moved calmly through the preliminaries: the witness's name, address, age (eighty-seven), marital status (widower), and children (one, who died in her twenties).

"And your profession?"

"Retired. Very retired."

"And before that?"

"Truck driver, laborer, dear. Don't know if those count as professions."

"Okay, now." Papadakis stopped abruptly, as though she'd just thought of something. "Where's your oxygen, Mr. Shaughnessy? Aren't you supposed to be using that?"

He waved a hand dismissively. "I left the little cart back there. I'm fine. I'm fed up with the damn thing."

"You're sure?"

"I'm fine." He coughed into his fist. "Better, actually."

Papadakis looked dubious. "Okay, then, Mr. Shaughnessy, let me ask you this." She paused, taking her time, looking down at the floor briefly and folding her arms. "Other than being a truck driver and laborer, sir, was there something else you did during a certain period of your life for compensation?"

"Yes, my dear, I killed people." Shaughnessy frowned and shifted his shoulders.

The courtroom's faint sounds and random fluttering ceased. The air went still, and everyone's eyes fixed on the witness box.

"'Course I been out of that line of work many years now." Shaughnessy held his cane in front of him, gripping it hard with both hands. "Long time now, dear."

"I see. Well, Mr. Shaughnessy, I want to take you back to the spring of 1968, okay? In the weeks before Robert Kennedy's assassination."

"Terrible time."

"Do you remember that?"

"Very clearly." He closed his eyes, perhaps thinking back. "Before you were born, dear." He shook his head. "Terrible."

"Do you remember anything in particular that happened around then?"

"Yes, Tommy Gallagher called me."

"And why did he call you?

"He wanted somebody taken care of."

"I see. And who was that?"

"Cop named Scanlon, my dear." Shaughnessy winced again and took a deep breath, apparently warding off some pain.

Not more than twenty-five feet from the witness, Charles Scanlon's children sat in a tableau, staring at their father's killer, unmoving except for one of the daughters, who'd dropped her head and placed her hand over her eyes.

Noticing this, Shaughnessy lifted his chin in their direction. "Sorry. Long time ago."

"And do you recall meeting the defendant in this case, Dominic O'Connell, around then?"

Shaughnessy took longer to respond this time, closing his eyes and taking two or three deep breaths. Papadakis started to repeat her question, just as he managed to answer.

"Yes, poor kid." He coughed and cleared his throat. "Tommy roped him into the Scanlon pop."

"I see, and exactly when, if you recall . . ."

Shaughnessy produced another of his pinched leprechaun smiles and looked over at O'Connell, stroking his goatee. "We didn't hit it off too well, did we, Dom?"

Tarbell was on his feet instantly. "Objection!"

O'Connell had been staring hard at the witness. Now, from the bench, Judge Norcross could see him respond to Shaughnessy's crooked smile—frowning, shaking his head faintly, and looking down. It was a potentially devastating moment for the defense. Tarbell's fiercely asserted position was that his client had never met Shaughnessy, had never seen him, didn't know him. O'Connell's half-buried reaction made it very obvious that, in fact, the two of them had known each other, had met. Norcross couldn't tell whether any of the jurors had caught this very brief response from their angle. It was one of those fleeting moments that could arise in a trial, a form of evidence that would never enter the transcript, but that might make all the difference. Patterson immediately saw it and gave a head tilt to the judge, the courtroom equivalent of a wink. Tarbell, on his feet and focusing on the witness, missed the whole thing.

"Sustained. Mr. Shaughnessy, please wait for the question and don't interject."

"Interject?"

"Just wait for the question and answer it." Norcross turned to the jury. "Ladies and gentlemen, I instruct you to disregard whatever comment the witness made about hitting it off, or not hitting it off, or whatever that was. Simply disregard it. Put it out of your minds."

These moments in a trial were always a problem. He couldn't ask a jury to disregard something without telling them what they should disregard, and that risked emphasizing the very point they were supposed to avoid thinking about. Still, whatever its effect on the jury, his instruction would satisfy the court of appeals, if the case got up to them. He'd handled the situation appropriately, under the rules.

"Sorry. Getting old." Shaughnessy's words were sinking into a mumble. His chin was starting to droop, and he wiped his hand across his mouth. "Talk too much."

Papadakis picked up. "And when did you meet Mr. O'Connell?"

Shaughnessy said something Norcross couldn't make out, and he broke in, tapping the bench with his pen. "Could you speak up a little louder, Mr. Shaughnessy?"

Papadakis repeated her question. "When did you first meet the defendant?"

"Ouch." Shaughnessy sighed and stirred himself to sit up. "Couple weeks before we riffed the cop, my dear."

"And how would you characterize your relationship with Dominic O'Connell?"

"Cocky kid. Couldn't stand him. Stupid of Tommy to drag him in."

"I see and . . ."

"He was way over his head and didn't know it. Some people can do this kind of work. Some can't, my dear." He pulled at his goatee. "That's how it is."

"Objection. Move to strike."

"Overruled."

"Fact is, most people can't do it." Shaughnessy's voice grew faint. "Which is good, I suppose."

O'Connell sat, arms folded, looking down at the table. Tarbell, back in his chair, touched his client's shoulder and let his hand drop.

Papadakis turned to the side and raised her voice, moving on. "Okay, Mr. Shaughnessy, would you please describe the circumstances of your first meeting with the defendant?"

Shaughnessy nodded again and closed his eyes, apparently reaching back into his memory. His body gave a little shudder. The time drew out uncomfortably, and still Mr. Shaughnessy did not respond. Norcross checked on the jury. Several were exchanging anxious glances.

Papadakis took a step toward the witness box. "Mr. Shaughnessy? Would you like me to repeat the question?" The witness did not move or open his eyes.

Norcross broke in. "We'll take a short recess."

As the jurors made their way out of the courtroom, several looked nervously back at Shaughnessy. A stillness had gathered around him. At a nod from the judge, one of the deputy marshals hurried over to the stand.

O'Connell twisted around to look back at his wife. Norcross could not see his expression, but his wife's face did not change. The two men seated next to her glanced at each other, but their faces also remained completely deadpan.

The deputy shook the witness's shoulder gently, then placed his fingers on the side of his throat. After a few seconds, he looked up at the judge and shook his head. Brian Shaughnessy was gone.

PART FOUR

55

Two days after Shaughnessy's death, the government moved to dismiss *O'Connell* based on a lack of sufficient admissible evidence. When Papadakis presented the motion, she did not express her feelings in words, but her face made it clear that she was deeply angry. Judge Norcross's ruling not to permit Shaughnessy's deposition meant eighteen months of hard work down the drain and, to her mind at least, a murderer escaping punishment.

Sandy Tarbell naturally did not oppose the government's motion. When the judge allowed it, he reached over and gave O'Connell a businesslike handshake. The trial was over, and his client was going home. On to the next case. He did get a hug and a pat on the shoulder from the defendant's wife, which seemed to please him.

In the courtroom, O'Connell did not hazard a smile. He seemed almost baffled, as though he didn't believe it was really over. Two young women, both crying, both obviously daughters, gave him long embraces, and at the end of these O'Connell's face began to soften a little. His two associates stood off to the side, the red-haired one beaming and the other looking disgusted.

Like Papadakis, Judge Norcross was not at all happy with the dismissal. He did not blame the Scanlon family for the dark looks they shot him from the gallery. At the same time, he didn't permit himself to dwell too much on the bad, or unlucky, call he'd made about the deposition. In two or three days, a week at the most, the worst of his remorse would be behind him. He'd done his best. Making mistakes was part of the job.

Soon after that, Judge Norcross's designation to Boston ended, and he returned to Western Massachusetts, where his regular docket in Springfield immediately swallowed him up. Claire and Monica somehow got their manuscript submitted on time, and Claire's classes resumed. The summer slid toward autumn. In Amherst, the sugar maples were soon displaying dabs of red and orange.

Angie Phipps quickly resigned her position with the court, and one splendid September afternoon, in the backyard of the home she and Carl Alberti were renting in Lenox, Judge Norcross officiated at their wedding. Alberti was on disability, and Phipps had a job working as the office manager of a Berkshire County real estate agency. Norcross did not know, and did not ask, what Phipps's legal situation was. At the small reception in their living room afterward, Alberti limped over to inform him that the investigation into the deaths of the Doyles had concluded with no charges being filed. Alberti was still mending, but he looked happy, and Phipps was radiant.

True to his promise, David Kamau came out to Amherst that fall to observe Lindsay's softball practice, sitting in the bleachers next to Carmen Marquez, who was now officially acknowledged as Lindsay's girlfriend. Marquez had alert, intelligent eyes, brown hair so dark it was almost black, and very pale skin. She was polite but distant and formal with Judge Norcross—suspicious perhaps of his judicial role, especially in the immigration area—but unreserved in her delight at spending time with Lindsay's Kenyan half brother.

As much as he enjoyed seeing Lindsay, David Kamau seemed to make his strongest connection with Charlie, his *ndugu mdogo*, or "little brother." The boy adored him and would sit comfortably in Kamau's lap for fairly long periods—sometimes up to fifteen minutes—before squirming down. He loved looking at a big photo book with scenes of the Masai Mara National Reserve, fascinated by the lions, the giraffes, and the brightly striped zebras.

Kamau volunteered to come out and look after the boy if David and Claire wanted an evening off, but Claire was not quite ready for this. Her adjustment to the arrival of her unexpected stepson was steady but slow. She was clearly taking her time, finding words for her feelings, and getting used to her new reality. It was all good, but, as she told David, now and then she still felt on the periphery. An outsider.

One morning in October, Judge Norcross was sitting in his chambers proofreading a memorandum disposing of a Social Security appeal when he got a call from his old boss Bill Treadwell. Treadwell was going to be out in Western Massachusetts that afternoon. Could he drop by for a chat? He had something important to discuss.

When he arrived, Treadwell seemed thinner than Norcross remembered.

"Wow, Bill, looks like you've been hitting the gym. Good for you."

"Yes." Treadwell smiled wanly. "Seems I've lost some weight."

They took seats in a couple of club chairs drawn up around a low glass table in the corner of Norcross's inner office. As he was sitting down, Judge Norcross noticed that the lines in Treadwell's heavy face were deeper. His flowing hair had thinned, revealing glimpses of pink scalp. Time, it seemed, caught up with everyone eventually, even demigods like Bill Treadwell.

As soon as they got through their inquiries about each other's families, Treadwell leaned forward and put his elbows on his knees. He had some small object he was rolling around in the fingers of his right hand.

Norcross nodded. "What have you got there?"

Treadwell gave a half laugh and held up a shiny silver object. "Broke the post of one of my cuff links just now in the elevator. Fiddling with my cuffs, I guess."

"That's life." Norcross was in a good mood. He was back in harness, keeping up with his Springfield caseload, and it was a pleasure to see Treadwell. "Just a series of annoying tragedies."

"Yes. This pair was one of my favorites. My granddaughter gave them to me." Treadwell looked down, turning the cuff link in his fingers. "I had a particular reason for being here today . . ." He looked up. "Do you mind if I call you 'David'? What I have to say is not going to be easy, and that may help." His gravelly voice had slowed down.

"Of course. Sure." Norcross began to feel worried.

Treadwell took a breath, readying himself for his difficult topic, but broke off and looked around. "Goodness, David, here you are, hard at work in your lovely chambers. Seems like yesterday that you were arriving at the firm, the proverbial breath of fresh air, just out of law school."

"Well, thanks. You all were very kind."

"Remember that employment discrimination case you took? Right after you started? I forget the defendant."

"City of Boston."

"Right, our executive committee wanted you to turn it down."

"Really? I never knew that."

"We didn't do much of that kind of white-hat work, and those municipal defendants were tough. Proud to say I convinced them otherwise. After your big verdict, you were free to break your own path." Treadwell gave a strangely sad smile. "Years later, when you left to put on the robe, everyone was very sorry to see you go."

"I was sorry, too, but it was a good move for me." Norcross paused, thinking back. "I needed a calling, and I thought of judging—still think of it, actually—as a sort of secular priesthood."

"We've all been proud of you."

"Plus, I was a mess after Faye died, and I needed a change."

"We tried to do what we could to help."

"I'll always be grateful. You're a good man, Bill."

Treadwell gave a decisive nod. "Well, David, I hope you'll feel the same after you hear my news. I want you to get it from me before our friends in the media pick it up." He looked down at his hands, then raised his heavy face to Norcross. "Fact is, I'm going to be indicted any day now."

"Good God, Bill."

"I may already have been. They may be keeping it under seal. Sometime soon, someday sometime around sunrise I expect, the marshals will be coming to collect me."

Treadwell's anguished expression was painful to see. Norcross realized his mouth was hanging open, and he closed it. "What on . . ." He shook his head. "What on earth for?"

"I'm not sure of the precise charges. Bribery and conspiracy to obstruct justice. Something along those lines."

"How in the world . . ."

"Fact is, David, I deserve it. The firm used—that is to say, I used—Jack Taylor to steer some of our cases to selected judges. Just a few, but some big ones. At least two other local firms also used Taylor, and a couple of others around the country, Dallas and L.A. at least, that I know of. Maybe others. I expect we'll soon be seeing a raft of indictments. Bob Schwartz is driving the cases, but Buddy Hogan will take the credit of course. I hear he's calling it 'Varsity Green.'"

"I don't see how you—I'm sorry, but really—how anyone like you could ever do anything like that. Honestly, I can't believe it."

"I thought I could just take a small bite of the poisoned apple. The judges, of course, had no idea what was going on. In fact, on two occasions, after we'd sent Taylor a truckload of money, some colleagues of yours ended up ruling against us, anyway. Over the years, we had some good outcomes, but of course we never knew whether they came from the judge, the evidence, or whatever God of Comedy rules the courts. What counted was that the clients were impressed at our predictions, stuck with us, and paid our very large bills right on time."

Treadwell, who had continued fiddling with the cuff link, dropped it now, and it bounced on the thick carpeting, ending up at Norcross's feet. He picked it up and set it on the glass table. On its face, he noticed, were the scales of justice, white against black, in a ceramic design.

"I'm sitting here, and I still just can't . . ."

"I had my reasons, and they seemed good enough at the time. I made sure the firm used a big chunk of our cash flow in good ways. We were putting poor kids through college, paying medical expenses, creating programs to support immigrants. Lots of good things. How bad was a little innocent fudging in comparison with that? Everyone was happy. That's what I told myself anyway."

"Then people ended up dying."

"I was blind to that connection, David. I really hope you'll believe me when I say that. I dismissed Warren Armstrong's death as an act of terrorism and Sam Newbury's as a robbery gone bad. Very sad, but nothing to do with me." He closed his eyes, and his face sagged. "I was guiltless, in my own mind, every step of the way. Absolutely guiltless."

They sat for a few moments in silence before Treadwell continued.

"I doubt the U.S. attorney will try to tag me for the violence, but morally I am responsible, especially for Sam and poor Cynthia. I passed on the connection with Taylor to Sam. I have to live with that, and for that I deserve to go to prison, at least." He paused. "Assuming I live that long."

"What do you mean 'live that long'?"

"I just feel so . . ." He shook his head. "To get involved with someone like Jack Taylor. I'll never forgive myself."

"You're scaring me a little here, Bill."

"Oh, don't worry." Treadwell waved a hand. "I take my little pills, and they keep me mostly in balance. Give me a few hours of sleep at night. Besides, suicide would be kind of over-tidy, don't you think? I have to face the music, as they say. Plus . . ." Treadwell blew out a sour laugh. "The largest part of my estate is in life insurance. The premiums are enormous at my age, but the firm has been covering them. If I kill myself, it voids the policies." He looked at Norcross with a grimace. "I can face prison, David, but I can't face paying all that money to Boston Mutual for nothing. And, of course, I couldn't do that to Sandra. So, here I am, stuck in my life."

Norcross could think of nothing to say.

"I expect I'll die in prison. That may square things up at bit. I keep remembering the old story about the ancient Mafia capo. The judge gives him thirty years, and the old boy protests: 'Judge, I'm too old. I can't do that much time.' The judge looks down and says very kindly, 'Don't worry. Just do the best you can.'"

"Right. Classic judges' inside joke." Norcross sat for a few seconds before remembering again to close his mouth. "My God, Bill."

"I'm seventy-nine. I've done a few good deeds in my career, and that might shave some time off. If I'm very, very lucky, I may wobble back home in six or eight years to die. Not likely, but maybe."

A silence fell over them and deepened, until Norcross's inability to say anything became awkward. Having no idea what words he'd find, he tried to start. "I-I just . . ."

"I better go." Treadwell stood up, abruptly. "I thought nothing would be my fault, David. I was wrong. I am so very sorry."

Judge Norcross sat, dumbfounded, as Treadwell strode quickly out of the room. After the door closed, he continued to sit for some time, staring at the door, empty-headed. Finally, his eyes dropped to the coffee table, where the cuff link with the scales of justice lay. He briefly considered how he might get it back to Treadwell, but then realized he needn't bother. It was broken. He walked back to his desk, rolling it between his fingers, and gazed for some time into the blue-gray Berkshire hills. Finally, he sighed and leaned to toss the cuff link into his wastebasket. Then, he hesitated, looking down at where it lay in the palm of his hand, black on white. He put it in his desk drawer. He'd keep it, as a reminder.

56

As the season declined toward the end of the year, the grand jury continued to return fresh indictments, and Judge Norcross kept track of them. Graham Tarbell, William Treadwell, and Angela Phipps all entered into plea and cooperation agreements with the government, promising to testify against the holdouts, especially Jack Taylor. As part of the agreements, Bob Schwartz committed to recommending a five-year term for Graham Tarbell and eight years for Treadwell. Given Phipps's very early cooperation, which had broken the case open, and her near-fatal encounter with Dennis Doyle, Schwartz promised to recommend a three-year term of probation for her.

Of course, it would be up to the judges to make the final decisions. Jack Taylor's case was drawn to Roberta Stackpole, one of the most amiable judges in the district and by far the toughest sentencer. In time, additional indictments came down, directed at a number of big-firm lawyers: two in Boston, three in New York City, and one each in Los Angeles, Dallas, and Chicago. There was speculation that more charges might be in the works, including an indictment of Dominic O'Connell.

Cimarron was drawn, legitimately, to Judge Conti, who dismissed the case based on the complaint's failure "to state with particularity the circumstances constituting fraud," as required under Rule 9(b) of the Federal Rules of Civil Procedure. Graham Tarbell's deal with the devil, it turned out, had been entirely unnecessary. Conti's ruling of course went up on appeal. No one knew what the court of appeals would do with it, but an article in *Massachusetts Lawyers Weekly* suggested that the parties had no desire to find out. Their attorneys were working hard to wrap up a settlement.

A week before Christmas, Judge Norcross read in the *Boston Globe* that Dominic O'Connell had died in his bed at his place on Louisburg Square. His wife had been on the phone, calling 911, and according to the obituary his last words were to her: "Never mind, sweetheart. I'm fine." If Brian Shaughnessy had lived to complete his testimony, and the jury had found O'Connell guilty, the appeal would have eaten up at least another eight months, and O'Connell would never have survived to serve any prison time. Given this, Norcross's ruling on Shaughnessy's deposition seemed less dire, and the ache of that mistake bothered him less. Two members of the Scanlon family were quoted in the *Globe* article, one disappointed that O'Connell had "cheated justice," and the other grateful that the family had had its day in court and that their father was remembered. Further efforts at punishing or rehabilitating Dominic O'Connell, if any, would be taking place in another world.

When David suggested inviting David Kamau and Helena Toivonen out to Amherst for Christmas dinner, Claire said it was a fabulous idea, really fabulous—as long as David did the cooking. After some hesitation, David agreed and promptly texted Lindsay to come help him. To Claire's delight, both Lindsay and Carmen Marquez were added to the party.

Now, as Claire sat in the living room, trying to make conversation with Kamau and Toivonen, she could not help hearing the muffled bangs and occasionally urgent voices from the kitchen as David, Lindsay, and Carmen worked through the final, intense stage of preparation. Carmen had brought some traditional Mexican-American Christmas food—pork tamales and delicious little crispy treats called buñuelos—to supplement the standard turkey and trimmings. So far, no aroma of smoke was coming from that end of the house. Outside, a light snowfall was floating down, sugaring the hemlocks. The Christmas tree sat in a corner, and the room smelled of pine.

Kamau was sitting on the sofa with Charlie in his lap. He had turned the boy around so that they were facing each other, and he was teaching him to say "I love you" in Swahili.

"I believe he is getting a basic grasp." Kamau tipped his head down. *"Nah."*

Charlie looked up with bright eyes. *"Nah."*

"Koo."

"Doo."

Kamau looked at Claire. "See? The boy's a genius." Charlie was staring up at Kamau with bright, enraptured eyes.

"Now, the challenging part." He bent down and touched his nose to Charlie's. *"Penda."*

Charlie opened his mouth, made a face, and reached behind him for a large stuffed monkey sitting on the coffee table. Helena had brought it for him, neatly wrapped in elegant blue-and-white Marimekko paper. The monkey's name was Sibelius. The beautiful wrapping paper and the box were now scattered in pieces on the rug.

Kamau clapped his hands, joggling Charlie with a three-bounce rhythm. *"Nah-koo-penda, nah-koo-penda, nah-koo-penda."* After a short time, he stopped, leaned down, and whispered, *"Nakupenda sana*, little brother. I love you very much."

But Charlie had had enough school. He wanted his monkey, and he wanted his mother. He began to wriggle and make grunting noises, holding his arms out to Claire.

Realizing that her boy was trending toward one of his meltdowns, Claire hastily got up and scooped up both Charlie and the monkey. When she returned to her chair, Charlie settled down immediately into her lap and began making noises at Sibelius. Helena looked on, clearly pleased that her gift was a hit.

Claire spoke to her. "So, waiting for David to be released from custody, and then having him almost flying off to Kenya—all that must have been very nerve-racking."

Helena looked at Claire, her face blank. "I am a Finn. Finns do not nerve-rack."

Claire tried to think of some follow-up to this. "I see, um . . ."

Kamau broke in. "Rubbish, Helena." He nodded over at Claire and pointed at Helena. "You should have observed her behavior when I was released."

Helena pulled at her spiky blond hair and looked down. "You're right." She rubbed the back of her neck self-consciously. "That was a foolish thing to say. I was, of course, very, very worried. Many nights, I could not sleep."

"I can imagine. A few years ago, when David, my David, was in the hospital, I was pretty much a mess."

"The root of my name in Finnish is *toivo*, which means 'hope.' I am Helena Toivonen, of the Toivoset, the people of hope. Sometimes with our long winters, you know, things can become hard."

Kamau was beaming at Helena. "I think that's why your religion has such a wide margin of frost on it."

Helena waved her hand at him. This had to be an old argument.

"Perhaps," Claire said. "You could teach Charlie the word *toivo* too."

"I'm not yet skillful with small babies, but I could try." Helena looked at Charlie nervously. "What do you think, little one?" But Charlie was deeply engaged with his monkey and did not look up.

Claire looked at Kamau. "And your friend Godfrey? Where is he?"

"Godfrey is spending the holidays with his wife's family in Melrose. He is hopelessly addicted to American college football. He and his father-in-law actually make small wagers. It is beyond rational explanation."

David appeared in the entryway. His shirt was untucked on one side, and his face suggested that he had just come off some death-defying roller-coaster ride. He looked ridiculously vulnerable, and it occurred to Claire that she had never loved him more than she did at that moment.

"We're plating the meal as I speak." He noticed his shirttail and began stuffing it in. "Please come. Please. Please."

Once they had gathered at the table and were picking up their forks, David looked around distractedly and asked, "Would someone like to propose a toast?"

"Yes, I would like to." Claire stood and picked up her glass. "Some time long ago, some hundred thousand years or more, I guess, our ancestors, began spreading out over this earth . . ." She nodded at Kamau. "From East Africa, we're told. It has been a long, tangled history for the human race since then. Following our individual paths, we each of us have had our own tangled histories. So here is a toast to our big family on this planet and to our small family around this table, especially to my two sons." She raised her glass. "My *two* sons. Here is to all of us."

Charlie, seated in his high chair, threw his spoon down with an emphatic bang. David Kamau raised his glass. "Amen, Claire. Amen."

ADVISORY AND ACKNOWLEDGMENTS

First, the Advisory.

Part of the plot of this book involves a low-level clerk who takes bribes to steer cases to particular judges. Given the quality of our staff, and the safeguards in place, I know that this kind of misconduct has not happened in the District of Massachusetts. It may not have happened in any court. The point of this fiction is to highlight the fact that justice occurs at the intersection of principles and people. Adherence to principles matters. The character of the individuals applying those principles also matters a great deal. My story aims to illuminate this reality. Everything else in the plot roughly follows actual practice.

Now, the Acknowledgments.

Several friends took time to look over the manuscript and make suggestions, in particular my old and dear friends Ted Scott, Peter Shaw, and the wonderful poet Ellen Bass. Their steerage improved the book enormously. Other helpers included Esther Scott, former Assistant U.S. Attorney and now Justice of the Massachusetts Appeals Court Ariane Vuono, and two prize former law clerks, Justice Monica Marquez (now of the Supreme Court of Colorado) and

Josh Rovenger. My good friend Gordon Nicholson gave me advice on the finer points of cricket. My children, Anne and Joseph, offered advice on specific points within their expertise.

Several judicial colleagues graciously took their time to read the manuscript and make suggestions, virtually all of which I adopted. These included Chief Judge Dennis Saylor, former Chief Judge Patti Saris, Judge Douglas Woodlock, Judge Denise Casper, and Judge Richard Stearns. I also benefited from advice from my friend Rob Farrell, Clerk of the U.S. District Court for the District of Massachusetts, and from my friend and coworker of more than thirty years, Mary Finn. Deputy U.S. Marshal Richard Wisnaskas, Attorney Mark Sauter of the Department of Homeland Security, and Assistant U.S. Attorney Annapurna Balakrishna also provided important input.

My agent Robin Straus was her usual terrific self, providing steady, patient encouragement and agile guidance through the world of publishing.

My publisher Open Road Integrated Media has been a rock from beginning to end, especially Mara Anastas, VP for Publishing Relations, and Emma Chapnick, Publishing Coordinator. It is a pleasure to work with them and with everyone at Open Road.

Once more, this book owes its existence to my extraordinarily talented, tactful, and wise editor Maggie Crawford. She read every word more than once, made crucial suggestions, and guided me around the banana peels and out of the blind alleys I so often created for myself. Apart from everything else, she is a delight to work with. My gratitude to her is immense.

I need to mention the two people to whose memory this book is dedicated. The late Chief Judge Joseph L. Tauro was my boss, my mentor, my colleague, and finally my close friend. He still stands, and will stand for as long as I am standing, as my model of compassionate and dedicated service and as an example of a life lived with relish.

Hannah Njoki Kahiga, later Hannah Tiagha, was my dear friend—no more, no less—during the thirteen months I spent teaching in the Highlands of Kenya during college. She is the model for the remembered character in this book, Hannah Nyeri. Hannah was one of the brightest, most delightful, most generous-spirited people I have ever known. She eventually came to the United States and obtained her Masters in Social Work from Columbia University and her PhD from Adelphi University. For many years, she worked for the United Nations in Ethiopia. Very sadly, and much too early, she died in 2012. Her 1966 essay entitled "A Model Day During the Emergency" is a searing description of the brutality that she and her family suffered at the hands of the colonial regime during what the British called the "Mau-Mau Revolt" and what Kenyans call the "Emergency." Her essay can be found in *Women Writing Africa: The Eastern Region*, Amandina Lihamba, et al. editors (Feminist Press at the City University of New York, 2007).

Last, and most importantly, there is my wife Nancy Coiner—my eternal love, my writing bud, and the best of companions. This book, along with the great majority of what makes my life rich and happy, would not exist without her.

ABOUT THE AUTHOR

Michael Ponsor graduated from Harvard, received a Rhodes Scholarship, and studied for two years at Pembroke College, Oxford. As an undergraduate, he spent a year teaching in Kabete, Kenya, just outside Nairobi. After taking his law degree from Yale and clerking in federal court in Boston, he began his legal career, specializing in criminal defense. He moved to Amherst, Massachusetts, in 1978, where he practiced as a trial attorney in his own firm until his appointment in 1984 as a U.S. magistrate judge in Springfield, Massachusetts. In 1994, President Bill Clinton appointed him a life-tenured U.S. district judge. From 2000 to 2001, he presided over a five-month death penalty trial, the first in Massachusetts in over fifty years. Judge Ponsor continues to serve as a senior U.S. district judge in the United States District Court for the District of Massachusetts, Western Division, with responsibility for federal criminal and civil cases in the four counties of western Massachusetts. *Point of Order* is his third novel featuring Judge Norcross.

THE JUDGE NORCROSS NOVELS

FROM OPEN ROAD MEDIA

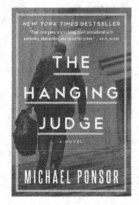
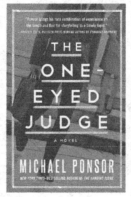
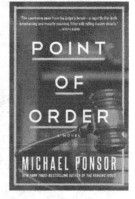

OPEN ROAD

INTEGRATED MEDIA

OPEN ROAD
INTEGRATED MEDIA